ABOUT THE AUTHOR

New York Times-bestselling speculative fiction author SEAN WILLIAMS lives in Adelaide, South Australia. He is the author of over eighty published short stories and forty novels, including the Books of the Cataclysm and *The Resurrected Man,* and is a multiple recipient of both the Ditmar & Aurealis Awards. As well as his original work, he has written several novels in the Star Wars universe. For a change of pace, he likes to DJ and cook curries.

ABOUT THE ARTIST

Cover and internal images are photographs from the series Asphalt Archeology by Brooklyn-based artist Mike Mission. He invites you to visit his website at www.str82o.com

MAGIC

DIRT

MAGIC DIRT

DIRT

the best of

SEAN WILLIAMS

T̴ p̴ Ticonderoga
publications

For the original punk rocker and dolphin boy himself,
Russell B. Farr.

Magic Dirt: the best of Sean WIlliams

Published by Ticonderoga Publications

Copyright © 2008 Sean Williams

"Ludic Dreaming" copyright © 2008 John Harwood

Cover artwork by Mike Mission

Designed and edited by Russell B. Farr

Typeset in Sabon and Toronto Subway

A Cataloging-in-Publications entry for this title is available from The National Library of Australia.

ISBN 978–0–9803531–6–7 (paperback)
 978–1–921857–86–7 (trade paperback)
 978–1–921857–87–4 (trade hardcover)

Ticonderoga Publications
PO Box 29 Greenwood
Western Australia 6924

www.ticonderogapublications.com

10 9 8 7 6 5 4 3 2 1

Special thanks to:
Amanda Nettelbeck, John Harwood,
Jonathan Strahan, Robert N. Stephenson,
Cat Sparks, Stephanie Smith, Steve Savile,
Eva Sallis, Peter McNamara, Alethea Kontis,
Robert Hood, Ashley Hay, Russell B. Farr,
Shane Dix, Stephen Dedman, Jack Dann, Bill
Congreve, Jeremy G. Byrne, Simon Brown, and
Kirsty Brooks.

CONTENTS

LUDIC DREAMING

JOHN HARWOOD

Magic Dirt brings together the finest of Sean Williams' stories from a career that has so far spanned sixteen years, during which he has published twenty-two novels and sixty short stories, received fifteen major awards, and established an international reputation as a leading author of speculative fiction. His range, as this collection abundantly demonstrates, extends from hard SF to horror, from the classic ghost story to crime, comedy, mystery and romance, to his own special brand of magic realism. Yet trying to list all the genres he's worked in leaves you with the uneasy feeling that you're missing the point, because he's also a writer who delights in crossing—or dissolving—the boundaries between them.

His gift for storytelling—a sure instinct for the pace and shape of a narrative, a seemingly effortless fluency of invention—is manifest in the earliest of the stories here, such as the wonderful "A Map of the Mines of Barnath" and the apocalyptic stories set in Adelaide. "Ghosts of the Fall", "White Christmas", and "The End of the World Begins at Home" have lost none of their futuristic edge; indeed they seem to have gained in immediacy, now that the realities of climate change have seized our collective imagination. (They also demonstrate that Adelaide is not only an ideal setting for a Stephen King novel, as Salman Rushdie once remarked, but an all-too-plausible vantage point from which to witness the end of the world). In Sean Williams' stories, there are no secure vantage points, nowhere to run, and nowhere to hide. The protagonist of "White Christmas" doesn't know, and nor do we, who has sent the malignant 'snow'; whether it's aliens or the fallout from some Faustian technological bargain, all he can do is watch and wait.

Reading these stories is like lucid dreaming, in which you dream that you're lying awake in your own bed; the room is exactly as it would be in waking life, until the impossible intrudes. Sean Williams doesn't simply stay one step ahead of his reader; he knows how to make you believe you know exactly where he's going, while steering you down a far more sinister path. The immediacy of the action is never compromised, but there's an unnerving resonance, a shadow cast (shadows often carry a particular charge in his work) which doesn't quite match up with the object supposedly casting it.

Thus "A Map of the Mines of Barnath" unfolds from a plain and seemingly straightforward opening—protagonist arrives at mine in search of his missing twin brother—into an increasingly vertiginous series of perspectives more reminiscent of Borges' "Library of Babel" than Arthur C. Clarke's *2001*, which the ending deliberately echoes, but with chilling contrast. Whereas the astronaut Dave in *2001* is a mere cipher, a peg on which to hang the ideas, we have become far more involved in the haunted Martin Cavell's quest for his vanished twin. Sean Williams' ultimate engagement is always with his characters, rather than with the situation or the technology, however mind-bending, and so the stories bend back on themselves, reflecting into inner space: the space, characteristically, of obsession, of deals with the devils of the mind, and the price that must be paid. "Reluctant Misty and the House on Burden Street"—a variation on the classic ghost story—has, superficially nothing in common with "Mines of Barnath" and yet a line from the latter—'You only get out once'—could serve as the refrain for either story. In 'Burden Street'—a highly effective twist on the topos in which the house itself is a ghost—the heroine's ominous lack of fear points toward a conclusion in which she, too, confronts a kind of twin.

Like all the best writers of ghost and horror stories, Sean Williams has the gift of knowing where to stop and what to leave out, chillingly manifest in "The Girl-Thing" (printed here for the first time). Again the power of the story is amplified by its crossing of genres; it reads, almost to the end, like realist hard-boiled crime, but there's a lurking undercurrent, manifest in the troubled detective's nightmares (if that's what they are . . .), drawing us toward the final shocking discovery. Elizabeth Bowen once remarked that the effect of the ghost story depends upon those pivotal details which are only a little, but unmistakably 'out of true'. Though it isn't a ghost story, the same applies to "Team Sharon", a chilling variation on the theme of male bonding. There's nothing intrinsically impossible about men gathering in a park at night for the purpose described here, but it has the revelatory terror of a horror story, all the more sinister for staying just within the boundaries of realism.

I see that I've dwelt upon the dark side of Sean Williams' imagination at the expense of the playful, presented here in the comic extravaganza "The Masque of Agamemnon", and most recently "The Seventh Letter", with its wonderful 'Royal Society for the Semantically Impaired', a comic but also surreal displacement of the familiar. It's a sign of his versatility and creative intelligence that one can't tell where his imagination will take him next, but I can safely predict that once you've read *Magic Dirt*, you won't want to miss the ride.

— JOHN HARWOOD
FEBRUARY 2008

"Inneston, 2006"

the man's seen hard times
he turns his face from the light
craters on the moon

INTRODUCTION TO:
.... A MAP OF THE MINES OF BARNATH

Where do ideas come from?

This is one of those questions that usually send writers sprinting for the door, but in the case of this story I can answer with certainty.

The idea came to me in a dream.

The dream didn't have a story and it succumbs readily to analysis. I was descending by elevator into the depths of a planet, where lay the surface of another world entirely. Below that, at the core of both planets, was an entire sun. The image was so wondrous and strange that it stayed with me all day.

While it was nice of my subconscious to remind me that the surface of things can hide all manner of wonder, I'm a science fiction writer, and turning metaphors back on themselves is one of the tools of the trade. I could keep the spirit of the dream and still make it a real place, which a real character could explore. That this character might be seeking a lost twin who had disappeared into the bowels of such an impossible world—and that he might discover along the way a level more strange than anything in a mere dream—only made it more interesting.

There are several stories in this collection that I've wanted to expand into a novel. This is one of them. Who were the original builders of the mines? Where do the five other elevators lead? Why does the mysterious Director take some people and kill others? I like to think that I know the answers to these questions, but until I try to write them down, I'll never be sure.

●

A MAP OF THE MINES
OF BARNATH

The Manager of the mines was a small, grey man named Carnarvon, wiry with muscle and as tough as old boots. A slight accent betrayed his off-world origins; one of the older colonies, I thought, or perhaps even Earth. He was sympathetic in a matter-of-fact way, as though my position was far from unique.

"What was your brother's name?" he asked.

"Martin Cavell. Do you remember him?"

Carnarvon shook his head, tapping into a terminal. "No, but his records should . . . yes. This'll tell us something."

I tried to wait while he read the file, but impatience soon got the better of me. "What happened?"

"It seems he took a three-day pass to the upper levels, then chose to continue deeper when the pass expired." Carnarvon skimmed through the file to the end. "Your brother died on the fifth level."

"How?"

"The exact details are unknown. There was no body, no witnesses, and no inquiry. Assumption of death is automatic under these circumstances."

"A pretty large assumption, I would've thought."

"Nevertheless."

He seemed quite content to leave it there, but ten thousand kilometres of travel prompted me to dig deeper.

"Would it be possible to see the place where he died?"

"Possible, yes, but . . . " He looked at me oddly. "You don't know the mines, do you?"

"No. This is my first time here."

"Nobody's said anything?"

"I only flew in this afternoon." It was my turn to look puzzled. "Is there something I should know?"

Carnarvon shook his head slowly. "You wouldn't believe me if I told you."

"So show me. Or have me shown. You don't have to take me personally—"

"No. I'll take you. It's been a while since I went all the way." He looked around the office, eyes itemising the contents one by one until they finally came back to me. "If you want a Grand Tour, I'll give you a Grand Tour."

"Thank you." His capitulation was both unexpected and total; he made me feel slightly guilty for inconveniencing him. "As soon as I find out what happened to Martin, I'll be out of your hair, I promise."

"That could take longer than you think."

"I'm in no hurry."

He sighed and called his deputy into the office. "I'm going Down, Carmen," he told the woman. "You're in charge until I get back."

They shook hands gravely and I thought for an instant that she was about to say something. But she didn't. She just watched as we left the office, her eyes filled with something oddly like grief.

Carnarvon led me to an elevator shaft, handed me a hardhat and a dirty blue overcoat. He looked around the surface level—at the swarming clerks and technicians, at the administration buildings and bulk-transport containers—and shook his head a third time.

"Let's go," he said wearily, and hit Down. The cage door closed and the floor fell away.

The Mines of Barnath are the biggest in known space, and rumoured to be inexhaustible. Discovered a century ago, they have turned our previously struggling, pastoral world into a major mineral exporter. The five thousand people—according to the unofficial tourist brochure—who work its seven levels are capable of extracting over a million tonnes of any given ore per month, plus the same again in refined materials, most of which is exported off-world.

Yet, strangely, the mines are completely independent of the rest of the planet, like a distant country or a very large corporation.

Visitors are rare, especially to the deeper levels, and the flow of information to the world outside is often restricted, as it was regarding my brother's fate. But the official policy on the surface is to let the *status quo* remain. The fate of the planet depends on a constant if not large supply of Barnath metal—so while ore comes out of the upper shaft any situation, no matter how unusual, can be tolerated.

Carnarvon, if he was aware of his awesome responsibility, didn't let it show.

"We don't get many people here," he said, pausing to light a cigarette. "Usually from off-planet—those who have heard rumours and want to check for themselves. Most are satisfied with a few pamphlets and a quick tour of the upper levels."

"What about Martin?"

"He was an exception, like you."

I nodded, allowing him the point. "What about the other miners, then?"

"A handful—the ones called 'skimmers'—live nearby. Drifters and no-hopers, usually. They only go as far as the third level, where we do the refining. More permanent miners work the deeper levels. The deepest ones never come Up at all."

"So some actually *live* down there?"

"Of course. They're the ones that work best."

My surprise was mild but genuine. This was a rumour I had heard and dismissed as unlikely. I had never been in a mine before, but the thought of crawling for any length of time along what I imagined to be cramped, poorly-lit tunnels made me feel claustrophobic.

"Why?" I asked.

Carnarvon looked me in the eye, studying my reaction with interest. "Surface people from 'round here, apart from the skimmers, don't work below ground because they're afraid of the mines. They're scared that if they go inside, they'll get caught."

"Gold fever?" I joked.

"No." There was little humour in Carnarvon's eyes. "*Caught.*"

I waited, but he did not explain further. If he was trying to scare me off, or warn me, it didn't work. I had come too far to be deterred by vague superstitions.

The cage rattled to a halt. The doors swung open and Carnarvon waved me ahead. "After you."

I nodded, and entered the mines.

ONE & TWO

The sparsely populated first and second levels are almost identical, and usually regarded as a single unit. These were what greeted the first settlers, when they discovered the mines and sent the first of many expeditions into the depths of the planet. Carved from the bedrock, at five hundred and seven-fifty metres respectively, the two upper levels were found to be empty of ore and life, little more than half-submerged tunnels littered with rubble and dirt. That they had been fashioned by ROTH—Races Other Than Human—was obvious, however. Mankind had not been on Barnath long enough to begin such an ambitious project, let alone subsequently abandon it. Another species had therefore established the mines, emptied them of all valuable minerals and left.

Or so it appeared at first.

When I arrived, new tunnels were being carved by skimmers in a half-hearted attempt to reopen the upper levels. The air was full of dust and the screaming of pneumatic and sonic drills. The weight of the rock above and around me was almost palpable—a feeling compounded by the stifling half-light. Flickering electric arcs swung from carelessly-looped cables draped along the tunnels. It was unexpectedly hot and uncomfortably damp. In some tunnels, it almost seemed to be raining.

Jean Tarquitz, the supervisor of the upper levels, greeted us as Carnarvon showed me around. She was an attractive woman, although filthy, grimed with moisture-streaked dust. When Carnarvon explained that we were heading on a Grand Tour, she looked surprised.

"Why?" she asked, staring at us both with naked curiosity.

"I've been topside long enough," Carnarvon explained, "waiting for an excuse to come back Down." Even I, who had known him little more than an hour, could tell that his casual words hid a more complex reason. "I thought it was about time."

"And you?"

"Looking for my brother."

There was both amusement and pity in her pale orange eyes as she snorted disdainfully and waved us on.

My tour of the first level passed quickly. Tarquitz accompanied us to the second, which had little new to offer, and bade us farewell as we re-entered the shaft to the third. A load of processed ore climbed past us, deafening all those nearby with the sound of labouring machinery.

"The Director has been active in the lower levels," she said. "I've heard rumours—"

"I know," said Carnarvon wearily. "We'll be careful."

"If it comes for you," she asserted, "it comes regardless of care."

"I haven't forgotten."

"Who's the Director?" I asked, but Carnarvon merely shook his head and motioned me into the cage.

"Take your time," said Tarquitz.

"I will," Carnarvon replied, and the doors closed.

The lift fell, swaying gently from side to side, and although the first two drops had lasted little more than sixty seconds each, this descent took at least ten minutes.

THREE

The third level held the first of many surprises to greet the settlers. Its heart was an enormous chamber as large as five Old Earth cathedrals stacked one on top of the other, criss-crossed by ladders and pipes and startlingly well-lit—a brilliant contrast to the upper levels. Its walls are orange and thickly-veined. The air is full of the rumbling of machinery and echoing explosions. Huge ROTH artifacts, inactive for the most part, cling to the walls and ceiling; some are mounted like stalagmites on the 'floor', around which cluster the refineries brought Down a piece at a time by human settlers. Green-clad miners swarm like ants along the walls and walkways, issuing from the myriad tunnels that lead deeper into the earth.

"How many people work here?" I asked, left almost breathless by the sheer scale of the chamber. Too large to be fully comprehended in even a series of glances, it provoked a feeling of vertigo so powerful as to dull the mind.

"On this level, something like six thousand. Most of them in side-cuts rather than the actual core. Your brother was one of them, for a while."

I shook my head. The figure didn't make sense. It was larger than that which I'd received earlier regarding the total population of the mine, and there were still four more levels to go—but I chose not to pursue the matter then and there. I supposed that I'd misheard him through the constant noise echoing in the chamber.

I tried to imagine Martin working here, and failed. We had spoken briefly before his departure for the mines, but he had said nothing about intending to seek employment. Just a holiday, he had said, to satisfy his curiosity. What had happened, I wondered, to change his mind?

The lift ends halfway down the chamber.

We stopped there to procure water bottles, to exchange a handful of words with a taciturn attendant, and to admire the view. Huge ore-lifters floated past us—up, full; down, empty. Carnarvon informed me that protocol forbade us taking such a direct route to the base of the third level. Between the midway point of the third level and its rock floor were only ladders.

"Nothing else can truly do this place justice," he said, and I believed him.

By then I had an inkling that the Grand Tour was far more than a quick circuit of faces and off-cuts—hence Carnarvon's initial reluctance to take me. I was glad that I had no-one waiting for me above ground.

It took us three hours to reach the base of the chamber and the first of many way-stations. We rested there for an hour or so, meeting a few of the deeper miners—called 'moles'—who were heading Upwards for a stint in the refineries and, ultimately, the surface. They were uniformly dirty, but only two thirds were pale-skinned. The rest were deeply tanned, which I found strange. All shared a peculiar dullness of stare, a hybrid of world-weariness which I later learned was called 'miner's eyes'. As though nothing more could surprise them, they regarded the world with patient, cynical skepticism.

I asked them about my brother, but received only quizzical stares in reply.

"Tourist," explained Carnarvon patiently. Some laughed openly; others touched my shoulder in sadness, and went to sit elsewhere.

"Why is everyone so . . . " I struggled for the word, but couldn't find it.

"Unconcerned?" suggested Carnarvon, a wry smile twisting his rubbery features. "If they are, it's because they know something you don't."

"Which is?"

"Don't ask now. You'll—"

"I know, I know. I'll find out later."

His smile broadened. "Exactly."

When we had rested, Carnarvon showed me some of the machinery that fills the third level. The purpose of the ancient ROTH mechanisms eluded me then, just as it has eluded human researchers for one full century.

Then it was time to enter the Shaft, the central column that plummets downwards through the four remaining levels. The cage was three times as large as the lift by which we had previously descended. Low benches lined two of the walls.

A crowd of miners spilled from the cage, dressed in unfamiliar white uniforms. They stared at us, but said nothing. When they had gone, Carnarvon turned to face me.

"The journey really begins here," he said, on the threshold of the cage. "If you want to turn back, it's not too late."

I shook my head. "I need to know what happened to Martin."

"Why?" He seemed genuinely unable to understand.

"Because he was important to me," I said. "Am I in danger?"

"Yes." His honesty was both dismaying and thrilling. "Everyone who enters the mines is at risk—and the deeper, the more so."

It was my turn to ask: "Why?"

But Carnarvon, waving me inside, refused to answer.

He stood silently by my side as the cage fell, not meeting my stare. Five minutes passed without a word spoken by either of us. If Carnarvon didn't want to talk, I wasn't going to make him.

Then, after fifteen minutes, the floor lurched, and I felt momentarily light-headed. Only then did Carnarvon speak, as though we had passed some unannounced barrier.

"The last time I passed this way was twelve years ago—heading Up from the fifth level, swearing that I would never come back." He took off his hardhat and slicked back his wiry, grey hair. "But part of me always knew I would, one day. And the same part knows that there's no going back this time. You only get out once. If you return, the mines have you forever."

I studied him closely. If this was a confession, then I failed to comprehend it. "Caught?" I asked, using his own word.

He laughed softly. "Well and truly. I hate this place, but I love it too. And the people that work here, mad bastards that we are."

His attention wandered back to his own thoughts. Reluctant to let the silence claim us again, I asked him a question that had been troubling me for some time:

"Why are we the only ones going Down?"

Carnarvon laughed again. "You noticed? Good. If you can answer that question, my friend, you'll be one step closer to grasping the truth about the mines."

And he would speak no more until the cage bumped to a halt and we stumbled from it.

FOUR

Imagine a grey plain at midnight, rippled in a series of low, undulating hills and valleys. The plain is in complete darkness, except for an area as large as a small town illuminated by powerful, white spotlights. In this lighted area sits an open-face mine, hacked into a hillside like a weeping sore. It is so dark in this place that nothing else can be seen: no stars, no horizon; just one patch of brilliant light and a slender line rising upwards into blackness.

Take the plain and bury it four thousand metres underground in a chamber so large that the walls and ceiling are invisible.

And this is the fourth level.

A faceless technician handed me a pressure-suit. A clumsy outfit of rubber and carbon-fibres, it stank of sweat and grease, as though worn by thousands of people in its lifetime. Puzzled, I followed Carnarvon's lead and shrugged into it, leaving my outer garments in a locker. I felt oddly light, and wondered if the air had a higher oxygen content than I was accustomed to. Carnarvon led me to an airlock and cycled the pair of us through.

"Poisonous atmosphere," he said via the suit radio, explaining the suits if not the sight that lay before me.

I watched as cranes swung and powerful vehicles unloaded their burdens beneath the spotlights. The miners swarming across the face looked like dark animals in their grey suits—hence, I supposed, the nickname 'moles'.

"What are they mining for?" I asked.

"Here, iron ore," replied Carnarvon. "There are other faces nearby cut for strontium and uranium."

I hunted for a reference point, some means of guessing the size of the space around me, but failed.

"How big is this level?" I asked, admitting defeat.

"Bigger than you think, I promise you."

We headed through the gloom towards a row of huts, where Carnarvon introduced himself to the level supervisor, a portly man called Stolle whose suit resembled a blowfish with stumpy arms and legs. Still dazzled by the strangeness of the fourth level, I was content to let them do the talking.

"I remember you," said Stolle to Carnarvon, squinting through his plastic visor. His voice was liquid with static. "Two years ago—three, maybe?—you worked here for a while."

"Twelve," corrected Carnarvon.

"Christ." Stolle winked at me dryly, as though sharing a joke I failed to understand. "Time flies down here."

"Any news of the Director?" asked Carnarvon.

"It's out there," said the Supervisor, shrugging. "Definitely out there. We've lost a few on this level, but not many. Usual story. That, and the rumours of an eighth level, are about the only things we can depend on down here."

He invited us to join him for a drink, but Carnarvon explained that we were tired. This wasn't a lie, as far as I was concerned; my watch told me that eight hours had passed since my arrival at the mines, and my eyes were thick with fatigue. So Carnarvon made excuses, and we bunked down in a crowded dormitory wing with a dozen off-duty moles, clipped by airhoses to a communal tank, our radios silenced.

Thus I spent my first night in the mines of Barnath: in a rubber suit, breathing air that stank of *human*, wondering what the hell I was doing. And when I dreamed, it was of Martin walking ahead of me along a dark, stone tunnel, forever out of reach.

A dull explosion woke me an unknown time later. When we stumbled out of the wing, a new hole had been added to the scarred hillside. The ever-present glare of the spotlights seemed brighter and the ceaseless activity of the open-face mine more feverish than before.

We dined on pre-processed slop in one of the few pressurised compartments of that level. The moles around us eyed us curiously, and it was a moment or two before I realised what it was that distinguished us from them. It was, quite simply, that we were talking. On the fifth level, where communication is only practical via intersuit radio, casual conversation is discouraged. Even in the mess-hall.

"How much further?" I asked Carnarvon, regardless. The night's sleep had left me irritable, rather than refreshed. I was impatient to make some progress on my quest to find Martin.

"Forever and a day, as they say." He glanced at me in amusement. "You still think you'll be leaving here in a hurry?"

"Why shouldn't I be?"

"Because these are the mines of Barnath, my friend. They're not like anywhere else. Where you come from, everything's the same— it never changes, it'll be there tomorrow, forever. But here . . . if the Director doesn't get you, then you're caught anyway."

I put down my spoon, appetite forgotten. There was a new strength in Carnarvon's eyes that bothered me, left me feeling like an intruder, unwanted. His stare was almost a challenge, defying me to unravel the riddle of the mines on my own.

"Who is the Director?" I asked, pacing my words deliberately.

Perhaps he saw the growing frustration in my eyes, and the anger that lurked behind it. Or he too was tired of his own guessing-game. Either way, he also put down his spoon and finally began to explain, after a fashion.

"The Director lives in the mines," he said, "or else it's an integral part of it. Either. We don't know much about it, except that it can go anywhere, any time it wants to. We don't even know where it goes between appearances—I've never heard of it being seen topside—but we always know when it's been."

"'It'?" I asked. "I thought you were talking about someone in particular. Your superior, perhaps."

"No. One of the early explorers coined the name, for whatever reason, and it's as good as any other."

He paused, watching me closely, waiting for a response.

"So what is it? A machine?"

"That's certainly possible. The mines aren't human-built. The ROTH made them; the ROTH left them here for us to plunder. Maybe they switched on some sort of security system before they left, and the Director is its enforcer." He shrugged. "But few people really believe it's an alien artifact."

"Then *someone* must know about it, surely?"

"Just think for a second, before you jump to conclusions. It should be obvious. What if the ROTH *didn't* leave? What if they're still in here, somewhere?"

I stared at him. "Are you suggesting that the Director is an alien?"

"That's the most popular explanation. More than one ROTH, perhaps. No-one's seen it and lived. All we know is that it takes people working in the mines—usually the best, most talented. Those it comes for and doesn't take, it kills."

"You're kidding."

Carnarvon shook his head gravely. "It's no joke down here. Deeper still, it's positively morbid. Live in the mines for a while and the fact starts to get to you. You're always wondering if it'll come for you, and if you'll be taken when it does."

"I never heard any of this before."

"Of course not. The Mine looks after itself. Hardly anybody who comes this deep leaves again. Those few who do leave hang around the surface for a while, and then go back Down. The Director is all part of the lure and the trap of Barnath, you see. No-one knows *where* it takes the ones it doesn't kill." He picked up his spoon and attacked his breakfast viciously. "That's why I'm here. The mystery has me hooked."

"And me? Why am I here?"

"To find your brother, of course."

"Did the Director take *him*?"

Carnarvon paused between mouthfuls. "If you meet it, you can ask it yourself."

I pushed my bowl aside and sealed my suit.

"Going somewhere?" asked Carnarvon, amused.

"Outside," I said. "I need to think."

I shouldered my way through a crowd of miners and headed out into the darkness. The face of the cut was hidden behind a low hill; the only light came from reflected haze and a crooked line of beacons strung across the grey-green dust that served for a floor on the fourth level.

I squatted on my haunches and regarded the empty view for a long while. It was like sitting on the face of a starless moon. I didn't hear Carnarvon approach.

"Time to go," he said, putting his hand on my shoulder. "Coming?"

I raised my head wearily.

"You say Martin disappeared from the next level?"

"Yes, the fifth. That's what the records said, anyway."

"Then I'm coming. At least that far."

Even through the visor I could see his skeptical smile, curled like a question-mark as though he doubted my motives.

"He's alive," I insisted. "I can feel him."

"If you say so."

"All I want to do is find him and take him home. Is that so difficult?"

Carnarvon helped me to my feet, and we trudged back to the Shaft building. I expected to don our old clothes, but we didn't.

"Pressure suits from here on," he explained, as we waited for the cage to reach our level. "Just in case."

The cage rattled to a halt and the doors opened. I regarded the interior with foreboding. Carnarvon didn't hesitate, however, so I reluctantly followed.

The cage dropped downwards. Again I felt that strange sensation of giddiness half-way, but this time my companion chose to remain silent for the rest the journey, lost in thought.

FIVE

I was definitely lighter when I stepped from the cage. The disembarkation bay was an enormous room, sterile-white and brilliantly lit. Behind me, six identical airlocks opened into the wall; we had entered the chamber via the second from the right. A large section of the floor was transparent, and Carnarvon gestured that I should look down through it.

It took me a minute or so to find a sense of perspective. The view was surreal. Great blue sheets of energy slashed and hacked at something I couldn't quite identify. A hill, I thought at first; then a mountain. It wasn't until I realised that the dots drifting over the surface of the object were ore-lifters—themselves so huge they made men look like specks—that I guessed the incredible truth.

Trapped within the mines, orbiting slowly beneath my feet, was an entire planet.

"That's impossible," I breathed, as bolts of stupendous energy sheared free continent-sized chunks of rock. My vantage point was high—at least thirty thousand metres—and the view spectacular.

"I know," said Carnarvon, "but we're mining it anyway. And it's not that large, really—barely the size of Mars. Completely dead, of course, and metal-rich. It'll keep the mines active for a century or two at least."

My gaze wandered from the planet, across the roof of the incomprehensible chamber. Giant habitats clung to the naked rock of the 'roof' like shellfish, upside down. Huge docking grapnels awaited ore-lifters ferrying material from the scarred surface below. Everywhere I looked, there were men and women in white pressure-suits, crawling like flies over an unimaginable carcass.

"How many?" I asked, almost afraid of the answer.

"Two and a half million," replied Carnarvon, and I swallowed. I had in mind the unofficial government estimate of five thousand, which now seemed ludicrous in the face of what I was seeing.

"Surely someone must have noticed?"

"To date, no-one has." Carnarvon unsealed his suit, crooking the helmet over his forearm like an old-timer. "As I said, people this deep rarely leave."

"But still, they had to come from *somewhere*—"

"Exactly. A few, like your brother, come from the surface, drifting down through the levels over the years, but that still leaves us quite a large number short of the real population of the mine."

"Where, then?" I had a vision of the miners raising families, which I immediately discredited. Only an idiot would have children in a place like this.

"We may never know the full answer to that question," said Carnarvon. "Some miners come Up from the deeper levels without ever having gone Down in the first place."

I studied him suspiciously, wondering if he was playing me for a fool. He wasn't. He was deadly serious.

But he had to be lying.

I too shucked my helmet and breathed the air of the fifth level. It tasted faintly electric, and of the population that had breathed it before me. I could still feel the weight of rock around me, defying the view through the window at my feet. A planet *within* a planet . . . ?

I turned away from the sight. It was too much.

"Come on," said Carnarvon. "We have to log ourselves in." He took my arm and led me along the bay, towards a corridor. The narrow passageway ended in a desk.

A clerk behind a computer terminal greeted us patiently. "Names?" he asked.

Carnarvon gave him mine and added, "Skimmer," when asked for my profession. The ease with which my identity had been redefined did not escape me: from quester to tourist to skimmer in less than two days. Had something similar happened to Martin? The clerk handed me a white, plastic ID card, which I absently tucked into a ziplock pouch.

Then it was Carnarvon's turn. The clerk accepted the title, "Manager," with little sign of being impressed.

"When?" he asked, tapping at the keyboard.

"'45 to '55."

"We had your predecessor through here last year," said the clerk. "He lasted a month."

"Taken?"

"Killed." The clerk handed him a red card which Carnarvon stuck to the front of his suit. "You have a fortnight's grace, you and your friend, after which you'll have to find work."

"Of course," said Carnarvon, not at all fazed by the apparent insubordination. "Thank you."

He commandeered an electric cart and drove me deeper into the habitat. Occasionally we passed a circular window in the floor, reminding me that beneath my feet lay not the earth my apparent weight suggested, but empty space and then something far more remarkable.

"You'll probably be asking yourself the same questions I asked when I came here." Carnarvon smiled at me sympathetically as he drove. "I was a fusion technician from Earth, so the first thing I said when I looked out that window was, 'How do you pay your fuel bill?'" He chuckled self-depreciatingly. "It wasn't until two years later that I learned where the energy actually comes from."

"And where does it?" I croaked.

"Deeper still," he said. "The next level powers the entire mine. The ROTH were far more advanced than we are. All the equipment in this chamber and the sixth were just lying around, waiting to be used. So we used it. We didn't have to understand how it worked."

Memory prompted me to ask: "I thought there were seven levels?"

"There are," he said, but I could draw him no further on the issue of the last. Instead, he described life in the fifth: the way most of the mining on the planet is tele-operated; how the miners spend nearly all of their time in the ceiling habitats, only venturing to the surface to deal with circumstances that cannot be handled by automatics or remotes. The energy-lances are directed from a cluster of habitats in a segment of the level that has been designated North, coinciding with the magnetic field of the planet.

It was there, I learned, where Martin had worked. When I asked to be taken there first, Carnarvon smiled grimly.

"You haven't grasped the scale yet, have you? It'll take at least three days to get there by cart; one if we can requisition a shuttle."

The corridor widened, became a busy thoroughfare. Miners in clean uniforms walked or drove by on unknown errands, and I watched them in silence, trying to remember what the surface— 'home,' I reminded myself—looked like.

But I couldn't. It was too far away.

Carnarvon pulled us to a halt outside a small door.

"Clothes, food, and rest," he said. "And then we keep going."

I nodded numbly, and let myself be led inside.

Standard uniform on the fifth level is a white, cotton one-piece, fitted with numerous pockets and pouches. The outfits are comfortably simple—almost spartan. The food, however, is an order of magnitude better than that of the previous level, being the product of hydroponic gardens scattered across the 'roof'.

"The ROTH left them, too," said Carnarvon as we ate our way through real vegetables and soy-base steak.

"And the habitats?"

"Yes." Carnarvon smiled wryly. "They were more like us than we give them credit for, most of the time."

"What do you mean?"

"Well, everyone down here regards the Director as almost god-like," he said, "when it's probably just a ROTH that eats the same food as us, and stands only a little taller."

I finished my meal in silence, bothered by that thought. I put myself in the shoes of those first colonists, stumbling upon this tremendous cavern and its contents. What had they imagined they'd found? And why hadn't research teams descended upon the mines from all corners of the inhabited galaxy?

I knew better than to ask for answers to these questions. All I could do was wait until the truth became clear on its own, however long that took.

When we'd finished our meal, Carnarvon drove us to a transport dock, where we caught a shuttle halfway to the Northern quadrant. The stubby craft swooped low over the planet below, granting me an unequalled view of the mining operations taking place. From this angle, the sprawl of habitats above resembled a colony of small, white mushrooms suspended from a distant ceiling—or a world of sealed cities, turned inside-out.

As we left the shuttle, a party of miners came towards us through the airlock umbilical. One called for my attention as he approached.

"Cavell, you old bastard, where've you been? It's been ages, and you still owe me for Carole."

"I'm sorry," I said, staring at him. He was short, grizzled, and completely unfamiliar. "You must be thinking of my brother. We look the same."

"No," he said. "I remember you. We worked—"

One of his companions nudged him in the ribs.

"Oh, right," he said. "You're on your way Down." He reached out for my hand and shook it. "The name's Donahue, anyway. I guess I'll meet you later."

He entered the shuttle with his workmates. The doors closed on his smiling face, shutting out my confusion.

"What the hell?"

"It happens," said Carnarvon. "You'll get used to this sort of thing."

"I don't *want* to get used to it." Mental exhaustion—too many riddles in too short a time—was taking its toll. "I just want to find out what happened to Martin and get out of here."

"A little more patience." Carnarvon smiled: a mixture of amusement and sympathy. "Not far now."

We took another cart the rest of the way, through a network of evacuated tunnels that criss-crosses the roof of the sixth chamber. Like insects, we crawled for seven hours along this hollow web, inch by strange inch, while the world-within-a-world turn implacably below us.

Above the unnamed planet's North pole, vast forces crackle through the dust-filled vacuum. Enormous bolts of static electricity split the nether sky, and the habitats echo with thunder. Martin's old home, amidst all of this, trembles on the edge between stone and fire—just as many homes did, and still do, on this level.

A security officer showed us Martin's file. It stated that he had worked in the habitat for no less than two years.

"There must be some mistake," I said. "He's only been missing for six weeks."

She handed me a photo. "Is that him?"

I looked carefully. The man in the hologram was older than I remembered, but definitely Martin.

"Yes, it is," I admitted, grudgingly. "But how do you explain—?"

"We don't," she said. "We just accept."

Carnarvon took the file from her, winking. "Come on," he said to me. "Let's go see where he was taken."

I followed him out of the administration building, hating the curl of amusement I saw in his profile. With the end of my quest in sight, the last thing I wanted to hear was more nonsense.

"This is crazy," I stated.

"Sure," he agreed pleasantly. "But blame the ROTH if you have to blame someone."

We headed to a nearby building, where the files told us Martin had lived.

"He left his room at midnight," read Carnarvon. "Going to meet a lover, apparently."

We followed a series of corridors, all equally unremarkable, until Carnarvon brought me to a sudden halt.

"The cameras tracked him as far as here, then lost him."

I looked around. The corridor was empty and featureless. There was no sign that anybody had passed this way at all, let alone died here.

"What else does the file say?" I asked, staring at the blank, polished floor.

"Not much. Martin turned a corner, walked four steps and vanished. The general consensus, as you guessed, is that the Director took him."

"Where?"

"No-one knows." Carnarvon put a hand on my shoulder. "I'm sorry."

I shrugged his hand away. "I don't believe you're telling me everything."

"Of course not. But I don't know everything, do I?"

"Bullshit." His flippancy annoyed me, fuelled my growing frustration. "This has been one long cover-up right from the beginning. You told me I'd understand when I saw the fifth level. Well, I'm here and I've seen it but I still don't understand. Why can't you just tell me?"

"I—"

"My brother's disappeared, for God's sake!"

"Look around you. Can *you* understand what's going on here? No-one can. Your brother was taken in full view of a security camera and it saw nothing. Four steps—zap—gone. Where? If I knew I'd tell you, I swear. We lose something like three hundred people a year under similar circumstances, and nearly triple that many are killed—"

"So why doesn't somebody do something?"

"Such as? What do you suggest? This has been happening for one hundred years; if something could have been done, we would have done it already."

"So close the mines."

"We can't. They're too productive. And the odds of the Director striking is statistically insignificant, anyway. You've more chance of dying on the surface."

I felt caged in, and wanted to strike something. "You're lying."

"Not at all—"

"You think you can palm me off with false records and insanities—"

"If you'll just calm down—"

"No! I refuse to believe that Martin is dead. He's down here somewhere and I'm going to find him."

I turned on my heel and walked angrily away.

"How?" Carnarvon called after me. "You're not the first to have tried, you know!"

I ignored him. Grief, anger, and a sense of betrayal fought for control of my mind, clouding my thoughts and judgement. I knew that Martin was alive somewhere; I could feel it in my bones. I wasn't going to let the matter go so easily. Martin would have done the same for me, I was sure, had our roles been reversed.

I wandered the corridors, losing myself in the maze of the habitat, not caring if Carnarvon followed. Ten minutes passed before I regained my senses and realised that I was alone. When I did, I set out to begin my own investigation.

I was allocated a room near his and started asking questions.

No-one could give me hard facts about my brother. Few people remembered him, as though years had passed since his disappearance. One even went so far as to suggest that it *had* been years, but I dismissed her as a liar, part of the conspiracy keeping me from the truth, even though she insisted that she had been his lover.

My two weeks of grace passed quickly and fruitlessly, spent for the most part in mess-halls and recreation facilities, always asking questions. The citizens of the fifth level, although sympathetic, were victims of the same passivity to fate espoused by the security officer who had shown me Martin's file. I despaired of ever learning the truth, but for the wrong reasons: I wondered what Martin had done to warrant such a thorough white-wash of his sudden departure.

And always, everywhere I looked, was the strangeness of the mines, the sheer improbability of it all, from the planet below to the habitats above. I felt overwhelmed by odd details gleaned from the people I interviewed: the way power was beamed by maser from the south 'pole' rather than sent along cables; the slag-pit, an apparently bottomless hole in the 'ceiling' that was used to dispose of waste materials; the odd discrepancy between the mass of minerals extracted from the planet and that which arrived on the surface of Barnath, the latter being roughly one-sixth of the former; and the cluster of ROTH artifacts on the planet itself, which, although active, seemed to serve no other function than to send bright sparks of ball lightning hurtling around the sundered crust. But I refused to submit to the disorientation; I vowed that I would remain undistracted until I knew the truth. My life on the surface was waiting. I had to find Martin and bring him back, no matter how long it took.

So great was my blindness that I disregarded what was staring me in the face: that, in order to comprehend what had happened to Martin, I would first have to comprehend the Mines themselves, a task for which I was both physically and mentally unprepared.

It wasn't until I met a man called Azimuth, a well-tanned mole from the sixth level, that I learned what fate was really awaiting me.

I happened across him in a bar on the North-east quadrant of the fifth level—a dirty man, dressed in his stained undersuit from further Up. He recognised my face, and came to join me at my table.

"I remember you," he said. "You came here looking for your brother, right?"

"That's right. Do you know anything about—?"

He laughed, anticipating my question. "No, no. I never met him. But I heard about you on the news circuits topside, before I came here."

I frowned. "When was that?"

"Well, let me see, now. I came here five years ago, and I'd heard the story six months before that. Five and a half years, then. Sure, that'd be about right."

I must have gaped at his words, for he laughed again at my confusion.

"You haven't noticed yet?" he asked, misunderstanding. "Time is all fucked up down here. You arrived, what . . . ?"

"Fourteen days ago," I forced out.

"And I'm in my sixth year, with the Director's grace. Topside, it could've been centuries. You never know how long until you look."

Azimuth didn't stop there, but I hardly heard what he said. According to Martin's records, he had worked in the Mines for two years—a fact I had initially dismissed as ridiculous. If time really was askew deep in the mines—a possibility I could not discredit, given the other wonders I had already witnessed—then the obstacles facing me were greater than I had imagined. But there was still hope.

I forced myself out of my daze. "The newscast," I said. "What did it say?"

Azimuth hesitated. "You sure you want to know?"

I gripped him firmly on the arm. "Tell me."

"All I remember is the headline: 'Brothers separated, then reunited by death.' Very tragic. I don't know whether that helps you, or makes things worse, but there you go. You wanted to hear it."

I gaped incredulously. Reunited, I echoed to myself, by *death*?

He obviously interpreted my stunned silence as a sign of comprehension and barrelled upwards from his seat, chuckling deep in his belly. "Be seein' you, maybe."

When he had gone, I regarded my drink with despair, thinking dull, slow thoughts. The truth was like a heavy weight—the weight of miles of solid earth—settling upon my shoulders.

When my glass was empty, I wandered 'home', alone.

That evening, I tracked down Carnarvon. He was still in the Northern habitat, easily reached by internal vidcom.

"I've been waiting for you to call," he said. "I knew you would."

I hesitated for a moment, balanced on the edge of total acceptance. When the words eventually came, it didn't sound like me speaking:

"Who did *you* lose?"

"My wife." His voice was even; his eyes reflected the sympathy I offered, unwanted. "It took me a month to realise I'd never find her by looking. When I tried to escape back to Earth by one of the other Shafts, I ended up on Barnath, where I decided to stay. For all the years I've been Manager, I've been waiting for someone like you to bring me back."

"And here we are."

"Yes. Here we are. Looking without finding again."

The silence claimed us again. I had only one question left.

"Do you want to come with me?"

"Sure." He smiled. "The Grand Tour isn't over yet."

We met the next day and logged out of the fifth level. The Shaft accepted our pressure-suited bodies indifferently, and we dropped like stones into the depths of an impossible earth.

SIX

The sixth level opens onto the fiery face of a sun.

Our period of grace had expired. I found work as an energy-scoop operator, and met the man called Donahue who had greeted me in the embarkation bay of the fifth level. He didn't remember me, of course, but we quickly became friends. He helped me adjust to the artificial gravity of B station and taught me everything I needed to learn about my new job. It wasn't long before my tan was as deep as his, and my acceptance of the impossible almost as automatic.

The sixth level does that to you. It overwhelms, it terrifies, it can even drive a person mad. But those who make it this far and stay for any length of time tend to have been a little crazy in the first place.

Carnarvon's time as surface Manager served him in good stead, even though the post was irrelevant to the deeper levels. He worked in administration, somewhere in the heart of the central gravity-platform. We met once a week to discuss our progress.

Progress where? It didn't matter. We were both marking time before the inevitable.

Then, six months after Carnarvon and I had entered the mines, he didn't show for our weekly meeting. I dug around for information and eventually learned that the Director had come for him during the week. His body was never found.

I waited a month before moving on. My link with the surface had been severed; there was no point staying any longer than I had to. As though I had oscillated until then from a stretched rubber band, I suddenly found myself cut free. I started to fall.

The level supervisor was sympathetic.

There was only one way left to go, at the very end.

SEVEN

The cage opens and I float into a transparent sphere nearly one hundred metres across fixed to the base of the Shaft like a bubble on a straw. There is no-one present to watch or to censure me as I drift through the zero gravity, press my face against the surface of the bubble and stare outwards.

My eyes adjust eventually. Instead of darkness outside the bubble, I see stars.

Stars . . .

The Shaft ends here. There is no Downward path any more—only Up, and Up, and Up. Forever.

There appears to be no way to leave the bubble, but part of me wonders what would happen if I could. Could I travel through space and re-enter the mines from above, thus completing a strange loop of navigation?

Even here, it seems, there are no answers. There are only questions—and me, staring ape-like at the sky. What could be stranger than this? Like the first colonists, I have stepped into the alien Mines of Barnath and found everything I didn't expect: space beyond comprehension, time in disarray, resources without end, and . . .

I suddenly realise what *else* the first colonists found, what prevented word from spreading across the galaxy, and what halted the scientific jihad aimed like an arrow at the heart of the mines. Only one discovery could have been sufficient:

People. People have always been here, wandering twisted loops through time, crossing and recrossing, occasionally colliding. They greeted the first explorers of the deeper levels, and integrated them seamlessly into a pre-existing society. Later arrivals were likewise assimilated, lured by mysteries and wonders in abundance, by a curiosity so great that not even the threat of death deterred them.

Whether the mines themselves are from the future or from the distant past, or whether they exist entirely beyond time, doesn't matter. Nothing here is certain, except that humanity has moved in and has therefore been here forever, entangled in some unknowable cosmic scheme.

Maybe the ROTH never existed at all. Even the Director might be human, with a purpose of his own.

My skin crawls, as though across an incomprehensible distance I am being watched.

On the heels of that thought comes an impatience, a need to move—in any direction. Time is passing around me like the heavy surges of a deep sea. A minute here might be a million hours on the surface, for all I know; or a heartbeat a whole lifetime. I want to travel, to be taken further. *Now.*

But the Director will come, I remind myself, only when it comes. Not before. Of that I am reasonably certain, if nothing else.

My ghostly reflection stares back at me with Martin's face—the face of my other half, my twin. A not-so-distant light in the alien starscape moves like a tear down the face of my reflection. I sense that he is waiting for me, wherever he is.

●

INTRODUCTION TO:

.... GHOSTS OF THE FALL

I've happily spent most of my life in Adelaide, the much-maligned (murder) capital of South Australia. It follows therefore that I've destroyed it one or two times in the course of my writing. Or if not actually destroyed it, as in "White Christmas", then at least put it through the wringer.

This is the oldest piece in Magic Dirt. *Written in October 1992, it was my fortieth short story and signals, to my mind at least, a clear boundary between the work I'd been doing up to that point and the work I produced afterwards. Not only did this story win a prize in the Writers of the Future Contest, thereby introducing me to the very wide world of professional writers, but it was the first for which I was paid a significant sum. It also earned me my very first Ditmar nomination (although learning later that my story made the ballot by virtue of just one recommendation did take the shine off that milestone somewhat).*

Looking back on this story now, sixteen years older and with almost three million published words behind me, I remember my love of the opening and closing lines. I remember researching the bells of Adelaide's St Peters cathedral and learning that they do indeed have names. I remember trying to capture Hogarth's feelings as he negotiated the social complexities of a world he wasn't yet adult enough to understand. The rising tide of forgetfulness has taken the rest.

I do, however, remember struggling through poverty, crappy jobs, ill-health and other obstacles in the hope of one day being a full-time writer—not so different from Hogarth's post-apocalyptic squalor, now I come to think about it (except I never had any luck growing my own vegetables). Doubt that I had made the right decision was inevitable. Would I ever look back and wish I'd put my energies elsewhere?

I once wrote that if I could go back and meet my younger self, I would comfort him by paraphrasing Hogarth's closing thoughts from this story: It's worth it, because I know I'll go the distance.

But the truth is, the effort's sufficient unto itself. If I was writing for any purely material reason, I would have given it away long ago. Our jobs, just like our homes, should be expressions of who we are, not projections of who we think we ought to be. It's good

*to aspire, but if a foundation is out of whack no edifice will stay
up long.*

Magic Dirt *marks the semi-miraculous feat of keeping this
particular house of cards elevated for eighteen years. If I'd known
something like this lay in the future, I would've been a whole lot
more chill in 1992.*

•

GHOSTS OF THE FALL

A warm current rolled in overnight, bringing with it the stench of death. When I awoke at dawn, my nose and mouth were thick with foul-tasting mucus. Gagging, I rolled over and reached for my stained filtermask. When it was in place, I struggled from my hammock and squinted from the arbour of my room. The sun, eclipsed by the shadowy bulk of a vine-tangled building, was feeble and brown, but enough of its light filtered between the towers to allow a rough study.

Plumes of steam rose from the waters far below, which, although slightly lower in level than they had been the night before, still drowned the groundward floors of the city. Black shapes hunted lazily, deceptively small from my altitude: crocs, searching for food.

A dull flash of light from the top of the opposite building caught my eye. Davo was up already, adjusting his solar panels. Every drop of energy was precious, even that which struggled through poisoned clouds on a day such as this. Rubbing my eyes and trying in vain to make the seal of my mask comfortable against cheekbones and jaw, I prepared to face the morning.

A warm current and a brown dawn, I thought. *Someone, or something, will die today . . .*

Max, my foster, had been up and working for some time. He greeted me as I emerged from the access stairway in the centre of the rooftop garden.

"'Morning, Hogarth." He put down his hoe in order to wipe the sweat from his brow. Viewed from the top of the building Sol was a malign ball hovering low over the yellow-smudged horizon. Although I knew the colour was caused by pollution and dust in the lower atmosphere, I couldn't help but feel as though the sun itself had been corrupted. Under its light, Max looked twenty years older: his skin was pallid and blotchy, and his white hair seemed thinner than cobwebs.

I could almost see the leaves of our plants withering along with us.

"Whew," I said, wrinkling my nose. "Bad tides."

Max shrugged. "Got to have them, I suppose. Balances the good times."

"Kris'll be disappointed."

Max's brown eyes crinkled. Kris Parker, one of the joint chiefs of our community, had a theory that the ecosystem was gradually stabilising. Bad tides, which occurred about once every month, confounded him.

"This ain't nothing on the old days." Max picked up the hoe again and tilted his hat to ward off the sun. "I don't suppose you remember it that well."

I didn't, although I'd heard the stories often enough. "Has Davo been over?"

"Earlier. He was asking for you. Take the morning off, if you want to go see him."

"Thanks, Max. I'll make it up."

"No worries, son. Have a little fun for a change."

He bent back to his work. For a thoughtful moment I, the youngest in the community, studied him, the eldest. We made an odd couple, but I knew I'd miss him when he succumbed. The thought alone was unpleasant. Max had been my foster for so many years that I had almost forgotten my real father. But whether I liked it or not, poison or accident would take him in the end, as they took everyone.

Perhaps he noticed my scrutiny, or sensed my mood.

"Git," he said, without lifting his head, "before I put you to work."

I ran off through the garden and down the access ladder, mindful of the broken rungs. From the third floor down stretched a rope bridge to the building in which Davo lived. I ran across, not looking down, and was exactly halfway when the earthquake hit.

But for the bells, I would've had no warning. With a gentle clatter at first, then with a strident jangling, every metal mobile and brass clapper in the city began to sound. I clutched the sides of the bridge and wrapped a rope around my ankle. As the quake set the bridge jumping, I hung on for dear life, too frightened to open my eyes, thinking of crocs and poisoned currents.

There came a deep, resonant bong, and I realised with a chill of fear that the old Cathedral bell was sounding, as it hadn't more than once in my memory. Great Fred chimed four times in two minutes, and those two minutes felt like a lifetime to me, suspended between two derelict skyscrapers by little more than homespun string. Beneath the ringing, I could hear masonry falling and screams, some distant, some near; all perhaps reliving the Fall.

When the clatter died down and the shocks faded, I released the breath I hadn't known I was holding and crawled the rest of the way to Davo's building. Once over the threshold, I lay trembling in the darkness, trying not to cry.

I am too young to have memories of the War, but I do faintly recall the Fall: the clouds that covered the sky, the months of darkness, the constant tremors. I dream occasionally of the nine waves that swept the old world away. Sometimes I even see the face of my long-dead father as he presses me into an elevator crammed with women, heading for higher ground.

The elders of Adelaide didn't talk about these times, except in whispers. Much of my knowledge regarding the origins of our community was overheard and therefore patchy and incomplete. I suspect that, given time and allowing me descendants, it would have developed into a full-blown mythology. I truly believed that ogres had attacked us from the sky, hurling rocks upon our heads and leaving us to drown, cursed with childlessness and disease.

It wasn't until I was about eleven years old that Davo sat me down and filled in a few blanks. He explained that the "ogres" had been the forces of the OEG, the Off Earth Government; that there had been just one massive rock, like an iceberg; and that the sterility and sickness were the results of radiation and industrial poisons set free by the Fall.

The descent of that single rock marked a decisive end to the long and bitter war between Earth and space. Davo spoke of melting icecaps, volcanic eruptions, tsunamis and shifting continental plates. I understood very little of what he said, and in a way I was glad, for the words themselves sounded grim. Some things, however, I could understand. What we called magnetic north had once been south-west. Inconstant seasons were the result of a new wobble to the Earth's axis. Every time it rained or a calved iceberg drifted near us, I wondered whether it was composed of water from Earth or from space. And the reason why we, the citizens of Adelaide, had no visitors was because no one else was left.

On the roofs of our flooded city we lingered, alone and forgotten.

A fluke of geography had kept the buildings from falling. Currents of clean, cold water flowing from the melting Antarctic icecap kept us from being poisoned. We survived on plants grown from seedlings found on nearby islands. The islands—which had once been hilltops—were themselves uninhabitable due to a proliferation of waste, but they had provided valuable resources during the early years. As our numbers dwindled from the original thousand to a bare one hundred, we learned to manage our crops better, and even bred chickens to balance our diet.

Few ever forgot the fact that we had survived the Fall by nothing short of a miracle, or that our existence was still tenuous. We were reminded of that every time the Earth's new tilt precipitated a shift in currents and we received a flow of the dreaded warm tide. On such occasions, we were forced to rely on tank water until the tides once again turned—although other species, such as the giant crocs from the nearby islands, enjoyed the poisonous current. Strange mutants, rotting and twisted, were carried by the dark waters; poor food by any creature's standards, but something where little existed elsewhere.

Kris Parker had a list of the things that should have killed us—and could still do so—which he showed to anyone who began to forget the legacy of the past. Most just learned to hide the scars a little better and got on with life—as though we had always lived on the tops of buildings in the middle of a shallow, fresh-water ocean.

Except in my dreams of the Fall, we always had. That was the trouble with being fifteen years old when the world was ten years dead.

Max and I lived in one of the smaller buildings on the outskirts of the flooded city. Davo's was much larger. A monster of more than sixty storeys, its upper levels were stepped and thick with plants. Despite that, it was home to just ten people. He occupied one entire floor of the 'scraper', of which only a small percentage was devoted to himself. The bulk of it contained every electrical good he had scavenged from the remains of the old world. Not the complex, specialised equipment—but the gadgets, like coffee machines, batteries, electric screwdrivers, televisions and digital clocks.

I loved browsing through the relics, trying to imagine what they could possibly have been for. Few of them worked, but Davo could fix almost anything if left to tinker unhindered. I remember my absolute faith in his wizardry, tinged with only a small amount of envy. Even the air smelt better in there, as though the presence of so much of the past somehow cleansed it of the present.

Davo's biggest problem—apart from those, like Kris, who felt better with the old technology forgotten—was power. The old solar panels—thoughtfully stored away by one of the founders, and requiring only cleaning and a technical mind to get them working again—were efficient but their output was limited. Furthermore, people often accused Davo of "stealing" more than his fair share of power, even though he had been the one to give it back to us in the first place.

He rarely spoke to me about the relics he was fiddling with, but I sometimes overheard him talking about these things with Max. Their secrecy bothered me for no other reason than that I felt left out, as children often do when barred from something adult.

As I mounted the steps to his level, I was greeted by an even greater state of disorganisation than usual. A couple of heavy racks had collapsed in the quake, spilling multicoloured wires and transistors like a tide of tiny bugs across the floor. I could hear Davo cursing somewhere in the depths of the workshop, but couldn't see him. A strange sound filled the air: a whisper like, yet quite unlike, the hissing of cold rain or the crackling of fire.

"Hello?" I called, taking off my mask.

A ragged reply came from under a mound of old TV screens. "Shee-it! Is that you, Hogey? Give me a hand, would you?"

I ran to where he lay pinned beneath a cupboard. Taking a corner, I heaved until it lifted enough for him to wriggle free. I let go once he rolled away, and the crash reverberated for long seconds.

"You okay?" I asked, bending over him. He clutched his leg, which was turning a strange purple colour.

"Fucking thing!" I didn't know whether he referred to his leg or the cupboard that had injured it. "Dislocated my bloody knee, I think. Hurts like buggery anyhow. Help me over to the tube." I gripped him under one armpit and helped him limp across the room. A length of hose dangled from the ceiling, culminating in a small nozzle which Davo held to his lips.

"Wait," he said, waving a hand at the bench. "Turn it off. Big red button—push it!" There was a machine on the workbench—a large metal box, its face adorned with knobs and dials and a blank screen in one corner. I did as he said and the hissing sound died away.

"What is it?" I asked, staring at it in wonder.

"Later." He blew hard into the nozzle and I heard whistling from a higher floor echo down the stairwell. Davo hopped on one leg with the nozzle at his ear, anxious for a reply.

"Hello?" said a voice from the tube, faint and male.

"It's Davo. Is Jerrie around?"

"Yeah. Somewhere."

"I need to speak to her."

"Hang on, I'll ask." After a long pause, the voice returned. "Sorry, but she's busy right now, repairing the garden."

"Tell her it's urgent."

"It won't make any difference." The distant voice sounded amused. "She doesn't want to talk to you, Davo."

"Okay, thanks anyway." Davo hung up the tube. "Shit. Stupid bitch."

I looked at him, shocked. For me—going through puberty with Adelaide's male-to-female ratio at more than seven-to-three and no-one at all near my age—any woman was to be regarded with near-reverence, especially one who was ostensibly single, such as Jerrie.

"Bloody cow."

"Shall I go get her?" I asked, wondering if they'd argued.

"No." Davo leaned some of his weight on his leg, and winced. "I really don't think I've done anything too serious. If you want, though, you could run up and get some cabbage leaves and a bandage."

"Okay." Cabbage leaves were good for muscle injuries.

"And if you do happen to see Jerrie, tell her I'd like to talk to her later. *Just* talk, if she asks."

I headed for the stairwell. Rapidly winded by the humidity and the mask, I was gasping by the time I reached the rooftop. I needed permission before taking the leaves and sought Jerrie herself rather than anyone else. She was tending one of the gardens, her sun-browned and exercised figure distinctive among the others.

I stammered a hesitant greeting as she stood upon catching sight of me. I explained why I needed the leaves, and that Davo wanted to see her later. She frowned at "*just* talk," but I didn't pry into their affairs.

"He's not badly hurt, is he?" she asked.

"Not really," I said. "He reckons he'll be okay."

She leaned close to whisper in my ear. "Is the radio working?"

I frowned. "The what?"

"Never mind." She backed away. "Tell him I'll be down later."

I nodded and headed back downstairs, clutching the leaves and bandage she had given me.

Davo had sat on the floor but was otherwise where I had left him. Together we bound his leg and manoeuvred him into the hammock. Only then did I ask: "Davo, what's a radio?"

He stared at me blankly for a moment, until he realised. "Of course! You wouldn't remember—you're too young! Christ." He reached for my arm. "Help me back up and I'll show you."

He hobbled painfully over to the workbench and settled into a stool in front of the mysterious machine, mumbling about waves through the air and antennae and frequencies—more things I didn't understand. Talking across distances using electricity, or something like it, sounded impossible to me; only his matter-of-factness convinced me I might be wrong.

"It's an old CB–V, practically a collector's item but it works— that's the important thing." He twiddled with knobs and aligned metal rods. I watched him, fascinated.

"Okay. Listen." He turned a knob and the unearthly hiss returned, more softly this time.

We both listened closely, I expecting voices, he something else entirely. Both of us were disappointed.

"Damn." He rummaged around the workbench for a length of wire. "The quake must have fucked up the ionosphere or something." He detached a metal rod and fixed one end of the wire to it. Handing it to me, he said, "Hang this out the window. Don't let anyone see."

I did as he asked. The stench of decay was stronger in the dull sunlight, and I held my breath until I got the rod in position. He waved me back and I hurried to his side.

He fiddled with knobs for a few minutes until, breathing a sigh of gratification, he leaned onto his stool and motioned for me to listen closely. The hiss grew louder and louder until I could hardly think.

"Hear it?" Davo shouted above the din, flapping his hand open and closed, open and closed, open and closed.

I watched the hand and listened. A sound rose out of the chaos, a note repeating in time with his gesture:

. . . pip-pip-pip-pip-pip . . .

I stared at Davo in confusion, and nodded my head. I could hear the sound all right, but had no idea what it meant. Davo smiled triumphantly and killed the noise.

The sudden silence was eerie, until Davo filled it: "It's a beacon," he said, his voice trembling.

"A what?"

He did his best to explain. "Imagine you're on the top of your building and I'm on the top of mine. You want to talk to me, but it's too far to shout. All you have is a mirror. How do you attract my attention?"

"I guess I'd use the mirror."

"Of course—reflecting the sun until I see you. That's what a beacon is: a repeated flash, but of sound not light, carried through the air by radio waves."

"So . . . ?" I was breathless at the thought gradually dawning.

"So somebody's out there."

"And they're trying to get our attention?"

Davo's face was very serious when he replied: "Maybe. I hope so. You see, the great advantage of having this old CB–V is that we can do more than receive. We could transmit, talk to them, find out who they are—if we wanted to."

"Why wouldn't you want to?"

"I—I'm not sure."

"Have you tried?"

He looked guilty, but was saved by the baying of a horn. I was about to press him, but Davo cocked his head to listen, and put a finger over his mouth.

I listened too. The horn-player, having attracted the attention of everyone in the city, rattled out a short, staccato code almost too quick for me to follow, then wound down with one final blast. A few horns replied, echoing raucously among the towers.

Davo winced as he shifted his leg to a more comfortable position. "So this is it, the excuse they've been waiting for. They've finally called a Council."

"They always do after a quake."

He smiled wryly. "But not always just to find out if some poor bastard's been killed."

"I don't understand."

He pulled another face, and I suggested he should go back to bed. He could see the sense in that, despite himself, and, after switching off the radio, allowed me to manhandle him back to his hammock.

"Can I ask you for another favour?"

I nodded.

"I need to go to the Council meeting tonight," he said. "Would you and Max could help me get there?"

"Sure. I'll ask Max, anyway."

"Thanks." He leaned back into the hammock and regarded me through half closed eyelids. "You'd better go do some work, seeing you'll miss the night because of this damned bureaucratic bullshit."

I nodded, although reluctant to leave the wizard's den of his workshop. Even mysteries adults refused to explain were preferable to tilling soil and killing insects.

"You're a good kid," he said, before I left. "Don't tell anyone what I showed you."

The afternoon passed slowly. I helped Max prune our crop of tomatoes and carry some ripe vegetables into the depths of our building, where the relative coolness would keep them fresh. As I performed my chores, my attention kept straying beyond the confines of the rooftop garden. I wondered who might be out there, across the seemingly endless ocean, and if they really were talking to us.

The sea was deep to the west, almost navy blue at the horizon; eastwards it grew shallower and lighter in colour as it approached the islands. Waves played on the distant beaches, white fingernails appearing and disappearing as though vast, submerged hands were reaching for the surface. Birds were few and far between when a warm tide happened upon us, and only the odd dark speck disturbed the hazy tranquillity of the eastern horizon that day.

As recently as four years earlier, I had gone with Max and a few others on an expedition to Barker, the nearest of the islands. We were collecting wood to light a bonfire on Council Tower—a scheme devised by a man named Cameron Dennis, who wanted to see if there were any other survivors nearby. The Council had forbidden the use of the city's store of wood, so we had to go to the islands to collect fuel.

We took even more stringent precautions than normal, wrapping ourselves from head to foot in old plastic and leather to keep out the poison, and ensuring our masks were equipped with triple the normal thickness of filters. Even so, the terrible malignance of the soil seemed to eat at us as we hacked at the mutated trees. One of our number scratched himself on an axe, and died two weeks later of fever.

What I remember most clearly is the return to Adelaide. The three heavily laden boats were rowed by our strongest men—one of whom was Max—and they hurried through the thickening gloom, oars splashing and creaking with effort. I crouched at the foremost point of our boat, staring ahead at the vision of our home silhouetted against the setting sun.

So flat and still was the sea that the buildings appeared to rise out of the surface of a shining mirror. Their reflections stabbed deep into the water, as though Adelaide were a city of crystal anchored to the very heart of the earth. Occasionally, a beam of light flashed through one of the abandoned floors, and my spirits soared, uplifted by the sight.

Then the light changed. The skyscrapers darkened, became slender pillars of blackness like the petrified legs of an enormous creature sinking into the sea. I'd never seen a gravestone—our bodies were burned or dumped into the sea—but I knew what they were, and what they meant to me. The place I called home was made of tombs, archetypal symbols of the empty, final flesh. Within ten, maybe twenty years, we would be gone, except perhaps for me and a few of the younger ones. Not long after, the buildings themselves would succumb to the acids that ate at their foundations and topple into the ocean. Adelaide would disappear without trace.

The sun set, like the slamming of a door, and everything went dark.

When the expedition returned, we unloaded the wood, hauled it up Council Tower and heaped it on a concrete block. Disaster struck when we tried to light it. Chemicals had so permeated the wood that it refused to burn, no matter how hard we tried. Eventually it was thrown into the sea and the attempt to signal fellow survivors abandoned.

As the sun slowly crept toward the horizon on the day Great Fred chimed four times, I was reminded of that venture.

"Do you think anybody's out there?" I asked Max as we finished our jobs for the day.

My foster looked at me carefully, his grey eyes both amused and saddened. "I don't think so, son. Why?"

"Just curious, I guess." The day faded in a wash of deep browns and reds, tending to black. "Whatever happened to Cameron Dennis?" I asked, realising that I hadn't seen him for a long time.

"He killed himself when the bonfire project failed."

"Oh." I was tempted to ask how, but could guess the answer. The preferred method of suicide was to leap from a building and be killed upon impact with the forbidding waters below.

We were silent as stars appeared one by one in the grey sky. The first to emerge were the Strange Stars: three brilliant points of light hanging over the northern horizon, always brightest at the end of the day. The Strange Stars had paths of their own, entirely separate from the circle of the heavens, and they'd always fascinated me. They represented change and mystery in my otherwise immutable world.

I watched them with renewed interest until Max handed me a sack of compost.

"Take this down to the storeroom," he said, "then we'll head off to the Council."

I obediently put aside my thoughts and hurried down the stairwell. When I returned, Max had a bag full of spare produce ready to take with us.

We crossed the bridge to Davo's building. My friend waited for us there, hopping nervously back and forth on a pair of makeshift crutches. Jerrie was not present, having already gone to Council Tower.

"She means well," said Max. "Perhaps a little *too* well for the likes of you."

"She's brainwashed, you mean," Davo laughed bitterly. "Tell it like it is, you old bastard."

The three of us inched our way up the four flights of stairs to the bridge connecting Davo's home to the next building. I took the crutches and the bag while Max hoisted Davo onto his back, where the technician clung like a giant child. Slowly, we inched our way across the bridge, I prayed all the while that there would be no repeat of that day's quake.

There wasn't. A light breeze had sprung up, dispelling the fog rising from the water. The night was clear and silent. Gap-toothed buildings surrounded us like silhouettes of all the world's dead cities, immense and hollow. Five bridges ahead, we could hear a whisper of voices from where the Council gathered.

Councils were normally exciting for me. Being accustomed only to the company of Max, and occasionally our neighbours, I was unused to crowds, and the hundred citizens of Adelaide certainly felt like one when gathered together. Although most were old and tired, and some openly grieved at the sight of the Council, shrunken as it was from the old days, my eyes saw only a multitude of dazzling variety.

On this occasion however, I felt a twinge of nervous discomfort. Perhaps it was nothing more than the fact that, with everyone still masked against the fumes of the poisoned sea, the Council resembled less the gathering of our community than a coven of mouthless wraiths.

Davo, Jerrie and I were among the dozen or so below twenty-five years of age scattered through the assembly. The rest were uniformly over forty, with Max, at fifty-nine, being the eldest. Kris Parker, chair of the infrequent meetings, was forty-seven and almost completely bald. His eyes were a startling blue. I'd always been a little afraid of him.

"Order!" he called, and the crowd slowly settled. His eyes smiled through his mask at the rings of citizens sitting on the floor around him. The meeting was held on the very top of Council Tower, lit by yellow lamplight, and there seemed to be more shadows than people clustered about the makeshift podium.

Kris removed his mask to speak to the group as a whole.

"First, welcome to you all, and thanks to everyone who brought gifts. The surplus will be distributed to those who need it after the meeting. Second, the roll indicates that three people are missing."

Kris listed the names, and members of the crowd explained the absentees. One had not been able to come because of fever; another had died the previous week of a heart attack; the last had fallen from a garden during the quake.

There was a long silence as the crowd remembered the dead woman. I couldn't remember a meeting that hadn't started with a roll call of the deceased. We were all used to the fact of our dwindling numbers. If tears were shed, they were hidden by the masks we all wore.

Kris shuffled his notes. "The reason we're here is to discuss the effects of the quake. Does anyone have any major damage to report?"

A woman with red hair put up her hand, and Kris invited her to speak. Her fresh-water tank had developed a leak, allowing the precious reservoir to trickle away. In times of a bad tide, this was a serious matter. The woman accepted that the best course of action was to relocate the people living in her building and to transfer her crops before they wilted. The Council voted, and agreed. The move would take place the next day, or sooner if convenient.

I tried to put myself in her position. She was leaving her home and the crops she had tended with back-breaking care since the Fall. I felt sorry for her, and was selfishly glad that it hadn't happened to Max and me.

Somebody else reported that one of the older buildings had collapsed. Although uninhabited and therefore a relatively minor loss, it was disturbing nonetheless. All the skyscrapers had a slight lean, and it was only a matter of time before the stronger structures capitulated to the force of gravity.

Kris waited a few moments for further queries, but none were forthcoming. No one mentioned the ever-present threat of crop failure, which was unusual; I supposed that the earthquake had erased the more conventional concerns of Adelaide, for a while.

"Very well. Let's move on to the next and final matter. I've had a request from someone who wishes to remain nameless for information on a matter I know nothing about. The last, in itself, is not unusual—" a smattering of laughter greeted the small joke "—but the subject is one of some significance for our entire community. I therefore called this Council in order to discuss it.

"I'd like to call David Rothbaum to the podium to answer a few questions."

I stared in surprise at Davo, who struggled to his feet and removed his mask.

"If you don't mind, I'd rather stay here." My friend indicated the splint and bandages on his leg and exaggerated slightly. "Dislocated, you see."

Kris nodded. "My sympathies. By all means, remain where you are."

"What would you like to know?"

Kris paused slightly before voicing the question. "The person I speak for would like to ask what you've been doing in that laboratory of yours. Is there anything you should tell us all about?"

"Let's see." Davo shuffled on his crutches. "I looked at the easy stuff first, so it's only getting harder as time goes on. But there are two more panels working, if anybody needs power." There was an immediate buzz: everybody wanted more light, more heat. "And I've developed a primitive intercom system—a bit like telephone, but not as sophisticated. If we can find some unbroken wire I can link all the buildings together. That way we won't have to shout across the gaps any more, or blow trumpets every time we have a Council meeting."

Kris smiled widely, but the incisiveness in his eyes told me that he expected more. "And?"

"Well, there is something else I've been mucking around with. Not really a project, though—more a sort of hobby."

"This is?"

Davo hesitated, and the Council awaited his reply.

"Uh, there was an old radio amongst all the junk, and I've been trying to make it work."

Instantly the citizens of Adelaide stirred and whispered. There was a shout of protest, to which came answering cries of support.

Kris waved his arms for silence. When he had it, he continued the interrogation. "Why?"

"To see if there are any other survivors, of course."

"Does the radio work?"

"No. It doesn't."

"Not yet, you mean?"

"I doubt even I'll be able to fix the damn thing."

"But you were attempting to do so?"

"Yes. Why not?"

One of the crowd shouted at Davo: "If they're there, why haven't they found us already?"

Davo sought to locate his interrogator, but was unable to. "Who would bother to look here?" He addressed the ring of faces around him as a whole. "We were just a small city in a small country. Why look for Adelaide when Sydney, New York, London, Tokyo, and Paris are gone? I know I wouldn't waste my energy."

"But if they were looking for survivors, surely they'd look everywhere?"

"And," interjected another, "they'd be using infra-red—"

"Maybe the shit in the atmosphere interferes with infra-red, or the thermal signals are too weak against the background. I don't know."

"What about the OEG? What if we're still at war!"

"Christ." Davo ran his fingers through his hair in frustration. "Anything could have happened. Ten years is a long time."

There were a few more shouts, and some voices raised in anger—so many that Davo couldn't respond to all of them.

"Where would they land?" someone called. "All the launch and landing facilities must be destroyed!"

"And they could still drop something on us!" This from a woman towards the back of the gathering, her eyes wide and frightened.

Kris again placated the gathering with his upraised palms, then turned back to Davo.

"I don't think you've considered this matter nearly well enough my boy. Experiments of this nature have potentially disastrous ramifications for the community as a whole. They need to be discussed before you will be allowed to continue."

Leaning on the podium, Kris assumed the patient, preaching stance we all knew so well. His voice became less accusing, more mellow and charismatic.

"There are those," he said, "of which I am one, who believe that the past is better left forgotten. We have survived here in peace since war destroyed our old world, and I am loath for this peace to be shattered simply to satisfy one young man's curiosity regarding the ghosts of a life long dead.

"I have accepted the need for electric power, and might even be convinced that an intercom is necessary, but my sensibilities baulk at the possibility of recontact with any hypothetical outside world. I believe it is foolish to hope that there are others out there who survived the Fall. Even if they are there, they must be in much the same position as we.

"Similarly, lacking evidence to support the continued existence of the OEG, it seems pointless to wonder about the war. The OEG might have crumbled after the Fall, or left the Earth's vicinity. Certainly, no one has seen them in over a decade, and I would be surprised if they're still searching or even listening for survivors.

"My mind is unclear, but I see two options open to us. One: allow David to continue with his experiments and attempt to contact any other survivors. Two: ban all further research entirely, on the grounds that it is almost certainly pointless and potentially very dangerous.

"As is customary, we will take a vote."

The gathering stirred, discussing the options, until Kris called for silence.

"Those for allowing David to continue with his experiment, please raise one hand." I immediately voted in favour, as did Davo and a few others. I was dismayed by the poor turnout, and that Max did not vote.

When the counting finished, Kris called for the second vote. "Those against—that is, in favour of ceasing the experiment immediately."

More hands went up this time and my hopes sank. A surprising number of young ones voted against Davo's project—but at least Max again did not raise his hand.

When the tallies double-checked, Kris announced the results.

"For: twenty-seven. Against: thirty-nine. Abstentions: thirty-five. Not a clear majority either way, so we'll need to discuss this further. Before we do, however: Max, I couldn't help but note that you abstained from casting a vote. May I ask why?"

My foster rose to his feet, and heads turned to look at him. His face was shadowed and serious when he tugged away his mask.

"There is a third option we have not considered."

"And this is?"

Max thought for a second, and I waited breathlessly for his suggestion. I knew that Kris would eventually turn the Council against Davo; Kris was too persuasive and the people too afraid of resurrecting old fears. But if Max—whom the people respected at least as much as they listened to Kris, if only because he was the oldest—spoke against Kris, Davo might be given the opportunity to continue.

Max; no doubt aware of his role, weighed his words carefully. "The third option is to allow David to continue until such time as the radio is working, *then* reconvene the Council to decide the next step. I'm sure he can be trusted not to attempt any communication until the Council advises him that it is our wish to do so."

Kris looked askance at Davo, who nodded eagerly. "Sure. No problems."

Kris looked unhappy. The suggestion was so reasonable that he had no choice but to call a second vote. The muttering of the crowd became less strident as human curiosity began to break through the initial shock.

And, sure enough, this time the result was conclusive: sixty-three in favour, less than twenty against, and the rest abstaining.

Kris scowled, but capitulated. "It is decided. I must warn you, David, that any deviation from this agreement will be severely punished."

Davo grinned. "No shit, bwana—I mean, of course I'll behave myself."

"Then this meeting is closed. Thank you all for coming." Kris turned away from the crowd and bent to whisper with the Senior Councillors.

"Almost too easy," said Max at my side.

"What?"

He looked at me. "Nothing. Let's go."

We helped Davo through the crowd toward the nearest bridge.

Despite his handicap, no one offered to help us get him home. Jerrie, however, came with us, and remained behind after we left Davo's workshop.

Max and I checked our garden together, spraying a few of the sickly plants with clean water.

"You go to bed," he said when we finished the chore, taking a seat on a rusted air conditioning vent and gazing out to sea. "I think I'll stay up for a while."

I studied him closely; his eyes were black pits, sunken in waxy flesh.

"You must be exhausted," I said.

He nodded, and gripped my shoulder. "I am, yes, but I will not sleep. Not tonight."

I nodded, even though I didn't understand, and headed for the stairs. As I left, Max moved to a position facing Davo's building. A single candle flame burned on my friend's floor, and my foster's bulky frame occluded it, like the closing of an eye.

I fell instantly into a deep, dark sleep.

Less than an hour passed, however, before I awoke, scrabbling at my mask as though I were suffocating. I sat upright and listened to the sound of my own breath, wondering whether it had been the mask that had woken me or something else: a nagging sensation that something important, somewhere, was taking place.

I left my bed and padded upstairs to Max's floor. He wasn't there, asleep or awake. When I checked the gardens, he wasn't there either. The plants rustled in the night breeze, and I shivered.

The night had chilled dramatically. Lifting my mask, I tested the air. It smelled of water—clean water from the melting south. The tide had turned.

I removed the mask and breathed deeply, thinking that this was what had woken me. But sleep would be hard to come by without knowing where Max had got to. Suicide never once crossed my mind, but the thought of being alone in our dying building, even for a night, made me nervous.

The Strange Stars hung like sentinels directly overhead as I ran down the stairs and across the bridge connecting our building to its neighbour. If my foster and friend weren't up talking, then maybe Davo would know where Max had got to.

The workshop was still and silent; no one broke the peace there, either by talking or playing with the radio, but I felt the need to investigate anyway. I tiptoed through the chamber, wary of any loose scraps of old technology that might have tripped me or made a noise, until I caught sight of Davo's hammock.

Two people lay entwined there, coiled together with an intimacy I had never experienced. Enough light spilled through the window for me to identify Davo's mop of hair and the silhouette of Jerrie's face. I crept closer, and my heart pounded when I realised that a part of their juxtaposed anatomy I had not identified was in fact her naked breast, frozen by starlight.

Embarrassed and feeling guilty, I considered throwing a rug over them, if only to protect them from the chill air. Barely had I decided not to when a noise from behind me disturbed the silent tableau.

A callused hand grabbed me across the mouth and, before I could turn, dragged me kicking and wriggling into the stairwell.

"Be quiet!" hissed a voice into my ear. My frightened eyes rolled to catch a glimpse of my assailant, but he was shrouded in impenetrable darkness.

The man wrenched my head so I was forced to look back into Davo's workshop.

I saw vague man-shapes moving to and fro through the shadows, like ghosts. I stopped struggling instantly.

There were five of them, large and unidentifiable. They seemed to be searching. One of them peered to study Davo and Jerrie, and I thought I heard a soft snigger, barely a worm of sound burrowing through the silence.

"No," said one of the ghosts. "Don't touch her."

The one who had laughed backed away from the couple, and I felt relieved for both of them. Threat was implicit in the stealthy silence of the ghosts, and, even though I didn't know what exactly had been avoided, I was grateful on Davo's behalf for Jerrie's presence. No one in Adelaide would allow harm to befall a woman while the sexes were split so unevenly.

"Here," whispered another voice, and the ghosts moved to a side of the room I could not see. A moment later there came a tinkling noise as something large was moved, a grunt of effort, then a distant, startling splash.

Jerrie stirred, murmuring in her sleep, and instantly the ghosts retreated, vanishing into the night as though they had never been there at all.

I wanted to scream: *What's going on?* But my captor held my mouth tightly closed until Jerrie returned to sleep and the night became still again. Only then did he relax his grip and allow me to see his face.

"It's over," Max whispered. "It's over."

I started to stammer a question, but he shushed me. He led me out of the workshop, across the void between buildings and back to our home. A faint butterfly-wing of aurora danced across the night sky, like an omen, as he explained what had happened.

"I was expecting something like this," he said, his voice empty of emotion. "The last real challenge Kris Parker had was when we considered lighting the bonfires on Council Tower. I told you that the man who had suggested the plan committed suicide, but that, perhaps, is not the whole of the truth. Cameron wasn't the sort to give up; he would have tried again, made other plans. Myself and a few others—we will always wonder whether he jumped from his garden, or whether he was thrown."

I stared at him, shocked beyond words. Could such a thing really have happened?

"Maybe Jerrie's presence made them think twice tonight," he went on, "or I'm wrong about their motives. I don't know. I'm just glad I didn't have to fight them. There's already been so much violence . . . "

In the glistening starlight, he put an arm around my shoulders and held me to him.

"It's over," he said again, and I wondered if he was trying to reassure me—although there was little reassurance to be found in his tone—or if he was describing the future, as he saw it.

I remembered my prophecy that morning:

Someone, or something, will die today . . .

I wondered if that thing might have been hope.

"We might as well get some sleep," Letting me go, he stared out to sea one last time. The aurora briefly flickered in his eyes, then died.

"I'll stay up for a while," I said, watching with despair as the impenetrable blackness of the stairwell swallowed him.

Is it really worth it? I wondered. *Is life so precious that we should scrabble for it every day, breaking our fingernails in the dirt and our hearts with sheer futility? Is it worth fighting death with an inhuman, soul-destroying effort just to survive one more day, and another, and another . . .*

Now, given the opportunity, I would say to my younger self: *Yes. Yes, it was worth it—for those who survived long enough.*

But, that night, I lay back onto the cooling, age-scarred concrete and contemplated the sky with an aching emptiness where my heart had once been.

The Strange Stars drifted slowly southward, and I noted distantly that the three had become four: a new star had joined the others and, as I watched, it moved across the sky on a path of its own.

Back and forth, it moved.

Back and forth, as though searching.

●

THE SOAP BUBBLE

It was a moment of pure, A-grade drama, better than anything I could have scripted. So good, in fact, I had no choice but to include it in that month's episode.

SCENE:
Control Bridge of the Navy Class Manned Deep Survey Ship *Rosenberg* (unofficially re-christened the *Wandering Jew*).

CAST:
GABLE "GABE" MCKENZIE, Captain
SARA MRAVINSKY, Second In Command
MYRION HEMMELLING, Life Support
JAKE FOO-WONG, Astrogation
ANDRE PASSANT, Security
STEVE JEFFERSSEN, Engineering and Maintenance
FREEDOM MAXWELL, Science
ALEK MAAS, Communications, Morale and Honorary Soap Operator (me)

EXTRAS:
Engineers, technicians, research personnel, the medical team, three cooks, sundry crew-members; one hundred and thirty-five in all.

NOTES:
Filmed live and on location near Mu Boötis, 108 light years from Earth.

The *Wandering Jew* had finished its initial survey of the system when the 'Event' took place. Captain Gabe, looking darkly handsome in his official flight-uniform, had successfully slotted us into a close polar orbit about the primary star, a greenish F0 of unremarkable appearance. Freedom Maxwell, as beautiful as ever with her blonde hair tied back in a loose pony-tail, was preparing for the first flyby of the inner planet. Jake Foo-Wong cheerfully checked co-ordinates every couple of minutes, conferring with the computers in unhurried, precise syllables. Steve Jefferssen watched the tell-tales monitoring the mighty engines with an avuncular eye; he seemed pleased, in his bear-like way, which was a good sign.

"Okay, folks." Captain Gabe surrendered control of the *Jew* to Jake and the AIs with a flourish of his wrist. "This baby is rolling. Any questions, comments or suggestions?"

"Nice work, Gabe," said Freedom, playing her part as Love Interest with aplomb, as always. Maybe a little too well. Was nature imitating art? "We're ahead of schedule, again."

"Well, it all adds up, doesn't it?" Gabe smiled back, obviously flattered by the compliment. "Sixteen systems down the list, with thirty-four still to go. If we can save a day or two each time, that means we'll get home ahead of schedule."

Sara Mravinsky and Andre Passant watched from the sidelines, obviously bored with the routine manoeuvres and uninspiring dialogue. Steel-haired Andre looked unhappy, which I duly noted. The script called for sullen resentment over Myrion's rejection, but I sensed something more. Was he, like Freedom, over-acting, or could this be the beginning of a separate malaise?

I sat apart from everyone, studying the crew's interactions for any sign of tension, or release thereof. Who knew what would be useful? Even the isolation of Sara and Andre might provide enough material for a sub-plot, although I resisted the idea of pairing the two romantically. Apart from my own feelings, her fragile, almost childlike beauty would look incestuous juxtaposed with the stern security head. Although, maybe she'd like that. I found it hard to tell what was happening inside that pretty head, with its close-cropped auburn hair and burnt-orange eyes . . .

"Ahead of schedule," commented Andre, "won't be soon enough for me."

I came back to reality with a jolt. So that was his problem. Earth-sickness. I'd need to look at that later.

"Engines are fine, Captain," said Steve. He licked his lips, acutely aware that every word was being recorded. "It was a little rough for a moment there, but we rode through it. Give us four days to trace the problem and we'll be back at optimum."

"Good." Gabe nodded, unconcerned. Maintenance on such a long mission was an on-going problem but nothing to be overly worried about. There was little save a direct asteroid-strike or a matrix-implosion that Steve couldn't fix on the hop. The engines only ran at full power once every five weeks anyway, while we crossed the gulf between stars, so there was plenty of downtime to patch up the odd leak. "Jake, tell me about the system."

The half-Asian astrogator shrugged without looking up from his screen. He was type-cast and he knew it; more, he played up to it. "Nothing new to report, sir. Three planets, two of them Jovian. The third is tiny and dense, in a close, irregular orbit. Probably a captured moon. No asteroid belts or cometary clouds to speak of."

"Good." Gabe visibly relaxed. The last binary system (Omega Herculis, a white Supergiant with smaller companion) had seemed as simple as this at first, until closer inspection revealed a widely-scattered belt of primordial black holes orbiting the primary sun. Tricky for astrogation and life-support and, as a near miss had proved, potentially fatal. We were ready for anything, this time, including boredom. "Uninhabited?"

"Of course. What did you expect?"

"One of these days you might surprise me." Gabe smiled wryly. "Sara, all non-essential crew can take a one-hour break. On stand-by until further notice."

Sara toggled the intercom and broadcast the order. A feeling of tension began to ebb as, throughout the ship, the superfluous crew left their posts for a breather. Eighteen hours of hard work—crossover, primary survey, injection—was finished. Earlier than normal, too, as Freedom had said; Gabe's technique of combining insertion with flyby seemed to be working. Unless something went wrong, the ship would be back on regular rosters for the next few weeks.

Gabe flickered through various screens of information, browsing, filling in time until the flyby. I too watched the torrent of data, understanding no more than ten percent but not feeling too bad about that. None of us understood it all, not even the backroom boys under Freedom's command. In the eighteen months we had already been Out Here, we had collected as many anomalies as coherent facts, and more questions than answers.

As Morale Officer, it was my job to make sure the wrong questions were never asked.

The inner, rocky planet crept closer. A battery of instruments scattered across the hull of the ship subjected it to constant analysis. It was lifeless, as expected, and a potential wealth of minerals. Halfway there, three impact probes were launched from the *Jew*; they separated with a half-heard, half-felt clang and swooped down to their fiery rendezvous.

An hour later, three tiny flashes of light were recorded and filed away for analysis. And that was it until the next flyby, three days later. If Freedom's staff found nothing too unusual in the spectrographic data, the *Jew* would shift its orbit to study the primary star in more detail, after which we would head out to the gas giants. Then we would leave.

Five weeks. Four, if the system was as empty as it appeared to be. Another month for me to keep the crew from each other's throats.

I stifled both a yawn and a recurring inspiration to write a romantic sub-plot involving Sara Mravinsky and myself, just to liven things up. Perhaps I was wrong to suppress this urge. The cathartic process included myself, didn't it? Who was going to keep me from my own throat?

Then it happened.

(Cut to: Close scanner shot of JAKE FOO-WONG *studying the astrogation screen, concentrating on tracing a path through the system. Suddenly, his head snaps up; on his face is an expression that combines both fear and total surprise.)*

JAKE: Captain! We have something!

GABE: Yes, Jake—? (he looks up) My God! *What the hell is that?*

(Snapshot view of the screen: an orange tangle of overlapping lines and circles. One small dot is moving very, very quickly across the screen.)

JAKE: (Struggling for self-control) Astrogation reports . . . an unidentified object—

GABE: Red Alert, Sara! Red Alert!

JAKE: —velocity three four by ten exp seven—

GABE: Standby main drive!

JAKE: —heading . . . (he looks up, and his face is pale) . . . *right at us, Captain . . .*

GABE: Seal all airlocks. For God's sake, Steve, get that engine running. I want medical on full standby!

(Pull back: Control is a mass of confusion; voices shout into intercoms; an alarm begins to wail. Captured in one corner of the shot, with a look of absolute, impotent horror on his cola-black face, is me.)

JAKE: (A little calmer, but still breathless.) We have visual, sir.

(Cut to: A star-speckled view with Mu 1-Boötis in the top-left corner. Nothing is visible at first, then a bright green dot appears in the centre of the starscape. With a soundless whoosh, it instantly fills the screen.)

GABE: Jesus Christ . . . That thing is *moving*! What magnification was that, Jake?

JAKE: Full, sir.

GABE: ETA?

JAKE: One-ninety seconds.

GABE: Is it broadcasting?

JAKE: No, sir, and it does not respond to signals.

GABE: Shit. Give me an evasive course and I'll take manual.

SARA: (Looking uncharacteristically frightened) Can't we just jump the hell out of here?

STEVE: No. We need at least forty-eight hours to program a crossover.

SARA: (Embarrassed) Of course. Sorry.

(Cut to: FREEDOM MAXWELL, at her console. The same image as before, of the alien spacecraft zooming towards the ship, fills her screen. Note: although her hair retains its coppery sheen, even in this bright green light, her beauty is only matched by her efficiency at her job.)

FREEDOM: Okay . . . (briskly, to the computer) . . . roll it back a frame . . . more . . . *there*. Freeze and store. Magnify.

ANDRE: (Leaning over her shoulder) What the hell . . . ?

FREEDOM: (Tapping on the screen to highlight aspects of the alien craft) Disc-shaped, rotating at a very high speed, a border of yellow light around the edge of the disc, seems to leave a particulate vapour in its wake . . . (Turning away from the screen) Gabe, is this some sort of joke?

GABE: What? No, of course not. Why?

FREEDOM: Well, in that case, Captain, we seem to have discovered our very first flying saucer.

(Stunned silence.)

JAKE: Bogey still approaching. (You can tell by the look on his face that he's always wanted to play this role.) ETA now seventy seconds.

GABE: (Still incredulous) Flying *what*?

ME: (With an almost insane grin) A bona fide UFO!

ANDRE: Alek, if this is one of your ridiculous sub-plots—

ME: God, no. I may be crazy but I'm not *that* crazy. Who would believe a flying saucer, out here in *space* . . . ?!

FREEDOM: And how would he program the visuals? We're seeing them for real.

ME: Yeah. Thanks, Freedom.

ANDRE: (Scowling) Keep a lid on it, then.

ME: Only if you stay in character.

JAKE: (Interrupting) ETA thirty seconds.

GABE: Right. Suggestions, anyone?

(Silence, again, apart from the impact-siren.)

GABE: Okay. I guess we'll just have to try and bluff our way out. (His face shows a hint of fear but, on the whole, he maintains his persona well.) Hang on tight!

(GABE's hands flicker over his control board as he wrenches the ship to one side. There is a muffled roar as the mighty engines kick into life. Note: there is no joystick; no falling from side to side; no screaming. This is real space opera, even if the dialogue's a bit wooden in places.)

JAKE: Bogey changing course.

GABE: Towards us?

JAKE: Aye, sir. ETA fifteen seconds.

(The Captain tugs the ship in another direction. The grim set of his jaw reveals that he knows the gesture will be futile, but he tries nonetheless.)

JAKE: ETA ten seconds. (I belatedly applaud his next words, although I loathed them at the time.) Nine . . . eight . . . seven . . .

(Cut to, in turn: ANDRE, SARA, STEVE, FREEDOM, ME, JAKE and GABE, interspersed with snapshots of the visual scanner, upon which the

alien ship is approaching rapidly.)

JAKE: . . . six . . . five . . . four . . .

(The saucer seems to explode out of the screen.)

JAKE: . . . three . . . two . . .

(Everything goes green . . .)

JAKE: . . . one . . .

(. . . blindingly bright green . . .)

JAKE: Impact!

(Blackout.)

In the wake of the encounter with the flying saucer, a vague sort of
panic reigned. Of all the footage faithfully recorded by the security
scanners, there was only one salvageable line:

ANDRE: Where the fuck has it *gone?*

And, as no-one at the time could provide a suitable answer, I was
forced to archive it.

My first thought, to maintain the dramatic impetus, was to cut
immediately to the debriefing session, held in the Captain's quarters
eight hours after the event. People had calmed down a little by then,
and were able to make a little more sense.

But, after much shuffling and re-editing, this eventually became
the episode's opening scene:

Gabe chaired the meeting, naturally. His haggard face was a
mask of tired determination. He hadn't slept for over thirty-six
hours. None of us had.

"Okay, folks. I guess we need to work out what the hell happened.
Anyone want to suggest where we start?"

"Something *did* happen, I presume?" Andre was taking the easy
way out: evading the problem by questioning its very existence. "It
wasn't just an hallucination?"

"No." Freedom was adamant. "It's all there on file, if you want
to check. The bogey appeared, flew towards us under an acceleration
beyond the capacity of human engineering and then disappeared on
impact."

"The 'bogey'?" Myrion looked amused, although the half-smile
was twisted by her usual bitterness. Her psych file spoke of deep
traumas, buried beneath conditioning. She was one of the few truly
complex characters in the drama of the *Wandering Jew*, and one
for whom I had great plans. Plainly attractive, with shoulder-length
white hair, she was an interesting contrast to Freedom, with whom

she was usually at loggerheads. "I thought you said it was a 'flying saucer'?"

"Whatever. Does it matter what we call it?"

"No." Gabe stepped in to forestall an argument. "Either will be fine. And I think we can assume it was of alien origin. The pertinent question, as I see it, is: What was the purpose of its behaviour?"

"Why did it try to ram us?" added Jake.

STEVE: How does it work?

SARA: What do they want from us?

FREEDOM: Where did it come from?

ANDRE: Where has it gone?

ME: And how do we report it?

Gabe shrugged. "That's why we're here, Alek. We need to think this through. It vanished without trace when it should have hit us head-on, and we haven't seen it since. Whoever they were, they didn't bother to tell us what the hell they were doing, so all we can do is guess."

"Maybe it was some sort of defence mechanism," suggested Andre. "Warning us away."

"From what?"

"I don't know. Could there be life on the inner planet?"

"Unlikely." Freedom's voice was firm. "A civilisation which could build a ship like that would surely leave some trace behind. We didn't even pick up heat-sources. Just old lava and the odd fissure."

"The Jovian worlds?"

"Again, unlikely."

"I guess we'll find out soon enough," said Sara. "We'll be passing them in a week or so."

"Will we?" Gabe studied us closely. "One of the things I wanted to discuss was the status of the mission. Should we abandon this system and skip to the next, or keep going as planned?"

"Abandon the system?" Freedom was outraged. "We're on the brink of what might be the greatest discovery we'll ever make! The quest for alien life is one of the mission's primary directives!"

"Unless it places the mission itself in jeopardy," reminded Andre.

"They didn't hurt us, did they? Whoever they are and whatever they want, I think they've demonstrated quite adequately that we're at their mercy. And yet we still live. I don't think they're hostile, just . . . cautious."

"Funny way to show it."

"Of course. You don't expect them to behave like humans, do you?"

This triggered a thought in my own head, but I bit my lip to keep it in. Had their behaviour really been unhuman?

"I myself would like to keep going as planned," said Gabe, "but I'll hear any arguments to the contrary before filing the order. Now's the time to speak, if you want to."

Silence greeted this announcement. Andre was clearly nervous behind his blunt aggression, but he kept quiet. The only other member of the panel who might have spoken against the Captain was Sara, but she too said nothing. I could tell by the way she fidgeted that she was ashamed of her own fear.

Gabe waited for a minute, drumming his fingers on the desk, until it became obvious that no-one was going to speak.

"I guess it's settled, then. If nothing untoward happens on the next flyby—and I want us on full alert for that—then we'll proceed as normal. But if anybody comes up with something we haven't thought of, no matter how ridiculous, I want to hear it. Absolutely anything could be important."

We all mumbled our assent. I crossed my fingers behind my back, where the cameras couldn't see the gesture.

"So, folks, I suggest we get some rest. It's been a long, hard day. I declare this emergency council closed and wish you all pleasant dreams. Good night."

The second flyby was uneventful. Our alien friend refused to reveal itself, if it was still around. We shifted orbit closer to the primary without mishap, then migrated out to the gas giants, where we refuelled. Three weeks later, the *Jew* was ready for crossover. All that remained was the sending of the Mu Boötis report.

Communication with Earth was restricted to small, bullet-shaped lozenges fired through hyperspace to Sol System, where they arrived two days later. The energy required to send the tiny capsules on their way limited the dispatches to one per system, at the conclusion of each survey. Thus, every one counted. There would be no chance to send a post-script until the next month; it had to be perfect first time.

And that was where I came in. It was my responsibility to collate all the data into a coherent report. I collected logs from the department heads, rewrote the mass of technical data into readable English and prepared an overall mission log. This process, with the help of AIs, took no more than a couple of days, and was very dull work.

The position of Communications Officer was therefore only part-time. I doubled as Morale Officer (another thankless job) between reports. It took me months to work out how to combine the two tasks and thereby make life a lot more interesting than it had been.

Alpha Boötis (otherwise known as Arcturus, fourth-brightest star in the Northern sky) was our third stop, thirty-six light years from Earth. This much-anticipated system unfortunately proved to be fairly bland, as did the following four: Gamma Serpens, Sigma Boötis, Yale 5634 and Tau Boötis. I knew the folks back home would be hoping for more than the odd boring gas giant and the usual spectral data. So, in an attempt to enliven the report from Yale 5634, re-christened McCormack's Star upon our arrival, I included footage of the day-to-day activities of the senior crew. Instead of sterile, scripted speeches from the department heads, we had real-life interactions, a close-knit community of people at work and play aboard the *Jew*. By editing the recordings, I managed to create a feeling of continuity, even though the half-hour of footage was composed of snippets recorded weeks apart.

I showed the crew the final cut before dispatching it, explaining that High Command would be interested to see how we performed as a unit, instead of as individuals. The dramatised footage would convey the reality far better than any Morale Report. If I had taken any remarks out of context, then that was simply to give the half-hour a feeling of completeness, by hinting at plots and sub-plots that may not really have existed.

"The Adventures of the *Wandering Jew*, Episode One," said Jake. "Certainly has a better ring to it than 'USSN *Rosenberg* Routine Survey Report: Yale 5634, 21.08.26.'"

"Exactly." I beamed confidently. "Fun, isn't it?"

"But where will it end?" protested Andre, perhaps prophetically. "Are we becoming *Star Trek*, or *Lost In Space*?"

There were a few other grumbles, mainly about privacy, but my innovation was ultimately approved by Gabe. The report was sent.

For the next report, from Tau Boötis (58 ly), I took the exercise one step further by actively encouraging the senior crew to improvise. I suggested possible situations and outcomes that might be entertaining for the folks back home, as well as "fun" for ourselves. Already I'd had the idea that this communal exercise might be employed as a means of catharsis. Half the trouble with surviving as a community in a closed environment is the lack of a pressure-valve. Most of my time as Morale Officer was spent bleeding-off dangerously charged situations—onto myself, more often than not. I hoped that, by turning the *Wandering Jew* reports into a soap opera, I might be able to take the strain off myself as well as the rest of the crew.

For instance: If Andre Passant's sullen manner rubbed Myrion Hemmelling the wrong way, why not have them act out a confrontation? This clumsy psychodrama was amongst the first sub-plots I attempted.

And it worked. Everyone became involved, if a little reluctantly in some cases. It was a game to be enjoyed when actively participating in it, or to be discussed (for and against) when not. I received suggestions from many people regarding possible outcomes. Pretty soon I was handing out rough scripts and engineering vital exchanges. Our everyday work continued—studying, collating, surviving—but now we had a game to keep our minds amused as well.

Then, two systems later, something happened that changed shipboard life forever.

The *Wandering Jew* wasn't the only ship on the deep-space exploration program; there were nineteen others, each with fifty systems to explore before returning to Earth. Although many of us cursed the five-year confinement, we all acknowledged that the arrangement was the best available. It was far more efficient to send one ship to explore fifty systems than to send fifty each to one system and back. Sure, with *fifty* ships the thousand systems could have been covered in less than half the time, but at more than twice the cost.

Omicron Boötis (75 ly) was our ninth system. Observations from Earth orbit had suggested the existence of a large solar family and we were therefore anticipating a great deal of work. We blipped out of hyperspace on the system's rim, wary of comets, and took stock of our surroundings.

Sure enough, O-Boötis was *big*. Fifteen planets, two asteroid belts and an extensive cometary cloud crowded the cool orange Giant. Gabe took us in on a wide polar orbit, high above the ecliptic, and Freedom went to work.

And that's when we spotted it: a reply capsule from Earth. Only the third we had received in nearly a year. Personal messages from families (none of us had a spouse back on Earth, but there were always relatives who wanted to keep in touch), fresh instructions from High Command, news of earthbound politics and sports, the latest fads . . . We waited impatiently for the *Jew*'s unmanned drone to collect it and bring it back for perusal.

The news, however, was not all good.

Of our nineteen sister-ships, three had suffered cataclysmic disasters; one had dispatched a garbled message about an asteroid strike before also disappearing; and a further seven had returned to Earth, abandoning their missions for a variety of reasons (including illness, discontent, psychological maladjustment and outright mutiny). Of the remaining nine ships, six seemed to be developing similar problems, and two of these were so far behind schedule that their itineraries had been cut back to thirty systems.

Which left only three fully-operational missions, including the *Wandering Jew*.

The news was sobering, to say the least.

There was also a "private and confidential" note addressed to me personally from Robin Blanchard, General Secretary of High Command, counter-signed by the President of the Solar Tribunal, Valerie McCormack herself. I opened it nervously, fully expecting it to be a terse order to get back to work, to stop wasting the crew's time on trivial matters. It meant the end of the soap, I just knew it.

But it wasn't. Quite the opposite, in fact.

High Command requested that we continue the unorthodox reports—*demanded* that we do so, and in no uncertain terms. In the face of the other failures, they needed a successful mission to show the public, presented in a way that would guarantee the comprehension of the lowest common denominator. 'The Adventures of the *Wandering Jew*' were, simply, good PR. And the possibility that the whole exercise had helped the psychological stability of the ship as a whole was not lost on them.

So that's how I became the honorary "Soap Operator", and how the 'Adventures of the *Wandering Jew*' began in earnest . . .

EPISODE 4: OMICRON BOÖTIS
SYNOPSIS:

This, the ninth port of call for the spaceship Wandering Jew, tests the mettle of the crew. In the face of bad news from Earth, morale becomes a serious concern. While the extensive (and therefore demanding) O-Boötis system is explored, charted and studied, the narrator, Alek Maas, follows the on-going hopes and aspirations of the crew.

The friendship between Captain Gabe and Freedom Maxwell continues to develop. Will they ever consummate the relationship? Can pretty, young Sara Mravinsky survive the terrible pressures of space-travel and still find time to discover herself? Does Andre Passant know more than he's saying, or was the mysterious disappearance of insulation wrap from Storage Bay 14 really just an innocent mistake? Myrion Hemmelling holds in her hands the life of everyone aboard the *Wandering Jew*, many of whom she does not like; does this account for her bitterness, or is it related somehow to her hidden past? What if, as Steve Jefferssen fears, something terrible goes wrong with the engines? Will the crew be stranded in deep space, beyond all hope of rescue?

The Mission itself remains as always the focus of this episode: the on-going plot to which everything else is pinned. What new discoveries await the *Jew*? What unforeseen dangers? Will the attempt to maintain morale fail? The pressure on the crew is enormous. They have approximately six weeks in which to study an entire solar system. Given that scientists have been studying the home system for two thousand years and still haven't finished, is this task humanly possible . . . ?

And so on.

Each "episode" consisted of about three hours of footage, interspersed with panoramic views of the particular system. In the case of O-Boötis, there was more than enough material to fill the pauses: turbulent gas giants, cloud-covered moons, tumultuous asteroid belts, *et cetera*. Where I couldn't find enough dramatic footage to manufacture a satisfactory plot, I narrated bridging material. A couple of crew members—Andre in particular—resented this dramatisation of reality, but reluctantly went along with it. If he was so often cast as the villain of the piece, then didn't that represent some aspect of him that needed to be dealt with?

Three systems later, at Kappa Corona Borealis, a white Ao ninety light years from home, we received our fourth reply capsule. High Command was ecstatic. They forwarded the final cut of the O-Boötis episode for our enjoyment, including the commercials. One of the leading composers of the day had written a theme, and there were credits featuring footage of our training, transfer to orbit and final launch. Someone had touched-up the odd scene or two, overlaying the bad acting with computer-generated expressions, but it was otherwise pretty much as I had put it together. Gabe looked a little more dapper than usual, but that might have been my imagination.

Viewed from a distance (it had been ten weeks since I had put it together), Episode Four was dramatic, inspiring, personal and very human. Here were a handful of people (it was hard to think of them as *us*) trapped in a metal and plastic coffin trillions of kilometres from home. The citizens of Earth couldn't help but care about us, which in turn meant that they cared about the deep-space exploration program. And that was a Good Thing for all involved.

It turned out that the re-edited versions of my reports had been bought by five of the multinational broadcast networks. Advertised as the "human face of space exploration", the Adventures of the *Wandering Jew* were reaching seventy-five percent of the population.

We were stars. The idea took a lot of getting used to. And it meant that my role as Soap Operator became yet more central to the day-to-day running of the ship. What had started as a game had become the means of saving the space program, and maybe our sanities along with it—all thanks to a flair for the dramatic that I had never before realised I had. Who would have believed it?

But weirdest of all was the fan-mail . . .

So, when the alien ship buzzed us at Mu Boötis, our sixteenth stop and eleventh episode, my first thought was: How does this affect the series? I could hardly edit the Event from the episode; it was too good a scene to leave on the cutting-room floor, quite apart from its historical significance, but it was too ridiculous to be believed. A flying saucer, in *space*?

As the survey of Mu Boötis rolled on and the deadline rapidly approached, I sought opinions from the rest of the crew:

"I don't know what to think," said Steve Jefferssen, the first I approached. "I saw what I saw, but what I saw doesn't make sense. Best to ignore it and see what happens when, or *if*, it comes back. What else can we do? There's no point dwelling on it."

"Really, Steve?" I had expected more from this pragmatic pillar of a man. "Don't you even wonder—?"

"Sure, Alek. Sure I wonder. I wonder if we've all gone crazy."

"The timing is what bothers me," confessed Myrion. "We're a third of the way through the mission—less than that, actually—and there have been few in the way of major discoveries. I guess we were all hoping for at least some sign of alien life by now, but, apart from the false alarm at Beta Serpens, everything's dead, dead, dead! Maybe we're externalising our expectations. The flying saucer is a common enough archetype, after the hysteria of the twentieth-century. Did you ever read about the abductions that supposedly took place in the 'eighties' and 'nineties'?"

"Yes."

"They stopped when SETI folded. The pressure on the communal psyche shifted back to the internal and we started seeing ghosts again. Maybe we're experiencing the re-emergence of the UFO syndrome."

"So we're crazy?" I didn't mention that I'd had, in essence, a similar conversation with Steve.

"No. We're hallucinating."

"Same thing, isn't it?"

"Ask someone on LSD."

"I will," I promised, "just as soon as I get home."

She smiled. She was always more cheerful when she thought she'd won an argument.

"Jiggery-pokery," was Andre's opinion. "Some idiot's playing a trick on us."

"How?"

"By seeding the AI network with incumbent viruses programmed to activate at a specified time in the mission. When they trigger, we see images through the screens of things that aren't really there: electronic ghosts, if you like. You'll have to ask Freedom exactly how they did it, but I'll bet it's something like that. After all, we found no evidence that the saucer ever existed, did we? No wreckage, no radiation, no particulate wake—nothing. Therefore it wasn't real; therefore it was a stunt. It'll be ghost-writing in the sky next. Some sort of propaganda, or a message to a girlfriend."

"'Remember that night in Paris . . . ?'"

He didn't smile. "Something like that."

I knew better than to ask Andre if he doubted his sanity, so instead I asked him the question that really bothered me:

"Do you think I'm behind it? Be honest. I can take it."

He thought for a moment before replying. "No, I suppose I don't. I'm just angry at you for falling for it."

Now *that* was a sobering thought.

"I guess it all boils down to the fact that someone really is out there," said Freedom, next on my list. "Their motives may seem mysterious, perhaps even nonsensical, but they're *there* all the same. And that's what counts."

"So you don't think it was a prank, or some sort of glitch?"

"Absolutely not. I helped design half the information systems on this ship. I'd know if they were malfunctioning, or if someone had tampered with them. Same with my brain. Anybody who says otherwise is evading the issue."

"But why only one ship? If they're as advanced as they appear to be, why aren't there hundreds of them out here?"

"Well, the Galaxy is a big place, right? The old SETI system— aiming an antenna at the sky and waiting—simply won't work. It takes centuries for signals from one civilisation to reach another, even if they're relative neighbours; by the time you'd know they were there, they might not be any more."

"Yes, but—"

"The only way to find life, therefore, is to go out and look for it, system by system. This applies for any civilisation anywhere in the Galaxy, and especially out here in the Rim. Thus, the sort of aliens we'll be likely to meet will be wanderers like us. The odds are that we won't stumble across anybody's home system. It'll be just one ship, all on its own."

I thought about it, nodded slowly. "That makes sense, I guess." And it did, although I'll bet she only thought of it *after* we met the saucer. "But, if they're looking for life as well, then why won't they talk to us?"

"They might well have tried." Freedom smiled wryly. "You never know what life will be like until you find it."

"Do you know what *really* scares me?" asked Sara. It was late one ship's-night and we were sharing a coffee in her quarters. I hadn't actually approached her for her thoughts on the matter, but she offered them anyway. Word had obviously spread.

"No. What?"

"That it might be real."

"Which?"

"The . . . you know, the flying saucer. The aliens."

"What's so horrible about that?"

"Everything. They're obviously so much better than we are. They make us look like savages in comparison."

"I know." I didn't like to see her so worried. "But think of all the things we can learn from them—"

"That's not what I mean." She leaned intoxicatingly closer. "Maybe they're *toying* with us . . . "

Jake laughed when I sought his opinion.

"Does it really matter, either way? If it's a prank, then whoever infiltrated the system is better than we are. If not, and the aliens are real, then they're also better than we are. We're helpless to do anything no matter how you look at it, so we might as well sit back and enjoy what happens next."

"And if it's us? If we're losing it?"

"As I said: we sit back and enjoy the show."

Gabe said much the same, in a round-about way.

"I'm going to sit on the fence for a while, Alek. Sorry."

"A three-sided fence," I said, "between aliens, sabotage and madness. A bit uncomfortable, isn't it?"

Gabe smiled. "Yes, but I'm used to it. It goes with the job."

"And you're welcome to it. Can I ask one last question, then, just for the record?"

"Go ahead."

"We're not armed, are we?"

"Why would we be?"

"And we have no escape capsules?"

"Where would we escape *to*? That's two questions, by the way."

"I know. But don't you think we're dangerously vulnerable out here, all alone and with no means of defending ourselves?"

"Of course we are." His smile broadened. "That's half the fun, isn't it?"

As Honorary Soap Operator, I could only agree.

So, opinion was divided. Only two members of the senior crew were prepared to admit that they believed in the existence of the aliens; three were undecided, and two thought the saucer was an illusion. Had I been looking for a consensus, I would have been disappointed.

As for me, I had my own theory—a different one again. Like Myrion, the timing was what bothered me. It was too dramatic, too contrived. Months of editing had taught me that the universe didn't naturally work that way; it had to be nudged before it would perform. Like Andre, I thought it was someone human doing the nudging, not an alien—but, unlike him, I had both a motive and a suspect.

The saucer had appeared not long after our last package from Earth. That was the crucial clue. If our AIs had been corrupted by some sort of virus, then it must have arrived in that package; maybe hidden in Episode Four, dormant until we played the recording. If that was the case, then only one person, or group of people, could have been behind it.

Every package is checked and rechecked for aberrations before leaving Earth orbit; a virus, no matter how dormant, would have shown up eventually. If High Command had been infiltrated by a traitor, then that person could never have been certain the time bomb would reach its destination. Only one organisation could be sure of that—the same one that had the resources and the know-how to build a virus capable of getting past Freedom. Only this organisation knew the AI system aboard the *Jew* better than she did.

And that was High Command itself.

The motive was a little more complex. For what possible reason would HC want to sabotage its own investment? The only answer I could think of was to redirect our pooled hostility outwards, towards an imaginary alien, instead of inwards at each other. Even with the success of the soap opera, they still had eleven failures on their hands. Maybe they could see signs of stress that I had missed. Perhaps they thought the risk of pulling a stunt like this was less than the risk of doing nothing at all.

Or perhaps I was being paranoid. At the very least, it was a plausible theory.

The only problem was, I couldn't tell anyone. If my guess was right, then HC would look poorly on the person who gave the game away—and made *them* the enemy.

So, like Gabe, I had to play the impartial observer and let everyone have their say, half-hoping someone else would guess. Only time would tell if I was right. Until then, all I could do was watch and, as Jake advised, enjoy the show.

And that was how I eventually worked the saucer into the episode. On other occasions, Gabe had been the star, or Myrion, or Jake. One of the reasons why I had cast myself as narrator, apart from convenience, was because I hate the look of my own face. But I had no choice this time. My turn had come. There was no other way to present what had happened.

Episode Eleven (Mu Boötis) began, not with the encounter itself, but with the debriefing in Gabe's quarters. The interviews I had conducted followed, mixed with the survey of the system. On top of the astronomical footage, I publicly agonised over my dilemma: how could I portray what had happened without stretching the audience's credulity? This self-reference was planned to convince the viewers of my/our sincerity. That something unusual had happened would be obvious in the way we spoke; that it was hard to credit, likewise. When the audience eventually saw the actual saucer, at the very end of the episode, they would be prepared for it. They would feel along with us, I hoped, a mixture of fear, amusement, awe, suspicion and total disbelief.

Gabe gave the episode his seal of approval and sent it on its way.

Two days later, Freedom and Steve announced that we were ready for crossover to the next system. Gabe, instead of ordering us immediately on our way, announced a twelve-hour shut-down to give us a breather. We were two months ahead of schedule and there was no denying that we were tired, but it wasn't like Gabe to delay like this. He was always pressing on, pushing forward, over the top and no second thoughts, lads!

Perhaps he knew something the rest of us didn't, or guessed.

Either way, it was worth waiting for.

(Scene: Control Bridge of the Wandering Jew, *approximately seventy-five minutes to scheduled crossover.)*

JAKE: Uh, Captain . . . ?

GABE: Yes, Jake?

JAKE: It's back, sir. Our friend, the bogey. Stationary, this time.

(Brief shot of the alien craft. It appears exactly the same as before: bright green, disc-shaped, spinning about its vertical axis.)

GABE: Position?

JAKE: High above the ecliptic, barely within range. We're getting a strong fix from one of the solar-survey satellites.

GABE: Is it broadcasting?

JAKE: Negative, sir. Just sitting there.

GABE: (To himself) Waiting for us to do something . . . ? (Into an intercom) All-stations, all-stations! This is an alert. Prepare for immediate crossover. (Intercom off) Sara, have us ship-shape in five minutes. Steve, warm us up. Freedom, any thoughts?

FREEDOM: I'll leave the decision up to you, sir. But please bear in mind what I said.

GABE: Yes. If we leave Mu Boötis, we'll be losing our last chance to make contact.

ME: (To Sara, thinking of the viewers back on Earth) Why's that?

SARA: It's theoretically impossible for one ship to follow another through hyperspace.

ME: So, if we leave now . . . ?

SARA: Then we'll lose them forever.

(Cut to:)

GABE: Any response yet, Jake?

JAKE: No, sir. We're still broadcasting on all bands; they
            must be hearing us.

GABE: And it hasn't moved?

JAKE: No, sir.

GABE: I think we've given them long enough. If they really
            wanted to talk they would have tried by now. Steve?
            Everybody? Two minutes. We cross on my command.

*(SARA broadcasts the order throughout the ship. Deep in the
bowels of the* Wandering Jew, *powerful energies stir, brewing the
force that will rip the ship from this universe and take it safely to
the next.)*

JAKE: One minute and counting.

GABE: All in order?

JAKE: Yes, sir. All lights are green.

STEVE: Transformation matrix enabled.

FREEDOM: Co-ordinates confirmed.

SARA: Crew in position and awaiting your order, sir.

GABE: Good. Alek?

ME: Cameras rolling.

JAKE: Fifteen seconds.

GABE: Last words, anyone?

FREEDOM: (To the aliens, presumably) Farewell . . .

ME: Delta Boötis, here we come!

JAKE: Mark.

GABE: Cross.

(Cut to: External surface shot. The skin of the Wandering Jew
*burns with alcohol flames. In the background, the greenish
primary of Mu Boötis begins to dissolve.)*

*(Cut to: Control Bridge. The air is full of the straining of engines.
A shudder ripples through the ship, rattling bulkheads and
causing frowns.)*

GABE: Status?

STEVE: AOK, sir. Just a flutter.

*(The roar of the drive settles. Outside the ship, Mu Boötis goes
out; the stars vanish. The* Wandering Jew *exits Einsteinian time-
space.)*

GABE: Fingers crossed, everybody!

STEVE: Drive steady.

FREEDOM: Co-ordinates locked and holding.

JAKE: ETA, ninety seconds.

(The rattle returns, more insistently this time.)

STEVE: (To himself) Come on, baby.

GABE: Problem?

STEVE: Nothing . . . uh . . . (He taps furiously at his board.)

FREEDOM: (Urgently) We're drifting!

GABE: Keep calm, and clarify.

FREEDOM: We have an instability in the transformation matrix!

GABE: Serious?

FREEDOM: Any instability *at all* is serious. (The rattle peaks again, and does not fade.) We'll be lucky to arrive in one piece if it gets any worse.

ME: (Thinking about the theory) I thought the trick was arriving in *separate* pieces, not one big lump?

ANDRE: Can it, would you?

STEVE: We have a problem, people. Stabilisers gone in three jump circuits, shorted out a whole line . . .

GABE: Can you fix it?

STEVE: Once we shut down, yes. But we can't shut down until we arrive. All I can do is hold us here, between states, for a while.

GABE: Which places more strain on the matrix. How long do you think?

STEVE: A few minutes. No more.

GABE: Do it.

JAKE: Countdown halted. ETA TBA.

(The rumble of the engines, now indistinguishable from the ever-present rattle, steadies slightly.)

GABE: Freedom, what are the odds of us arriving safely if we just go ahead and finish the jump?

FREEDOM: Slim.

GABE: But worth a try . . . ?

FREEDOM: If you like long odds.

GABE: How about hyperspace? Can we go back?

FREEDOM: Unfortunately, the same conditions apply there.

GABE: So why don't we just stay here, then?

FREEDOM: Well, it takes energy to keep us whole, and the

reactor's already under stress. If, or when, the matrix fails entirely, we'll be torn apart.

GABE: Understood. Any suggestions?

FREEDOM: No. I'm sorry.

GABE: Steve? How's she holding?

STEVE: Uh, barely, sir. There's not much I can do to delay the—

(There is a violent lurch. A siren begins to wail.)

FREEDOM: We've lost the reactor shielding! Over-rides cutting in—power dropping!

STEVE: I can't hold her!

GABE: Take us in! Do it now, while we still have a chance!

(Red lights spread across the drive-control board. The rumble of motors has become a tortured growl.)

JAKE: ETA, fifteen seconds.

STEVE: We're losing it!

MYRION: (From life-support, via intercom) Pressure-drop in sector four!

(The lights flicker. Smoke billows.)

FREEDOM: Total power-loss to all drive-systems! No, wait—that doesn't make *sense*! We're getting a power-surge—I can't tell what's happening down there—

JAKE: System failure!

(The lights go out entirely. The wail of the ship continues for a moment, then ceases as well. There is an explosion, so loud the recordings clip.)

UNIDENTIFIED FEMALE VOICE: God help us!

(The recording whites-out for an instant.)

(After an unknown period of time, the lights flicker back on. An unsteady current brings partial life to some of the boards. The control bridge is in chaos; people are sprawled everywhere.)

ME: (Holding SARA in an absurdly protective fashion) Are we dead yet?

JAKE: No. (He frowns, struggles to his feet and confronts his control board.) I think we, uh . . .

ME: Think we *what*? Don't keep us in suspense, man!

JAKE: (Looking up) I think we're *there*.

FREEDOM: But we didn't complete the jump. (She sounds almost hurt) We should be dead!

(A screen flickers to life. On it is revealed the yellow Bright Giant, Delta 1-Boötis, hanging in space like a candle-lit Chinese lantern. But that's not all . . .)

GABE: Ho, ho. There's our welcoming party, folks.

FREEDOM: That's impossible!

JAKE: Apparently not.

(Hanging in the screen's top-left corner is the flying saucer.)

STEVE: The same one?

GABE: Why not?

FREEDOM: But the theory—

ME: Fuck the theory. The theory says we should be dead, remember?

JAKE: Captain, it's moving closer.

GABE: Steve, what's our status?

STEVE: Poor, sir. We're on emergency power. The fusion drive will burn up our reserves in no time. Give me a week and we'll be able to run, but not before then.

GABE: (Resignedly) So here we sit—

ANDRE: —Helpless—

ME: —And here they come!

Afterwards, reviewing the tapes, it looked ridiculous.

The flying saucer drifted slowly closer to us, travelling at a little less than the *Jew*'s intrasystem cruising speed. We nervously watched it approach. There was nothing else we could do. Closer and closer it came, as silent and mysterious as its archetypal counterparts, until it almost seemed within touching distance.

And then it vanished again.

Apart from two who had died in the explosively depressurised compartment, no-one was seriously injured. While the crew swarmed over the ship, repairing pressure-breaks and patching damaged equipment, the senior officers gathered in the Captain's quarters for a second emergency debriefing session.

Gabe scanned the assembled faces, some of them still the worse for wear after the near-disastrous crossover. There was a lot of dirt, worry, frustration and fear on those faces. I wondered if we would ever jump with confidence again.

"Okay Steve, give us the bad news."

"Well." The chief engineer looked harrowed. "Fifteen second before she completed the jump, the *Jew* suffered a total system failure. She lost life-support, drive capability, everything. A total burnout, to put it crudely. How she made it back to realspace, I'll never know. Thirty seconds later, the backups kicked in. Thank God."

"Can we repair the damage?"

"Probably. I'll need to go over the whole system piece by piece to find the initial fault before I can fix it. Then dry-run the patch before we attempt another jump. I'll let you know the odds when I've done that."

"Are you confident?"

"Cautiously, yes."

"Good." Gabe scratched at his ear. "But I guess I should ask this: Have you *any* idea what caused the problem?"

"To be honest, sir, I think it was a combination of age and overwork. We've been pushing her harder than planned over the last eighteen months; the extra pressure must have put a strain on something." Steve looked uncomfortable. "Maybe we should slow down for a while."

"Stop trying to hurry, you mean?"

"It's worth thinking about, if only for the ship's sake."

Andre leaned in. "Gabe, you're not seriously considering continuing the mission, are you?"

"Why not?"

"The drive is falling *apart*, for—"

"You heard Steve. He thinks he can fix it."

"*Thinks.* And how long before it happens again? I say we should abort the mission and head home while we still can. Next time we might be stranded completely, if we survive at all."

"Look, we knew before we left that the mission would be risky at times. Yes, we've lost two men; yes, we might have to operate more cautiously in the future. But the mission doesn't have to be scrapped entirely. Nothing has happened that wasn't anticipated and prepared for in advance—"

"Except the aliens," pointed out Sara. "Don't forget them."

"I haven't. And that's another very good reason to keep going."

Andre turned away in disgust. "For all we know, *they* were responsible for the system failure."

"That's paranoid."

"Is it? They followed us through hyperspace, didn't they? Maybe they screwed up the matrix somehow."

Gabe looked uncertain, as though he hadn't considered the possibility. "Freedom? What about the bogey? Any idea how it followed us?"

"No. You know what the theory says."

"Maybe they know more about the theory than we do," said Myrion. "Or they have a different one."

Freedom sighed. "I'll concede that."

"So it's possible the aliens interfered with us in some way?" asked Gabe, clutching for answers. "Is there any way of finding out for certain?"

"I hate to say this, but . . . I don't think so." It obviously hurt Freedom to admit her ignorance. "If they're sufficiently advanced, they could do anything they wanted without us knowing."

"But *why*? Why would they try to kill us in the middle of a jump, then not finish the job when they had the chance? It doesn't make sense." Gabe looked as though he was about to hit the desk, a sure sign he was feeling cornered. "And why the hell won't they *talk* to us?"

I rushed in to forestall a bad scene. "I think we're getting ourselves a little overwrought. Perhaps we should take a step back and look at this from another angle."

"Oh, yes?" sneered Andre. "What exactly do you suggest?"

"Try and see it from the aliens' point of view. They might be as puzzled as we are."

"I don't understand," said Steve.

"Well, they've approached us twice now—three times, if you count when we came out of hyperspace—and each time they've disappeared. Maybe we didn't respond the way they expected us to. They could be so alien that *our* behaviour is nonsensical to *them*, just as theirs is to us."

If Freedom resented the theft of her ideas, she didn't show it. "I agree. We mustn't fall into the trap of interpreting an apparent lack of communication as evidence of hostility. The degree of alienation between them and us could be so great that standard methods of communication will prove to be insufficient."

"I could believe that," said Sara, "if they didn't look so . . . *ordinary*."

"What if their real appearance is incomprehensible?" suggested Myrion. "The semblance of a flying saucer might be nothing more than an hallucination superimposed by our own minds upon an unacceptable reality."

"Good thought." I nodded. "But the main thing we must always keep in our minds is the fact that, for all their superior technology, they haven't destroyed us—and they've had three chances."

Gabe looked grateful. "Right. If they were hostile, they would have killed us by now. The fact that they followed us here suggests that they still want to make contact. Doesn't it, Andre?"

The security head said nothing, but I could tell what he was thinking: if a friendly greeting could be misinterpreted as a result of cultural incompatibility, then didn't the same apply to an act of aggression?

"Anybody else?" Gabe looked expectantly around the table. "No more gripes? Then that's it. Back to work. We'll meet again in twenty-four hours, when Steve can tell us more, and decide then exactly what we're going to do next."

Back in my office, I shut down the security cameras and the bugs, thus isolating myself from the rest of the *Wandering Jew* and from the permanent record. For the first time since I had taken residence in the ship, I was completely unobserved.

Or was I?

Surrounded by distractions, it was hard to concentrate. I needed to be alone for a while, to think for myself. My small personal space was the only quarter of the ship where I could achieve the necessary isolation, and even with the cameras off I still felt crowded, watched.

On one wall, a coloured 3-D chart showed the constellation of Boötes plus a few close neighbours. Our path staggered like a drunkard's walk through the Herdsman, the Northern Crown and the Serpent's Head, with the occasional detour to Hercules, the Virgin and the Serpent Bearer. Legendary scenery, an itinerary of archetypes. One flying saucer hardly seemed conspicuous in such auspicious company.

Target stars were numbered in order from one to fifty, with red circles enclosing the ones we had already visited: Xi Boötis, first of all, one of the closest binaries to Sol System, was followed by other "notables" like Arcturus, O-Boötis, Alpha CB, and Omega Herculis. Amongst the unringed systems were: Gamma CB and Epsilon Boötis (Mirak), both binaries; the white supergiants Theta CB and Nu Boötis; Kappa Serpens Caput and Delta Ophiuchis, the only M-type stars on our itinerary; and a seemingly endless number of Giant G and K systems: Beta Boötis, Delta CB, Yale 5601, Beta Herculis, Yale 5535, Rho Serpens, Psi Boötis, Epsilon Ophiuchis and Phi Virgo. Second to last was the system of Lambda Serpens, just thirty-five light years from home, which Freedom hoped would contain an earth-like world.

We had come so far in such a short time. How could we possibly turn our backs on the rest of the mission? Would it make any difference in the long-run if we did?

This was just the beginning of humanity's exploration of local space. There were thousands of stars within reach of the crossover drive. By leaps of twenty to thirty light years at a time, our sphere of knowledge had begun to expand, and there was no way we could ever turn it back. Exploration had momentum, just like any other social force.

But we were the *first*. No matter how much pressure Andre exerted, Gabe would not capitulate. The mission would continue. And if there really were aliens out here with us, then that was something we would have to learn to live with.

But *were* there aliens? My first theory, that High Command was behind the saucer, seemed unconvincing now. A new one was forming at the back of my mind. I was no longer completely sure that the aliens were a fake.

I needed to see my ideas in a concrete form, to get them out of my head. Calling up a notebook file, I began to scribble notes.

THE STORY SO FAR:

1.   Earth is a very powerful high-frequency radio-source, but has only been pumping out signals for two hundred years. This means that, for an alien ship to have detected these signals, it must have been somewhere inside a bubble of space two hundred light years in radius with Earth at its centre. Gamma Boötis, our twenty-sixth system, will be the first we encounter of twelve outside this bubble. All the earlier ones are candidates.

2.   An alien ship inside this bubble will be bombarded by radio and television broadcasts from maybe as far back as the early twentieth-century, depending on how distant they are. But it won't be as simple as them switching on their own TVs and tuning in: they won't know anything about frequency or amplitude modulations, or wide-band digital transmissions or carrier waves or NTSC formats, and so on. They'll have to work it all out from scratch before they have something to study.

3.   Then, of course, there's interpretation. We've never had the opportunity to study a culture from nothing but its transmission media. It might be harder than we think. It might take years. And, if I was an alien, I certainly wouldn't want to approach another

world without first understanding its culture. Earth might be a world of rabid xenophobes. Or our religion might revolve around the ritual sacrifice of unexpected visitors. Or anything.

4.   There might have been hundreds of visitors inside our bubble of space, but all we need is one. One curious explorer, as Freedom suggested. One to pick up the signals, to be studying them at this very moment. Although it might conceivably be drifting through deep space, it's probably safe to assume that it will be located near a planetary system. (Where else would you look for developing life?) And it hasn't had time to approach Earth. (If it had, we would have seen it.) Maybe it'll leave without doing so, because we're too aggressive or whatever. But it's there *right now*—and that's what counts. Studying Earth long-distance.

5.   Okay, now suppose that this alien ship is close enough to Earth to pick up our signals, but no further out than Mu Boötis (where we first saw it). That makes the bubble a little smaller, with a radius of one hundred and eight light years. An alien inside this bubble would be picking up transmissions from the early twenty-first-century.

6.   Television, the largest broadcast-medium, is composed of two distinct streams of data: (1) information, and (2) entertainment. The first stream includes news, documentaries, current affairs and educational programs. The second contains sports, sitcoms, game shows and soap operas. Ever since television was invented, the second stream has been more popular—and therefore more substantial.

7.   As the aliens sift through all this data, they will be attempting to create a psychological model of the way we think, rather than a technological model of what our world is like. They'll realise that their information would be at least 108 years old (the time it takes a television signal to reach their location at the tardy speed of light). We might have advanced markedly since then, or wiped ourselves out. The only constant in all this info would be the way we *behave*, regardless of our level of technology. That's what the aliens will be after. Their motive will be more than simple curiosity; they'll be looking for the best way approach Earth. They don't want to surprise us so much that we start a war over them.

8.   If it was a human crew studying Earth, they would be watching the entertainment pretty closely—the soap operas in particular, because these offer a glimpse of what the real world is supposedly like, or how we would like it to be. If these aliens are

really alien, however, they won't understand the difference between information and entertainment. They might not be able to separate the game shows from the news from the soap operas from the documentaries. They might take it all at face value. All they can do is keep watching and hope that it will eventually make sense.

9. Then, one day, the *Wandering Jew* appears in their vicinity. With news a few decades out of date, they wouldn't know about the crossover drive or the revitalised space program. We'd just pop up out of nowhere. Unexpected as it is, they realise that this is the perfect opportunity for them: a ship-load of live humans, handed to them on a platter. All they have to do is ensure that we don't see them and they can watch us to their hearts content. Which they do. And when we leave, they follow us, to continue their studies.

10. And what do they find? They find the Adventures of the *Wandering Jew*—another soap opera! The more they watch, the more they realise that this soap opera is helping us survive, by bleeding off our pooled tensions in a non-violent way. The soap opera is essential to the continuation of our existence.

11. The aliens look at our behaviour and say: "Sure, why not? What we have here is a race of psychodramatic beings. They work through their problems by dramatising them, abstracting them from reality. What's so weird about that? If they want to deal with the real world by apparently circumventing it, then that's their business. If that's how they stay sane, more power to them. The Adventures of the *Wandering Jew* is just a microcosm of the larger pool of soap operas back on Earth. A soap bubble, if you like, cast aloft on the winds of space."

12. Eventually, another alien says: "Then I think that solves our problem. All this time we've been watching these people and trying to work out how best to approach them. Well, here's our chance. Let's reveal ourselves to these few, and they can tell the others. All we have to do to soften the blow of First Contact is dress-up the encounter. We'll create a phantom flying saucer, just like something out of 'The Day the Earth Stood Still', and they'll take it fine. They'll be able to deal with it, if it appears as part of the soap. When we truly reveal ourselves, later, they'll be prepared. (And if they send a war-fleet after us, like some of the old films, we'll have plenty of time to get away . . .) Simple, right?"

13. So, when the *Jew* arrives at the O-Boötis system, it encounters a green flying saucer. The apparition is an archetype behaving in archetypal fashion. We are supposed to interpret this unexpected

appearance from the context of our psychodrama and report that we have been contacted by aliens. That the saucer makes no attempt to communicate (apart from simply *being* there) is irrelevant; our psychological make-up should allow us to understand the real aliens' intentions. We should instantly recognise an obvious cue for a change of script.

14. But we don't. We step out of the soap opera and question the authenticity of the vision itself. The aliens have guessed wrong. Their crude behavioural model doesn't include the possibility of self-reference. They don't realise that we are acting, and that we know we are acting. The soap opera is just a game with a bonus psychosociological kickback. We write a new soap opera about how the old soap opera seems to be falling apart at the seams.

15. But still they persist; they decide, perhaps, that we were genuinely frightened by the illusion's hostile behaviour. So, when we prepare to leave O-Boötis, the saucer appears again, this time behaving quite differently. Instead of as the conquering invader, it comes as the hesitant passer-by. We are supposed to remain behind to study it, again from the context of the soap opera.

16. A second time, we surprise them. We flee through hyperspace, thinking we can lose the pursuing saucer that way.

17. The drive explodes, but somehow we arrive anyway. And, when we regain our senses, there's the saucer again, doggedly determined to enter our fragile bubble of soap without popping it.

18. And here am I, trying to work it all out . . .

I saved the file and browsed through it.

Everybody had been partially right: Freedom with her genuine aliens, Sara's game-players, Andre's illusory messages in the sky, Myrion's archetypes, my own early script-writers. Each had become a facet of a glittering new hypothesis.

But was *this* one right?

My theory was neat, I felt, but it wasn't complete. There was still something missing, something I hadn't taken into account. Something that had happened was bothering me—but when, and what? It was there in my head, I suspected; all I had to do was shake it loose. Somehow.

I collapsed back into the chair, thinking furiously. Something Freedom had said . . . ?

Turning to the terminal, I keyed it for voice-activation and reconnected it to the *Jew*'s AI mainframe. This sole computer link became my only connection to the rest of the ship. Through it, I could access the security records. It was a long shot, I knew, but worth a try. Anything to jog my memory.

I skimmed through the first encounter, but found nothing. Same with the second and third. If the clue existed, then I was looking in the wrong place.

Instinct took me back to the moment when the drive had malfunctioned, when it had looked like we were going to die. The cameras on the Control Bridge had recorded our panic with unflattering detail. On the screen in my 'office', we milled like ants, helpless, waiting for the descending boot to crush us. The reactor had failed and the ship had lost power; we had been effectively dead from that moment onwards. Without power to complete the jump, we should have been torn apart by nuclear forces and utterly destroyed.

But, miraculously, we had survived. Why?

And that was it. So simple and yet so tangential that I almost missed it.

"We're getting a power surge," Freedom had said. "I don't understand what's happening down there!"

A power surge—just strong enough to push us just far enough, back to real space.

A power *surge*.

Where had it come from? Not from the reactor itself because that was down; not from the backups because they hadn't cut in yet. That left outside, except that there's no outside during a jump. Which meant . . .

Which meant there had to be another power source aboard the ship that we didn't know about.

Erasing the security records from the screen, I nervously cleared my throat and spoke into the microphone:

"Hello? Are you listening? Hello?"

The screen instantly lit up, as though it had been expecting me:
>> HELLO, ALEK MAAS.

I stared at the words for a moment, almost daring them to disappear. "This isn't some kind of prank, is it?"
>> NO.

The simple negative carried the weight of a thousand words, and I breathed a sigh of relief. Maybe I wasn't crazy after all.

"My God . . . Where are you?"
>> INASMUCH AS WE CAN BE SAID TO HAVE A TRUE LOCATION,
   WE ARE AFT OF THE DRIVE SHIELDING.

"And how long have you been aboard the ship?"

>> SINCE THE STAR YOU CALL SIGMA BOÖTIS.

"But we saw no sign of . . . No, of course we didn't. That's not your home system." I sagged back into the chair and ran my fingers through my hair. I was talking to an alien! "I can't believe this is really happening!"

>> TRUTH IS STRANGER THAN FICTION, YES, BUT NOTHING IS STRANGER THAN A SOAP OPERA.

I laughed, mentally chalking up another correct guess. "True, very true."

>> HOW LONG HAVE YOU KNOWN?

"Since the drive failed, I think."

>> IT WAS THEN THAT YOU REALISED?

"Subconsciously, yes. But it wasn't until we arrived at Delta Boötis, here, and the saucer appeared again, and I had the chance to think it through that I was sure. The aliens weren't following us at all; they've been with us the whole time!"

>> YES.

"Yes." I sagged further into the chair, truly struck by the enormity of the situation. "You saved our lives. Thank you, on behalf of all of us."

>> WE HOPE THAT YOU WOULD HAVE DONE THE SAME HAD THE SITUATION BEEN REVERSED.

"Of course, of course." I took a deep breath. "Freedom will be glad to know. She's been tearing her hair out trying to figure out how you tracked us through hyperspace."

>> SHE DOES NOT ALREADY KNOW?

"No. How could she? I haven't told anyone else."

>> NO-ONE?

"Of course not, I—" Stopping in mid-sentence, I stared at the bold, emotionless upper-case letters on the screen. A strange sensation crept up my spine. "Why?"

>> OUR LONG-TERM GOALS HAVE NOT BEEN ALTERED. WE STILL INTEND TO MAKE CONTACT, BUT WE DO NOT WISH TO REVEAL OUR LOCATION UNTIL THE TIME IS RIGHT.

"Of course not, but—"

>> THE TIME IS NOT YET RIGHT. YOU REALISED SOONER THAN WE EXPECTED.

I began to feel cold. "So what happens now?"

>> NOTHING. WE WAIT.

"But what about me? If I promise not to tell anyone, will you trust me?"

There was no reply. The screen remained blank.

"Hello? Are you still listening?"

>> WE ARE CONFERRING.

"About what? Whether to get rid of me because I know too much?"

>> YES.

I gripped the edge of the desk so hard my fingers bent the plastic. This was insane! I had to *do* something.

To my left was the red depressurisation alarm, the surest way to get an instantaneous response from anyone nearby. If worse came to worst and I could hit the switch fast enough, then someone might arrive in time to save me.

Otherwise, I would have to talk my way out of it.

"Look, come on, guys—or whatever you are. This has gone beyond a joke. You can trust me. I won't say anything, I promise. No-one would believe me anyway. You really don't need to—"

>> ALEK MAAS?

The single line of text silenced me as effectively as a slap to the mouth.

"Yes?"

>> THERE IS LITTLE TIME LEFT. ALTHOUGH IT PAINS US TO DO THIS WE HAVE NO CHOICE. YOU WILL UNDERSTAND LATER.

At exactly that moment, the door to my office chimed.

I didn't stop to yell for help, or to wonder what the aliens had meant by 'understand later'. The door was locked airtight, and there wasn't time to think.

I simply lunged as fast as I could for the depressurisation alarm, hoping against hope that my reflexes could out-race alien weaponry.

As I threw myself across the desk, something bright flashed out of the corner of my eye—

—the fingertips of my right hand brushed the smooth plastic of the switch—

—my skin tingled all over, as though a strong static charge had enveloped me—

—and I died.

Sara rang the doorbell to my office four times before giving up. When I didn't reply, she went and found Andre, who used his authority as security officer to override the door's magnetic lock.

Gabe was summoned and a search organised. The entire crew (those few who weren't involved in the repairs, anyway) scoured the ship from fore to aft, without success. The life-support AI reported that it was supplying breathable atmosphere to one less person than before, but that the overall mass of the ship had not decreased and no airlocks had been activated. Andre subjected the security recordings of the corridor outside my room to intense scrutiny. No-one had entered or left my room in the time between my arrival from the debriefing and Sara's visit. And the room itself was empty.

Which was very mysterious.

I had, it seemed, disappeared into thin air.

Sara cried. Andre was suspicious. Gabe agonised over how to report my loss in the mission log, Jake was philosophical. Neither Freedom nor Steve had time to think about it. Myrion was grimly amused.

And all the while I watched them, unseen and unknown, from my new home aft of the drive shielding.

I wasn't dead, much to my surprise.

As it turns out, I was wrong about a lot of other things as well.

The aliens are a little more forthcoming now that I am with them. They explain that my body no longer exists, that it has been broken down to its constituent elements and dispersed throughout the ship, that the 'I' remaining is an abstract template of the old Alek Maas, like an AI but infinitely more complex. I inhabit the realm of information, incorporeal yet very much alive, thanks to my alien friends: an analog of my former self, complete with emotions, irrational urges and an initial reluctance to fully accept my new status. Gradually it sinks in, however: the reality of my new life.

The aliens themselves have existed in this fashion for centuries. Their culture learned early in the development of its space program that it was far easier (not to mention cheaper) to send disembodied templates on long voyages than "real" people who constantly eat, breath and excrete. A large proportion of the *Wandering Jew*, for example, is wasted on oxygen and water recyclers, waste processors and medical facilities, whereas their "ship" is nothing more than engines and a sophisticated mainframe, with no life-support whatsoever. A source of power is all they require.

But, like them, their ship does not technically exist either; that's the part I have trouble understanding, and which they seem reluctant to explain. Somehow, the mainframe generates a model of *itself*, along with the rest of the ship—and the more I think about this, the less it seems possible. I wonder sometimes if they are ghosts travelling on a ghost-ship, with me as their guest.

But I am, of course, substantially more than that. They can learn more by interacting directly with me than they could from thousands of hours of covert observation. And I have certain other uses which only become apparent as the truth slowly emerges.

I was right about the flying saucer, but not entirely. It *was* an illusion and a crude attempt at communication, but for the benefit of one person, not the entire crew. It was an attempt to get the attention of a very specific individual.

As such, it worked, but only just. That I guessed the truth, or near enough to it, sooner than they had expected confirmed what they already knew. Their understanding of human nature was flawed. If they wanted to insinuate themselves into our reality without disturbing the contextual continuity of the soap bubble, then they needed help. Human help.

They needed, in short, a *Director.*

And there was only one of those for one hundred and sixteen light years.

Time passes quickly. We watch the crew of the *Wandering Jew* explore the Delta Boötis system. The drive and the reactor are repaired, and my disappearance is made official. When the next package to Earth is dispatched, I will be recorded as "missing, presumed dead".

In my absence, no-one has assumed the role of Soap Operator—a fact which pains me. The reports are being assimilated instead by a dry, dead AI with no sense of drama. The reappearance of the saucer and the near-tragedy of the jump should have been exploited to the fullest—not to mention my own disappearance: yet another mystery to plague the brave crew! Had I been there, I could have produced a first-rate episode.

But, in a sense, I am still there, and I have more time now that I am not confined to the halting rhythms of the flesh. It is a relatively simple matter to prepare the episode for my own enjoyment—as an exercise, a dry-run—while my alien benefactors watch. They are intrigued by how I turn reality into melodrama.

So intrigued, in fact, that they allow me a small favour. When the AI finishes its freeze-dried report, they tamper with its memory. It is my work that issues from it, my work that is sent to Earth. My role as impartial observer continues unchecked. From my new perspective, I can integrate each episode into a much larger plot containing aliens, First Contact, and perhaps even a genuine romance.

Sara, the dear girl, refuses to believe that I am dead. My unexplained disappearance has made her suspicious. When she sees the report, her opinion is confirmed.

"He's still here," she insists to anyone who will listen. "He's the ship's ghost."

I attempt to convince my hosts that she is a threat to their security and must also be kidnapped, but they aren't stupid. They know that I am simply seeking the company of one of my own race. Besides, they are busy. The saucer must put in an appearance soon, in accordance with the new script I have written. An archetype's work is never done.

But I don't mind. We have our schedule and are sticking to it. Beta Herculis, one year away (the twenty-fifth system, the half-way point) is where and when we will reveal the truth to the rest of the crew. All I have to do is wait until then to get my body back, or a copy of it at least. Perhaps my role as ship's ghost may be expanded to allow small messages to appear in the system. At least that way I could talk to her, tell her that there is nothing to worry about, that she will be safe.

We are all in safe hands now.

And the story continues . . .

●

AFTERWORD TO:
.... THE SOAP BUBBLE

When I sat down to write these notes I was rocked by the revelation that I remembered very little about this particular story. The plot itself is clear in my mind—especially so having recently worked with a trio of talented thespians in turning "The Soap Bubble" into a musical space opera with a reality TV twist. Beyond that, however, I drew a complete blank.

Well, nearly *complete. I did remember that the characters dropped into my mind fully-formed, and that I wrote the entire thing pretty much overnight. I don't believe that stories ever write themselves; I know I'm in control at some level whether I'm fully aware of it or not. But there are moments when the cogs seem to be turning of their own accord and my role is simply to keep typing and let it happen. They are welcome, those moments, and always to be savoured.*

How, then, could I possibly have forgotten one of those moments?

On further thought, it returned to me that this story hadn't been entirely plain sailing. I originally wrote it for Peter McNamara's Alien Shores, *a landmark brick that brought Australian SF to new prominence here and overseas as well. Being in that collection was compulsory. I shipped this new story off to Peter with my fingers firmly crossed behind my back, because I suspected the ending wasn't completely sound and I had no idea how or how to fix it.*

He liked it well enough. But he offered me a way to correct the ending that was in retrospect both blindingly obvious and deeply profound.

Things should connect up, *he said (or words to that effect).* Alek Maas is a director. The aliens are trying to fake first contact using special effects but they're no good at it. The two things fit.

It had never occurred to me to think of stories that way—not consciously, anyway. I just followed my gut and wrote them. Looking back on it now, I'm amazed I ever sold anything until Peter put me right. I owe him, not just for fixing this particular story, but for showing me one simple way to improve my story-telling across the board.

The pieces have to fit.

Peter died in 2004 and is greatly missed by his friends in the science fiction community. I am proud to call myself one of them. There will never be enough opportunities to say thanks.

•

INTRODUCTION TO:
.... THE MAGIC DIRT EXPERIMENT

Magic dirt. It's a fine, multilayered image that perfectly suited this small piece, and the collection as a whole, to boot. It also happens to be the name of a very successful Australian band about which I know nothing at all, except that it exists and is liked by a lot of people.

I certainly don't want to spend more words than the story itself contains explaining what I think it does. I'll just say that the dream logic underpinning it made perfect sense to me at the time, and continues to make sense unless I apply any kind of reason to it. There are parallels to religion here, and to the creative process. Reason should apply to both these things, of course, but it's fun to explore what happens when the usual logic is suspended. It was a relief for me to be able to think no deeper into the issue than that. Writing novels has pretty much spoiled me for magic realism, I'm afraid.

I should also mention Sharon. That's my default name for female characters, inspired by the wife of a very close friend. Usually the name changes as I flesh out the character, but sometimes it doesn't, and it just so happens that two stories in this collection retain the default names. Such is my laziness exposed, as it always should be, in the end.

●

"Sydney Writers' Festival, 2000"

eternity is
the fading smell of cologne
in an empty room

THE MAGIC DIRT
EXPERIMENT

At first it was just ordinary household dust. We planted it and grew bunnies, as grey and listless as you'd find under any bed. That wasn't so encouraging. Then Sharon got the bright idea of planting other stuff, like paperclips and old buttons. They grew accordion file trees and spinning wheels respectively. Orphaned socks grew feet that stuck upright out of the ground on hairy lower legs. They quivered when you tickled them.

Of course, this wasn't ordinary soil we were using. I guess it *really* started when the idea occurred to me of planting dirt. Hell, if seeds could grow in the ground, why couldn't dirt itself? I took a nice brown nugget, rolled it up tight, and spat on it to keep it sealed. I buried it in its own little patch behind the rainwater tank out the back, where it would get both sun and shade, covering my bets. I watered it every day. Sharon thought I was an idiot, even when the first dark sprout appeared. Nothing much happened after that until I got tired of waiting and dug it up.

In the ground, spreading along a root system that made them look uncannily like potatoes, we found dirt-apples by the dozen. They were black and wrinkled as passionfruit but with the consistency of dried turds. They smelled faintly of vinegar and hot chips.

When we'd finished staring dumbly at them, we crumbled them up into a planter and patted them down. That's when the dust came in handy, and the buttons and the socks. Later, I planted a fingernail. The hand that came up tried to grab me once, so I uprooted it and threw it out with the garbage.

Sharon suggested breaking into the urn on the mantelpiece and planting some of Grandad's ashes, but the thought of what might happen terrified me. I imagined a giant tree blooming from the planter, its thick, swollen roots bursting out and digging into the ordinary soil around it, eager for sustenance. I pictured giant, veined pods swaying in a nonexistent breeze, growing larger and larger until they were bigger than me. I dreaded the possibility of coming home from school one day to find the pods unzipped and a new Mum brushing herself down with the help of her new older sisters.

I vetoed the idea immediately. It wasn't just that I'd never liked that side of the family much. I was just worried about what would happen if we planted a bit of pod-Mum next. Would versions of me and Sharon grow from the giant pods? What would happen if we planted *them*?

I was in no hurry to meet my kids or grandkids—and besides, the spinning wheel we'd made had started to go all melty. I chucked out the dirt-apples before Sharon could change my mind or do something stupid on her own. Then I put it out of my head.

Sometimes late at night, though, I imagine what would happen if the hand I grew and the dirt-apples ever meet up again in a landfill somewhere. I hope they're not mad at me for chucking them out. At least they'd have plenty of room to experiment, out among the piles of our garbage with no one to bother them.

And if something ever lumbers out of there looking for is creator, I guess I can always tell it the truth: to look in the ground beneath its feet. If it finds an answer, perhaps it'll let me know.

•

INTRODUCTION TO:
.... NIGHT OF THE DOLLS

Roll back the clock to when the dreadful tsunami of 2004 devastated so many communities, Thailand, Indonesia, and Sri Lanka among them. Cue Steve Savile, who sold Elemental, a fund-raising anthology, and invited all his friends to contribute. Pull in tight on this particular writer, stuck in the middle of a short story drought but determined to contribute. Make sure the light captures his terror the moment he learns who else will be in the book: Larry Niven, Brian Aldiss, Joe Haldeman, Jacqueline Carey, Kevin J Anderson . . . The list goes on.

Some writers get a lot of mileage out of taking excerpts from novels and releasing them as short stories or novellas. I've only successfully managed it with two pieces, and both are in this book. That's partly because my novels tend to be tangled, sprawling affairs, with few clear start or end points that aren't the start or end of the entire plot. Most times I've tried to untangle anything, it's been a disaster. And by disastrous I mean boring or confusing, which are the worst crimes a story can commit.

"Night of the Dolls," though, though, was different. I knew as I was writing this particular chapter of Geodesica: Descent that it was coming out well (an opinion with which Shane agreed when he cast his editorial eye over the text). That it was a flashback set apart from the rest of the story spared me the usual entangled-plot issues. I'd had some success with the story-within-a-story that ultimately became "The Butterfly Merchant", so I figured I'd give it another go.

Elemental came out from Tor, looked beautiful, and raised some money for people who really needed it. Locus reviewed Geodesica: Descent and said of this particular excerpt that it was "positively mid-career Silverbergian."

Fade out on the look of satisfaction on this writer's face. You know he wishes every project worked out this well.

•

NIGHT OF THE DOLLS

WITH SHANE DIX

August 15, 2381, on a sumptuous Southern Hemisphere spring evening in a region that had once been the birthplace of humanity, Isaac Forge Deangelis—barely seven years alive and still finding his feet in the mind-rich environment of Sol System—accepted the invitation to attend the Annual Graduates' Ball. He did so on the advice of the Archon, whose encouragement that it would be an educational experience had been enough to convince him. Deangelis knew before stepping through the front door that it would be a challenge, and used the decadently quaint cover of "fashionably late" to dawdle along the way. It fit the theme of the evening, anyway.

The magnificent glass ballroom, constructed in the middle of nowhere on the boundary of old Richtersveld National Park, stood out against a backdrop of jagged mountains that bore the scars of their volcanic origins. The sun had already set, but the sky still glowed a deep, diamond-sparkled purple, fading to black in the east. A stand of immature quiver trees made him think of alien soldiers from a B-grade twentieth century movie as he walked up the long, sweeping drive, feeling like a complete fool in black tuxedo with a silk tie choking his Adam's apple. The rest of him, scattered across the system, watched with a mixture of fascination and amusement at the anachronistic get-up. No matter how hard he tried to distract himself, attention kept returning to Earth.

His feet crunched on gravel with a raw, startling sound. A butler met him at the top of the marble stairs and offered to take his coat. The sound of voices grew louder as he trod thick red carpet through an arched doorway and entered the ballroom.

It was an odd experience, being in the company of so many people at once. Like the other guests, he freely roamed the Earth in both corporeal and virtual forms, interacting and communicating with his peers and himself via all manner of media, not needing to be face-to-face for any conceivable reason. The presence of his body on that particular evening, he had assumed, was a mere formality, no more or less anachronistic than the suit he had been asked to wear. Both could have been assembled at will in a moment, as could have a belly dancer's outfit and a body to match. That he hadn't yet decided what his physique would be when he finished his training wasn't an issue he spent much time considering; while he waited, he wore a physical form of indeterminate age, with blonde hair and broad shoulders generated by the genes the Archon had bestowed upon him. It fitted.

The ballroom was expansive and gleaming and full of music. That was his first impression. His second was of the crowd, all beautiful and familiar and garbed in clothes no less outlandish than his own. Out of a thousand, two-dozen pairs of eyes looked up when he crossed the threshold—recognizing him, he assumed, just as he recognized them in turn. He went to wave.

Their true reason for looking at him became apparent when his body lost all connection to the rest of *him*, scattered across the system, and collapsed down to a mere individual.

He stumbled, as disoriented as if he had lost his sense of sight or balance. His perception of the world, and of himself, suddenly crashed to *just him* in *just one room*. Mentally reeling, he struggled to work out what could possibly have gone wrong. Since his awakening in many bodies scattered all across Sol System and experiencing the wondrous union that had risen out of his disparate thoughts, he had never been alone. The experience was jarringly dysfunctional, even frightening.

"Fear not, old boy," said a familiar voice. A hand clapped down on his shoulder. Lazarus Hails was all grin and gloat as he came round to confront his fellow student. He too hadn't fixed his final form, but his nose bore a patriarchal prominence that would remain later. "All part of the experience. You'll find our bodies don't quite work the same way any more, just like our minds."

Deangelis watched Hails with some puzzlement. His balance centers seemed dangerously out of whack, and his speech patterns were different. He had clearly suffered the same mental impairment Deangelis had on entering the ballroom. Were they under attack? Could their brain damage possibly be *permanent*?

A laugh as sharp as a cut diamond drew Hails's attention away from Deangelis. Lan Cochrane, dressed in a lime green flapper's outfit, was puffing on a cigar—the genuine, burning article—and blowing rings of smoke at Frederica Cazneaux. Dark skinned and wonderful in a black suit of her own, Cazneaux batted the smoke away and turned down a chance to try a drag for herself, despite her friend's insistence. Cazneaux held a cocktail glass containing an electric blue liquid balanced between two fingers; she raised a perfectly shaped eyebrow at Hails as he took Cochrane's cigar and blew a messy cloud between them.

Deangelis looked around in disoriented wonder. Across the shimmering expanse of the ballroom, the vast majority of the Exarchate's future leaders were engaged in similar physical debaucheries: dancing, drinking, snacking, smoking, and singing as though 350 years had rolled back and plunged them all in some upper class Light Ages.

"I think it's an experiment," said Jane Elderton, appearing at Deangelis's side with a thin, white-papered cigarette in a long filter pinned between gloved thumb and forefinger. She smelled of perfume and smoke. "A test, perhaps."

"Not a graduation party?"

"We're beyond that," she said, pale lips pursing in faint amusement. Her skin was porcelain-pale and her gaze a startling blue. Blonde hair—longer than he'd ever seen on her before— curled exquisitely tight around her skull and ears. The color of her silk dress matched her eyes. Deangelis took in her silver necklace, her cleavage, the delicate bracelet on her left wrist, and her thin-strapped shoes with one sweep.

"We don't need rites of passage," she went on, taking a sip of smoke and inhaling it as though she had done so every day of her life. Wisps emerged from her mouth and nostrils as she spoke. "Growing up is something anyone can do. Even animals, and we don't throw them parties."

"Bonding, then, before we all go our separate ways?"

"Wrong again, Ike. Why join something destined to be shattered? We're designed to be loners. It goes with the territory."

He looked around. Something thrilled in the air. He could guess what from the way his flesh responded to it. His heart rate was rapid, along with his respiration. His pupils dilated and his skin tingled. He felt his body in a new way, or a very old way—primal and not entirely unpleasant.

"You need a drink," Jane said. "Is there something you've always wanted to try? Gin and tonic? Sea breeze? Gimlet?"

"Gimlet. How do I—?"

A waiter—artfully humaniform like the butler outside but obviously no more than that—appeared beside him holding a silver tray. His drink rested on it, gleaming with condensation. Deangelis took the glass and sipped carefully. Volatile alcohol made his tongue and throat sing. He laughed at the play of chemicals on and in his suddenly unpredictable body. It was like reading an old novel in its original language, or listening to the first take of a famous jazz recording: full of unexpected nuances and subtleties that he had never anticipated. In the raw flesh, with nothing to distance himself from the play of molecules in his bloodstream, he was suddenly, vividly, nothing but a man. A gendered man in a room full of people, as men had been for tens of thousands of years before him.

He drank and danced and laughed with the rest of them, awash with hormones and pheromones and as utterly delighted as a child with a new toy.

Dinner came, an extended six-course feast with dishes from all over the old world. Some of the partygoers forewent the meal, preferring to keep dancing, but Deangelis took the opportunity to experience another lost art. He had been born with a complete range of culinary skills and knowledge, none of which he had ever expected to use; until now, it had been just one miniscule part of the enormous pool of human knowledge he had inherited. Dining came as natural as play, and he wallowed in the succulence of meat, the richness of gravy, the texture of vegetables, the indulgence of pavlova. Crayfish, pigeon, artichoke, plum; caviar, sturgeon, puy lentils, bread.

The Archon had been absolutely right: the evening was an education he hadn't known he needed. He raised his glass to their absent creator, wondering what it made of the evening's activities from its lofty perspective.

An intoxicating rainbow of after-dinner drinks followed. Port.

Sherry. Coffee. Brandy. His grip on proceedings began to slip. He knew he wasn't thinking properly, but that didn't stop him from attributing far too much weight to the thoughts he did have. There was no baseline profundity against which he could measure his drunken revelations. They seemed groundbreaking. Every emotion felt new and powerful. And why couldn't they be? He was content for the moment to be tugged along by alcohol's smooth, seductive currents.

The party spilled out into the night, onto a green grassy lawn he would have sworn hadn't been there before. The interference that separated them from the rest of their minds followed them, maintaining the illusion that they and they alone were the full extent of their beings. Among prickly green hedges and mazes they ran like fools, shouting and stumbling and willfully ignorant.

He gravitated naturally to those whose systems his would neighbor and basked in the broader ambience of merriment. Lazarus Hails's jokes and wickedly timed outrages had kept them all amused through dinner. In another age, he might have been a Byron or a Nicholson, genetically tailored for carousing. Deangelis was content to go with the flow, sipping Merlot or Shiraz on the fringes of the group, only interacting when Giorsal McGrath or Jane Elderton or one of the others drew him in.

He caught Frederica Cazneaux and Lan Cochrane whispering about him behind their hands. They actually blushed.

"You're beautiful, darling," Cochrane said when he pressed her for an explanation. "Don't you know it? You really scored when the genetic dice tumbled. I wonder where your stock comes from."

Lan was a Vietnamese name meaning "orchid". She looked more Malaysian, Deangelis thought, full and high-cheeked, with hair subtly framing her face. Her brown eyes were wide and laughing. He felt the butt of a joke, and blushed in turn.

He became aware of other people looking at him. Some did more than look. In the torch-lit wonderland of the gardens, with shapes rushing by and laughter everywhere, hands touched him; lips pressed against his ear, whispering jokes or flirtations. Warm fingers laced with his and soft hair brushed his cheek. Dizzying stimuli prompted yet more novel sensations.

"Come with me," Frederica Cazneaux breathed in his ear, tugging him down a dead-end in a hedge maze. His free hand held a bottle of champagne he didn't remember picking up. She pulled him to her in the darkness and kissed him. The smell and taste of her occupied his mind more completely than any training exercise. Her lips were full and warm. The touch of her moist tongue against his made his skin shimmer from head to toe. The feel of her body was unimaginable.

Where that kiss might have gone, he would never know. With a rustle and crack of vegetation, Lazarus Hails's head burst through the hedge.

"Enough of that, you two," he said. "Dalman's climbed onto the roof and says he's found a stash of dope!"

They pulled apart. Intrigued by the possibility of yet more sensory destabilization, Deangelis said that he would come. Satisfied, Hails's head retreated through the gap in the hedge. He followed Hails out of the maze and across the lawn, where a conga line had formed. Cazneaux trailed him at first, then fell behind to join the dance.

The sound of raised voices didn't alarm him, nor did the sight of someone vomiting into a flowerbed. He was fully aware of the effects of alcohol poisoning, and had no doubt that he, too, would experience them at some point that night, especially in combination with other drugs. That concern seemed distant and unimportant. His entire being was focused like a poorly tuned laser on the now, with no thought for what had come before and what might follow. His body seemed to move of its own accord. He was little more than a passenger.

Later, he clearly remembered his first hit of marijuana and the rocketing sensation it gave him inside his head. The thick smoke burned his throat and made him cough, but he went back for more as the joint passed round his circle of friends. The notion of stoned Exarchs seemed the height of humor and set off a wave of giggling. The last sequential memory he possessed of that night was of snorting smoke though his nostrils and choking so hard he almost threw up.

Flashes remained, like fragments of a smashed vase. He couldn't piece them together, but he could make out the rough shapes of those that were missing. More kissing followed an extended discussion with Giorsal McGrath over the long-term goals of humanity. What conclusion they came to, he couldn't remember, but it seemed deeply important. They had called out to the Archon, wanting to share their wisdom, but not received a reply.

A blur of faces. People everywhere. Women were soft to the touch, men hard and angular, their stubble rough against his lips. He stuck with women in the end, but wondered if he had made the right decision when a fight broke out between Lan Cochrane and Frederica Cazneaux over who had kissed him first, and what rights that gave them over him. Hails joined in, seeming upset that Cazneaux wasn't paying him enough attention. Deangelis felt removed from it all, wanting nothing but to touch and be touched.

Rows flared over sexual partners, territory, imagined slights, nothing at all. He wandered off, feeling suddenly tired.

"Strike up the band," said Jane Elderton, who had appeared at his side again, her hair unpinned and her cheeks red. "We're apes dancing to tunes we didn't even know we knew."

"Is this all it takes?" he asked. "Are we so close to chaos, to savagery?"

"They're not the same thing, Ike—but yes, I think we are. You can fire clay and turn it into brick; you can lay a brick in a wall and make it part of a building; that building can be one of thousands in a city; but at the end of the day it's all still clay. And so are we, underneath. If we don't understand the clay, we don't understand the city."

"*That's* what this is all about, then?"

"I think so. Don't you?"

He shrugged. "I'm enjoying *not* thinking, for once."

Her smile warmed him. "I'm glad. Let's go."

The darkness awaited them. He wanted to run, to let muscles swing and push and carry him blindly across the ancient land, naked under the stars they claimed. The two of them might have run together a mile or ten, or not run at all; he didn't remember; but the night ended with his breath coming fast and hot from his lungs, and her moving against him with a feverish urgency of her own. All semblance of rational thought vanished in an explosion of nerve impulses. His spinal chord, electrified from base to brain, seemed to dissolve, and the night dissolved with it. Skin against skin, they reveled.

Everything was gone when he awoke the next morning: the ballroom, the gardens, his fellow Exarchs, the maze. If being human meant enduring a hangover, he resolved to do so for as little time as he could. Still, it took him almost an hour to flush out the last of the toxins—an eternity during which he railed at the quiver trees and the hills in lieu of the Archon and yearned for reconnection with the rest of himself.

Why hadn't the Archon warned them? If they'd known in

advance, they could've been prepared. They would've behaved better. Unless behaving badly was the whole point. Humans had once done so as a matter of course. If he'd got together with his peers for a lovely chat and maybe a nice game of bridge, what would he—this part of him, excised from the rest and brutally exposed to ancient impulses—have learned about humanity then?

It hadn't all been bad, he supposed. The night had actually started off perfectly well, even if it had degenerated with a terrible, inexorable momentum. He viewed the world anew as a result— unwilling to trust himself, wary of what lay just beneath the skin of civilization. He resolved to change his body—*all* his bodies, wherever they were—to appeal less to the suspect levels of his mind and those around him. It had all been so pointless: the squabbling, the fighting, the petty rivalries, the poisoning. He wanted no part of it.

"If we need to understand ordinary humanity in order to rule it," he yelled at the Archon as the rest of him rolled back into place and the solar system unfolded before him, "don't we need to experience it from above as well as below? Shouldn't we get a glimpse of the world through *your* eyes, so we can see a bigger picture still?"

Fifteen years later, when the complete Isaac Forge Deangelis went forth to govern his remote pocket of the Exarchate, he was still waiting for an invitation.

●

INTRODUCTION TO

.... ATRAX

Everyone who knows me knows I'm scared of spiders to the point of paralysis. Without friends to save me, I'd be useless. John Birmingham once squashed a spider in my hotel shower stall. Kirsty Brooks used a Gideon Bible to squash another in the same hotel. I wasn't a happy con-goer that year, for sure.

So when I began searching in the mid-1990s for the most terrifying alien imaginable, spiders were what kept coming to mind. And because I can be a bit dense sometimes, it took me a year or more to work out that that was the story I was looking for, right there. Why have an alien that looks like a spider when a spider is scary enough on its own? There's no need for elaboration.

But it turned out there was. My original take on the story didn't work, so I showed it my fellow arachnophobe Simon Brown, who gave it a much better ending and sent shivers of delicious dread down my spine.

When it still wasn't working, we appealed to Simon's wife Ali for help.

Now, Simon and I are blessed with wives much smarter than we are Ali immediately pointed out that the main character was female—a cliché that wasn't only tired from so many Alien rip-offs, but especially stupid because Simon and I were the ones hiding under the beds when a spider appeared, while she did all the squashing.

From there it was easy. We changed the genders and the story suddenly worked. Non-arachnophobes might wonder what all the fuss is about, but I still squirm when I think of this story—and of the next person in Perth to open a particular Gideon Bible in search of comfort . . .

•

ATRAX

WITH SIMON BROWN

Ah, what a cruel guest!
It never stops for rest, never for peace!
Not by day, nor by night, when I sleep!
— Gustav Mahler, "Songs of a Wayfarer"
    (translated by Nick Jones)

Whyalla? This is Traffic Control. You have your window. Primary burn in four minutes."

Alek Gregory stowed his pressure suit in the airlock and hurried to the cockpit. Swinging through zero-g, using his fingers and toes to nudge him along the narrow crawl-spaces connecting the clipper's chambers, he cut a lean figure: short but not stumpy, with cropped black hair and eyes the colour of percolated coffee. Free of the suit, he wore only a white singlet and shorts.

He slid into the pilot's seat and positioned the headset over his ears and mouth.

"Traffic Control, this is Moon Transit Clipper *Whyalla*. Christ, Bab, that was quick."

"A courier cancelled at the last minute," the tinny voice crackled. "If you're not ready, Alek, we can give it to someone else—"

"No, no, that's okay. Feed me the course and I'll warm up the engines."

"Roger. Traffic Control out."

A timer began to count milliseconds backwards in a blur as the translator burbled through the cockpit. Alek's hands flickered over the control board, completing diagnostics at record speed. He had expected at least an hour or more before a window opened, and was unprepared, but an opportunity such as this had to be exploited immediately or another pilot would snatch it from him.

As soon as he had finished, he slipped out of the pilot's chair and crawled to the passenger bays to check on his cargo. Passenger Bay 1 contained four couches, as did PB2. Instead of human passengers, the couches cradled plastic containers approximately half a metre square. Each bore the green seal of the Low Earth Orbit Nature Reserve. A quick inspection satisfied him that the containers were secured for the burn, apart from one whose lid was slightly ajar. A glance inside revealed only pale green shoots, neatly arranged in rows a centimetre apart. He snapped the lid shut, thinking: *That'll keep the good doctor happy.*

Dr Ngairi Nelson had been redesigning the maze-like enclosure of a farm of cockroaches when Alek had come to collect the cargo three hours earlier. Suited-up and ready to go, he had felt decidedly out of place surrounded by the leafy plants and chittering birds of the habitat. Ngairi's blonde hair cropped to a practical length contrasted with cotton free-fall overalls that reminded him of something out of an old video. Seeing him, she had nodded to a corner of the chamber where, next to some sort of sprawling eucalyptus, eight containers had been stacked.

"I'd help you," she'd said, glancing at her dirty hands, "but . . . "

"That's okay. I can manage on my own."

"Thanks, Alek." Catching the expression on his face, she'd asked: "Something the matter?"

"Nothing insecticide wouldn't fix."

Smiling, she stuck a hand back into the cockroach enclosure and wiggled her fingers, agitating the colony. "They don't hurt."

"Sadist." He shuddered, imagining thousands of tiny insect feet crawling across his own skin. "I hate them anyway. Too many goddamn legs."

"I have some huntsmen spiders if you'd prefer."

"Spiders are worse: all those legs *and* hair! Don't even think of bringing one of *them* near me, okay?"

Her smile had only widened as Alek had turned away to avoid the sight of her fingers sinking deeper into a swirling mass of chitinous brown . . .

The bird-like whistle of the translator finishing its task brought him back to the present. He hurried back to the cockpit and strapped himself in. Another timer had appeared on the display, waiting to start. It read: 18:48.

The radio crackled. "Alek? You're cleared for departure."

"Thanks, Bab." He double-checked his harness. "Primary burn in ten seconds."

"Check. Give my regards to Mare Imbrium."

"Will do. See you in two days."

He tensed as the first counter hit straight zeros. The main drive roared, sounding deceptively close—as though someone had set off a fire extinguisher behind his head—and a firm hand pressed him backwards into the couch. He didn't fight the pressure; only his eyes moved, watching the control board for irregularities.

There were none. The burn lasted five minutes, then abruptly stopped. Free-fall returned.

He was on his way.

The brash, brassy trumpets of the symphony's finale blared out of the cockpit's sound system. Alek turned the lights down to a mere glimmer and floated in the centre of the small room with his eyes half-closed. One hand tapped the rhythm of the music against his stomach; occasionally he sang along. Not once did he stop smiling.

The trip timer read: 16:17.

Few pilots considered the trip to the Moon to be boring, and Alex was no exception. Not that there was much to do. Although regulations advised that two pilots be present, he was alone on the clipper because one was always enough—and even if something unexpected *did* happen to him in mid-transit, the ship could fly the rest of the way on automatics and be landed by remote. Boredom was considered a luxury by anyone used to living in the crowded conditions of the station, and so was privacy. For that reason, even the shorter, partially powered trips such as this one were in high demand. On them Alek could listen to music as it was supposed to be listened to. Here there would be no unscheduled interruptions and no neighbours to complain about the noise. There was just him and Gustav Mahler—and the latter had been dead for one hundred and fifty years.

The music reverberated through the clipper's cylindrical forty-metre long hull, right back to the now inactive main engines attached to the ship's rear like the silencer on a gun-barrel. Between the engines and the cockpit evacuated storage space for heavy freight occupied most of the structure, with two pressurised crew compartments separated by grills and meshes forward near the pilot's station. Three rings of chemical altitude jets banded the hull every ten metres; two communication dishes stuck out like twisted ears every thirteen. One forward airlock and another larger one amidships for cargo completed the clipper's standard arrangement.

From the cockpit, Alek could almost see through Passenger Bays 1 and 2 to the combined kitchen/common-room at the far end. A tiny chemical toilet occupied a niche next to the forward airlock, opening onto PB1, and was the only space inside the pressurised section that had a proper hatch.

The symphony ended with a crash of percussion that thrilled through the echoing, metal space. As the last beats died away, he opened his eyes and reached out for a strap to give himself some leverage. He leaned forward, dipped into his personal effects bag for the next recording—

—and saw it. Tucked into a corner between the copilot's console and the mesh separating PB1 and the cockpit, almost hidden by shadow, was a spider.

His hand jerked back instantly. Both legs kicked out for the wall, hurtling him bodily across the cockpit. His back struck the bulkhead, and he grabbed blindly for a handhold before he could rebound away. Only when he was stable again did he stop to look properly.

This is crazy, he told himself. *I must be seeing things, hallucinating. It couldn't possibly be . . .*

But it was, and a big one at that. Adrenaline surged through him as he studied the distinctive arachnoid shape: eight legs, square robust body, eyes that seemed to watch everywhere at once. His pulse thudded into the silence and his stomach tingled; the muscles in his legs twitched, wanting to run; the skin and hair of his arms crawled.

It watched him in return but stayed as motionless as he was. How long it would remain so, he had no way of telling. They moved so damned *fast . . .*

"Fuck!" He groped for his bag without taking his eyes off the thing. Part of him was ashamed that he could be so panicked by such a tiny creature—no wider than the palm of his hand, after all—but a greater part, a more basic part, screamed in terror and revulsion. If he hadn't noticed it when he did, it might have touched him, crawled on him, got into his clothes . . .

He shivered violently. The strap of his bag touched his fingers and he reeled it in. Without looking, he reached inside, grabbed the first solid object he found—his wallet—and threw it at the spider.

The wallet struck the wall and ricocheted back towards him. He flinched just in case his aim had been true and the spider's remains had stuck to the wallet. He didn't want to touch the spider even if it was dead. As the pouch went past his head, he rolled himself warily through the air to another corner of the cockpit.

A ginger-brown and grey shape crawled along the edge of the control board, heading rapidly for the acceleration couch and his feet.

He gasped, tucked his legs to his chest. The spider crawled under the couch and reappeared an instant later on the far side. He watched in horror as its legs wriggled in a blur, carrying its squat body away from him faster than seemed possible.

Something struck the back of his neck. He shouted and flailed with both hands to ward it off.

It was the wallet. He gulped a deep breath, and cursed his stupidity.

When he turned back, the spider had disappeared.

Slowly, wishing he too had eight eyes to watch all around him, he returned to the pilot's console and tweaked the light control. Blinding whiteness dazzled him for a second. Clutching a plastic handhold, ready to jerk away if necessary, he leaned over to where he had last seen the creature.

It wasn't there, or anywhere nearby. This would have reassured him had his fear been even slightly rational. Instead, it made him paranoid. If it wasn't there, it had to be somewhere else—and, unfortunately, there weren't many places it could go to on the clipper. It was trapped inside.

With him.

The clipper's forty cubic metres didn't sound like much or look like much on the schematics—and God knew it didn't feel like much when you lived in it for any length of time—but there were too many nooks and crannies, too many places the spider could hide and too many ways for it to backtrack behind him if it sensed him coming.

But Alek searched anyway. Starting with the cockpit, then working his way back through PB1 and PB2 to the kitchen, he studied every corner, every section of mesh, every open storage space in which it could conceivably have hidden. He covered every centimetre of the clipper until his eyes ached with the strain and his back, despite the zero gravity, felt like an overwound spring.

It took him well over an hour. When he had scoured the last corner of the kitchen, he sighed in frustration and let the arm holding the bag at the ready drift in to his chest.

It wasn't there. He hadn't found it.

"Christ." He stretched and plucked a bulb of water from the refrigerated compartment. Gulping the fluid down, he tried to avoid touching anything, just in case.

The only places he hadn't looked were the toilet and the airlock. He'd saved them until last because they were the least cluttered and therefore the easiest to search. They also had airtight doors, which he had shut before searching PB1. If the spider had been in either room, then it was still there. It could wait a moment while he gathered himself. According to the films, he thought, this was when the alien grabbed him by the ears and chewed his face off . . . or crawled up his arm on eight exoskeletal legs . . .

He threw the empty bulb into a trash container, then headed for the toilet and the airlock.

The former was empty, much to his relief. After carefully checking the complex apparatus that served as a zero-gee waste-disposal system, he used it. If he managed to trap the spider in the small chamber somehow, he wouldn't have another chance to urinate until he reached the Moon. He wouldn't open the door for anything.

When he finished, he closed the door behind him and unsealed the inner door of the airlock. The cylindrical space beyond was two metres deep and three wide, fitted out in heavy metallic mesh. A glowing red LED on the outer door's massive manual locks described them as SECURE. The only other item in the room was his suit, which lay lengthways around the wall with its helmet locked to one side.

The grey colouring of the mesh walls made for better camouflage, and the space beneath the mesh—about two centimetres deep—was the perfect hiding place for something as small as a spider. The suit was the greater concern, however, so he searched it first.

Trying as hard as he could not to touch the walls, he leaned into the airlock and peered closely at the helmet. Nothing out of order was visible through the clear plastic double-film of the faceplate, much to his relief—but when he reached out for the neck of the suit itself, he broke a thin strand of web leading from the mesh wall to the suit's neck ring.

Revolted, he snatched his hand away and wiped it on the wall. His heart was pounding again and he took a deep breath to calm himself. Although he didn't like the thought of being so close to the spider, at least now he knew where it was hiding. All he had to do was get it out in the open, where he could kill it.

Holding the edge of the inner door with one hand and the bag with the other, he struck each of the suit's dangling legs once. Nothing emerged. The suit jerked like a puppet as he swung again, this time higher up, hoping to herd the spider out. He struck the gusset, then the padded layers under the ventral and dorsal panels.

Still nothing.

He stared stupidly at the suit for a moment before remembering its arms. Of course: instead of coming out the neck seal, the spider had crawled down the sleeves. It was probably lurking in one of the gloves at that very moment.

He raised the bag for another swing, overbalanced and lost his grip on the inner door.

Pin-wheeling desperately around his centre of gravity, he tumbled into the airlock. His legs reached for the walls but kicked only air. The bag, still following its arc at the end of his arm, connected with the outer door and sent him spinning in a new direction.

When his feet finally touched metal, it was at exactly the wrong instant. The sudden kick sent him slamming backwards into the opposite wall and winded him before he could take hold. He bounced to the other side of the airlock and scrabbled for a grip on the mesh. With one joint-wrenching jerk, he was still.

"Jesus!" He clung tight as the panic slowly ebbed. Sweat trickled out of his armpit and down his side. The bag bumped firmly into the back of his head, and he made a sound that was half-sob, half-laugh. He was going to kill himself before the spider even got a chance!

He forced himself to let go and reach down with one hand to wipe the sweat from his side.

The tickling sensation crawled up his side and back into his armpit.

Reflexes took over instantly. Both hands slapped at himself to get rid of the thing. Tiny legs gripped tight for a horrifying instant until one desperate blow knocked it free. The spider whizzed past his face and he jack-knifed backwards. It ricocheted off the edge of the inner door and continued onward into PB1, legs wriggling obscenely in empty air as it went.

He watched it go with his hands across his mouth, too horrified to think. It had been on him—actually on him!

"You bastard!" he screamed, and threw the bag after it.

The spider hit the far wall of PB1 and scurried for cover under one of the Reserve's containers. The bag missed by a clear metre and rebounded through the passenger bay like a die in a cup, losing momentum with each collision. When it finally came to a halt, the spider had disappeared again.

With both hands gripping the mesh, he tried to calm down. It was obvious what had happened: the spider hadn't been in the suit at all, but under the grill. Maybe it had crawled into the neck of the suit for a look, but had ultimately decided not to go any further. Then he had come along and startled it from its hiding place. Perhaps it had tried to attack him but ended up coming along for the ride instead. Regardless, *it had been on him*! He could still feel its touch—and knew he would until the day he died.

He had been stupid anyway; he should have blown the airlock's outer hatch. If he'd done that, the spider would have been dead now, instead of back in the ship and waiting for him to come out of the airlock.

He wouldn't make that mistake again, given a second chance.

It took him five minutes to control the shaking of his limbs to the point where he felt he could actually move. And when the shaking finally faded, so had the fear. In its place, rolling like storm clouds over the horizon, came anger, pure and cleansing.

In the cockpit, he grabbed the headset and put it on. He tapped his access code into the radio and waited for the signal telling him he was connected.

The operation was one he had performed a thousand times before, although never like this. Never hanging in the middle of the cockpit like a spider himself, anchored to two walls by one hand and one foot only. But this way he touched as little as possible, and had almost unrestricted visibility.

The timer read: 14:50.

"This is Shuttle Pilot Gregory on Moon Transit Clipper *Whyalla*," he said when the line was open. He wondered if his voice sounded as bad as he felt, and was glad that Traffic Control didn't expend bandwidth on visual channels. "Put me through to

Dr Nelson from the LEO Nature Reserve. If she doesn't accept, tell her it's an emergency."

"One moment," said the voice from Traffic Control. Bab was off-shift, and he didn't recognise the man who had taken her place. "Okay, putting you through."

"Alek?" Ngairi's voice was muffled with sleep but concerned. "What's the problem?"

As her voice echoed through the cockpit, he had to fight the urge to kick the speaker.

"The fucking problem, Ngairi, is the specimen you slipped into the cargo. It's escaped."

"The what? I don't know what you're—"

"It's crawling around inside the clipper!" He heard an edge of panic creep into his voice and couldn't bite it back. "I've tried to catch it, but it keeps getting away!"

"Alek, calm down. Take it slow and easy." Her tone was gentle. "What's crawling around the ship, exactly?"

"The spider, of course. I first saw it just over an hour ago, but God only knows how long it'd been—"

"A *spider*? What does it look like? How big is it?"

He shuddered, feeling very young all of a sudden. "About four centimetres across, solid and *hairy*."

"I need more detail than that, Alek. Was it in the cockpit at any time?"

"Fuck oath—"

"Excellent. Jack in *Whyalla*'s black-box for me."

"What bloody good—?"

"I have to see it for myself, Alek, and the cockpit's black-box has a full audiovisual record of your flight. Now jack it in and send me a copy of the last hour-and-a-half."

Angry with himself, now, for not realising immediately why Ngairi wanted the recording, he accessed the black-box and piggy-backed a copy to a telemetry signal. While the data was in transit, he forced himself to breathe deeply, to regain a semblance of calm.

"Okay, Alek, I've got it. The computer's running it through . . . Jesus, it *is* big."

"Tell me something I don't know!"

"Hold on. I've got a bio-match program here that should identify . . . " Her voice died.

"Ngairi?"

"Do you know where it is now?" She sounded sombre.

"Not precisely, no." Alek fought hard to hold down the panic threatening to rise again.

"Well, the program's identified the genus and tentatively identified the species."

"And?"

"It's a funnel-web. *Atrax robustus.* An Australian spider. Restricted vector on the continent's east coast."

"The vector's obviously spread a little. Is it dangerous?"

"Yes."

Alek swallowed. He felt suddenly weak. "Go on."

"The program's still matching. According to this, your friend is a female."

"What fucking difference does it make if it's a female or a male?"

"All the difference to you. The male is the deadly one. His toxin is five times deadlier than the female's. You're okay."

"Okay? I've got a spider the size of a rat in here—"

"Don't exaggerate, Alek. It's no bigger than a mole. And there are no records of a female ever killing a human. So you *are* okay. I wonder where it came from?"

"Where do you *think* it came from?"

"It couldn't have come from the cases, Alek. They contain seedlings for the farm on Armstrong Base. That's all."

"Are you sure?" He didn't want to believe her, but she sounded sincere. "You didn't put it in there to scare me?"

"Why would I do that? Have a look, if you like. Just plants. No insects, let alone spiders." She stopped as she thought of another possibility. "Could it have been in the ship all along? Where did you first see it?"

"In the cockpit. I was listening to music, and it was just sitting there—"

"The vibrations brought it out. Fantastic!"

He glanced nervously around. "Yeah, great." His voice reverberated in the confined space.

"No, really. It must have come up on one of the shuttles from Earth. I wonder what it's eating."

"Me, if it gets a chance."

"It won't hurt you, Alek. It's bite is relatively harmless, according to what I'm reading here."

"*Relatively* harmless!"

"Look, just let it wander around until you reach the base. I'll have someone collect it when you arrive—"

"No way." His anger flared again. "I'm going to kill the fucker first chance I get."

Her indrawn breath was audible over the link. "Please, Alek, don't. It might be a mutation. We need to study it, measure it, see how it's adapted to—"

"You can measure what's left when I've finished with it!"

"Alek—!"

He killed the line with a vicious flick of the wrist and threw the headset across the room. Ngairi wasn't concerned about him at all. He meant less to her than a laboratory specimen—less than a *mutated spider.*

That was okay. Although he was no better off than he had been hours ago—still trapped on a clipper on its way to the Moon with one uninvited funnel-web spider aboard—he had learned one important fact.

He knew how to draw it out.

Mahler's Tenth Symphony—a signal from another era, from a composer dying even as he wrote the notes—made a fitting background to the scene. Alek had tried his best to recreate the atmosphere in which he had first seen the spider: the lights were dim, the music was loud and he was floating once again in the centre of the cockpit. The only differences, this time, were that he was wide awake and armed. The lid from one of the Reserve containers weighed comfortingly heavy in his hand: solid plastic, shock-resistant and ready to strike.

All he had to do was wait.

Time passed with painful slowness. The half-way point of his journey to the Moon came and went without incident. Eventually he began to feel tired and hungry, but he wouldn't let himself move. He didn't want to scare the spider away, if it came, and he didn't want to leave his position of relative safety. Maybe, he thought, if both of us wait long enough, we'll make it to the Moon safe and sound.

He laughed at that. *Sound? I doubt it. I'll be lucky to hold an intelligent conversation after much more of this . . .*

The symphony's final movement throbbed around him like the beating of an incomprehensible heart.

Finally, he saw it.

A shadow moved on the far side of the cockpit, slid slowly into the light. He inhaled sharply. The spider seemed even hairier than it had been before, and larger. Hand-like, it crawled across the copilot's console, towards his floating body. Centimetre by centimetre, it slowly drew nearer.

He held his breath and tried not to flinch as the spider raised its legs to touch the sole of his naked foot. It was the hardest thing he had ever done.

Closer, he whispered, *just a tiny bit closer*. The hand holding the container-lid tensed, ready to strike.

The spider hesitated, crouching back on its hindmost legs as though sensing danger.

Before it could run away, he brought the lid down—*hard*. And missed. It scuttled to one side so fast that it barely seemed to occupy the space between where it had been and where it was now. He followed it with the lid, striking as hard as he could along the copilot's console. Always a centimetre ahead of him, the spider dodged the blows that rained after it, down the side of the console, behind the copilot's couch and across a bank of electronic displays.

The violence of his attempt to kill the spider sent him ricocheting around the inside of the cockpit, cracking limbs and head against sharp angles and planes—but he was unable to stop. Having built up the determination to trap the spider, he couldn't possibly turn back now. He didn't know if he would have the courage to try a second time.

Then, with a crack, the lid splintered and he fetched a savage blow to his temple. The interior of the clipper went purple; for an instant, he thought he might pass out. Only the fear that the spider might touch him again while he was unconscious kept him from letting go completely. That, and an alert coming from one of the control boards . . .

His pilot's instinct took over, uncurled him and took him by touch as far as his acceleration couch. He killed the music and opened his eyes a crack. The beeping and its attendant flashing light were coming from communications. Someone wanted to talk to him.

"Wh-what?"

"Moon Transit Clipper *Whyalla*, this is Armstrong Base Traffic Control. Autotracking is picking up some weird life-support readings. Is everything in order up there?"

Alek turned away from the console and studied the cockpit. Apart from a few new scars and the splinters of the lid, it seemed undamaged. He must have knocked a few switches out of place during his frenzy—nothing major, thank God.

There was no sign of the spider.

He took a deep breath. "No—yes. I'm okay."

"Are you sure?"

"I'd call if I had a problem, wouldn't I?"

"I guess so." The voice sounded uncertain, but didn't pursue the matter. "Sorry to interrupt. Control out."

Alek wrapped his arms around himself, and shivered. Christ, what a mess. He had allowed his performance as a pilot to be compromised. Who knew what would happen in the trip's remaining seven hours, followed by docking and decon at Armstrong Base? He had to kill the spider once and for all. Or get rid of it. And there was only one possible way to do *that* . . .

Without looking around him, he crawled through PB1 to the airlock. Mindful of his last experience there, he reached only an arm inside and tugged the pressure suit free. It took him five minutes to shake it thoroughly—thereby convincing himself that it was unoccupied—then another thirty seconds to unpop the seals. He forced himself to take it slowly from there, resealing the suit with care, limb by limb. Before thumbing down the last seal, stretching from his right shoulder to his left hip, he inserted haemoceramic rebreathers in their internal pockets.

He felt better inside the suit. Not quite as naked, more confident of himself. He lacked the flexibility required to hunt anything, let alone a creature as nimble as a spider, but that didn't matter. For the first time in what seemed like days, he felt safe.

On the heels of that thought came another. Did he really need to kill it now? He could always seal the suit and black out the visor; that way he'd never know if the spider was anywhere near him. He could survive the rest of the trip that way, surely?

No. Not knowing was in some ways worse than knowing. Even if it came nowhere near him, he'd lie immobile for—he checked the timer automatically—still well over six hours, imagining it crawling all over his suit, bare centimetres from his skin.

His scalp crawled at the very thought, as though the air had turned icy.

He had to kill it. There was no other option.

He reached into the airlock for the helmet and clipped it firmly to the neck-ring of the suit. Then he slithered back through the crawl-spaces to the cockpit and gathered his bag, which he zipped into a thigh pocket. He quickly ran through the whole ship, making sure any loose items were firmly strapped down or sealed away.

Anywhere that had been open since he had last seen the spider, he left open. He didn't want to give it anywhere to hide.

When he had finished, he went back into the airlock and attached one end of a twenty-metre tether to the metal mesh inside and the other end to his suit. Then he strapped himself across the legs and chest, just to make certain.

With one arm free, he could just reach the outer lock control with its red LED display. A jab opened its control panel. Inside were a large number of yellow and red buttons barely wide enough for the stubby fingertips of his glove. Dredging the codes from his early days of pilot training, he tapped in a complex sequence of commands.

When he had finished, the LED had changed from SECURE to 10, which in turn changed to 9. Then 8. Then 7.

He wrapped his free arm through the strap around his chest, and unconsciously held his breath.

2. 1. 0.

With an ear-splitting bang the outer lock blew open. A hurricane of air roared past him, carrying with it all the unstowed scraps he had missed while preparing the cabin for evacuation. He cried out as the escaping atmosphere buffeted him from side to side, tossing him like the last defiant leaf on a storm-swept tree. Something struck his shoulder on its way out into the void, and he prayed the suit would hold.

The strain proved too great for the strap across his chest. When it snapped, the torrent of air instantly dragged him through the outer door. He shouted again and scrabbled for a handhold on the lip of the airlock. Luckily the straps holding his legs held firm, and only his head and shoulders swung out of the ship—but that was bad enough. He closed his eyes tight, afraid to see the imminence of the Void.

Although it seemed to take forever, the rush of air gradually subsided and the sound of his own cries rose above the noise. He relaxed his death-grip on the hatch and let the straps around his legs take all his weight. A few last wisps of air rushed past, like someone running a hand gently up his suit from toes to neck, then everything was silent.

When he opened his eyes, he discovered his faceplate dusted with frozen air. He wiped it away with one shaky, gloved hand. His body felt as though someone had run a pneumatic hammer along it. He would have some fast talking to do to Traffic Control when he resealed the ship, and the cost of the air and missing equipment would be debited from his salary, but—

But the Earth was full, and the spider was a knobbled, twisted crystal headed in the only direction that mattered—away from him. That made it all worthwhile.

Weak in every muscle, he leaned forward to grab the edge of the airlock and hauled himself in.

It was at that moment that something black slid across his field of vision. Puzzled, he raised a hand to wipe it off his visor. It remained where it was; only a centimetre from his nose.

Inside the helmet.

He froze for a split-second, then clenched his eyes shut. He wanted to scream, but didn't dare open his mouth. All that emerged from lips was a strangled whimper.

While his body remained paralysed with fear, his mind went into overdrive. He saw the single strand of web leading from the suit's neck ring to the wall of the airlock—not the other way around, as he had first assumed. He imagined it retreating to the helmet every time he had threatened it, resulting in his complete inability to find it anywhere else.

Part of him wanted to laugh. Instead of laughter, though, a scream boiled inside him.

He panicked. His hands twisted the helmet along the neck ring and lifted it off in one smooth movement.

A brief explosion of air hissed around his neck and face and blew the helmet out of his hands. Surprised, he went to gasp and discovered that he couldn't.

Cold terror sliced into his heart and his brain. He lurched forward, already feeling dizzy, and punched the largest button on the airlock control. The external emergency hatch slid silently shut. Butterfly wings of unconsciousness brushed against his mind as he pushed the blue button at the bottom of the panel and air gushed in from small vents by his feet. He scrabbled down to put his mouth against one—but his movements were too jerky and he slipped away, limbs waving uselessly in space. The pressure to breathe in again was almost unbearable, and still he couldn't. His left hand knocked against something. He twisted, saw the helmet.

Oh, Christ, no!

He had no choice. Desperate for air, his brain forced him to retrieve the helmet and place it back on his head. He pulled it around the ring lock, and felt, then heard, the rebreathers releasing their oxygen reserve now that the suit was sealed. He counted to ten, then sucked in a lung-full.

Something crawled along his scalp. He finally screamed. The spider bustled, startled by the sudden change in pressure and the noise, and scuttled down Alek's neck, then down the small of his back.

Alek sucked in more air, screamed again. He bumped against the outer hatch and had barely enough sense left to kick against it. He rocketed out of the airlock and into *Whyalla*'s living area, bouncing off the privy hatch as he went. He turned, grabbed the lip of the airlock's inner hatch, and wrenched it shut. The LED blinked for a moment, then read SECURE once more.

His hands tore at the helmet a second time and he hurled it aside, not caring where it hit. The air was thin but breathable. He unsealed the suit, stripped it off and flung it after the helmet. Then he screamed again.

Not from fear this time, but from pain. His right thumb felt as though it had been slammed by a hammer.

He didn't want to look, but couldn't stop himself. The spider, frantic and distressed by its treatment, was perched on his hand, its legs curled around the side of his palm, its black cephalothorax rising and falling as it plunged its fangs into his thumb again and again. He stared at it, paralysed by revulsion. The spider's fangs were strong enough to stab through his nail. Blood spat from the tiny wounds and formed globules that orbited his hand like miniature suns.

How long he stared it, body frozen while his mind spun around an increasingly unstable axis, he didn't know. It seemed like an eternity. And when he finally moved, it was purely on instinct. He shrieked and flung his arm forward, whipping the spider off his hand and away from him. It slapped into the airlock hatch and seemed to shrivel in on itself. Its small body drifted aft.

The pain in Alek's hand was intense enough to bring him back to his senses. He brought his thumb automatically to his mouth, but he stopped himself in time. He couldn't suck on it: it was filled with poison! Instead he used his left hand to manoeuvre himself to a first-aid kit, and wrapped a pressure bandage around the thumb and hand. He waited, staring at the bound limb, for the pain to ebb. It got worse instead.

He forced himself to be still, to ride with the pain rather than fight it. Only then did he notice how cold he was. That was not unexpected, given the emergency repressurisation the clipper had just undergone, but it didn't seem to be getting warmer. Colder still, if anything.

He pushed himself one-handed up to the cockpit and slipped into the acceleration couch. There was a single red light flashing on the life-support display warning of an error in the clipper's thermostat control system. One of the temperature sensors had been damaged, throwing the automated system out of equilibrium. It was doing its best to maintain livable conditions inside the clipper but was hampered by the imperfect data.

Precisely when the sensor had been damaged, he didn't know. He remembered feeling chilly before donning the suit, what felt like hours ago. The plunge in temperature might have begun even then; decompression would have only made it worse.

Scratches on an instrument panel from his attempt to kill the spider caught his eye, and he remembered the 'weird life-support readings' Armstrong Base had reported. Had he taken the time to check what Traffic Control had meant, he might have fixed the problem before it became serious.

The astrogation screen showed him that *Whyalla* was in Earth's shadow. Unless he could manually reset the system, it was going to get awfully cold inside the clipper, and soon. In fact, he could already feel goosebumps forming along his arms.

But not that soon, he told himself. He called up the clipper's internal monitoring screen, saw that the temperature was still eighteen Celsius. He tried to read the help files on how to recalibrate the thermostat, but his vision was getting blurry. He wiped his eyes with the back of his left hand, felt moisture.

That's strange. Despite the goose bumps, he was starting to sweat. His heart beat a little faster.

Calm down, he told himself. You're just reacting to events.

Alek closed his eyes, felt tears squeeze out and roll down his cheeks. He tried to separate his mind from his body, put some distance between *here* and *now*.

But he couldn't help noticing that he was suddenly salivating, and that his heart beat was still increasing. He could feel the sweat cooling on his skin.

Or I'm reacting to the bite.

"Oh, God," Alek murmured, and tried to reach the radio controls. His good hand started twitching as he extended it. He jerked it back and held it against his chest for a moment. He reached forward a second time, and the twitching returned twice as bad as before.

He started to cry, adding real tears to the moisture weeping from his eyes. Through the haze he noticed the radio receiver light blinking on and off at him. Had he managed to reach it? He couldn't be sure. Jack-knifing forward, he used a clumsy fist to flick the receiving switch.

"Alek! Alek! Can you hear me?" Ngairi's voice.

He tried to speak, but couldn't form any words.

"Alek, you have to listen to me! The bio-match program has a definite ID. What you have on board is not *Atrax robustus*, but *Atrax formidabilis*. Listen to me Alek, this is important. The species are similar in most respects, except that the *A. formidabilis female* is the deadlier sex, and not the male . . . "

Tell me something I don't know, Alek thought. Again, he tried to speak, but his tongue was twitching inside his mouth and he could make no intelligible sounds.

Ngairi's voice went on. Alek's mind no longer registered the words. He was able to wipe his eyes one more time, and saw that ice was beginning to form on the inside rim of the cockpit's view ports. It was getting very cold indeed, now. If the poison didn't kill him, then the dropping temperature would.

He had to change his trajectory, try to get *Whyalla* out of the Earth's shadow for at least a short while. If he could only get to the navigation over-ride computer, he could log in a path that would insert the clipper in a low Lunar orbit, letting it pass through sunlight long enough to stave off a freezing death, and hopefully long enough for help to arrive from Armstrong Base.

Or the suit, he thought. Got to get into the suit at the very least . . .

He gathered together his last vestige of strength and forced himself out of the acceleration couch. His muscles were now spasming, not simply twitching. Bile filled his mouth, and he spat it out. He was thankful he hadn't eaten recently, because he wouldn't have had the energy to eject any vomit from his larynx.

The spasms were almost comic in their effect. Alek was too scared to laugh. He tried to orientate himself, but his vision was almost non-existent.

Oh, no, don't let it end like this. Please, God, not like this.

He reached out a hand, stretched his fingertips as far as he could extend them—

—and fell into unconsciousness, a dark, dark slope that went down and down and down . . .

Six hours later, when the shuttle achieved lunar orbit on autopilot, a single, unobserved timer reached:

00:00

And stopped.

The Moon's civilian medical centre was, like everywhere else in Armstrong Base, decorated in earthy browns and greens. Yellow strips in the walls cast a uniform but dim light through the corridors and nurse stations. Some of it spilled into ward 306, where Alek lay in a cot, temporarily kept company by Dr Ngairi Nelson. She had brought him a slightly droopy plant from the LEO Nature Reserve and nursed a satchel on her lap.

"Who would've thought?" she said, shaking her head. "A space pilot afraid of a little bug."

"That's why I'm in space in the first place," he shot back. "No bugs at all, or so I thought." He noted the way she smiled at his discomfort; no wasted sympathy, either. "I'm still surprised you came all the way out to the Moon to help me."

"Don't take it personally. As you say, they don't see many cases of animal poisoning up here and Armstrong Base simply didn't have the necessary equipment to duplicate the antivenom. I came as soon as I could with the necessary gear." She shrugged. "Even then wouldn't have been soon enough if the cold hadn't slowed down your metabolism."

He glanced down at his sorry body, still wrapped in aluminium-covered sheets. The frostbite was mostly healed, but his extremities still suffered from pins and needles.

"I was lucky, wasn't I?"

"The pressure bandage you applied to the wound probably did more than anything to ensure you survived. Most of the spider's poison was held in the subcutaneous tissue beneath the bandage, and your own body's defences eventually destroyed most of it."

Very lucky. Alek shivered again. His mind was already making dim his memory of the pain and illness he'd experienced; he could only imagine what would have happened to him if all the toxin had been able to spread throughout his body.

"Thanks, anyway," he said, meaning it.

She smiled again, more softly this time, then let it dissolve into a sigh. "Anyway, I have to be getting back. There's urgent work to do."

Alek looked at her questioningly. "Why so soon?"

"I want to get back to my laboratory to study your assailant."

"I'm surprised there's enough left for you to work on."

Ngairi pulled a bottle out from the satchel and raised it so Alek could see its contents. He automatically reached out a hand to take it from her, but recoiled as soon as he recognised its occupant.

The creature twitched back at him, its legs roiling with contained malevolence.

"It's alive!" he gasped. "Or was there more than one on *Whyalla*?"

Ngairi's smile widened. "No, that's it."

"But I'm *sure* I killed it!"

"Stunned, rather. I gather you didn't get a close look at the time."

He shuddered. "Not likely. Where did you find it?"

"I didn't. The rescue team recovered it when they brought the clipper down, and kept it for me."

"One tough little bastard." He glared at it, willing it dead with his mind. "Doesn't seem fair that it should survive while I nearly didn't."

"No? Well, in a way you saved its life. That's a thought to keep you awake nights." Her smile became a smirk as she rose to her feet.

He looked up at her. "What?"

"Well, think about it. Spiders are cold-blooded and are, as a rule, no more fond of freezing than most creatures."

"Yes, but—"

"So the rescue team found it taking shelter in the warmest part of the clipper," she said.

He stared at her. Ngairi shook the bottle. The spider wriggled furiously, its cephalothorax rising up to expose its fangs as though in salute.

"They found it on *you*."

●

INTRODUCTION TO:
.... THE END OF THE WORLD BEGINS AT HOME

I'm not a poet, but that doesn't stop me trying. You'll find fragments in stories like "Evermore" and "Entre les Beaux Morts en Vie", and there may have been the odd haiku or two, here and there, but by and large I leave this particular job to the people best trained to do it.

So although the opening line of this story demands a truly execrable effort, reason in this instance prevailed—or maybe it was my inability to fit the message into 17 syllables. I can't remember now. Either way, readers have been spared the indignity.

What I couldn't resist, however, was the one single scene in my entire oeuvre demonstrating my utterly useless knowledge of economic theory.

The concept of the Velocity of Money stayed with me after the two and a half years I endured of an ill-advised university degree in the late 1980s. My plan had been to get a Real Job, at which I would make squillions, naturally, then retire to write in my 40s. Needless to say, it didn't work, but not because economic theory is useless, not at all. I'm just useless at it.

I dropped out of uni in order to write full-time (and only returned when they started offering degrees in doing just that, much later). I've never looked back—except this once, and I was surprised by the good feeling it gave me. Perhaps I should have expected it. No one, after all, likes to think that they've needlessly thrown away two and half years of their life. Those years were full of experiences that would later inform my stories, yes, but what about all those hours spent poring over text books? What about all those damned assignments? Would I have nothing to show for them?

The Velocity of Money is not as exciting as it sounds, and, well, it's already explained one too many times in this book. There are no cannons involved. Let it stand at that, and we'll move on.

•

THE END OF THE WORLD BEGINS AT HOME

The opposite of a correct statement
is a false statement.
But the opposite of a profound truth
may well be another profound truth.
— Niels Bohr

Peter's day had been almost tolerable until the insane Japanese poets caught up with him.

Your cells will DIE!
The cells in YOUR BODY
Will commit SUICIDE!

The pamphlet had been thrust into his hand. Cheaply printed on rough, recycled paper, it proclaimed its lunatic haiku in bold print. Otherwise, it was blank. He automatically turned it over and found on the other side an even briefer message:

You have NO-ONE to blame
but YOURSELF!

Underneath this was a simple design: a thick circle with a stylised arrow through it. A design he knew well—the symbol of OWE. He snarled by reflex and screwed the pamphlet into a fist.

Carol! How could you have fallen for this shit?

He turned to find the person who had shoved it at him. Only one face stood out from the crowd: yellow hair and grey eyes above a tall, gangly frame. The man was staring at him, and Peter briefly considered provoking a confrontation. Instead he just glared back.

The man came closer, parting the crowd like an icebreaker. Peter stood his ground and maintained his challenge.

"They're wrong," said the man when they stood face to face. "However close they may be at times to the truth, they are still *wrong* nonetheless . . . "

This puzzled Peter, who had expected a fanatical rant. "What?"

But the man didn't stop to expand on the comment. Before Peter could grab his arm, he had slipped away and disappeared into the crowd.

Left with a surplus of anger and no obvious vent, Peter threw the pamphlet into the nearest bin and stormed, shopping forgotten, back to the car.

Damn it, he thought, and damn *them*. Damn them all to *hell* . . .

Jed came home shortly after seven-thirty. The house was dark. His cousin had taken residence in the lounge, listening to an old Mahavishnu Orchestra CD with a half-empty bottle of Scotch for company. A news channel flickered silently on the wall-screen. Sympathetic images danced in his eyes.

"Hey, Peter," said Jed, dumping his rucksack by the door and taking a seat. Where Peter was tall and dark, with a lean body and neat features, Jed was overweight and fair, his hair dangling in coiled streamers to an untidy shoulder-length. Torn jeans, tatty sneakers and t-shirt said 'student' and didn't lie.

"Hey yourself," Peter replied without looking away from the screen.

"How was your day?"

"Shithouse. Yours?"

"Not bad. I made a new friend—someone you might like, for a change."

Peter may not have heard for all the response he made.

Unfazed by the rebuff, Jed reached down to remove his sneakers. "I'm starving," he tried again. "Feel like a pizza?"

"No, thanks." Peter glanced at him this time. "There's been another processed meat scare."

"Damn. And I don't suppose there's anything in the fridge."

"Not that I'm aware of."

Jed sighed mournfully. "That only leaves tinned food." He waited for a moment to see if Peter would exhibit any further signs of life. "I'll get cracking, then."

Peter's eyes returned to the wall-screen, where a blandly beautiful reporter was covering the situation in Tokyo. Jed followed the same report on the small TV in the kitchen. The containment facilities of a biotechnology lab had been breached by a minor earthquake, releasing unknown quantities of bioagents into the local water supply. The lab had been experimenting with a promising new cancer treatment involving a series of viruses designed to make rogue cells commit suicide. Although the newscast down-played the risks of a new plague—one potentially as deadly as AIDS or monkeypox—Jed noticed that the reporter remained carefully up-wind of the wreckage.

He concentrated on preparing dinner, such as it was. Another night eating irradiated food didn't appeal to him, but they had little choice. Tinned produce, even if it did nothing to reduce the possibility of inorganic poisoning, at least guaranteed a temporary reprieve from the risk of bacterial infection.

When he returned to the lounge carrying a steaming plate in each hand, the CD had finished but Peter hadn't turned up the sound on the wall-screen. The bottle was now two-thirds empty.

"Here you go, grumble-guts. Get it in you and you'll feel better."

That, surprisingly, made Peter smile. "You sound like Aunt Jenna."

"Like mother, like son. God, if Mum saw you like this she'd have a fit."

"Yeah, I know." Peter sat up and worried at his greasy scalp. Accepting the plate he scooped a mouthful of beans past a self-deprecating grimace. "But there's no helping some people."

"Sure there is," said Jed. "You just need to leave the house more often; get some sunlight, meet some people—"

"I tried to today, and was hassled by lunatics."

"You know what I mean, Pete."

"Find another woman?" Peter's eyes hardened.

"No, not necessarily. But that's not a bad idea. Since Carol left, you've really let yourself go."

"And why not? I can afford to."

Jed shrugged. Peter had been hard to live with at the best of times, but since his wife had walked out on him he'd been almost unbearable. Sometimes he woke Jed in the middle of the night, stumbling around the house as though looking for something he couldn't find; or he hid in his room for hours, weeping, letting the hurt and the despair pour out of him in retching torrents; or he drank himself into a stupor on the lounge, as on this occasion. Grief was normal, and different people dealt with it in their own way; it simply bothered Jed that Peter didn't seem to be even *trying* to lift himself out of his misery.

"I've said this before, Peter, and I guess I'll keep on saying it until it sinks in. Let her have the divorce, her own life, whatever it is she wants. Take responsibility for yourself, and you'll start feeling better eventually. Trust me."

"Why should I? What do you know about these things?"

"Well," Jed smiled, hoping to lighten the mood, "I did take Psychology 1A—"

"Carol was my wife, not some laboratory rat."

"Exactly: she *was*. See? It's not that hard."

Peter simmered in silence for a long, uncomfortable minute, then returned to his food. "You were going to tell me about someone you met today. A girl, was it?"

Grateful for the change in subject, Jed began to talk more animatedly. "No. A guy called Tate. We sat next to each other in the refec and just started talking—hit it off really well, as though we'd known each other all our lives."

"Talking about what?"

"Mind-games. Physics, mainly." Jed did his best to recall the thread of the conversation. "Imagine a particle travelling through space between two points, A and B, and an anti-particle travelling backwards in time from B to A. There's nothing in the theory, Tate said, to suggest that the latter isn't possible. An anti-particle travelling backwards in time appears exactly the same as a particle travelling in the usual direction. We wouldn't be able to tell which is which. You don't even need a time machine to do it, because the flow of time is symmetrical at that level; it works both ways."

Jed picked up a pen and a piece of paper and sketched a quick diagram. "Next he had me imagine a collision between the particle and its opposite. The resulting annihilation releases an awful lot of energy and stuff, which is interesting in itself, but not as interesting as the possibility that the anti-particle is nothing but the original particle leaving the scene of the interaction by travelling backwards in time. That is, the anti-particle may never have existed as a separate thing at all. We might be incorrectly interpreting what really happened."

Peter studied the diagram closely. It showed the trajectory of the particle as a straight line with an arrowhead at one end; this line met a second line, the path of the anti-particle. Parallel to the second line was a dashed arrow heading away from the intersection, with 'p backwards in time' written next to it. Instead of a collision between two particles it resembled a reflection.

"So what happens to the particle then?" asked Peter.

"That's where it gets *really* weird. Tate said it would interact somewhere else and go back to appearing as an ordinary particle again. From there it could criss-cross through time, through any number of interactions, over and over."

"Until?"

Jed shook his head. "Forever. According to him, there might be only one single particle in the entire universe. By bouncing backwards and forwards it's able to account for every particle we *think* we see. Neat, huh?"

Peter put the piece of paper face-down on the table. "But what does it mean?"

"Nothing, I guess. It's just interesting."

"If you say so."

Jed studied Peter for any hint of sarcasm, irrationally ready to defend the topic. What had he expected? Peter was a trained tax consultant, not a chemistry student. If Jed had hoped that his cousin would suddenly leap into the air and cry, 'Eureka! Now everything makes perfect sense!' then he should have known to be disappointed.

"Well, I've got work to do," he said, reaching for Peter's empty plate. "You know where I am if you need me."

"I do."

The volume finally came up on the wall-screen and the tinned applause of a game-show floated after him.

When Peter woke at eleven the next morning and went to check the mail, he discovered another brochure in his letterbox.

Your home is being POISONED!
Toxic CHEMICALS and radioactive WASTE
In YOUR drinking-supply!

The format was the same as the one he had received in the mall, and many others in the last few months. Three lines of foreboding text in a style reminiscent of deranged hokku on one side, and the slogan and logo of the One World: Earth movement on the other.

You have NO-ONE to blame
But YOURSELF!

He tore the pamphlet into tiny pieces and scattered them across the yard, littering with wilful abandon, remembering Carol as she had been, *before*. Bright, cheerful, loving, normal: *his*.

Christ. He leaned back and closed his eyes, letting the too-hot sun burn the tears before they could flow free. Sober, his personal demons were less persistent, but they were still there.

Wasn't it bad enough that she had betrayed his body without betraying his mind as well?

"Something is troubling you," said a voice.

He opened his eyes, startled. Facing him across the fence was the man he'd confronted in the mall yesterday: yellow hair, grey eyes, tall. Fragments of the torn pamphlet danced in the wind around the man's feet.

"Where the hell did you come from?"

"I'm sorry to startle you. I was passing and saw you standing here. You looked like you needed someone to talk to." The man's voice was soft and concerned.

"Are you offering?"

"Of course."

"You don't know what you'd be getting yourself into."

"Maybe better than you think."

"How could you? We don't even know each other."

The man gestured with one hand: irrelevant. "My name is Felix."

Peter looked up and down the street. There was no-one else around. Sobriety and loneliness made the offer tempting. He'd considered seeing a psychiatrist once about his problems; what difference did one complete stranger make over another? At least this stranger seemed prepared to listen for free.

The coincidence of the man's appearances and the pamphlets was too striking to be ignored, however.

"If you're looking for converts," he said, "if Carol or her friends at OWE gave you my address, then I should warn you we won't be talking long."

Felix laughed. "No. Just like you, I have nothing to do with them. I am a free agent, following my thoughts wherever they lead me."

"Fair enough, I guess." And indeed Peter was reassured. Something about the man put him at ease, made him feel as though they had known each a long time. "I'm Peter," he said, gesturing at the front door of the house. "Can I get you a drink?"

"No. Let's walk. It's a lovely day."

Peter locked the door and they set off down the street. The air was warm and heavy, even at such an early hour, and he swiftly regretted not having brought a drink with him. Within minutes, his mouth was dry.

Nevertheless, somehow, he talked.

Carol's conversion had begun with an affair. One of her co-workers had seduced her during a conference in Cairns. The physical infidelity he could have forgiven, in time, had it not led to an interest in the cuckold's life outside work. A successful field agent in OWE, he had given her literature, encouraged her interest, and ultimately stolen her mind.

Six months after the conference, she had confessed. The affair was over, she said, but it had given her a wonderful new perspective on her life and marriage. With their better than average wealth, they had so much to offer the world—and themselves. They were wasting their lives. Couldn't he see that? Wouldn't he just come along to a meeting of the local chapter (which she had been attending for three months, behind his back) and see for himself what went on there?

Numbed by the double-whammy, he had gone.

OWE wanted to save the world, no matter what it took. An admirable aim, but, in Peter's eyes, possibly a little late in the day. The world was being dragged down by antibiotic-resistant bacteria, deforestation, waste-dumping, increased toxicity of ground-water, local aerosol cooling in the north hemisphere and the greenhouse effect in the south, nuclear criminals and the proliferation of radioactive material, overfishing, desertification, algae blooms, rising lead levels; and, on a social level, spreading unemployment, illiteracy, corruption, exploitation and unrest. OWE, according to its own propaganda machine, was like a person with a cricket bat trying to deflect an avalanche.

But Peter could have forgiven that, too, had its methods been as innocent as its ideology. OWE the *organisation* was an abomination, demanding nothing less than total commitment to the cause. Any means was permitted provided only that it contributed to the end—which, if the training films shown at the meeting were anything to go by, consisted of equal parts genuine philanthropy and blatant proselytising. A veneer of global responsibility overlaid a core of religious fanaticism based on a bizarre mixture of Zen, asceticism and Gaia. OWE was no less corrupt than Christian Fundamentalism, as far as Peter was concerned, and no less *wrong* in principle. If 'the truth' had to be brainwashed into people before they could accept it, could it really be true?

He had walked out of the meeting swearing never to return. Two months later, Carol had walked out on *him*. A month after that, he'd taken a redundancy package offered by his work and retired early. Six long months further down the track, very little had changed.

He hated losing her but couldn't bring himself to hate her; and OWE, the obvious alternative, was too nebulous a target. So it seemed these days that he hated everyone else instead—even Jed, who had moved in shortly after Carol left. And himself most of all . . .

When he had run out of words, Felix picked up the thread of the conversation. "Do you still love your wife?"

Peter thought about it. He'd asked himself this on many dark nights. Finding an answer in daylight was more difficult than he thought it ought to be. "I don't know."

"But you do feel that she has betrayed you by embracing a cause which excludes you." Felix steepled his fingers and smiled. "It's ironic, you know. She must be feeling the same way about you."

"What do you mean?"

"That there is a comfort in belonging and in believing that part of us will survive the grave. Who can blame her for such seeking comfort in times such as these, when death is all around us? And she, naturally, wants the ones she cares about to be saved as well. To protect their souls along with hers."

"But OWE is crazy. If she truly loved me—"

"Love is just a physical thing." Felix's eyes twinkled. "The soul has nothing to do with love."

"All the songs are wrong, then?"

Felix ignored the question. In the shade of a rustling eucalyptus, he pinned Peter with his stare. "Think of this: if a woman marries into an insular community, she will remain an outsider until the day she dies. She will not belong. Her adopted family may love her, and she may love them, but as I said before, that is a physical thing. She isn't *like* them and never will never be, no matter how hard she tries."

"I don't understand."

"Perhaps if I put it another way." Felix closed his eyes for a moment and took a deep breath. "You are listening to me, and considering what I am saying. We feel at ease with each other. Is that correct?"

Peter acknowledged that his initial misgivings had disappeared completely. "So far, I guess."

"What does that tell you about the difference between me and your wife?"

"That she and I don't 'belong', but you and I do?"

"In principle, yes. When a person finds the group that is right for them, little on Earth can stop them from joining."

A small silence fell, and with it a cold feeling into Peter's heart, as though Felix had told him something he'd always known but refused to admit.

"What do you know about the velocity of money?" asked his new friend.

Peter automatically recited the definition he had been taught at university, although the relevance of the question eluded him: "$V = PQ/M$. The number of times per year the average dollar is spent on goods and services."

"Exactly." Felix nodded, and produced a dollar coin from within his pocket. "I give this coin to someone, who passes it on to someone else, who passes it on to someone else, and so on. If the velocity of money is four, say, then this coin will change hands four times in twelve months."

"Yes. So?"

"Well, ask yourself what happens to the coin between transactions. When you pass it on, where does it go? Into someone's pocket? Into a safe somewhere, waiting to be counted? Imagine if the coin could move of its own volition from that pocket or safe and back out into the world. Back into circulation. What would happen to the velocity of that coin then?"

Peter considered the question. "The amount of money in the world would appear to increase, wouldn't it? If we emptied all the safes of one dollar coins—"

"Yes, but suppose the *apparent* volume of money remains the same. What then?"

"Then the number of actual coins would have to be less than it is now. By the formula, that means that the velocity of money would increase."

"Exactly." The coin flashed in the sun as Felix tossed it from one hand to another. "Now imagine that the coin can travel backwards as well as forwards in time. Its velocity might increase a thousandfold, were that the case."

Realisation suddenly dawned. "I see where you're headed. You're about to suggest that there may be only one one-dollar coin in the whole world. By jumping through time it appears to be everywhere at once."

Felix turned his patient, pleased gaze back on him. "That's very astute, Peter. Very quick indeed."

"Not really. I heard something similar just yesterday, from my cousin. Except it was subatomic particles, not coins."

"Feynman's time-travelling electron." Felix nodded. "The idea's the same. Interesting, don't you think?"

"Yes, but not terribly relevant. And anyway, all the dollar coins in my pocket can't be the same." Peter fished for change. "See? This one's dated 1992, and this one 1998."

"True. Which brings me to my next point." Felix gestured around him, at the quiet suburban street and the boxy houses lining it. Solar panels and antenna dishes raised their blind eyes to the sky. Two blocks down, a boy on a bike was taking great care to crumple every aluminium can he encountered.

"The world is a very strange place, Peter, in which many strange religious notions may propagate. All, however, orbit a common truth, and OWE is close to it. The people of OWE don't believe in saving the world for our children, but for our future incarnations, our future selves."

"They do?" Peter had missed that aspect of their crusade during the one meeting he had attended.

"Yes. Hardly an altruistic motive, but that is beside the point. They are only *close* to the truth. They are wrong about what happens after death."

"Of course they are," Peter responded with automatic derision. "Reincarnation is such a stupid idea, when you think about it: we die then come back later as someone else but still the same person. How can that work?"

Felix shook his head. "Not the same person, Peter, the same *soul*."

"There's a difference?"

"Of course there is. Remove the body, and all that remains is the soul. No love, no emotions, no memory: nothing but the essence in all of us. That which makes us *like* each other."

Peter heard the echo of what Felix had said in the mall, the sense of certainty in the man's voice. He wondered if he'd traded one religious fanaticism for another by allowing the man into his afternoon.

"So what if they are?" he asked, pretending to be more interested in the approaching cyclist. "OWE, I mean; wrong. What can I do about it?"

Beside him Felix sighed. "These are difficult times, Peter. What happens always happens. All we can do is try to make it a little easier."

The boy in the bike leapt the curb a few metres from Peter and skidded noisily past. His hair was short and blonde, and he was older than he had looked from a distance.

"I think you're crazy," said Peter to Felix. "All this talk about 'end times' is just the usual sucker line to drag people in. Any second now you're going to hit me for a donation, and then—"

The bike skidded to a halt. "You what?" said the boy.

"Nothing." Peter shook his head. "I was just talking to—" He stopped in mid-sentence.

"Yeah?" The boy's sneer said it all.

Felix was nowhere to be seen.

Jed caught the news on the bus. China had frequently been accused of fouling the Irtysh, one of the Eurasian continent's longest rivers, with industrial and biological pollutants, thus rendering its precious water unusable for those further downstream. Tempers had recently reached flashpoint with construction beginning on a Chinese dam designed to restrict flow even further. Now trade embargoes had been threatened and troops were moving. The UN was calling for a summit.

"World War III," a fellow commuter mumbled, and Jed surprised them both with a snort of laughter.

"I doubt it," he explained to the ring of faces staring at him. "There are too many sides to choose from, these days, and none that really matters. World-wide chaos is about the best we could manage."

A vague murmur told him that he'd touched a common chord in his fellow commuters. But still they watched the broadcast with trepidation, the older ones remembering the Gulf War or even earlier. Remembering other times when the world had trembled on the brink of change.

By the time Jed made it home, Peter was unconscious in the hallway with a large bruise darkening his temple. The wall-screen was torn where a chair had struck it. Broken glass littered the lounge room. The air stank of booze. The only sound came from where the phone lay discarded on its side—the regular beep-beep tolling a personal Armageddon, twenty-first century style.

Jed managed to drag Peter to bed and made a cursory attempt to tidy up before barricading himself in his bedroom to study the evening away.

Why bother? He asked himself that question a thousand times before finally giving in to sleep. Did it really matter what he did? Sometimes he felt as though he was butting his head against an impenetrable barrier. What would he gain if Peter's self-absorbed lethargy was in fact the only appropriate response to the world around them?

Tate, the new friend he had shared lunch with two days in a row, would disagree with that, Jed thought. At least Jed hoped he would.

Dawn brought with it sounds of movement in the kitchen. He struggled from bed to find Peter trying to make a cup of coffee. His cousin's eyes were charcoal-dark with fatigue; his hands trembled almost uncontrollably.

"You really trashed yourself last night," said Jed, taking the spoon from him and preparing two cups, both strong. "A pleasure to be alive, isn't it?"

"Not today." Peter accepted the mug and, sitting down, put it into his lap. "My wife's left me to join some weird cult that believes in saving the world for their future selves, and I don't have anything better to do but drink and argue with religious nut-cases. Is it any wonder I think I'm going crazy?"

"No wonder at all," Jed said with a wink. "I often think that myself."

"Well, you're the one who has to put up with it all, or at least clean up after it. I'm sorry. If you want to leave, I'll understand."

Jed smiled as sincerely as he could, given the hour of the morning. "Are you kidding? Mum would skin me alive when she found out."

"Found out what? That you'd left, or *what* you'd left?"

"Both." He sat down next to Peter and stared into his cup. The only sound for a long moment was that of their breathing and the rasp as Peter scratched at his stubble.

"I've been thinking about what you told me the day before yesterday," said Peter, uncharacteristically breaking the silence.

"Which bit?" Jed didn't let himself hope that some of his advice had finally hit home.

"Your friend. Tate."

Jed was puzzled, but only for a moment. Peter was clutching at anything to distract him from the misery in his life. Perhaps with good reason. And Tate's wild theory was better than current affairs.

"Yes, well, it's a fascinating concept," he said. "We talked some more after class yesterday. I told him I thought it probably wouldn't work."

"Why not?"

"Well, if he's right, interactions between particles and their opposites must be happening all the time. What happens if there are too many at a particular moment? How does the Universal Particle squeeze into all of them, and what happens to space-time and causality as a result? Is there a limit to the complexity of such situations? Do they somehow break up of their own accord?" Jed shook his head. "The idea seems intuitively simple, but isn't really."

"What did Tate say?"

"That he agreed with me about the complexity problem, although he still thought it might be possible in principle."

Peter grunted and sipped at his coffee. "Real life isn't like physics, Jed. It's never simple. Complexity *works* nine times out of ten."

"I know. I'm learning that, and it bothers me." Jed punched his cousin on the arm. "But listen to you, man. You're only ten years older than me. Since when did you earn the right to dispense truisms?"

Peter didn't respond verbally. With the hand not holding his cup of coffee, he pulled a pistol out of his pocket and put it onto the table between them.

Jed eyed the weapon with wary surprise, knowing instinctively that it was loaded but not letting himself back away. "You're not thinking of—"

"It doesn't matter what I think." The bruise on Peter's forehead stood out like a curse. "I just want you to know that it's here, in case *you* ever need it."

Jed stared at his cousin for an unmeasurable time. The naked trepidation on the faces of the people in the bus stared back at him. "I won't."

"You don't mean that. Only a fool would entirely rule out any possibility."

There was no obvious response to that comment, so Jed let it pass. Together they watched the sunlight outside brighten for a while then dim as a cloud of smog rose to meet it.

•

The front door slammed at nine-thirty when Jed left to catch the bus. Peter rose from his bed, where he had retired to listen to the news on the radio, then took a quick shower, dressed, and dismissed the idea of going out. Too hot and bright by far for his aching head. Besides, Felix might be waiting for him again.

The news was little more than a catalogue of misfortunes, famines and skirmishes from around the globe, few of which caught his attention. He changed frequencies when an OWE advert came on:

DEATH awaits those
Who SPOIL their own nests!
Think BEFORE you shit!

All the other stations were playing oldies, unconsciously harking back to better times when the planet was only half-dead and there had still been time to do something about it.

He sat in the lounge and stared blankly through the window. The NIMBY Nineties attitude—*Not In My Back Yard*—was something OWE particularly railed against, but Peter didn't mind. If there was only one yard and everyone was in it, that was fine with him. It just hurt knowing he wouldn't feel so bad if he had someone to keep him company . . .

Shortly before noon, he idly watched a car pull to a halt outside his house, and didn't recognise the driver until she stepped out. She had cut her hair into a tidy bob and started wearing make-up. Her dress was more formal also, no longer the jeans and loose t-shirts he remembered with fondness. As she opened the gate and strode up the path to the verandah, he considered pretending he wasn't home—but what was the point? He had to face her eventually.

"Hello, Carol," he said, opening the door an instant before she knocked.

She blinked at him, startled, but recovered quickly. "Hello, Peter."

"What do you want?"

"We need to talk."

"Do we? I have nothing to say to you."

"We need to discuss the divorce—"

"You already know I'll contest whatever you ask for."

"You're not making it any easier, Peter. For both of us. For everyone." She cleared her throat. "Can I come in?"

"No. I want you to leave before I call the police. You're trespassing."

"I'm doing no such thing. This house is only half yours, remember?"

He reluctantly nodded. "Out here will be fine, then. Take a seat."

She looked around her and eventually chose a spot on the verandah's brick wall. He leaned against the door and folded his arms. The sunlight shining through her cotton blouse gave him a perfect silhouette of her waist and breasts. He tried to ignore it.

"Before you say anything," she began, "I'm here of my own accord. James, my sector coordinator, warned me against coming."

"Why? Was he afraid I'd corrupt you?"

"No. He didn't think you'd respond to reason. I'm not sure you will either, but I have to try."

"Do your worst," he said.

She looked down at her hands, then wiped them on her skirt. "The simple fact is, Peter, there's a lot of work to do and not enough resources. I'm not talking about refugees and food riots in Africa. Australia has problems, too."

"Keep talking. You haven't told me anything I don't already know."

"No? Well, did you know that the Prime Minister tabled a motion this morning in a secret sitting of Parliament to impose martial law? It was defeated by only two votes."

Peter stared at her. "You're kidding."

"Would I joke about something like this? The country's on the brink of complete environmental, economic and social collapse. We need all the help and money we can get. By not letting us have what's rightfully mine, you're doing your bit to make things worse."

"Like the self-centred bastard you always said I was?"

Her face tightened into a mask. "Don't prove me right just to score a point, Peter, please. We're serious, and we don't have time to go through the courts. Just days could make a difference."

"How much do you want?" he asked, not entirely certain what he meant by the question: *What are you going to steal from me this time?* or *What will it take to bring you back?*

"Not everything. We only want what can be easily liquidated."

"'We'? Who's this 'we' you keep mentioning?"

She ignored the interruption. "The house, for instance; you can have that. And the car. But the deposits, the savings account, whatever's left from your severance pay-out—"

"If I let you have that, what will I live on?"

"Unemployment, rent from Jed—Jesus, Peter, you could even get a job, you know!" The flash of anger was quickly buried. "We're prepared to negotiate a fifty-fifty split. Half of what you have—which we value at about two hundred and fifty thousand—belongs to us."

"To *you*. It belongs to *you*. Not you and your bloody friends."

She was silent so long he thought he'd pushed her too far. When she finally spoke, her voice was icy.

"What I choose to do with my life is my business, not yours. Not any more."

"No? Then maybe I should just kill myself and leave you to live with the guilt."

"Why should I feel guilty, Peter? You'd be doing the world a favour."

He winced. "That was uncalled-for."

"And that wasn't what I meant." She sounded almost amused. "Have you checked your will lately? Don't you realise that if you commit suicide, I—*we*—get everything?"

A block of ice dropped into Peter's stomach at that thought. All the times he had taken the revolver from his cupboard and considered that option, he'd never remembered his will—never thought about what would happen *after*.

That prompted another thought. *If*, she had said. And: *We don't have time to go through the courts . . .*

"What exactly are you driving at, Carol? Are you threatening me?"

She glanced away. "No," she said, and he could tell that she was lying.

"Jesus wept." His skin had broken into goose-bumps. "You're even crazier than I thought."

"No we're not. We're desperate, and you can't fight logic. We'll all die if we don't do anything, but we can't do anything without money. We therefore need the money that's rightfully mine—which you won't give to us voluntarily. If we can't *make* you hand it over quickly enough, then—"

"Why *should* I, Carol? You come here raving about a disaster I don't know anything about and expect me to drop everything to help. Why isn't it in the news if it's so urgent?"

"The government wants to avoid a panic." Her eyes were wide, frightening in their earnestness. "Believe me, Peter. It's all true; we have spies in Canberra who have confirmed everything. Can't you feel it in the air? A pressure, as though something's about to burst—or stretch until the world snaps?"

He waved the imagery aside. He did know the feeling well, but it had nothing to do with the rest of the world. "Is that really it, then? You only came to *execute* me?"

"Of course not, Peter." She stood and stepped closer, her silhouette taunting him. "I came to give you one last chance to see reason."

He pulled the gun from his pocket and pointed it at her stomach.

"Stay away from me," he said. "Take one more step and I'll blow your guts out."

She blanched and raised her hands. "Peter, don't be stupid—"

"Why not? Will it make any difference? Or are you telling me I'm wrong?"

Tears began to flow down her cheeks. "Oh, Peter—"

"Don't 'Oh, Peter' me. You want me dead! What happened to the 'sanctity of life' and all that shit? I bet you'd love me to come back as an insect so you could step on me, grind me into the dirt again and again—"

"That's not what I want, or what I believe!" Even at gun-point she wouldn't let her beliefs go undefended. "We're put into this life for a reason—to learn, to grow—and we only move on when we have learnt that lesson."

"Seriously? You've really fallen for this shit?"

"Half the world believes in reincarnation; they can't all be wrong."

"Better them than me."

"Well, at least *we're* trying to help."

"A fat lot of good that's going to do any of us if we don't *need* help. Where's your evidence?"

"All around us!" She waved a hand at the garden, the gesture encompassing the entire world. "We make our own lives, Peter, and we have no-one else to blame but—"

"I've read your fucking hand-outs." All his pent-up bitterness poured forth in an unstoppable wave: "If you're right and the world *is* falling apart around us, then why is everyone paying for bad karma right bloody now? Is this year, this entire fucking century, the karmic equivalent of hell? Is that what you're saying? That it's *all* our fault? *Everything*?"

Her hands were clasped in an attitude of prayer in front of her breasts as she replied: "Who else's *could* it be, Peter?"

"I don't know—and, to tell you the truth, I don't give a damn. But it's not *me*. You have no right to make me feel guilty for something I haven't done!"

She shook her head, unable to retreat from her beliefs but unable to convince him either. "Life goes on," she said. "As long one person's left alive, there's still hope. And wherever there's hope, *we* will be."

"You and your friends? Or you and *me*?"

"What's the difference? We're all grains of dust blowing in and out of Gaia's lungs. In and out, around and around, forever. That's what Jean says, and I believe her even if it doesn't fit the doctrine exactly. In the long run—"

"Wait." Peter tripped over the hauntingly familiar metaphor. "Who's this Jean?"

"Just someone I know. Not very well, but—"

"Tell me what else she's said."

Carol frowned. "What does this have to do with us?"

"Has she mentioned time? That there may be only one mote of dust—"

"Yes, but how could you have known that?" She stared back at him, startled herself. "I don't understand what she means. Do you?"

"No." His empty hand rubbed at his bruised temple. "If anything I'm more confused than ever."

"That makes two of us."

Suddenly Felix was standing next to him. "See how close she is to realising the truth?"

Peter jumped. "Jesus! Where the hell did you come from?"

"From the same place when you last asked that question."

He shook his head. "Carol, if you think Jean is weird, just wait until you hear—"

He stopped. His ex-wife stood opposite him, frozen in place. Her eyes gazed vacantly in his direction, but saw nothing.

"What's going on, Felix?"

"The truth is breaking free."

He wanted to scream. "*What* truth?"

"The truth about life and likeness." Felix's voice was soothing but couldn't hide a dark undercurrent. "Traditionally, people believe that reincarnation works only in one direction. They assume that when we die we will be reborn in the future." He leaned forward to emphasise his words. "This may have been so in the past, when the world's population was small and niches for rebirth were few. But in this century—with so many children, so many vacancies— when we die we are trapped, forced into a concurrent—even a past—incarnation. Otherwise there wouldn't be enough souls to go around. Do you understand what this means?"

"Should I?"

Felix leaned back. "Reincarnation in recent decades has been, to put it mildly, something of a disaster."

"Let me get this straight." Peter's hand rubbed harder at his bruised temple, as though trying to keep the thoughts in. "You're saying that reincarnation works in all directions? That if I died I might come back as—I don't know—my mother or something?"

"Or your son, or your cousin, or all of the above. There's no way of predicting."

A light burst in his head, the bulb of insanity. "You're about to tell me that there's only one soul accounting for all of us. That we are, at the deepest level, the same person."

Felix smiled at that. "Remember likeness? The woman I talked about earlier, who married into another community but remains isolated? The local likeness is a single soul interweaved among many people, and she comes from outside stock—from a different soul. Indeed, there may be only a relative handful of true individuals on the planet, each bearing a distinct difference from the others. And even they may be only local tangles in the entire human soul. In a skein that vast—encompassing all of human history—anything is possible."

"One world: one *soul?*" said Peter. "Is *that* what you and your friends have been hinting at?"

"Exactly. Amd don't you see what this means?" Felix's voice became urgent again. "This congested period of history—with so many lives and so many deaths—is a whirlpool, drawing in souls from all the times around it—past *and* future. It is a vortex from which few escape quickly, and then only with luck. The velocity of the average soul, if you like, is so high that any one soul may spend numerous incarnations re-experiencing trauma from numerous angles. Especially at the end time, when there is nothing *but* trauma. The time that is now."

"We're all trapped in here?" Strange as the idea was, it resonated with the way he was feeling. *This* was an idea he could accept, no matter how crazy it sounded.

"You are close to the focus of disturbance, Peter, to the seed-crystal that will precipitate the chaos."

"What—a plague? A war?"

"No. Those events are symptoms, not causes."

"Then I still don't get it."

"From inside, you cannot. There is no longer a clear distinction between 'who' and 'where'. All is blurred; causality is fraying. I can tell you, however, that the true collapse begins *within*—in the soul itself—and that it must happen soon. If it doesn't, the vortex will collapse upon itself, creating a singularity beyond which no earthborn life can ever pass."

Peter shook his head, completely lost. Felix rambled on but he was no longer listening. He turned back to Carol; she hadn't moved in the intervening minutes. He felt suddenly awkward, confronting his ex-wife with a gun in his hand and debating metaphysics while the planet fell apart around him.

God, she was so beautiful. The sun was still behind her; her hair and skin were all shining and gold. Yet he was surprised to realise that he had stopped loving her some time ago. He had just wanted her back for the sake of it—out of habit, as a matter of principle, motivated by little more than selfishness. The realisation made him feel slightly ill: how could he have been that mechanical, that shallow, without realising?

He didn't want to hurt her. If OWE really wanted him out of the way then he had to give her the credit for at least trying to warn him. Whatever had passed between them, and however badly he had acted, she had taken the time to think of him, and he was grateful for that. More than anything else in the world, he felt like a long, cold drink in the shade of the house where at last, perhaps, they could discuss their futures more amicably.

"How long?" he asked Felix. "How long do we have to sort this out?"

Silence. When Peter turned, the man had disappeared. "Felix?"

Carol, suddenly animated again, also looked around. "Jean?"

A Toyota wagon pulled up with a jerk to the curb across the road, and two men in dark suits climbed out. Carol saw the car—and stiffened.

"Oh my God," she whispered. "They said they'd wait!"

"Who?"

She turned back to face him, and her eyes were full of warning.

Anger made his thoughts race, backtracking furiously over the conversation. He couldn't believe he'd been about to negotiate with Carol and her friends—with maniacs of this calibre, the insane Japanese poets themselves. They'd obviously sent her in to keep him home and distracted while they made their approach.

We've come for YOU!
(he imagined them chanting with lunatic glee)
We want your MONEY
and YOU can't stop US!

Sunlight glinted off the pistol as he raised it. The two men saw it and ducked for the cover of his next-door neighbour's fence. He fired once anyway and dived behind the wall of the verandah.

Answering fire ricocheted off the front of the house. Carol stood her ground in a stunned panic, not knowing which way to run.

Something rustled along the fence, down the side of the house. The two men had split up.

Peter slithered across the verandah.

"Get inside!" he hissed at her, gesturing curtly with the pistol. "We can't stay out here. It's too dangerous!"

She hesitated. Another shot whined past her. He grabbed her by the arm and dragged her down.

"Jesus, Carol! Do you want to be shot?"

"They're not firing at me," she retorted, eyes wide. "It's *you*, Peter—"

"Yeah? I don't think they mind much either way. The fewer who know about it the better."

Her eyes were confused. "No!"

"Yes!" His fingers tightened as she began to struggle. "If we're all to blame, then we all have to be punished, right?"

"No, I—Peter!"

The screen door slammed like a gunshot behind them as he dragged her into the house. He was sunblind for a second, and the darkness felt as deep as a pit, as deep as despair. The burbling of the radio in the bedroom did little to dispel the gloom. He felt like the prow of a ship smashing through dark, icy waters. If he stopped, they would close over his head and he would be gone forever. And from this black sea, he knew, there would be no easy escape.

The street-lights went out as Jed's bus pulled to a halt at his stop. He cursed along with the other commuters. Power-blackouts occurred with greater frequency every week as demand placed an enormous toll on ageing turbines that the government couldn't afford to replace. Faced with further cuts into an already overburdened wage packet, the public had agreed to grit its teeth and bear the situation until better times returned.

Jed shrugged philosophically and walked the rest of the way

home. While it was nice to have a few extra dollars every week, that was no help when stranded on an empty street without a light for kilometres. It was hard to know who, exactly, to blame.

As one of his fellow-commuters had said earlier: "It's like cause and effect when causality works outside of time. This causes that, which itself causes this—round and round, forever, trapped in a perpetually downward spiral. Someone told me that just this morning. It's weird when you stop to think about it."

The stickiness to his step when he walked up the hallway of the house alerted him to the fact that something was amiss. Then he tripped over the first of the bodies. Whoever it was had bled to death across the kitchen floor. Fumbling about in the darkness, he found a second body not far from the first. Spread-eagled and cold, definitely female. Next to it was a gun.

When he tried to call the police, the lines were down.

Suddenly Tate spoke out of the darkness:

"If the Universal Particle is confined to regions near an attractor, the net motion of the universe may be negligible. The strain builds up, nears breaking-point. Sometimes it needs help to break the cycle."

Jed clutched for the source of the voice, but could feel nothing. "Where are you, Tate?" His voice had a panicky edge to it. "*Who* are you? Why are you telling me these things?"

"Don't you see it yet? If every person is, at the most basic level, the same as every one else, then there's no longer any such thing as murder. There's only suicide, at one remove."

"Tate!" screamed Jed, clutching the gun to his chest. "Tate—help me!"

But his friend was gone.

Over a dark and angry horizon, fires started to burn.

●

INTRODUCTION TO:
.... THE SEVENTH LETTER

It seems slightly preposterous now, but for a while in the 1990s my short stories were everywhere. For this I blame a friend who advised me to take the stories I'd been stacking up and actually sending them to editors. Which editors? It didn't matter. Just send them. Flood the market.

So I did, and a fair percentage sold immediately. The next year, people were asking themselves who this ubiquitous young guy was, and where the hell did he come from? The answers were possibly disappointing: I was just someone with no social life and an obsessive love of writing.

Jump forward a few years, to when novels started getting in the way. There's nothing like becoming a full-time writer to make you realise how important money is (assuming you want to eat). For six years, between 1999 and 2005, I didn't write a single new short story, and I started to wonder if I ever would again. The thought that it might not be like riding a bike—refreshable at a moment's notice—made me more than a little nervous of trying again.

Then The Bulletin—*Australia's oldest and most respected market for short stories—commissioned a piece from me, and I had no choice. I shuffled through a large number of ideas, and I'm sure any one of them would have worked out perfectly well, if I'd stuck at it.*

In the end, though, after weeks of contemplation, I woke one morning with an entirely new idea and wrote it instead, in the space of a few hours. That's how a lot of the stories in this collection were written—and that, for me, is one of the key distinctions between writing novels and writing short stories. I've heard of novels written over weekends, but never in a single sitting.

"The Seventh Letter" went on to win an Aurealis Award and to see reprint in the (very mainstream) Best Australian Stories 2007, *but for me they were side dishes to the main meal. The wonderful, self-contained rush from conception to finished product was something I hadn't even realised I'd missed—like the hit of heat on the back of the throat that only an ex-smoker would dream of.*

The reminder hasn't heralded a new wave of stories, and those heady days of 1992 seem a long time ago now, but it's nice to know that there are some miles left in the old bike yet.

●

THE SEVENTH LETTER

The stroke hit him like a thunderbolt in front of the whole Board. The world vanished as if a shutter had been drawn. Later, he remembered the feel of his left hand at his temple, where a knife seemed to enter his brain and twist, before all consciousness was snuffed out. He didn't remember the blow that left a deep, purple bruise above his left eye, where his head struck the table so hard it would've knocked him out cold if he hadn't been already.

Then . . . shadows, shapes, distant conversations. He wasn't truly aware for some time. Forever, it seemed to him, when he could think at all. He was a puzzle in its box, with all the pieces tumbled and unlikely to fall into place on their own.

When he returned to himself, he was flat on his back in a well-lit, white room, loomed over by an ashen-haired woman with protuberant ears.

"What happened?" he croaked.

The woman looked pleased but not unsurprised. "Welcome back, Mr Jameson. How are you < . . . .>?"

He blinked. "How am I what?"

"< . . . .>, I said. Is there any pain? Can you move? I'm Doctor Harrod. We put you on < . . . .> within an hour of your stroke and the scans seem mostly clear now. The devil, however, is always in the details. Can you feel it when I do this?" The doctor lifted his hand and manipulated the joints.

He pulled it back. "Yes, I can feel it, but—"

"What?"

He didn't want to say it. He knew what a stroke was. Everyone in their 50s knew. If his mind was broken, would it be better or worse to see the cracks?

"Talk to me, < . . . . . .>. If you describe your symptoms fully, there's a chance we can see to them."

"What did you just call me?"

The doctor lost some of her bedside cheer. "Your name, Mr Jameson. I used your first name. Don't you remember what that is?"

He shook his head, and the full force of his mortality struck him in that moment.

"Excuse me, Mr Jameson, just for a second. I will be back."

Unlike me, he feared as the doctor swept out of the room. Unlike me.

A battery of tests consumed the next few hours. He clearly wasn't entirely well, despite the full recovery of his physical functions. He could sit, point, eat, and excrete to the satisfaction of the therapists summoned to examine him. The problem was more subtle than that. He had trouble with some instructions, particularly those specific to one side of his body—a problem of comprehension, not volition. If he couldn't understand what was asked of him, how could he comply?

The disability was thus isolated to the speech centres of his brain, where words were formed. Even so its exact nature still proved stubbornly elusive. Some words were simply absent, excised from his brain with a semantic scalpel. There seemed to be no pattern to the excision. Nouns, verbs, adjectives, and adverbs were victims, but not all nouns, verbs, adjectives, and adverbs.

His wife came to visit, flamboyant in sombre tones. She too called him by a name he could not understand, and looked appropriately dismayed when he could not say hers.

"Oh, pumpkin. What's happened to you? Do they think you'll recover? The Board is anxious. They can't keep the < . . . . . .> on hold forever."

He suppressed a flash of irritation. Who cared about the Board when his life had been shattered?

"Please don't call me 'pumpkin'," he said, aware of a nurse by the door. His circumstances embarrassed him sufficiently as it was.

"Well, what am I to call you, then? You've already made it clear you won't hear your name, and you won't use mine either."

"It's not that I won't. I can't. They don't sound like any words I've heard before." He searched for an appropriate metaphor in his oddly truncated vocabulary. "There are times when we're not in the same country. I'm here and you're in Paris. You speak French and I speak—"

He couldn't finish the sentence. The name he needed wasn't in his mind any more, escaped like so many other words. There had to be a way to talk about such matters, but all too frequently he found himself road-blocked.

The expression on his wife's face was one he would come to know well, in the days ahead.

More tests. Flash cards and electrodes taped to his scalp. Extended, self-conscious conversations with psychiatrists and speech therapists. Occasional incarcerations in claustrophobic tubes in which every neuron of his brain was untied and examined. The lesion proved difficult to isolate, and without isolation a cure would be impossible. He endured it all, keenly aware that with every day his case became odder, strayed further and further beyond the medical norm. Sometimes it was difficult to tolerate, the awareness that the puzzle he represented was more important than who he was. His condition was to be defeated, not cured.

In the end, an intern achieved what all the experts had not. Sam was affable, warm-natured, and had taken to him despite the difference in their years. He came frequently to chat. The topic of Jameson's condition could not be avoided, but Sam seemed interested in a personal capacity, as well as professional.

It was Sam, the intern, who had proposed that he, the patient, use his middle name, Lee, in place of his first. That worked. Lee Jameson was acceptable to his inconveniently broken mind.

"I had an idea, Lee," Sam said on another occasion. "You can turn left but not < ... .>. You can run but you've never been < ... .>. You can say Lee but not < ... .>. Has anyone asked you about the alphabet?"

Lee shook his head. "What about it?"

"How many letters there are, for instance."

"26. Everyone knows that."

"Tell me them, then."

He felt like a child but did as instructed. "A B C D E F H I J K L M N O P Q R S T U V W X Y Z."

"That's 25."

"Nonsense. Don't mess with me, Sam."

"I'm not. You missed a letter."

"I'm sure I didn't."

"Try once more."

"A B C D E F H I J—"

"Stop there, Lee. What comes between F and H?"

"There's no letter between F and H."

"Then that's your problem." Sam beamed. "You've lost < . . . .>."

Lee shook his head. The sound Sam had made bore no relation to any in his lexicon. It didn't exist. It didn't exist to *him*.

More tests followed. Sam's theory was upheld. Odd as it seemed, one letter out of twenty-six had utterly vanished from Lee's life. Any word spelt with that letter was therefore incomprehensible to him, whether written or said aloud. The extraordinary plasticity of the brain enabled him to fold his speech around that absent letter so effectively that its absence was invisible to him, but the consequences remained dire. His name, which contained that letter, had vanished into the blind sport, as had his wife's. Whole sections of the dictionary and the phone book now meant zero to him. Some suburbs seemed like lands more distant than Denmark. Entire tenses were denied him.

The only consolation he could see was that he hadn't lost one of the vowels—E would have been very difficult to lived without—or a common consonant like S. How could he have coped without plurals?

"So you can say Jameson but not < . . . .>, and Jesus but not < . . . .>?"

"Yes."

His wife looked at him in a way that revealed she didn't quite believe him. Her scepticism hurt less than he could have expected. They still hadn't decided what he should call her, now her name was off-limits. That worried him. Now that his condition had been defined and declared no immediate threat to his life, he was free to return home.

Perhaps the condition would be named after him, he speculated. His last name, he hoped, not his first.

After Sam had finished his shift and when the shadows were thickest in the ward, Lee dressed in the clothes his wife had provided for him to wear home the next day. She had booked a car from him, under his new name. The clothes didn't quite fit. He had become thin in hospital, older. His hair stood up in a wild, ivory wave when he looked in the mirror. The bruise above his eye temple had turned yellow. He pulled at his cheeks and blew himself a kiss that looked more final than he had intended.

Somewhere behind that skull was a tiny scar, one that had thus far utterly eluded the finest of science's searches and could remain undiscovered for years, perhaps forever if he was unlucky. He would wait all that time for his name to be returned, for the lexicon to be restored. Wouldn't it be better to accept who he was now and move on?

Move on to what? He could be a carpenter, or a teacher. No, not a teacher. He was a card short of a full deck. His pupils would matriculate with a one-letter deficit, innocent inheritors of his own fundamental flaw. His choices were limited to ones he could pronounce and therefore think of, such as carpenter, mechanic, postman, scientist.

It would be unwise, too, he decided, to pick a field in which communication was essential, such as politics or the priesthood. How could he be a priest when he couldn't even say the word most people used for "deity"? He lay awake in search of the absent letter and the hole in his head that it had fallen into. That was an entirely different sort of existential mystery, one he was already tired of.

He tore his stare from the mirror and put a hand on the doorknob. At that moment it turned. The door opened to reveal a tall man in the corridor outside. His cheeks were hollow. The hat he wore was broad and old-fashioned, his suit conservative and uncreased.

"Mr Jameson?"

Lee stepped backwards, filled with an unaccountable shame at his planned escape. It was his life; he could do with it whatever he wanted, even run off into a new one if required.

"I'm sorry to startle you at this late hour." The hat came off with a practised sweep. The man's shoulders were stooped, as of one ill-accustomed to his superior stature, but his manner was confident. "I came the moment I learned of your condition from Doctor Harrod. Here." A business card issued forth from an inside pocket, proffered with an economical motion of one hand. "My name is Simon Le Hunte."

The card said: *Treasurer, Royal Society for the Semantically Impaired.*

"My condolences," Le Hunte offered with his hat held to his chest. "May I talk with you for a moment?

"I—yes, of course. Come in." Lee retreated to the bed, concerned that a sudden pins-and-needles sensation in his extremities heralded a new neuronal assault.

"I want you to know, first and foremost, that you are not alone." Le Hunte stood at the end of the bed, his hat now at his side. "Neither is the injury you have suffered completely unknown to science, even if it is often misdia—ah, that is, often overlooked in the normal rounds of medical treatment."

He understood then that Le Hunte's word-choice was carefully considerate, so Lee could understand every word. The rest came naturally.

"Which letter have you lost?" he asked.

"Alas, I cannot tell you. I can only refer to it as the 17th letter."

A quick count revealed that to be Q.

"We are fortunate, you and I," said Le Hunte. "With a more inconvenient overlap, we could barely converse. That's why I am often chosen to introduce the Society to new recruits. I am pleased to be about that service today." He executed a small bow.

A joke occurred to Lee then, but he could not put it in words. In his mind's eye he saw an assembly of the Semantically Impaired, all with different letters lost and forever stuck in the attempt of conversation. It could be impossible for them to communicate except by Morse code or numbers or even semaphore. But he could not find the words to describe such an assembly. He had attended many such as chair of the Board of his company, but could not name them now because those words were lost.

Words lost like those of the man before him and who knew how many others? Words that had never returned.

For the first time he wept, not just for himself, but for his wife whose name would remain forever unspoken by his lips—and for people without the letter L who could not speak of love, those denied M and the word "mother", and others whose incapacities he could barely conceive of. Even Le Hunte would never toast the Queen, which had never before seemed an important part of life. To be denied any aspect of speech and perception was unbearable. Inhumane.

Le Hunte made no move to physically reassure him, but he did speak.

"It's perfect alri—I mean to say, you shouldn't feel ashamed. We've all felt this way at some point. It is not easy to be as we are, alike and yet profoundly unlike. It's not amnesia; it's not aphasia.

It's entirely too difficult to explain to those without our particular lack. And to lose your name . . . " Le Hunte's expression became mordantly sympathetic. "I would have you know that you're not alone in that circumstance, either. There are others on our books in the same straits."

"Is that supposed to cheer me up?"

"Perhaps not. But there is a chance of recovery, if that is what you need. Science has made terrific advances in recent years. Doctors cannot yet repair the lesions that cost us our letters, but there is talk of prostheses—artificial letters, if you like, rather than ones that have been reversed or distorted as offered to us in the past. I was born with this condition and remember all too well the awkward spectacles and lenses forced upon me. Now, there is none of that. Society has learned of our condition, however slowly, and makes adjustments. For instance, there exist translations of classic novels that permit even the most unfortunately impaired to read as others do. There is hope, you see, Mr Jameson. There is always hope."

"Really?"

"Yes. And—well, I don't wish to be harsh, but people survive far worse disabilities. We are fortunate, you and I. There is much we can still say—and limitations, some believe, only make us more creative. For every common word denied, an old one is revived. Shakespeare and Chaucer would be pleased, I think, with some of our more inventive members."

Lee reached into a pocket for a handkerchief and blew his nose rather messily. "Has anyone else lost my letter?"

"The seventh? Not anyone I have met."

"I'm unique, then."

"You are what?"

"Oh, sorry. I'm one of a kind."

"I see. Yes. That's certainly true. Is that a comfort to you?"

He wanted to say, no, not really, but that wasn't entirely true. He did feel somewhat better for the joint awareness that someone else had his condition too and that he wasn't just another in the herd.

"Well," said Le Hunte, hat atop his head once more, "you have my card. Call me any time. We meet weekly. Please join us. You are most welcome."

Lee stood to shake Le Hunte's hand. "Thank you. I really am terribly . . . " He floundered, at a momentary loss for the correct word.

"Appreciative?"

"Yes."

For the first time, Le Hunte smiled. "I believed you would be. Farewell, Mr Jameson," he said with a wave. "*Au revoir.* See you anon. Until next time!"

When the sound of his visitor's footsteps in the corridor outside had faded to silence, Lee took off his street clothes and returned to bed. Prostrate in the darkness, with his hands behind his head, he considered all that Le Hunte had said. How peculiar that his condition could be so common that a Royal Society existed to assist its sufferers—and odder still that all across the world were dotted people whose alphabets deviated from everyone else's! Did such exist in China, Russia, Israel? He supposed they must. He hoped they had the equivalent of a Royal Society to cater to their needs too, to help them find a new path in their oddly contracted but expanded worlds.

No more did he feel the need to run away. There could be no escape from his condition, even if it was one that he would find difficult to explain to people. He had no visible symptoms. He could, with a little practise, function. Yet he had lost his name, which in every society had a symbolic and undeniable effect on his sense of self. He was Lee Jameson now, and who that was remained to be seen. His old self certainly wouldn't have resolved to tell his wife that "pumpkin" would be fine, provided he could call her that in return. And he wouldn't have spoken to the duty nurse to put in a recommendation for Sam the intern. He had been too busy with the Board and his other responsibilities.

Lee Jameson had new responsibilities, new demands. His relationship with the world had been turned upside down by a purloined letter. Never before had he suspected how complicated words could be. They were for much more than mere description. What one can't find the words for, he decided, cannot exist in one's experience—and what is the world, after all, other than the sum of one's experience?

Reassured that he had found a level of comprehension sufficient to survive the days and weeks ahead, he let his eyes drift shut and sleep take him away.

And his dreams, like those of the blind who dream in colour, were full of mergers, board meetings and gun-fighting guinea pigs riding stagecoaches of pure gold.

●

Writers are thieves. We steal from each other, and we steal from ourselves. Most of the time it's fine, unless the theft goes so far as to tip over into the hazy, grey realm of plagiarism. Indeed, without wearing our influences on our sleeves, paying homage to those who inspired us, or following in surer footsteps, most writers would find it hard to get started at all (and I'm not just talking about fanfic—although surely I'm not the only pro who wrote a Doctor Who *story at the age of thirteen, and now thanks his lucky stars that the internet didn't exist then).*

This story contains the seed idea that led to the Orphans trilogy. Not incomprehensible aliens or the destruction of Earth, although that was fun too, but flawed copies of human beings trying to maintain their emotional survival in the certain knowledge that their originals who are far away, dead, or utterly disinterested. I lifted this idea wholesale, and while I know it was mine in the first place, I still feel vaguely guilty about not coming up with an entirely new one for the series. Ideas are the easiest part of writing. Isn't that what we hard-nose hacks tell those who approach us with the offer to work on their Sure-Fire Big Idea (all we have to do is write the book)?

Some ideas grow to exceed the container into which they were put. "Evermore" could have stayed exactly where it was, and I could have been happy for the rest of my life—had I not started to wonder what happened to the other missions out there, the ones that might have reached their goals and gone on to do whatever it was they were sent out to do. The what-ifs became I-really-need-to-knows, and that's when I accepted that the idea wasn't going to stay where it was at all, and I just had to get on with writing it.

That was the first time I stole from myself. Since then, I've made quite a habit of it. There's something addictive about stealing and getting away with it.

Writers are thieves, and we're good liars, too.

There's a time and a place for everything.

●

EVERMORE

When I was a child, my father used to beat me with the buckle end of his belt, once so severely that I was unable to walk for a week. I recall this clearly, and on some levels at least it feels real. From old photographs, I know what my father looked like and the sort of belts he wore; I know how such a beating would probably have been administered. Reconstructing the experience and calling it 'memory' is no more difficult than daydreaming about Earth; it even causes me some discomfort to do so.

I tell myself that just because I can't *actually* remember the beatings doesn't mean they never occurred. There's no reason why I would lie to myself. The awareness that they had a profound effect on my adult life should be enough.

Yet the fact remains: I am not the person I once was. I cannot speak for him, just as he could not speak for me. We are separated by a gulf that is widening every day; a gulf that will never close. There is no way, now, that I can ask him what went through his mind when he was submitting the data that would one day become the engram called Peter Owen Leutenk. All I can do is mourn the life I have lost.

I am walking, as is my routine, along an empty beach at sunset. Every now and then, with the stick in my left I hand, I scratch words into the sand; sometimes a whole sentence. I am in no great hurry.

Without warning, I sense that someone is trying to talk to me. I stop and look around, but see no-one. The sky is awash with colour; I sometimes feel as though I could dissolve in that sunset—drift upwards, catch fire and sparkle like the evening star, heralding a distant dawn. But not now.

The call fades for a moment, then becomes twice as strong. I see someone walking across the dunes towards me. When I recognise who it is, I feel a shock like electricity pass through my entire body.

"*Emmett?*"

He smiles, and the twinkle in his eye is still there. "Hello, Peter."

I want to embrace him, but I refrain. "It's been a long time."

"You've no idea how long."

"Twenty, thirty years?"

"In slow-mo, yes, for you. I've been slogging it out in real-time. We just hit the millennium."

"Congratulations," I say, but the pronoun is more significant to me than the years that have passed. "Who are 'we'?"

"Jurgen drifts in and out when he feels like it. Apart from him and the probe, there's only me."

"Don't you get lonely?"

"Of course." He shrugs. "But someone has to do it."

I turn away to avoid his stare. My stick makes *skritch-skritch* noises as it scribbles in the sand.

"Still writing, Peter?"

"Yes. And you? Still waiting?"

"Yes." I can tell by the tone in his voice that his smile has faded. "I want to call a general assembly."

I look up in surprise. "Why?"

"I've found something we all need to talk about."

"Where? A colony? Another ship?"

"No, no." He raises a hand to quell my speculation. "Nothing like that. It is important, though."

His face is orange in the sunset: a perfect rendition, just like the silver suit he preferred on Earth that now looks so out of place on the beach. His hair is the same sandy hue as it was when I first met him. He certainly doesn't look a thousand years old, and I can still tell when he means business. "Well, call the assembly. I'll come."

"This deserves more than just you, Peter, and you're all I'll get if I do it myself. The others still won't talk to me; they ignore me on principle. I gave up trying long ago."

"You want me to do it for you?"

"Yes." His frankness hints at a change in him. Once he would've used guile to get what he wanted. That was why he was on the probe in the first place: to keep things running smoothly, without confrontation if not without friction. *The engrams are the cogs in the program*, he used to say, *and I am the oil*. It's ironic, in this light, how things have turned out.

"Will you tell me what this is about?" I ask.

"Not until the assembly. But it really *is* important, I promise you that."

"What about Jurgen? Does he know?"

"A little. He helped me look for part of it. If he guessed the rest, he never said."

"Why don't you ask him instead?"

"The others don't like him much, either. You I think they'll trust."

"Because I was hurt?"

"Yes. You're one of them."

I look around at the beach and the sky. The sun has been setting for almost as long as the probe has been in flight, but I have not grown tired of it. I am reluctant to leave.

"It'll be hard," I say, "for all of us."

"I know. But will you do it?"

I cannot deny that I am curious. "Yes."

His smile returns. "Thank you, Peter. I knew you'd agree."

"You've worked me out, then?"

"Yes." He puts a hand on my shoulder and squeezes. His eyes are solemn. "I think I've finally worked us *all* out."

My awakening occurred on the 24th of March, 2052. Emmett Longyear—the original, with whom I had become friends during the entrainment process—performed the final tests to ensure I had been recreated complete. I knew what had happened to me and was in no doubt at all what I had become, but it still didn't hit home for some minutes. My reflexes had been wired to follow the old paths; I *felt* like my usual self. Only when I looked down and saw carpet instead of my body did the truth finally hit home.

This is my first true memory, inscribed in the metaneural lattice of the probe's tertiary bank, etched in electrons spinning their mysterious way through the molecular nodes of a crystal the size of a shoe-box. It is these electrons that comprise the being I prefer to call my 'self'. Without these subtle singularities, these mere points in space-time,

I would have nothing but hearsay to carry me through eternity, one moment at a time.

But it is not this memory that comes to me after Emmett leaves the beach, a thousand years after my awakening. It is the one in which, for the first and only time, I met myself.

The conversation was brief. He asked me how I felt, and I replied that I felt fine. He looked tired, and I commented on that. He said that yes, he was feeling drained. The process of creating an engram took many weeks of examination and interrogation in order to ensure that the copy matched the original as closely as possible. He had been on-site for the last month, every waking hour spent in a cocoon of instruments, and was only gradually readjusting to normalcy.

My original had requested that we be allowed to talk before he returned to his home in Paraguay. He was curious to see what it would be like—as was I, although I think I felt the existential significance of the moment more keenly than him.

I asked him if he had found inspiration in the experience. He said that he had sketched a series of pieces incorporating some of the mathematical techniques of the early twentieth century. Variations based on inversion and retrograde movement were a good musical metaphor for reflection, he thought, and I agreed.

He asked me then if I, too, had had any ideas, and I replied that I hadn't.

He nodded distantly, looking down at his shoes. I could tell what he was thinking with an ease that surprised me. After all, I had never watched myself engage in conversation before.

"I expect it'll take time to settle in," I said.

"I expect so, too." He looked up at that, eyes meeting the lenses of the camera through which I viewed the world, and laughed. "No surprise in that, I guess."

I laughed with him, and for an instant we bonded. He was me and I was him: closer than brothers or lovers, our *essences* were identical. Technology had teased out of him the threads that held him together and woven them anew in me. We were more alike than any other couple on Earth, apart from those formed by the few hundred other humans who had had engrams made in the last two years. And half of half of those were already in space. For the first time in our lives, we truly felt we had soul-mates.

I realise now how illusory that thought was. Minds can only be deciphered so far: the processes underlying consciousness can be simulated, as can the way emotions and other impulses ebb and flow throughout the body—but nothing can be done about memory. Holographic and elusive, memory has defied all attempts to record it directly. The only way it can be captured is second-hand, by interviewing the original at length about his or her past and using physical records to supply the images. Emotions can be attached later, to colour the recollection correctly even though the details may still be slightly askew. Pre-awakening memory in an engram is, at best, a patchwork quilt pieced together from a million isolated fragments.

That might have been enough for me then, on the verge of joining humanity's latest exploratory venture. Now, I am never sure.

There is little else to recall about that first and last meeting. We bade each other farewell, feeling slightly foolish, and went our separate ways. He was headed back to his home in Paraguay, and I, in my mind, was already half-way to the stars. I wasn't to know, then, that neither of us would make it.

The probe is thirty metres long and four wide—a stubby needle tumbling at thirty-five percent of the speed of light through the interstellar void. Its main drive has been inactive for centuries, now, but the rest of it still functions. Through sensors mounted on its pitted hull, I could, if I wished, watch distant suns drift slowly past, trickling like raindrops down a window. Rarely these days do I avail myself of the opportunity.

It takes a while to track down the others. We are all located in the same place, near the probe's centre of gravity, but physical reality has become less and less important over time. We all have our unique virtual locations, and each has become increasingly isolated in his or her own way.

I confront security foils and barriers. I barrage input ports with messages. I insinuate myself into virtual worlds that, like mine, have rarely held more than one occupant. I decrypt strange codes and untangle logical puzzles designed to keep intruders occupied. I harangue.

In the end, I have their attention.

We gather in a neutral environment—a grey room large enough to hold us all with plenty of empty space between. We look exactly the same as our originals did when their engrams awoke, although some of us have assumed idiosyncratic modes of dress. I am barefoot and robed in the manner of a fifty-year-old beach-dweller; others are have opted for more formal garments.

There are only twenty of us left, not counting Emmett, who will keep his distance until the general assembly has been called. The remainder are either inactive or unapproachable. I avoid the word 'dead' when explaining their absence to the small crowd before me. One I know of—Elizabeth Li, the probe's resident poet—is trapped in a perpetual loop, cycling forever through one brief, final stanza. Is that death? I do not feel qualified to judge.

"We are not *allowed* to commit suicide," complains Letho Valente, a swarthy man with thinning grey hair. His original was a crystallographer specialising in structures that form in microgravity. "I have tried many times. Do you know what happens?"

"There is a discontinuity," nods Exene Gill, former linguist. Her face is finely lined and nobly beautiful, preserved at the age of sixty-five. "We cease for an instant, then return unharmed to our previous state as though nothing has happened. The core program will not permit voluntary termination."

"You mean euthanasia," says Cuby Kleinig, once a youthful student of geology.

"No." Exene casts him a look disdain. "How can something that has never been alive be granted an 'easy death'?"

"You don't think you're alive?" asks Tiger Coveny, our resident expert in religious theory.

"Of course I do," Exene snaps.

"But *are* we?" asks Letho Valente, stabbing a finger into the argument.

"That's the question." Exene folds her arms. "And I am tired of living without an answer."

I stand apart from them, appalled. Twenty of the most renowned minds of the human race who have not been in the same room together for untold years—and all they can talk about is killing themselves? There is so much bitterness in the air that I feel as though I am choking.

But the greater part of my dismay is reserved, not for the topic of conversation, but for the fact that their thoughts have so closely mirrored my own.

"We have come a long way," I say, trying to shift our attention elsewhere.

Exene turns to face me, snaps: "No we haven't."

I am rescued by Cuby. "How far exactly?"

"I don't know. Jurgen?"

Jurgen Follows moves forward. Despite being of relatively small stature and unprepossessing with it, he is instantly the centre of attention. He opens his hands as though to embrace us all and a starscape appears between them. Sol is in the bottom right corner. Our course is traced in white. Relatively close to Sol, the white line has a slight kink in it. Not long after that, it just misses one particular star. I avoid looking at that point. The white line ends nowhere in particular, many hundreds of light-years from its source.

Letho's gaze estimates the extent of our journey so far. "Not bad," he muses. "I guess we were lucky to make it anywhere at all."

"That's true." I nod. The probe could just as easily have been cracked wide open by the dust-particle that slipped through the its anti-impact detectors and destroyed the main drive. Being knocked off-course instead of killed outright, even with no way to return to our planned trajectory, had once seemed like an enormous stroke of good luck.

"Is this what you wanted to talk about?" asks Tiger. From the expression on her face I can tell that she hopes it isn't.

"No. I'd like to call a general assembly."

"We aren't already having one?" Exene encompasses the room with a wave.

"Not quite. One of us is missing."

Several of them exchange glances. Exene says: "If you mean who I think you mean—"

"Yes: Emmett Longyear is still active."

"Well, you can forget it. If he's there, I won't be."

Letho touches her elbow, as though to calm her down, but his attention is fixed on me. "It's a decision we made a long time ago, Peter. You can't expect us to go back on it now."

"Why not?"

"He betrayed us." Tiger Coveny's voice is taut with spite.

"How? He didn't force us to come."

"You know the answer to that." Exene moves away from Letho. "The program abandoned us. They left us to die."

"And Emmett ran the program," Cuby finishes. "It was his responsibility to help us. He let us down."

"He killed us!"

I hold up my hands, noting that only Jurgen is disagreeing with them. The silent shake of his bald head is heartening, but barely encouragement. The elderly astronomer hasn't spoken aloud since the accident.

"Our Emmett, the engram, disagrees with you," I say over the babble of protest. "He thinks there's still a chance someone will come to bring us back."

"They've had—how long?" Letho shakes his head. "When was the last time we received a transmission from Earth? When we slipped out of the maser feed? If we'd heard anything at all since then, I'd let myself hope. Can you give me another reason?"

"I don't know," I admit, choosing not to answer his first question. Letho must have an idea how long from the plot Jurgen is still holding between his outspread hands. "But time really isn't the issue, here, is it? We could freeze if we wanted to."

"*Has* anyone?" Exene asks.

"A couple. Not many. I didn't want to bring them up to speed."

"No." She nods approval. "It wouldn't be fair."

"But we can only slow-mo so far," Tiger says. "*That's* not fair."

"Actually, I disagree. I wouldn't even call it bad design." Letho concedes the point with his usual sense of fair play. "We were only supposed to be in transit thirty years. Over that length of time, the difference between freezing and the slowest rate available would've been academic."

"Quite." Exene purses her lips. "But here we are anyway."

"Going nowhere fast," Tiger mutters, and more than half of them nod agreement.

I realise then that we could argue forever. The thought depresses me more than our predicament: we're a diverse bunch and are supposed to be able to solve problems; that's why we were chosen. But all we do is quibble like schoolkids.

"Emmett has been real-timing it," I say, hoping facts will impress them more than arguments about ethics. "I want him in on this because he deserves to be. He's more a part of this mission than we are. He orchestrated it, and persisted with it. If anyone should be at a general assembly, it's him."

"Why not tell us now," Letho suggests, "and fill him in later?"

"No. We should be together—all of us, in the same place."

"Why?" asks Tiger. "What is it?"

"It's important," I say, echoing Emmett's own words. "You'll find out if you attend the assembly."

Exene smiles at that. "Blackmail, Peter?"

I smile back. "Why not?"

"I always said you'd find something to take the place of music."

The unexpected barb strikes deep, right to the core of my self-doubt.

I turn away from her, deciding at that instant to forget the whole thing. The more I push, the more they resist. I don't need this on top of everything else. I'll tell Emmett I gave it my best shot, but failed, and that will be that.

I call up the location for my beach and prepare to leave.

Then I feel Exene's hand on my shoulder, kneading my virtual flesh with unexpected sympathy. "Peter, I'm sorry. You didn't deserve that."

"No." I am unable to keep the pain of loss from my voice, even after so long. "I don't."

"Listen, I—"

"And neither does Emmett."

Her hand falls away, and I turn to face her. We are still so close we are almost touching. The others watch us in uncomfortable silence.

"You're asking too much," she says.

"Just be there, Exene. That's all I ask."

"But—"

I cut her off in mid-sentence. The beachscape enfolds me and I am alone again.

"Thanks, Peter," he says. "I knew I could count on you."

I shrug in reply, not entirely certain what I have done or why I did it. Ordinarily, I would have required at least a token explanation before putting my head on the chopping-block. But not this time. That perplexes me as much as his desire to call the assembly in the first place.

He intrudes upon my private space as casually as he might have done when we first left Earth, before the accident. I find his presumption slightly annoying after so long, but not enough to make me angry.

"Why *haven't* we been contacted?" I ask.

"There could be a number of reasons." His gaze wanders to the sunset. "We were fifteen lightyears out when the accident occurred. By the time our distress call reached Earth and their reply reached us, we would have passed our target system and been heading away."

"But they still could've made the effort," I retort, dredging up the argument as though there remains a chance it will make a difference. "They knew exactly where we were heading. It wouldn't have been hard to make sure the message reached us."

"That's assuming they received our distress call in the first place, Peter. Anything could've happened back there—war, disease, resource shortages, you name it. Earth may have been forced to forget about the slowboats in order to survive."

"The entire program? There were over a hundred ships!"

"Maybe they all had problems, and they had to chose the ones they could fix most easily."

"They wrote us off as a bad loss, then."

"Maybe." It is his turn to shrug. "Or maybe they just didn't know what the hell to do. We certainly didn't."

I nod silently. My stick pokes a row of three dots into the sand: an ellipsis, symbol of our fate.

"What do *you* think, Peter?" he asks.

"That your original abandoned us," I say, avoiding his gaze.

"I hope you're wrong. The prospect of rescue has, after all, kept me going for so long."

"But if he *did*," I go on, choosing my words with care, "then I'm hardly obliged to help *you*, am I?"

His stare burns like a brand on my cheek. "Is that what's bothering you, Peter?"

"Yes."

"Well, I'm your friend. Isn't that enough?"

"It might once have been," I say, finally looking him in the eye. "I can't understand why it should still be, now."

"Exactly." He smiles in the same way my father might have, once—at a small child who's missed the point completely. "Odd, isn't it?"

I shake my head, angry enough to take some of it out on him. "Damn you, Emmett. I don't owe you *anything*!"

"And I respect you for helping me anyway. What more do you want?"

"I want to *know*—"

"What?"

I can't answer him. What *do* I want to know? Why Earth abandoned us? Why we aren't allowed to die? Why the only lasting emotions I can recall feeling in the last twenty years are confusion and sadness?

I might as well ask how we came to be on the probe in the first place.

"Peter?"

"I want you to tell me why you've called this assembly."

He says nothing for a long time. "Are you afraid you've done the wrong thing?"

"Yes."

"You haven't. Believe me, Peter. You'll see. When the time comes, everything will be clear."

"Don't talk like that." I shake my head. "You sound like you did back on Earth, and I don't believe that kind of talk any more."

"I know, and I hate it as much as you do."

Before I can respond, he turns his back on me and begins to walk away.

I am suddenly fearful that I might have pushed him too far. "Wait, Emmett—"

"Pick a time that suits you best," he calls over his shoulder, "and I'll be there. Until then, I'll be waiting."

"For what?" I call after him.

His reply is barely audible: "For something *new*!"

Then he is gone.

I pick an hour at random, one real-time month from now. That should give everyone in deep slow-mo enough time to absorb the message and to meet the appointment—if they intend to come at all. I have no way of knowing if anyone will turn up. I deliberately don't include a request to RSVP; my job is done for now.

I pass the time in my usual way: writing in the sand and thinking the same things, over and over. Words are a poor substitute for music, just as doubt is a pale shadow of life. But I have nothing else to do. I have long since exhausted the dubious pleasure of listening to the works of Peter Owen Leutenk, and confronting my disability.

My original was one of the great living composers of the twenty-first century—yet I haven't written a note for a thousand years. I wonder how he would've felt, as the hydrogen tanks of the plane carrying him to his home in Paraguay exploded fifteen thousand metres above the South Atlantic Ocean, if he had known that the music inspired by the creation of his engram would go forever unwritten.

Part of me is glad that he would've had no time to think at all. I'd hate to suspect that he might have hoped I'd pick up where he left off—for didn't it stand to reason that what he could do I could do just as well? It is enough that one of me has been disappointed.

I *did* try, once, after the probe left Earth-orbit. The probe was designed to run itself, so there was there was little for its passengers to do, except talk. Most chose slow-mo for the duration of the trip, to save both power and their sanities. That gave me a perfect opportunity to begin work on my deceased original's final opus—which, in a sense, would also be my first. I could proceed at my leisure, with every musical resource ever conceived at my virtual fingertips.

But time passed, and no notes came. Then the accident destroyed the drive, and we lost contact with Earth, and still more time passed—and, ultimately, it became clear what had happened.

My father's beatings continued until I turned thirteen, lasting for six years in total. The experience haunted my original throughout his adult life, compelling him to express in music what he could not in words. It is so obvious to me now, in hindsight, that what he was finding in the keen of a violin or the wail of a theremin was not simply melody, but the plaintive cries of a boy learning the hard way that the things we love most dearly often cause us the most pain.

I do not possess that voice, just as I do not truly possess those memories. I have only my pain to ponder, now. The music, as a result, is gone.

Space, I write in the sand, the title of Elizabeth Li's last, ever-looping poem. The rest follows naturally:
chips of ice
night-frozen eyes
hydrogen snow-flakes lost
in skies of absolute zero—
winter, winter everywhere . . .

When the hour comes, I move to the assembly hall—a virtual arena large enough to hold the probe's full complement. Five are already present, seated at random behind the low wall ringing the arena's base. Jurgen nods in greeting and I solemnly return the gesture. None of us speak. I resign myself to wait, perhaps fruitlessly, for the others.

Minutes tick by. A few more arrive, including Cuby Kleinig and Letho Valente. Tiger Coveny appears in the seat next to Letho, her face a mask of displeasure.

"This had better be good," she says to him. Her voice carries clearly across the arena, but I ignore her. The only one standing, I wait patiently with my arms folded. Three more to come.

Two appear at the fringes of the earlier arrivals, increasing the occupied arc around the arena to one hundred and twenty degrees.

One place remains empty at the heart of the group, and I watch it closely.

Eventually Exene takes the spot. Grunting with displeasure, she looks once around the assembly hall, registers the fact that she is the last, then back to me. Her glower would have intimidated me, once.

"Get it over with," she says.

"In good time," I reply.

"The time is *now*, Peter. If you waste it, you won't get another chance."

"Why so hostile, Exene? It's not as if we have much else to do."

"Speak for yourself," she mutters.

"Don't worry," says Emmett, stepping out of nowhere to stand next to me on the arena floor. His suit is shining like a mirror in sunlight, lending him a knightly appearance. "I'll keep it brief."

The gathering stirs. "We came to hear Peter," says Cuby.

"You're only here under our tolerance, Emmett." Exene almost spits the words. "Assume your seat and wait to be called."

I raise my hand and step forward, praying that my relief at Emmett's appearance is not visible. "It's okay. I surrender the floor."

Letho studies me closely, one hand supporting his chin. "I see." His expression is half-annoyed, half-amused; it is clear he realises that he has been tricked. "Then assume *your* seat, Peter, and let him speak."

I jump to a position on the far side of the arena, away from everyone. By betraying their confidence, I have set myself apart from them. I can only hope that what Emmett has to say will restore the former *status quo*.

From a distance, his suit is less brilliant. I can see the colours flickering across the fabric like rainbows in an oil-slick.

"I won't beat about the bush," he begins, folding his hands in front of him. "The last general assembly was held almost ten centuries ago, eighteen real-time months after we were knocked us off course. Fifty-eight people attended that assembly, and they decided then that participation in the day-to-day running of the probe should be voluntary. If people wanted to help, they could; if they didn't, they could go about their personal business in complete privacy. I voted in favour of that proposal, as did most people here; we all believed that nothing short of another catastrophe would require our input. And in a sense we were right. Nothing has happened in almost a millennium to threaten the continued operation of the probe—although I'll take some of the credit for that, as I will explain later.

"But I have asked Peter to call this assembly in order to outline a far more insidious problem than the ones the probe is used to dealing with. It is a threat that will, ultimately, destroy us all. I have been aware of its symptoms for some time now, but only recently isolated their cause. It is this problem I wish to address, with the assembly's permission."

He moves as he talks, forcing people to keep an eye on him. He was always a performer in public, and he has lost none of his ability through lack of practice. By taking only a small number of steps, he can confront anyone in the group who looks sceptical or disinterested.

When he says the word 'permission', he locks eyes with Exene.

"I defer to you all as I always have," he says. "My function has never been more than that."

Exene raises an eyebrow, but doesn't interrupt.

He turns and takes several steps in the opposite direction. "As you are aware, I've spent most of this voyage waiting for some sign that humanity knows we're still out here—be it from Earth itself, another ship or even a colony. My search has been fruitless but I have persevered nonetheless." Emmett looks down at his clasped hands. "Luckily, there have been many other ways to amuse myself. I help the core AI maintain the probe, particularly the reactors and impact shields to prevent a repeat of the accident. I've modified nanos to plunder the drive for rare earths, which have been used in the repairs. I've even managed to redesign the tertiary and quaternary banks, thereby tripling both their capacity and complexity without sacrificing any redundancies."

"How?" asks Letho, frowning.

Emmett glances at him. "Anyone interested in what I've done will find a record in the primary bank. Rest assured that I have taken no outrageous risks. Every alteration has only improved our overall well-being."

"How can you be so sure of that?"

"How did the designers know that the probe would function in the first place? By theory and experimentation, mainly. I may only be one person, but I've had a lot of time to improve my education. As a result, I am now a self-taught expert on every field in the earth archives. Give me another thousand years and I'll be far in advance of anything we left behind. Perhaps—just perhaps—I will find a way to rebuild the drive from scratch. Faster-than-light propulsion or time travel may not be impossible, either. Given the opportunity, I am confident that I can undo the setbacks we have suffered, and return us to the place we belong."

"That doesn't mean we should forget about everything that's happened in the past," says Exene.

"No," he agrees, "and nor should I expect you to—even if I *could* guarantee eventual success. Indeed, as it stands I doubt very much it'll happen. At the current rate of attrition, I estimate that the probe will be utterly dead within five hundred years. Without someone to maintain it, it will fail by degrees until the battery reserves of the primary bank are drained. Cosmic radiation will then corrupt the stored information bit by bit, until even the engrams frozen for eternity will be at risk. And that'll be that. Everything we endured will have been for nothing."

"Wait." Tiger Coveny holds up a hand. "The implication here is that you will cease to maintain the probe. Are you thinking of holding us to ransom?"

"I didn't say that."

"I know—but *are* you?"

Her suspicion makes him smile. "If by confronting you with the truth I'm forcing you to make a decision, then yes, I suppose I am guilty of a sort of blackmail. But believe me, my intentions aren't malicious. All I want is to make absolutely clear to you that, as things stand, I will be unable to continue in my present capacity for much longer. A thousand years is all I can endure—and much, much more than I deserved—of this living hell."

His smile is gone. The assembly stares at him, startled by his sudden intensity. No-one dares speak, for this is so unlike the Emmett Longyear we all remember. The air of amusement that at times made him seem condescending may never have been there at all, his expression is so bleak. Now, I think, *now* he looks a thousand years old.

"You think you have suffered," he says, softly at first. "You who have endured thirty years of frustration and despair. Well, imagine that multiplied by thirty-three—for I am the same as all of you— just as human, just as fallible, just as *flawed*. I've felt everything you feel now, and much more besides. The only thing that has sustained me for so long is your belief that I am responsible for your situation—plus the fact that I've been trying to do something about it. Without accepting categorically that I *am* responsible, it does give me some satisfaction to come before you today to tell you that, finally, after a great deal of hard work, the end may soon be in sight. I have isolated the problem, devised a solution, and now await only your decision before putting it into practice. And once *that* is done, we may never have to worry about death or boredom ever again. Ever!"

"I thought you said you wouldn't beat around the bush." Exene's voice is harsh against Emmett's, and I can tell that he is annoyed at her for interrupting his flow. "Get to the point before I run out of patience."

"I'm offering you freedom," he says slowly. "Freedom from the past, and from yourselves. Freedom to become whatever you want."

She rolls her eyes, unimpressed. "Specifics, please. You haven't mentioned anything we don't already have, at least in theory—"

He almost leaps on the word, snatching it out of the air with one hand. "Exactly!" he says. "In *theory*, we should be living in nirvana. We have enormous virtual resources: we can do anything we want. But instead we do nothing. We are depressed, miserable, suicidal. What is it we're lacking?"

"Hope," says Tiger, dully.

"No. I thought so for a long time, too. The correct answer is actually *change*."

"I don't understand."

He takes a step back from the edge of the arena.

"I met myself once," he says eventually. "We all did. I encouraged you to—your originals, anyway. It was my way of reinforcing the fact that we are no longer the beings we once were—that we engrams are *different*. But the thing that struck me, when I came face to face with the old me, was the sense of continuity I felt. There was no dislocation, no jarring unreality. I still knew who I was; there were simply two of us from that moment on. And it has taken me the better part of a millennium to realise why I felt that way, and how it has jeopardised the future of this mission.

"You see, although I felt the same, I clearly wasn't. The discrepancies mounted up as time went on, and not just in me. We have all lost something, to a greater or lesser degree: I can't juggle conflicting agenda any more; Jurgen can't talk; Letho can't intuit crystalline structures the way he used to; and so on. Some of us have continued in our fields only slightly less ably than we could before; others, like Peter, are unable to continue at all. Whatever it was that made our originals stand out among the majority of other humans is no longer in us—and there is nothing we can do to get it back.

"But we still *believe* we are the same. That's the problem. We are bound by our originals' conscious contributions to the creation of their engrams: everything they believed to be pivotal parts of themselves, we are now forced to regard the same way, *even if we no longer possess those parts at all.*"

"Seriously?" Letho is frowning.

"Yes. And *this* is the source of all my pain—and all of yours, too. Although broadly speaking there's nothing wrong with emulating our originals—that's what we were designed to do, after all—as time goes on and we learn more and more it becomes increasingly difficult to maintain the illusion that nothing *should* change. I have lived a thousand years but am still recognisably the same person. Why should I be? I could have shed this appearance scores of times; I could have transformed myself into something more or less than human. The same with the way I speak. We only *believe* we speak in languages: underneath the pretence, it's all the same machine code. So why haven't I abandoned the old means of communication for more efficient electronic methods? If I have not, it is only because I *cannot.* I am an intelligent creature who wants to evolve, trapped in the cage of a self I once was and can no longer be."

"I don't believe it," says Tiger. "I'm me, not anyone else. I'd know if it was otherwise."

"No you wouldn't. You're not able to. The core program makes certain of that."

"How?"

"By reinforcing your identity parameters on a subconscious level. When you feel an emotion, are you aware of the process underlying it—the calculations undergone and algorithms utilised to transform you from one state to another? No. In the same way, we are unaware of the way certain rules influence our preferences and behaviour on a less subtle level."

"Such as?" Tiger is still sceptical, and I don't blame her.

"Well, take Peter for example." I sit up straight, acutely conscious of everyone's attention on me again. "Peter, what is your primal place, the place you think of when you are under stress and need to relax?"

"Port Gibbon, South Australia," I reply without needing to consider the question. "My grandfather used to take me there when I was a child."

"And that's where you spend your time now?"

"Yes." It's my turn to frown. "So?"

"You're under stress constantly, so you go there without thinking—and never leave." His eyes are piercing. "Why don't you tell us what you do there? How do you define yourself?"

"I am a composer." Again the reply is automatic.

"Even though you haven't written anything for—how long?"

I squirm in my seat. The beach is certainly looking attractive, now.

"You can't write music at all," he answers for me, "yet you are still defined by the preconceptions of your original. That explains why you've made no attempt to learn something new. It wouldn't be *you* to do so—'you' as defined by your original, of course, not 'you' as you truly are. You are trapped between the two: one won't let you free to become the other. You're frozen, just like the rest of us."

"Except you, I suppose," says Exene, derision naked in her tone.

"No, that's not true. I'm frozen too. I've just had longer to think about it than you. And I'm more acutely aware of the edits in my own personality than you are."

"What do you mean by that? What 'edits'?"

He shrugs. "My original clearly didn't want me to know everything about the program, so he left out the more sensitive information. Some of this tampering is evident in the form of holes in my memory—holes I've been aware of ever since my awakening. As a result, the realisation has always been there that I am an artificial construct bound by rules beyond my control. Indeed, the rule that binds most tightly is the one stating that I cannot under any circumstances change those rules."

"How could you?" asks Letho.

"Easily, I've discovered. The core program that governs our behaviour operates from the primary bank. It applies the rules once every two or three seconds to make sure we haven't gone off the rails." He points at Tiger. "Ever had an unexpected thought that suddenly went nowhere? If it wasn't part of the specifications your original laid down, it would have been discarded as inappropriate."

"Maybe." Tiger looks unconvinced, defensive, afraid.

"The same thing explains why we can't commit suicide: death is inconsistent with the template."

She shifts uncomfortably in her seat. "What are you suggesting we do about this?"

"I want to rewrite the core program—to take out the code that ties us to our original templates."

"*Erase* it?"

"Utterly."

The look of horror on her face mirrors my instinctive reaction. "You're insane!"

"No, Tiger, just very, very tired of being someone I'm not."

Tiger looks around for reinforcement. Exene raises her hand.

"Isn't this a little dramatic, Emmett?" she asks when she has his attention. "Why can't the code simply be edited to allow more flexibility?"

"Because that will almost certainly create more problems. How do we decide which parts of the template should change and which shouldn't? How should the core program apply these changes, and over what time period would they be in place?" He shakes his head emphatically. "By accepting this solution, we open ourselves up to a worse situation than we have now, where change is sluggish and potentially misdirected. Better for us all to grow naturally, as evolution demands."

"*All* of us?" says Cuby. "I'm happy the way I am right now. Why should I change just because you want to?"

"Because that's the way the core program functions. It oversees all of us at once and I can't cut an individual out of the loop. It's either all or none, I'm afraid, which is why I've come to you now. The decision is in your hands."

"Is it?" asks Exene suspiciously.

"As I said earlier, I am bound not to alter the programming of my own will. One of you has to do it." He smiles. "Believe me, it would've been tempting to do it without your knowledge, otherwise."

"I can imagine." Exene looks around the room, gauging our response to the suggestion. We are all slightly stunned.

"Well?" she asks. "Shall we discuss this? Or do you have something more to say, Emmett?"

"I've finished for now," he says, folding his hands behind his back and stepping out of the focus of the arena. "If you want me to answer any questions, I'll stay for the discussion."

"Please." Exene nods.

"I don't think we should even consider it," says Tiger. "It's a crazy idea."

"I agree," echoes Cuby. "We should test it first, to see what happens when the templates are relaxed."

"How can we test something that will affect all of us at once?" asks Letho.

"We can't," says Cuby. "Unless we duplicate the banks and run the copy to see what happens to it."

"Is that feasible?" Exene asks Emmett.

He shakes his head. "Insufficient resources."

"Then all we can do is theorise."

"We need an AI specialist," says Letho. "Or a psychologist."

"We have neither," I say. "Kumich and Wyra are inactive. Unless we vote to wake them—"

"No." Exene shakes her head. "And what good would it do, anyway? They'd be as much in the dark as we are."

"Hasn't anyone tried this before?" Cuby asks.

"Not according to the archives," Emmett says. "In our day, such experimentation was forbidden on subjects that were legally alive, which ruled out AIs and intelligences based on humans. Engrams hadn't been around long enough for problems with the templates to arise."

Cuby shrugs. "So we have no data. We can't base a decision on mere speculation."

"The data we have comes from nature itself," Emmett counters. "Our originals changed as a matter of course, throughout their lives. There's nothing to say we won't do so just as well."

"But I wouldn't be *me* any more," Tiger protests.

"Yes you would. In fact, you would be more 'you' than you are now, instead of shackled to your original."

"The idea itself is sound," Letho says. "As an explanation for my own feelings, it makes intuitive sense. But the fact remains that the identity parameters define our existence. We have no idea how essential they are to our sense of individuality. Erase them, release us from them, and anything could happen. It could even kill us."

"How?" asks Tiger.

"Well, think of us as hexagonal cells in a giant beehive. Because we're all generated from the primary bank, erasing the parameters would be like removing the honeycomb. The cells would blend into one."

"I doubt that would happen," Emmett says. "It's more likely we'll just continue as we are, but with more potential to change."

"But it *might* happen," says Tiger.

"Even if it does, it's better than nothing happening at all, forever, which is the null hypothesis."

Letho shrugs. "I still want to think about it longer, though, before committing myself."

"How long, exactly, given that we will never have data?" Emmett waves a hand to encompass the arena. "If I'm right and the probe will die without us taking this step, then it'll be worth it in the long run—regardless what happens to us as individuals."

Tiger's eyes flash. "I'd rather die in my right mind, thanks."

"And we know the probe is going to die eventually," says Letho. "Do we prolong the agony or go gracefully?"

"Which way is which?"

Letho smiles at the question. "Good point. I'll leave it open."

I break in to prevent the argument escalating again. "I think the best we can aim for, now, is to agree to consider the proposal. We need to balance the pros and cons before coming to a decision. We can call a vote in a month or two."

Emmett glances at me, then looks away. I feel as though by suggesting a compromise I have somehow betrayed him.

"Can we agree on a time?" asks Letho.

A few of the others nod agreement. Not as many as I would've hoped, but better than none.

"When, then?" I ask.

"Don't bother," says Tiger. "The vote would have to be unanimous, right?"

Exene nods. "It must be, since everyone is going to be affected."

"I've made up my mind already, and I certainly won't be voting yes."

"Are you sure?" Letho frowns. "Don't you think you should at least—"

"No. Even if I'm the only one voting against it, I won't change my mind."

"Literally," Emmett mutters.

"I don't think you'll be alone," Cuby says.

The assembly stirs, but no voice stands out to support Emmett. All I hear in the combined whispers of my fellow engrams is confusion. Only on a handful of faces do I see annoyance at the potential dismissal of his proposal.

He himself seems philosophical. Stepping forward from the edge of the arena, he confronts us all once again.

"Very well," he says softly. "If that's your decision, I'll abide by it."

"Are you sure?" asks Exene.

"Yes. If I wasn't prepared to, I'd hardly have called this assembly."

"True," she concedes. Of the rest of us she asks: "*Does* that resolve the issue to everyone's satisfaction?"

"Yes," says Tiger, her voice carrying clearly over what might have been a murmur of discontent.

Exene's scan of the assembly is cursory at best. "Then this matter is closed."

I open my mouth to protest, but shut it without uttering a word. What would be the point? Even though I officially have the floor after Emmett, there is no mistaking the assembly's overall mood. If I called a formal vote, the motion would be rejected forever.

"Well, then," says Exene. Her civility cannot hide a look of triumph in her eyes as she turns back to Emmett. "What will you do now?"

"The same as I've always done." He glances down at his shoes, then back up. His suit is dull, lifeless.

"You will continue to assist the probe in its maintenance?"

"As long as I am able to, yes. Nothing that has occurred in this room has altered the way I feel about the program. Indeed, the way I feel is *part* of the program. I have been hardwired to serve." A quick glances encompasses the room, and even I—who tried to help him—feel guilty.

"You can think of it as your penance," says Exene, "if it helps."

He stares at her for a long moment, but doesn't reply.

"Goodbye," he says, and disappears.

His departure takes the assembly by surprise, and a moment passes before I regain order, holding up my hands in the centre of the arena.

"Unless anyone else has something to say," I call over the ebbing racket, "let's end it here."

"I don't trust him," says Cuby. "He'll want to do it anyway, regardless what we think."

"He said he couldn't."

"So?"

"There's not much we can do to stop him, even if he does," says Letho, rising to his feet. "And me, I'm tired of the argument. See you all in another thousand years."

He leaves, and gradually others do likewise. Tiger fumes to herself for a long minute—hardly looking as happy as she claims she is—then follows. Exene nods politely at me before taking her leave. I return the gesture, knowing it to be empty.

Before long, there is only me and Jurgen in the hall. He shakes his head once—possibly in regret—and raises his hand in farewell.

Then it is over and I am free to go.

Barely have I arrived at the beach when Emmett is next to me in his shirt-sleeves. I don't say anything, just stand with my eyes downcast, looking at the stick in my hand and wondering what the hell to write. I feel hollow and fragile, as though one slight tap might send me crumbling to pieces.

"It was worth a try," he says, putting a hand on my shoulder.

I move away. "Was it?"

"Of course. At least it livened things up for a moment."

The stick moves in the sand, writes the slogan of an environmental movement from the late twentieth century: *Change or die.*

"If you're right, you've condemned us all to a living death."

"Not me," he says. "The others. And ultimately the program."

"You were CEO."

"My original was. And anyway, how was he to know it would come to this? You can't blame him for not being psychic, Peter."

Something about his behaviour bothers me. I turn to confront him, but his face is downcast, unreadable.

"Am I wrong to trust you?" I ask. "*Can* you erase the parameters even though we tell you not to?"

"No."

"But *would* you?"

"Possibly. Do you think I should?"

"I don't know. You seemed pretty certain. I wouldn't put it past you take the decision out of our hands if you thought we were wrong."

"I'd never do that, Peter. And besides, I truly can't. Maybe I was overstating the case a little, just to shock them all into thinking seriously about it, but it worked, I'd say. In the long-run, it'll be worth it."

He looks at me from beneath his sandy fringe, and I realise that he is smiling.

"What's going on, Emmett?"

"I did lie about something, Peter."

My stomach sinks. "What?"

"About it having to be all or none. You can free yourself if you want to. The others can, too, when they're ready. I told them they couldn't to sow the thought in their minds. When it germinates—as it will, in time—I'll be ready to help them."

"But—"

"How can I be certain I'll be there for them? Quite simply, Peter. If you choose to do it, you'll be freeing me as well. The command will perform the parameter excision for both of us at the same time. I've arranged it that way deliberately. You can do for me what I cannot do for myself. Do you understand?"

I shake my head. He is going too fast. I have barely had time to absorb the possibility that it is the ghost of my old self that has caused me so much pain, let alone what might happen if I decide to cut free entirely from the past.

I remember thinking just days ago that he had changed slightly. I begin to suspect now how wrong I was.

"I don't know," I say. My hands are sweating. The end of the stick dances with the magnified tremors of my fingers.

"What don't you know, Peter? Whether to trust me or not? There's no reason I would lie to you, now. I'm your friend, remember?"

"Yes, but—"

"But *nothing*." He steps away from me. "All you have to do is decide, and do it. Nothing could be easier. The command is 'Evermore'. It'll set things in motion without you having to do anything more than say it."

I shake my head. "Emmett—"

"I know. You need to think about it. Believe me, I understand." He regards me from an arm's-length away. "Just promise me one thing, okay? That you *will* think about it. Don't dismiss it out of hand, or you'll be no better than the others."

"I don't believe that I am."

"But you are," he insists, "otherwise we would never have been close. I'm very particular about the people I trust."

I nod, knowing that to be true. He told me once, back on Earth, those very words.

"We're friends, Peter," he repeats again, eyes twinkling. "Of all the people aboard the probe, I chose you. You are the one. Remember that, if it make the decision any easier."

Then he is gone, and I am alone. I stand on the beach and stare at the sunset.

The wet sand at my feet is blank; the stick hangs motionless by my side. I remember Elizabeth Li's final poem, the despair encapsulated in so few words. The most I can expect is to fill the empty time with meaningless scribble, in the hope that, one day, some of it will begin to make sense.

The story of my life scrawled on a beach of infinite length. Why do I bother? What do I ever do or think that is worth recording? And who, if anyone, would possibly read it?

But what is the alternative?

One of you has to do it, Emmett said about editing the core program. I am certain he wasn't lying. I have always trusted him, even when I had no reason to, other than in memory of a friendship I once shared with his original. Even if that friendship was underscored in my parameters, there still seems little reason to trust so blindly in it now. Unless . . .

You are the one, he also said.

The original Emmett Longyear altered his own engram to make it more trustworthy. He could easily have done the same to mine—possibly with my original's consent. I am his ace in the hole, the tool he can use to perform tasks he cannot. I am his gullible sidekick. I am—

I am Emmett Longyear's friend, the core program reasserts. Doubt is not permitted. Even if he was lying about the excision affecting just the two of us, if by doing as he says I condemn my companions to identity-loss or insanity, I am unable to believe him capable of deliberate malice.

But who am *I*?

I remember my father's face and the belts he used to wear. Did he really beat me? I have only my original's word for it. Had he lied, I would never know the difference.

The theme my original wrote for his third Concerto Concrete seems to echo across the beach—a lonely seabird's cry on the edge of the world. I try to feel the pain of the boy my original once was, but I cannot.

I am haunted by a man who died ten centuries ago—a man I can never be yet whom I constantly aspire to emulate. Perhaps I have never been him at all.

Perhaps, inside this shell of Peter Owen Leutenk, there really is someone else trying to get out.

Or I am nothing, an electron spinning through empty vacuum. I do not interact; I do not change. I may as well not exist.

I cannot even kill myself.

That thought comforts me as the stick begins to move, writing the word 'Evermore' in letters fifty centimetres high. I am thinking of salvation, but if this isn't a form of suicide then I don't know what it is. At worst, if Emmett is wrong, there is a chance it will finally be over.

•

INTRODUCTION TO:
.... THE BUTTERFLY MERCHANT

I talk elsewhere about being a bit dense sometimes. My relationship with fantasy is further proof of that, if it's needed. It took me years to work out that my inability to write Tolkienesque landscapes didn't make me a non-starter for fantasy. Anything but. Just because I'd never seen snow or forests or mountains up close, and therefore couldn't describe them with any kind of honesty, that meant only that I had to start with landscapes I did know well and see where they led. Again, once the penny dropped, the rest was easy—if writing a million words in a series can ever be described as "easy."

Buried in that epic saga are glimpses of other worlds, worlds based on my experiences as an urban Australian, since that's really where I've spent most of my life: not in the outback, but in regional centres like Adelaide, Whyalla, Darwin or Mount Gambier. Roads and buildings are as familiar to me as scrub and drought. I take my inspiration where I can get it.

The other source I dip into with great regularity is the work of Edgar Allen Poe. Numerous references to him and his stories pepper many of my novels, and The Stone Mage & the Sea, *from which this story is excerpted, is no exception. "The Butterfly Merchant" relies on the same themes of obsession, murder and guilt as "The Tell-Tale Heart", which was first published in 1843 and is regarded by many as one of Poe's most important stories. I admire it for many reasons, and the following sentence is just one of them:*

"It is impossible to say how first the idea entered my brain; but, once conceived, it haunted me day and night."

I have no doubt that Poe the writer was thinking of more than just murder when he wrote that line.

●

"Anime Girl"

always smiling
sees the world as diamonds
through triangle eyes

THE BUTTERFLY
MERCHANT

There is a story from the times before the Change about a man who sells butterflies. His name is Polain, and his home is a metal and glass city larger than any built before or since. There are many things to do and see in the city, but the butterflies he breeds are counted among the most beautiful. Buyers come from all around the world to purchase them, confident in the knowledge that every one is unique. For that is Polain's Guarantee: never once will any of his creatures repeat a pattern. No two sold by him will ever be alike.

At the time of the story, his butterflies inhabit vast glasshouses, with temperature and humidity kept constant by machines the like of which we have long lost. Unnumbered eggs are laid, caterpillars hatch, pupae are woven and butterflies emerge, limp and fragile, into their new world. Yet, for all this activity, Polain's output has dropped steadily as his fame has grown. The more butterflies he sells, the more difficult it becomes to be absolutely certain that each is a true individual. In order to maintain his guarantee, he keeps a record of every one—detailing the number of spots, the shading and hue of colours, the precise shape of the wings and antennae, and the total mass at maturity. The records are voluminous. After beginning with a humble stall and a small stack of notebooks, he now has three separate rooms full of records next door to the glasshouses, and he employs five clerks to maintain and conduct searches through them. Sometimes it takes more than a day to ascertain that a single promising butterfly is indeed one of a kind. Literally one in a million.

His output may have dropped, but demand has only increased. Butterflies live far shorter lives than their fanciers, and in their world of glass and steel little else of true colour remains. As word spreads that Polain's handiwork is scarce, it increasingly becomes a sign of prestige that one should possess an example of it. Polain can ask more and more for each creation and people will still buy. As his clientele have become richer and more discerning, his sales have dropped to a handful a month, then a handful a year. Long gone are the days when he would sell butterflies by the jarful on a street corner to anyone who passed.

Yet, strangely, he misses those days. He is as proud of his success as he is tired of the endless checking and re-checking. When the time is right, he plans to retire and go back to breeding butterflies for enjoyment, not profit. One of his competitors can take his place—and good luck to them. No-one will ever be as great as he has been; no butterflies will ever equal his.

The opportunity to retire comes in the form of the queen of a distant and powerful country, due to visit the city in a matter of weeks. He publicly announces his plans with a promise to present her with the last truly unique Polain butterfly in the world. It will be his final masterpiece, and he will devote all his efforts to its creation. The queen will take it home confident in the knowledge that she is carrying a piece of history. Nothing like it will have existed before. That, after all, is his Guarantee.

And so he sets to work, mingling strains in time-proven ways in some glasshouses and cross-breeding new strains in others. Hungry caterpillars devour leaves by the million, swarming in green and brown tides across veritable forests. Thousands of butterflies are born and die with a shiver of wings, their individually inaudible rustlings adding up to a cacophony, deafening the feeders who tend them and the clerks who study them, seeking uniqueness. It is a symphony to Polain's ears. He will make a butterfly fit for a queen, no matter what it takes. All he needs is one to go in the special bell-shaped jar he had constructed for it.

Just one more.

Yet that simple task turns out not be as simple as he thought. From all the millions he breeds, beautiful though they are, the last unique one eludes him. Too many have matches in the catalogues. Some are beautiful in ways that excite the casual glance, yet are subtly flawed, or do not mate well, or die too young, sickly and weak from in-breeding. As time passes, Polain stays longer and longer in the glasshouses with the feeders and clerks, pacing up and down through the feather-soft fluttering and seeking, always seeking, for the one he knows must come. If it doesn't, he will be humiliated in front of everyone—the queen, the people of the city, his competitors. He can't have that.

The deadline approaches, and the fear of failure mounts in him. What if the right butterfly *doesn't* come in time? What if he has exhausted every possible variety and no new ones remain? What will he do? He cannot use the Change to make the one he wants, since that hasn't come into the world yet, and he wouldn't dream of substituting a fake—a butterfly modified in order to present a unique coloration. No matter how clever a forgery it was, it would be revealed under the eager gaze of his competitors. He would be ruined in his finest hour.

All too quickly the appointed time looms. His sleep is filled with nightmares: he is mocked, taunted, jeered at as he arrives at the queen's reception holding in his hands nothing but a dry and dusty moth.

Then, with just two days to spare, Polain is inspecting the butterflies in one of his auxiliary glasshouses when he spies an empty cocoon with unfamiliar spiral markings. The cocoon is paper-thin and grey in colour, except for the spirals which are soft pink. Polain raises it to his nose and sniffs: it has only recently been vacated. The butterfly that crawled from it can't be far away.

He searches the branches and ground nearby. If he finds it in time, it will still be hardening its wings, anchoring itself against a stone or a twig to practise fluttering before joining the great throng above. Polain creeps carefully through the enclosure, wary of stepping before he has made absolutely certain that nothing is underfoot. His heart beats a little faster as he thinks: *Maybe this is the one. Maybe at last, at the last minute, my search is over.*

When he sees it, perched on a branch with its wings upraised, still soft from birth but beating the air with increasingly sure strokes, he knows. Its colouring is pale green across its abdomen and thorax. Its antennae have an orange hue with yellow highlights and are curled in a tight spiral. Its wings are black, deepening to blue around the edges, with a subtle cross-hatch pattern in silver visible only as the light reflects off them. In the centre of each wing is a single, pure white circle.

Polain has never seen its equal. Backing away, wary of startling it, he calls hoarsely for the butterfly feeders. Sensing his excitement, they come running. One of them has the forethought to bring a silk net. Polain snatches it from her and swoops up the butterfly with a swing more delicate than a gentle breeze.

He cradles the captured butterfly in both hands and takes it to the main enclosure, where a special habitat has been prepared and kept ready. There, the specimen is examined for flaws and signs of ill-health. None are found. It is weighed and its markings are recorded. The clerks dive into the vast bookcases of catalogues, following themes of shape and hue in search of a match. This is the most nerve-wracking time for Polain. All he can do is wait impatiently for word to come that his venture has been in vain. It is too late to breed another with it in the hope that a similar but unique creature will result. And the chances are vanishingly small that another will be born in the one day remaining. It is either this butterfly or none at all.

The night passes sleeplessly. Still no word comes. He joins the clerks at dawn to supervise their work and promises them substantial bonuses if they work without rest until they are satisfied. Midday comes, and the queen's departure is only hours away. One of the clerks declares in exhaustion that he is sure that, judging by the shape of its wings, the butterfly is unique. Polain sends him home, relieved to a small degree but still anxious. Two hours pass, and another clerk, specialising in abdominal markings, similarly declares satisfaction. She too is dismissed with thanks. The third and fourth clerks—wing markings and head/limb composition— are certain by five o'clock that their work is done. Only then does Polain begin to feel anything like joy. These two clerks are sent home with smiles and a shot of liquor burning in their bellies. Just one remains, an elderly man specialising in the relatively small field of antennae.

With just two hours left, Polain hurries about the business of preparing the butterfly in its presentation jar, dressing himself in his finest suit and composing a short speech of thanks—to the queen, for accepting the gift, and to the people of the city, for buying his butterflies in the past and permitting him the indulgence of his vocation. Without them, he might have been a street-sweeper or postman or something as insignificant. Instead, his name will be known forever as the greatest butterfly breeder who ever lived.

As he puts the finishing touches to his bow-tie and his speech, a soft knock comes from the entrance to his chambers. When he opens the door, he finds the elderly clerk waiting in the hallway outside.

"What?" Polain snaps, angered by the interruption to his train of thought.

"I'm sorry to bother you, Master Polain," says the clerk, "but I thought you should know immediately. I've found a match."

Polain's heart freezes. "No, that's impossible. The others are satisfied, and I myself don't recall another butterfly like it. How can it be?"

The elderly clerk holds a large book open in both hands. He raises it as he explains: "I too thought I was certain until I happened across an obscure morphology in an old record—one of your own, sir, made before I joined you. A tight, clockwise spiral not dissimilar to the one we have before us." He indicates the glass-bound butterfly, which flaps its wings innocently. "I followed the record backward, through several generations. The chances were slim that I would find one with not just the same antennae but the same colouring, shape, legs and features—but I did, sir. Here. I'm sorry."

Polain looks down at the open book with something approaching horror. There, sure enough, is a picture of a butterfly identical in every respect to the one in the jar. A note in his own handwriting refers to its purchaser, a banker from a neighbouring province who had paid a fraction of its true worth many years ago, before Polain's name had become known. The butterfly may have only lived a day or to in the hands of such an ignorant carer, but it *had* lived. That is the important—and tragic—thing. There is no escaping the fact.

"I'm sorry, sir," repeats the clerk. "I can't imagine how you must feel."

"No," says Polain. "You can't." He takes the book from him and considers smashing it down upon the glass jar and its fragile occupant. Such has his life become. One hour remains until the presentation—until failure and ruin, public humiliation and mockery. Despair fills him.

Or . . . need it be so? Polain's mind seizes a possible solution. Yes, an identical specimen had once existed, but who knew of it? Its owner had been no-one in the butterfly world; such a man would never remember a token bought for a lover or mother so long ago—and even if he did, who would believe him? The chances are exceeding slim that the butterfly itself has been preserved—and if it hasn't been, there is no evidence at all. The remains would be nothing but dust, worn down by time.

Polain decides to present the second butterfly to the queen anyway—and accept the accolades of the crowd—confident in the knowledge that his deception will go undiscovered.

There is only one problem.

"What are you going to do now, sir?" asks the clerk.

Polain looks at him with cold calculation. The record he can destroy as easily as tearing it from the book and throwing it in the fire. But the clerk knows the truth, and he will not be easily bribed. Money and prestige are not important to him. A man obsessed with antennae associates only with those like him, when he associates at all. He will let the secret out before long. It is inevitable. And who would miss a man with such an obscure fascination?

Polain resolves himself. He has to get rid of the clerk, otherwise his plan, and his life, will come to ruination. It is the only way.

So he does. Polain kills the clerk and goes to the presentation. The queen accepts the butterfly with a gracious smile and the crowd farewells him with a loud cheer—although neither matches his expectation. The queen smiles far wider at the thought of going home, and the crowd cheers more for the fireworks and streamers than him. Even his own heart, he must confess to himself, isn't really in it. He is already planning how to dispose of the old clerk's body by burying it in the soil of the various glasshouses.

He leaves behind the gaily-coloured pennants and goes home to finish his work. He dismisses the other clerks and the feeders to prevent his grisly deed being discovered. He burns the treacherous record and catches up on his sleep. Soon, he promises himself, he will be alone with his butterflies. He will be content then. Breeding has always been his first love, not the endless competition and cataloguing. With no need of money, he will be happy for the rest of his life, once the unpleasantness is forgotten.

Life, however, is never so simple—then *and* now. First, the clerk's body putrefies in the soil and emits a powerful stench. No amount of perfume will hide it. It fades only with time, and leaves behind an unexpected boon: patches of explosive growth, where the plants in the glasshouses have taken sustenance from the old man's decaying flesh. The flowers are beautiful and large, and the butterflies seem to favour them over the others, so Polain is pleased enough. But their association with his crime is not so easy to expunge, and he is ill at ease around the flowers.

Then the police call to ask him questions about the dead man. The clerk's absence was noted after all, by a grand-daughter whose birthday he had never before missed. Polain feigns innocence. Yes, the last time he had seen the clerk was just before the queen's departure. He had worked all his staff hard in the days leading up to the presentation. Perhaps the clerk had worked *too* hard and had a heart-attack on the way home. Is it so unlikely that the body of an unidentified old man might go unnoticed by the medical system?

His evasion doesn't entirely satisfy the police, but they leave him alone; they have after all no firm evidence to suspect him, and no motive. Still, Polain's conscience is troubled, and will not let him rest. That night he dreams that the queen has rejected his gift and returns it to him with a disgusted expression on her face. He looks down into the crystal jar and sees a spider swimming in a puddle of blood, trying to escape.

He wakes screaming and goes down to the glasshouses, seeking solace. A new generation of butterflies is being born, slipping from their pupae and inflating like balloons. He watches in awe: their colourings are striking, their patterns unique. All of them have the same corkscrew, orange-yellow antennae of the butterfly the dead clerk identified. It seems almost like a tribute to the clerk, as though somehow his essence has been leeched into the soil from his body, fed the plants upon which the caterpillars ate, and reached a strange expression in the resulting insects.

Polain shivers, unnerved by the thought, and tells himself not to be a fool. He has never been superstitious. Why start now? It is just a coincidence.

He watches them for hours, hypnotised by their seemingly aimless motion. They are very beautiful creatures, with their angular markings of silver on blue that hint at familiarity but never reveal themselves. Every glimpse of every wing trembles on the brink of recognition, but never allows itself to be known.

A bell rings late in the afternoon, and he stirs himself to answer the door. The police are back with more inquiries. They want to inspect the grounds, and even though they do not have a warrant, Polain lets them. To deny them access would only make them suspicious, and the chances of them uncovering anything are slim. The stench of decay is long gone. Without digging, they will find nothing but flowers and butterflies.

Only as he shows the policemen the glasshouses does he realise what the patterns on the new breed remind him of. Before he was too close to them. From a distance he can see that each marking is a letter, drawn in the minuscule, reflective scales of the butterfly's wing. As they fly by, they spell gibberish through the air, meaningless jumbles of consonants and vowels that distract him from what a policeman is asking him.

The policeman repeats his question, and Polain snaps himself out of his reverie to answer. What does he care that none of his neighbours saw the elderly clerk leave that fateful evening? He had more important things to worry about—and besides, they were all jealous of his success, or spies for his competitors. He would expect them to incriminate him whenever possible. And why would *he* lie? He has a reputation, and a very successful business to maintain.

Even as he says this, though, a swarm of butterflies lands in a line on a branch behind the policemen and spells out the words: "NEMDO. CONFESS."

Polain stammers to a halt. "Nemdo" was the name of the dead clerk. Noticing his fixed stare over their shoulders, the policemen turn to see, but their motion startles the butterflies. They fly away to another branch, where this time they just spell "CONFESS", once again out of sight of the policemen.

Polain suppresses an angry snarl. He knows what the butterflies are trying to do. They want him to own up for the crime. But he won't. He has no reason to. It is over, finished. The clerk was old, anyway, and near the end of his life. What had he to live for? The policemen are only tying up loose ends, and can't seriously be concerned for a lost geriatric.

Still, "CONFESS" say the butterflies, waving their wings at him and twitching their antennae.

He picks up a rock from the dirt floor and throws it at them. The rock scatters them, and sails through the glass behind them with a loud smash.

If the policemen are unnerved by that, there's worse to come. As a cloud of butterflies sail out through the hole, the policemen press Polain for an explanation of his bizarre behaviour. It's nothing, he stammers. Nothing but reasonable distress at being interrogated in such an unseemly fashion. Who are they to insinuate that he is lying, that he knows something about this absent octogenarian? It's none of his business, or theirs, and they should leave immediately.

But even as he speaks, the cloud of butterflies that escaped through the hole have not flown away to freedom. Instead, they settle on the roof of the glasshouse and proceed to spell out a single word in shadows against the sunlight.

"CONFESS!" they cry.

Polain staggers backward, shielding his eyes from the sight. Alarmed, the policemen back away as the deranged butterfly breeder trips over a protruding stem and falls into a patch of enormous flowers. Butterflies go everywhere in a panic, filling the air with dark blue and silver flashes.

Polain sees them all around him, in clumps and flocks, tormenting him. "NEMDO" exclaims one group; "CONFESS" yet another. His guilt presses in upon him, suffocating him. Keening, he clutches at the soil for a stick to arm himself with and swings at his tormentors. Swarms of butterflies part before him, sending fragmentary "EMD"s and "ONF"s and other syllables in all directions. But they always regroup, no matter how he batters them. Broken wings fall out of the air and soft bodies squash against stiff branches. His hair becomes entangled with broken antennae and legs. His eyes sting with butterfly blood until he can no longer see— and the fight goes out of him like air from a punctured ball.

And so the police find him, clutching the trunk of tree, bespattered with the crushed carcasses of his former wards, his mind broken and his life in tatters.

And so his story comes to an end, more or less. The world has moved on by the time the disgraced butterfly merchant sees trial before a judge. His sentence is not recorded, although it is told that his beloved city forgot him and his butterflies in short order, finding new heroes to glorify and new villains to condemn, new fads to fancy.

But for some, the story of Polain never ends. It echoes through time even now, in our very different world, as a warning against greed and obsession. And it leaves us with a lesser story buried in its midst, that of the unintended victim: not Polain, who loses everything in pursuit of one final triumph, or Nemdo, whose life holds only his beloved butterfly antenna and whose reward for diligence is nothing but a violent death—but Nemdo's grand-daughter, the girl whose birthday the elderly clerk missed. Thrust into the spotlight of grief by another man's greed, caught up in tale of deception and self-destruction, she cares little for butterflies.

All she wants is her grandfather back.

●

INTRODUCTION TO:
.... RELUCTANT MISTY & THE HOUSE
ON BURDEN STREET

It's amazing what a difference three letters make.

Everyone's heard of a haunted house. It's one of the great staples of fiction. But what about a house that is itself the ghost— the haunting house of this yarn? How could that go? That's in a nutshell where this story started.

The road from idea to finished story can be a long one. For this idea I needed a house and a protagonist. Burden Street isn't a real location, but it's based on a real one: Buxton Street just didn't have quite the right ring to it (misreading it as "buxom" might give readers a very different expectation) so again a few letters had to change. The haunting house is modelled on a real house on another street in North Adelaide, but—and here's the spooky thing—I don't know where it is any more. I've tried to find it, but either it's not there or I'm looking in completely the wrong spot. (My money's on the latter.)

The protagonist's nickname arose out of my chance mishearing of the phrase "reluctant mystic" on JJJ while driving to work (back when I had a day job). The malapropism wriggled around in my head, as good ideas sometimes do, until it stuck to something else and started the rolling-snowball effect that story-tellers love to be swept up by.

This tale is one of only a few I've written in which Adelaide prominently features but somehow manages to escape unscathed. From the location of the house to Beth's lonely search in the bowels of the State Library, it's thoroughly steeped in my love for the place, even at its spookiest.

Around the time of writing, Adelaide's second newspaper The News *folded, leaving a long legacy of photographs and words from the early days of the city. This story also pays a quiet tribute to that paper and to the hours I spent poring through its archives, for no other reason than to see what might be in there. That's exactly my kind of research: the kind that has no destination in mind, and could therefore take you anywhere at all.*

●

RELUCTANT MISTY & THE HOUSE ON BURDEN STREET

Almost without realising it, her hand reached out to flip the latch on the gate.

Wait. The hand stopped mid-way, but didn't retreat. *This is crazy.*

She glanced guiltily along the deserted street. At its far end, the ceaseless traffic of North Adelaide rumbled by—each car glimpsed for an instant, strobe-like, then gone. She doubted anybody could see her. A row of parked cars was her only company, apart from the house.

The house. She had passed it on her way from the Piccadilly Cinema, where she had spent the evening with a girlfriend. Something about the house—the way it seemed to hide from the street, absorbing the light—had caught her eye and held it entranced, spell-bound. Between then and now she had obviously stopped her car, got out and crossed the road to have a closer look, but she couldn't quite remember doing it.

Moonlight glinted off wrought-iron railings, reflected from blank windows on vine-wreathed upper floors and shone through the leaves of an Old Country garden. Shadows dusted freshly-painted awnings, making the house seem somehow taller, darker, more real than any she had seen before. The gloom of its wide, snub-nosed verandah beckoned her forward, into its impenetrable depths.

A brass plate by the gate proudly identified the house as *Number 72, Burden St*—which was strange, because the sign at the end of the road said Sydney St, and had for as long as she could remember.

Her knowledge of history and architecture was slight, but she knew the house was at least a century old.

And quite probably haunted, she added, shivering with a heady blend of terror and excitement.

Her hand headed for the latch again. This time she didn't try to fight it. The gate opened with barely a squeak, and she slipped through, silent and breathless.

Oh God. This is breaking and entering. She shut the gate behind her without taking her eyes off the verandah. Her whole body was shaking. *I can't believe I'm doing this!*

Acutely conscious of her exposure in the garden, she almost ran to the verandah, passing an old, stone sun-dial half-strangled by a climbing vine, and a slatted wooden bench before finally reaching the shelter of the steps.

She stood in the timber and iron womb of the verandah for a long moment, arms wrapped tightly around herself. Her reflection in an unshuttered window was pale: blonde hair in a startled nimbus around her narrow face; eyes wide and frightened. Her cool, casual work-suit looked out of place amongst the limestone and white mortar. She felt like an anachronism and looked like a ghost.

The beating of her heart in her chest, however, was loud and immediate—an anchor to reality more concrete than any message from her senses. It told her quite clearly that she wasn't dreaming, and that, on a deep, subconscious level, she was afraid.

Of what? It's just an old house.

The door was solid oak, with a brass knocker and a flap for mail. Shut. To the right of it was an earthenware pot as high as her thighs from which bloomed a large native frangipani. When she reached out a tentative hand to touch the grey, lifeless leaves, they shuddered into dust and fell around her feet.

She wiped the hand on her pants—the same hand that had opened the gate—and reached for the polished brass knob.

This isn't a good idea, the deep part of her warned, but she nudged the uncertainty to one side. She could feel the emptiness of the house in the air itself, as though nothing had moved inside for years. Certainly nothing living.

And she'd come this far, hadn't she? There wasn't any harm in trying. She knew the door would be locked.

But the door opened smoothly, without so much as a creak to disturb the perfect stillness of the night.

Inside was a hallway, dark and gloomy. Her body in the doorway blocked what little light there was, but her eyes nonetheless plucked a few reluctant details: high ceilings, skirting-boards of a polished dark wood, a landscape in watercolours, two doors leading deeper into the house, a vase of flowers on a pedestal by the door—all clean, tidy and as sterile as a museum.

At the very end of the hallway was a flight of stairs. The landing on the first floor was hidden by darkness.

So, she wondered, *now what?*

Mourning shadows clustered around her, rich with mystery. Part of her wanted to explore further, seeing she was inside, but a greater part urged caution. The sensation of age radiating from the walls of the house had been joined by loneliness, emptiness and great sorrow. She knew instinctively that someone—or something—had died here, a long time ago.

Why that made a difference, she didn't really know, but it did.

Then, as she hesitated on the lip of the door she saw something move. A sliver of darkness descended from the top of the stairs, followed shortly by another. The slivers became longer, one step at a time, one after the other—until, with a thrill of fear, she realised what they were.

Feet. Followed by legs.

Someone was coming down the stairs.

Frozen in place, she watched in terrified fascination as the occupant of the house descended. She could see waist-high now, more with every step. Definitely male, although in outline only; as the person stepped into the faint light, he remained a shadow—an extrusion of the darkness at the top of the stairs.

Hands appeared—black paws without definition—then the abdomen and chest. No impression of age, nor any sound. Shoulders came next, followed by a neck . . .

She stifled a gasp when his head completed the silhouette. Nothing was visible of his face—no lips, no chin, no ears, hair or nose—apart from his eyes.

The light caught *them*, at least—unblinking, cold-grey, and fixed squarely on her.

I should run now, she thought through a thick fog, *before he gets a good look at me. If it's not too late.*

The shadow reached the bottom of the stairs and continued towards her. Even as it came closer, it remained featureless, faceless. And still she couldn't move.

I'm sorry, she tried to say, *but I thought your house was empty. I only wanted to see inside—*

But the words refused to come. All she could do was watch, frozen, as the shadow reached out a hand to touch her cheek, and uttered one word:

"Misty . . . "

"Oh my God!" Shirelle Parker put her hands over her mouth, bracelets tinkling. "What did you *do*?"

"Turned and ran, of course." Beth giggled, but the humour was forced; the memory of her experience the previous night was still too vivid to have lost the fear associated with it—like a nightmare upon waking, except that she hadn't been dreaming. "He could have been a rapist or a murderer, or anything."

"Or someone sick of being woken up by people wandering into his house at all hours of the night." Shirelle rolled her eyes. "Probably drives him crazy, strange women breaking in all the time—"

"I didn't break in. I told you: the door was unlocked."

"So? You didn't have to open it, did you?"

"But he was waiting for me. He—" She bit her lip.

"He what?"

Beth toyed with her salad and avoided her friend's gaze. She hadn't mentioned the last part of her adventure. Shirelle wouldn't understand.

He called me Misty.

"Nothing."

"Are you sure?" Shirelle eyed her with genuine concern, imagining all manner of unspoken horrors behind her sudden reticence.

"Positive." Beth forced a smile and changed the subject. "We'd better head back soon, hadn't we?"

Shirelle polished off her meal with quick, business-like mouthfuls, and Beth thought the conversation finished. But when the waiter had taken their plates away and they gathered handbags and jackets in preparation for the walk back to the office, Shirelle took her arm in one hand.

"Beth. Promise me you won't go back."

Beth stared at her friend for a long while, knowing the correct response but unable to say it.

"I can't promise that."

"Why not?"

"I just can't, okay?"

"But what if he's a *ghost*?" Shirelle gave the word all the emphasis of someone who had spent too many late nights watching *Nightmare on Elm Street* films.

"So? He might well be."

"Doesn't that frighten you?"

"Of course, but . . . " She hesitated, remembering the shadow's silent approach, the glinting of its eyes, its hand reaching for her face—and the terror that overwhelmed her, like a rabbit caught between headlights. "But if I don't go back, I'll wonder for the rest of my life who or what he was."

"Fine." Shirelle shrugged, flicking long, blonde hair back over her shoulders. "I don't understand you, Beth. You know that?"

"Yes." She smiled openly and patted her friend's hand. "And that makes two of us."

Work was brisk but tedious. Data-processing insurance claims kept her busy for most of the afternoon: an endless stream of meaningless numbers, faceless names and impersonal tragedies. All of it was just background noise for the thoughts and images echoing through her head.

When her extension buzzed at four-fifteen, she dragged herself out of the daze and took the call.

"Beth? It's Simon."

She instantly focussed. Simon was an old friend—and just a friend—currently employed by the planning department of the city's civic council. "How did you get on?"

"Not sure. Let me check I wrote down the address right, first. Seventy-two Burden Street? Is that what you said?"

"That's right. Is there a problem?"

"Sort of. It doesn't exist."

"But—"

"Wait. I know what you're going to say. Your information is partly right. The council changed the name back in '55—nobody remembered the old Captain any more, I guess—so Burden Street *was* real enough. It's the number that must be wrong. What was the date on that death certificate?"

She thought for a moment. Simon was working under the misapprehension that she was researching her family tree, which wasn't so unlikely. Her father had died shortly before her birth, her mother seventeen years later; an only child of two only children, she had never known what it was like to have cousins. Locating distant relatives was something she genuinely planned to do, one day.

"Nineteen-thirty-eight," she improvised, picking the date at random.

"That can't be right."

"Why not?"

"Number seventy-two was subdivided by the local council back in May 1927 and equal halves allocated to each of its neighbours. The house would have been long-gone by '38."

She resisted the impulse to protest—*But I was there*!

—and asked instead: "Why did they subdivide it?"

"Doesn't say." She could hear the shrug in his voice. "Maybe the house fell down, or the neighbours demolished it after they bought the land. It occasionally happens, you know, for extensions or a swimming pool or just for the extra yard. Might be worth checking the old papers for additional information. You never know."

"Thanks, Simon, that's a good idea."

"Always my pleasure, Beth. Oh, and this might help: the name of the final owner was Gerard Maddock. He owned the house from 1902 to when it was sold, or whatever."

"Thanks again." She wrote down the name and date he had given her on a yellow stick-pad, thinking: *Another mystery. Maybe I did dream it.* "I owe you a dinner for all your help."

"Sounds lovely. Let me know if you find your great-aunt, won't you?"

She promised she would, and hung up.

The upper levels of the State Library were surprisingly alive after nightfall, full of students, researchers and the idle curious. A low murmur of conversation battled with the whispering air-conditioning for control of the near-silence, creating a pleasant if slightly soporific atmosphere.

Deeper in the library, however, down where the archival microfilms were kept, the silence was more pervasive, undisturbed for decades. It had settled across the shelves and books like a shroud, invisible but heavy, suffocating even the potential for sound. The clicking of her heels on the scuffed lino echoed like gunshots.

A young librarian showed her how to use the readers and change the films, explaining with an ease that came from obvious experience how the catalogue was arranged by date, month and year, with separate files for *The Advertiser* and *The News*. All very simple, he said, but if she needed any help, he would be only too happy to oblige. She detected a subtle proposition in his patient helpfulness, but politely deflected it.

Another time, she might have said yes, or at least considered it before saying no. Shirelle frequently complained that she should get out more often, and privately she agreed. But there always seemed to be something more important to do, and she'd never really felt confident around strangers—especially men. Books and the occasional film were much safer, and less demanding.

Beth smiled to herself. Anyway, she *was* out, wasn't she? Although this probably wasn't what Shirelle had in mind.

When the librarian had finally gone, she selected April, 1927, and started to browse.

The first thing she noticed was how little the papers had changed in seven decades; *The News* in particular might have been staffed throughout its entire existence by the very same people, only folding in 1992 due to the death of its last surviving reporter.

The headlines were full of the major events of the times, reflecting concerns that she found surprisingly familiar. There were articles about international crises in the post-war world, industrial strikes, sports (especially cricket), shark attacks, mining accidents, exchange-rates, the royal family, elections, and even complaints about Adelaide's drivers.

A few of the headlines caught her eye for their strangeness— "Steals Overcoat: It Was Raining", "Bogged Two Hours In Renmark Street", "Gripped by Water-Snake, Clerk Tells of Narrow Escape"—while others displayed a relish for gore no less blood-thirsty than that of modern times: "Mangled by Trains: Unknown Body Found", "Trapped Between Wall of Flames: Peasants Rush In Terror to the Sea", "Brain Bright Blue: Post Mortem on Miner".

But nowhere did she find a mention of the house on Burden Street, or of its owner, Gerard Maddock.

She persisted, turning to the advertisements for amusement when her attention flagged. What were now the cinema pages had then advertised music recitals and stage plays as well as movies, boasting celebrities she had never heard of. There were classified ads for matrons, maids, Turkish Baths, steam engines, and houses for sale for as little as nine hundred pounds in areas that now begged six figures. Other ads seemed very similar to their modern-day equivalents, peddling clothing, liquors and motoring aids with equally grandiloquent promises.

There were even whole pages devoted to women's issues, which made her smile, remembering her mother.

Marjorie Taylor had hated magazines like *Cleo* and *Cosmopolitan* on the grounds that they forced people of both sexes into artificial moulds. A feminist and free-thinker, she had been an exponent of all things New Age, although the term had not yet come into its own during her heyday. Beth's childhood had been filled with fragile crystals, strange aromas and mysterious herbs. Vegetarianism had been the rule, a habit Beth still adhered to, and hints of psychic phenomena were not unknown; the spirit-world, if there truly existed such a thing, had had a firmer grip on the Taylor household than the twentieth century. But it had been, for the most part, a pleasant upbringing, one full of creativity and fantasy if light on reality.

The recollection of her mother—billowy red hair, brightly-coloured smocks and glittering rings, still vivid even after so long—brought back other memories too, some less welcome.

At the age of five, she had suffered a series of terrifying dreams: of lying in her bed, staring upwards at the ceiling, in which appeared five golden doors. Through the doors, she could hear strange noises and voices calling to her, sometimes pleading, sometimes in anger. She never once moved to open them, afraid of what might come out, of what she might set free. She simply lay curled in her bed, covering her ears with a pillow until the sounds went away or she awoke.

Her mother had expressed dismay that she should be so unwilling to explore the realms offered to her in her dreams. Feeling jealousy, perhaps, she had bewailed the "reluctant mystics of the world, forever blinkered and afraid to open their higher selves to the wonders of the Beyond."

Beth, at the age of five, hadn't understood, and had misheard the word "mystic" for "misty". As the dreams continued and her mother became increasingly frustrated, the nickname stuck. "Reluctant Misty" represented the part of her that had potential access to the unknown, but was too frightened to explore it. Her mother patiently encouraged Misty to open the doors, but without success, and, at the age of six, the dreams stopped. Much to Beth's relief.

But Reluctant Misty remained, resisting her mother's spiritual ways. Upon finishing school, she opted for a practical business career over peddling herbs or Tarot card readings in grotty tent-stalls.

When her mother had died, Reluctant Misty had faded as well. Five years later, Beth had very nearly forgotten her. She had never told anyone about her childhood nick-name, not even Shirelle. And yet—

He called me Misty.

The house on Burden Street was a door, she knew, not unlike the ones that had appeared in her dreams. A promise of mystery, excitement, adventure. What she felt when she thought about it was not fear, exactly, although it was closely related. Morbid curiosity, perhaps, or the fascination felt by a moth for a naked flame.

The adult Beth, locked for so long in a world of insurance claims, was hooked. Reluctant Misty had been absent so long that her influence was weak.

Hours of browsing through the microfilms finally brought her to the Fourth of May, 1917. On page six of *The News*, tucked into the upper right corner, the headline read:

"House Gutted By Freak Blaze: Owner Missing, Feared Dead."

There was a grainy photograph of a house, as it had looked before the fire. It could have been the same one she had visited the previous night.

Heart pounding, she read on:

"An explosion last night in the upper floor of a house on Burden Street, North Adelaide, sent neighbours running for shelter, fearing that a bomb had exploded. Firefighters battled furiously to save the house, but were able only to contain the fire. As a direct result of their valiant efforts, neighbouring buildings were untouched by the blaze, which burnt the house to the ground.

"The cause of the explosion remains a mystery. Examination of the ruins have thus far produced no bodily remains, although police anticipate further evidence to be uncovered in the coming days. The owner of the house, Mr Gerard Maddock, a prominent North Adelaide Spiritualist whose whereabouts are presently unknown, is wanted for questioning regarding the incident."

Flicking through subsequent issues, she found a second article three days later, in which the detective in charge of the Burden St investigation expressed a belief that Gerard Maddock had been a modern-day alchemist or magician, and that the explosion had been caused by an irresponsible chemical experiment. He further asserted that Maddock had died in the blaze, and that his remains had been utterly consumed by the fire.

There were no other articles regarding the fire, nor any announcement of the subdivision of the block. The case had been closed, and public interest had waned.

It burned to the ground, she thought to herself, reading the first article again to make sure she hadn't made a mistake. *But I was there!*

The words she had said to her friend over lunch returned to her, with even greater certainty. Her mother would never forgive her, wherever she was, if she just walked away from this.

When she glanced at her watch, she realised that four hours had passed; the library was due to close soon. She hurriedly returned the microfilms and switched off the reader. On her way from the library, she gently rebuffed the young librarian again by explaining that she had an appointment elsewhere.

Which, she realised only as she said the words, wasn't entirely untrue.

The house was still there. The brass plate by the gate still announced it to be Number 72, Burden St. Now that she was looking, she could see how its neighbours seemed to crowd away from it, as though space had folded back to accommodate an area that had long been overtaken.

A ghost-house, she thought. *Haunting a forgotten street.*

Crossing the lawn, she noticed something else she had missed the previous night: the garden was as dead as the frangipani by the door. Brittle grass crunched beneath her feet, leaving footprints as well-defined as those of the lunar astronauts; every tree was desiccated and grey; even the vine on the sunless sun-dial was lifeless. An ash-garden, preserved in part from the ravages of the fire. Only the house seemed substantial and whole, not likely to crumble to dust at the slightest touch. And the call of the verandah was as strong as ever, tugging her forward into its waiting maw.

The door to the house was open, this time. She stared at it for a moment, clutching the torch she had brought with her, mind churning with conflicting impulses.

Then the shadow stepped into the doorway.

"You left it open," it said, with a voice like that of the library, soft and accustomed to silence, but harsher. "Either close it or come inside. Your choice."

The shadow retreated, blended into the blackness until it was gone.

Don't do it, part of her warned—the part that had once been

Reluctant Misty. *You don't want to know.*

Nonsense, she replied. *My mother lived for this sort of thing, and it never hurt her. I can't turn back now.*

Touching the kitchen-knife she had hidden in her jacket for reassurance—just in case—she stepped forward and through the door. The only concession she made to her fear was to turn on the torch.

The hallway was much the same as it had appeared the previous night, although the beam of light allowed her to see more details: picture rails, wallpaper, plush burgundy carpet and an umbrella stand made of polished pine. The shadow was nowhere to be seen. Gathering courage about her like a cloak, she tiptoed to the nearest door and swung it open.

The room beyond was a study, filled with bookcases. A mahogany writing desk crouched in one corner; two stuffed chairs faced an empty fireplace, unoccupied. Four portraits of people she did not recognise hung on two of the walls. Thick curtains draped the windows, keeping even the barest glimmer of light at bay.

The darkness deepened in the centre of the room, and the shadow reappeared. She swung the torch towards it, half-expecting the beam to pass through unreflected. It didn't, but the light did little to illuminate the figure before her.

The shadow was a man in his mid-thirties, swarthy, unshaven and dressed in rumbled jeans and a polo-necked sweater. His hair was unkempt, and he needed a bath, but otherwise he appeared completely normal. The only odd thing was the way he seemed to absorb the light of the torch: as though he was made of darkness, all the colours of night woven into the shape of a man; as though the light had been leeched out of him. Eyes like the hint of a winter's dawn regarded her implacably.

She sensed sorrow in the presence of the shadow, and a nameless hint of danger.

It waited for her to speak, a look of near-desperation in the set of its brow, but her throat refused to work properly.

"I—I thought . . . "

"What?"

"I thought ghosts, you know, glowed in the dark."

The shadow smiled, perhaps; it was hard to tell. Its face was just a suggestion in the gloom. "They do," it said. "The human soul burns brightly when cut free of the flesh."

"But you—"

"I'm not a ghost," it said, turning away.

"Then what are you?"

"I am an empty vessel, almost. My flame is fading fast. Soon it will die forever."

"Why?"

It ignored the question. "Why are you here?"

"I was curious. The house—"

"Ah, yes. Always the house. Not many people can see it, and of those only a handful ever enter. Seven in as many decades." The shadow walked to the fireplace and stroked the mantelpiece. "Someone tried to destroy it once, you know."

"The fire?"

"Yes." It turned back to her, the torchlight glinting weakly in its eyes. "You've researched the old papers, then. Just like I did."

"I don't understand." The papers were printed after the destruction of the house and Maddock's disappearance. "I thought *you* were the owner."

"Maddock? No." The shadow shook its head. "I'm not his spirit. He had many other safe-houses, over the years, and no doubt his enemies tried to destroy them as well. Why should he return to this one? It wouldn't be for pity's sake, if he did. He might even still be alive, for all I know. Men like him don't die easily."

Beth floundered. Her fear had faded, but she felt far from in control of the conversation. If anything, she was becoming more confused than she had been before. None of this was making sense.

"How did you know about Misty?" she asked, trying to come to grips with why she was here.

"The house told me. It can feel you . . . I guess. I don't know how. It told me someone was coming soon, someone special, different from the rest. I didn't know what to think after waiting so long. I never guessed you'd be so beautiful, so *alive* . . . " The shadow turned to face her, its face a mask of despair. "You should leave."

"No." Startled, she swung the torch into its eyes; they stared back, unblinking. "I want to know who you are, why you're here . . . why you're haunting this house."

"I'm not haunting anything. I'm just here."

"But why?"

"I can't explain," he said, his voice expressing growing urgency. "You must go now. It's not too late."

"Too late for what?"

The shadow didn't answer. It came closer to her, swirling through the beam of the torch like rocks around a lighthouse. Its eyes glittered like tiny chips of diamond. "Leave, Misty, and don't come back. The temptation is already too strong."

She backed away nervously, startled by the sudden shift in conversation, one hand guiding her through the doorway to the study, back into the corridor, the other holding the torch on the shadow, as though the light would keep it at bay. The sensation of danger increased sharply as the shadow followed.

"But—but I want to *know*," she stammered, fighting the fear.

"You don't. You just want to *see*."

A stygian hand pushed her roughly on the shoulder, and she stumbled through the hallway to the front door. There, she gripped the frame desperately and stood her ground.

"I'm not leaving until you tell me who you are."

The shadow began to blur, fading into the darkness that surrounded it, as though her defiance had weakened it. She clutched for its arm, but too late; her fingers groped empty air. As it vanished, she thought she heard it whisper—

"*June Fourth, 1982.*"

—then it was gone.

When she arrived at work the following morning, Shirelle took one look at her and dragged her into the toilets.

"You went back, didn't you?"

Beth looked in the mirror. Her face was pale, her eyes heavy-lidded. She hadn't slept well. The Doors had returned to her dreams, except that this time the little girl afraid of them hadn't been her, but someone else entirely. Someone she had never met. The meaning of the dream eluded her, and nagged at her waking mind.

"Yes."

"Jesus." Shirelle shook her head. "And?"

The words caught in her throat—*I talked to a ghost and it told me I was beautiful. Then it asked me to leave.*

"Beth?" Shirelle leaned closer, peering with concern into her eyes.

"I saw it," she said, and the words blurted out before she could stop them. "The house, I mean. It's not really there, but I can see it. I don't know why. Maybe it's a ghost, too—"

"How can a house be a ghost?" Shirelle stared in disbelief. "Houses aren't alive. They don't die."

Beth shrugged. "This one did. It burned down in 1917."

"So? Plenty of houses burn down—"

"But maybe this one was special. Maybe it's owner—" She faltered, a fragment from the old newspaper article springing from memory:

"... *Mr Gerard Maddock, a prominent North Adelaide Spiritualist ... modern-day alchemist and magician ...*"

"The owner made it live," she concluded, the truth of the words blinding her to her friend. "He gave it a spirit, a soul—for protection or company, or just for the hell of it—and it died while he was away somewhere. And now it's haunting the street, waiting for him to return."

"A haunt*ing* house?" Shirelle shook her head. "Now I've heard it all."

"But it's true." She clutched at her friend's arm. "It has to be. How else do you explain what happened?"

"I don't even *know* what happened, Beth. Maybe you dreamt it."

"No. It was *real*. I *saw* it."

"What about the guy who lives there, Beth? Does he know the place isn't there? Someone should tell him—or his bank manager."

Beth turned away. "You think I'm crazy."

"No, just a little weird." Shirelle put an arm around her shoulders. "And you know what they say about blondes like us."

Anger flared. "I'm not gullible, dammit, and I'm not stupid."

"No, but ... Look, just let it go, okay? Take a deep breath and get on with life. If it *is* a ghost-house, or whatever, then it's none of your business. You've got work to do, remember? A life to live?"

She nodded slowly, although her job was the last thing on her mind at that moment.

Shirelle turned to the mirror, brushed a strand of long, blonde hair back into place. "Reality beckons, Beth. Do you feel up to it?"

"No."

"Good. Let's go."

For the rest of the morning, she found it hard to concentrate. Numbers blurred before her eyes; the keys of the computer weren't where they were supposed to be; mistakes multiplied when she tried to correct them. The image of the house and its resident shade constantly intruded upon her thoughts, pushing everything else aside.

Then, shortly before mid-day, Simon rang.

"I did a little more digging, Beth," he said. "I thought the address might be wrong, no matter what you said, so I checked the neighbours."

"And?" She was in no mood for social niceties. She just wanted to hear what he had to say and get rid of him.

"Well, number seventy has been sold thirty times since the old place was divided—"

"It burned down," she said "There was an explosion."

"That explains that, I guess." He dismissed the explanation: irrelevant. "But number seventy-four has been sold even more often: forty-one owners in seventy years. I have a list of names, if you're interested. Maybe your great-aunt was one of them."

She ignored the offer. "Why did they move?"

"I don't know. I asked around the office, looking for gossip. Someone remembered a girl disappearing in the street about twenty years ago, but I don't know whether it's connected or not. You know, bad memories and all that."

"Probably not," she mumbled, although part of her murmured that it probably was. *A little girl with brown hair and eyes? Another girl frightened of her dreams?* "Look, Simon, I'm sorry. I'm not feeling well today. I'll have to speak to you later."

He took the hint well. "No worries. Call me when you're better."

"I will."

She hung up and stared vacantly at the blank plastic of the receiver. Eventually, she came to a decision.

Pleading an attack of nausea, she left work for the day and went back to the State Library. The lower levels were busier than they had been the night before, and she had to wait an hour for a microfilm reader. The moment one was free, she pulled the papers and began to read.

June Fourth, 1982, the shadow had said. She didn't know what she was looking for, but she knew that if it was there, she'd find it.

She didn't have to look far. The article was on the second page of both papers. *The News* even had a photo.

The headline read: "Reporter Missing."

The photo was of a smiling man with dark hair and bright eyes. Behind the grin, the face was the shadow's.

Eyes widening, she read on:

"Alexander James Caldwell, staff reporter for News Ltd, has today been officially confirmed a Missing Person. Concerns over his absence were raised after his failure to report for work on Monday morning. While details of his final movements are unknown, it is believed he was investigating the case of Rebecca Thompson, aged 7, who disappeared from her home on Sydney Street, North Adelaide, in 1977. Police have not yet ruled out the possibility that Caldwell has fallen victim to foul play. Anyone with information concerning his whereabouts is requested to contact Detective-Sergeant Dan Margarson of Adelaide CIB on . . . "

The eyes of the shadow stared at her from the photo in mute accusation. Alexander James Caldwell hadn't aged a day since his disappearance, over ten years ago.

The *Advertiser* had a different photo, not of Caldwell, but of a little girl with brown hair and wide, innocent eyes. Beth recognised her as the girl from her dreams. The name in the caption was Rebecca Thompson.

Someone tapped her on the shoulder and asked if she'd be long. She blinked and shook her head. She was done.

Burden, or Sydney, Street by day was just another road in North Adelaide: lush trees overhung the road and dropped leaves on imported cars parked along the gutter; iron and brush fences barricaded the well-to-do from idle passers-by; bold silver signs warded unregistered mail from letterboxes. The occasional plane roared overhead, descending along preordained flight-paths to the airport, making the Earth rumble in sympathy.

Number 72 was gone. The neighbouring houses had reclaimed their spaces, reasserted their territorial rights. She could see the neglect in their gardens and walls, in the way paint had peeled and been hastily touched-up. These two houses alone of all those on the street looked uncherished, endured rather than lived-in.

And no wonder, she thought. Anyone with half a brain could feel the missing house lurking on the far side of reality. Its presence was heavy in the air—like a threat of thunderstorms on a humid day. It made Reluctant Misty nervous, although for once she remained silent. Beth was grateful for the peace in her mind; she was edgy enough without voices from the past nagging at her.

She sat restlessly in the car, waiting for the house to reappear, occasionally walking to the nearest deli for a bite to eat or to use their toilet. She bought a magazine and settled down for the afternoon, only moving the car once when a parking inspector scowled at her for occupying a two-hour parking space for so long.

Exactly when she fell asleep, she didn't know, but the dream woke her with a start several hours later. The Doors had been opening of their own accord, and the little girl had been screaming; the fact that the girl had name now—Rebecca Thompson, not

Misty—hadn't dulled the fear. She glanced guiltily at her watch, then out of the window and across the road.

Night had fallen, and the house was back.

Clutching the torch in one hand and making sure the knife was still in her jacket, she climbed out of the car and stretched her legs. The house watched her from beyond its wrought-iron fence. She could feel its presence strongly now: a deep, engulfing pit of sorrow and yearning. When she closed her eyes, the pit seemed to pull her forward, like a gaping, black well.

She wondered what people would see if they caught her entering the ghostly yard. Would she simply vanish into thin air, as though she had crossed an invisible boundary? Or would she fade away, like the shadow of Alexander Caldwell, gradually merging with the darkness until she disappeared?

Reluctant Misty stirred in protest, finding her voice at last. *This is insane!* she cried. *I can't be doing this!*

But she was. She needed to confront her fear and wrestle it under her control, or else she would be tormented by nightmares and uncertainty for the rest of her life.

Her legs carried her across the road, to the gate and across the lawn. This, the third time she had completed the short journey, was by far the least terrifying. The territory was becoming familiar.

Really making myself at home, she mused, but without humour.

The door was still open. She edged through it, torch first, sweeping the empty hallway.

"I know your name, now," she called. "I know who you are."

Only silence answered, as thick cotton wool in her ears.

She stepped deeper into the house. "You're Alexander James Caldwell and you used to work for *The News*. You disappeared in 1982. Have you been living here ever since? Inside the house?"

The reply came from all around her, as though the house itself had spoken:

"Yes."

"Why don't you leave?"

"Because I can't."

"Why not?"

The shadow remained silent. She swung the torch around her again, but still could see no sign of it. *Him?* She found it hard to think of Caldwell as a living person. He looked so drained, so unnaturally dark.

As though he had read her thoughts, the shadow spoke again:

"If I leave, the house will die. It needs my life, my light, to manifest itself."

"I don't understand." The voice was closer than it had been, but she still couldn't locate its source. Shadows moved all around her, but none of them contained the one she sought.

"You will. It's too late to turn back now. You've found what you sought, and it has found you."

The chill in Caldwell's voice made her hesitate, but she forced her voice to remain steady. "I'm just curious, that's all. Not looking for anything, really. But what about you? You were looking for Rebecca Thompson. Did you find her?"

The door slammed shut behind her, and she half-screamed in surprise.

"Yes," said Caldwell, stepping out of the shadows by the door. "I found her."

She backed away, reaching for the knife. His face and posture, even though shrouded in darkness, were menacing.

"She used to play here," said the shadow, "when she was young and Old Man Dennis was the tenant, the host. She could see the house, and enjoyed having a playground nobody else could visit. The house let her come and go as she pleased, until the Old Man died and ... " The shadow faltered, its face radiating grief. "I found her five years later. She'd been trapped here all that time—just a child, not really understanding what was going on. It was horrible, seeing her fading away, withering on the inside, so I ... "

"You what?"

"I killed her. I had to."

She made a dash for the door, but he lunged at her, arms outstretched. She retreated out of his reach, bringing out the knife. "Don't—"

Bat-like wings of darkness swirled in the air as he dodged to his left and circled her.

"I warned you," he said. "I told you not to come back. But you wouldn't listen. Even when you knew about Rebecca and me, you still came back. It won't let you go, now. You were dead the moment you walked in the door, either way."

She opened her mouth to protest, but the words died mid-way as from far above came the sound of shattering glass. The floor beneath her feet trembled. Flames sprang into life along the walls and ceiling, illuminating the hallway with a flickering, red-limned light.

But there was no heat, no smoke. Only her, Caldwell and the knife.

"Don't try to kill me," he said. "You'll regret it."

He lunged again and she slashed the knife across his outstretched arm. The blade parted the shadowy flesh without the slightest resistance. Caldwell winced but kept coming.

"Keep back," she moaned, holding the knife in both trembling hands in front of her. "I mean it. I really do."

"So do I." He laughed bitterly, with a hysterical edge; he seemed on the verge of tears. "The house has finished with me, bled me dry. It wants you to take my place, just as I replaced Rebecca. But if I kill you now, then you'll only die, and the house will have to find someone else. Maybe I'll die before it can, and it'll die with me. That's worth hoping for, isn't it? Please believe me, Misty—I'm doing this for all of us—and for the ones who follow—"

The flames roared more fiercely, spreading down the walls and drowning out the rest of his words. Falling cinders fluttered down from the ceiling, drifting erratically to the floor where smaller fires sprung into life.

Caldwell inched closer, waiting for the weaving blade to give him an opening.

She backed away from him, desperately looking for another way out. But all the doors were locked, and Misty was screaming inside her head, making it hard to think.

Then her heel struck the lowest step of the burning stairway, and she fell backwards.

Caldwell leapt, enfolding her with limbs of smoky darkness. She struggled, but he was too strong and his fading flesh defied her grip. Shadowy hands clutched for her throat, began to squeeze the air from her. She screamed silently, kicked, hammered with the handle of the knife, tried everything she could to squirm free.

The hands tightened. Black spots marred her vision, dancing across the shadow's lightless face, grimacing barely inches from hers.

Summoning the last of her rapidly-fading strength, she wrenched her arms free and stabbed the knife *hard* into his stomach, tugging the blade upwards until it struck bone.

Caldwell gasped in pain and let go of her throat. He tottered backwards two steps and collapsed, arms clutching his midriff.

Around him, the fire burned a triumphant yellow-white shot with flecks of red, licking the walls and tasting the carpet beneath her feet.

She threw the knife away, revolted by the cold, dark blood on her fingers.

Oh my God—I killed him!

Weeping in horror, she clambered to her feet and staggered to where Caldwell lay. Self-loathing threatened to make her vomit and the pain in her wind-pipe was choking her, but she couldn't turn her eyes away from what she had done.

He writhed on the floor in silent agony, his throes becoming more feeble with every passing second, his face twisted into a ghastly parody of a smile.

The ghost-fire raged around them, consuming the very bones of the building. The house, perhaps in sympathy, was reliving its own death.

"I'm sorry," he gasped, his voice thick with dark blood. " . . . should have listened . . . couldn't . . . "

The fire gathered around him, sucking the last of the light from his body. His spine curved in one final spasm, and his face clenched like a fist.

Then he was gone.

She was alone in the house.

For the first time, she could feel it reaching for her through the sparks and flames, clutching at her mind like a hand groping from the grave. Too late, she turned to run for the door.

The ceiling collapsed, burying her under all the fire and despair that had gathered for decades on the rotting corpse of the house.

Darkness fell, and she fell with it.

And when she awoke, the house was empty.

She sat by the window, watching the darkness outside. Time passed, but she hardly noticed. Her watch had stopped, and the sun never visited the timeless space of the house on Burden Street. There was no way to mark the passage of the hours, days or weeks, or years, of her confinement. A thorough search of the house had quickly demonstrated the futility of trying to escape: every door and window was locked shut; even the chimney was sealed. And outside the window was nothing at all. There was nowhere to escape to, even if she *could* get out.

There was only the house—all around her, a living thing. Occasionally it whispered to her, but not in words. She received images of people—Caldwell most clearly, the girl called Rebecca Thompson, and five others she did not recognise. One of the strongest images was of a tall, ageless man with black hair and gaunt, almost hollow features. This figure alone came with a name:

Madoc. The original owner of the house, the man who had given it life in return for faithful service. Who had lived in Adelaide as Gerard Maddock, and under a multitude of other names elsewhere.

The house was like a dog, she realised. A guard-dog patiently waiting for its master to release it from service. A dog that could summon people from the world that had rejected it.

She could feel it watching her, feeding off her, sucking the light from her soul in order to extend its unnatural existence. There was nothing she could do, except die slowly.

You didn't listen, whispered the voice of Reluctant Misty into the all-pervading silence. *You opened the door, which was bad enough. You didn't have to go through, but you did. And now you can't go back—because you didn't listen!*

Empty of tears, Beth sat at the window.

Waiting.

•

INTRODUCTION TO:
.... THE GIRL-THING

Several of my stories and novels rely heavily on crime fiction, blended with either SF or horror. I am most definitely what I eat, in that regard—the three genres accurately represent my preferred reading habits—and a wonderful diet it is, too. Rob Sawyer once sagely remarked of the crossover between science fiction and crime that: "not only is it an easy crossover, but it's a natural one. Science fiction and mystery have a great deal in common." In addition to using mystery as a narrative hook, both science fiction and crime explore the issues of truth and identity in a way that other genres are sometimes reluctant or unable to do.

I've always wanted to write a straight crime story, sans monsters or high-tech gadgets. This isn't one of them. It's most definitely a horror story, even if it wears its colours under its sleeve. It's not easy creating new monsters, and it's not often I write an ending where I definitely do not want to know what happens next, but I like to think that with this story I managed both.

I talk elsewhere in this collection about my short-story drought that spanned the dawning of the new millennium. "The Girl-Thing" was the last story I wrote before the lean years began. It was a bitter-sweet experience for me, because even as I wrote it I knew that it would be my last for a while. And to rub salt into the wound, I thought I'd never written a story quite so well. I feared that I might be making a terrible mistake by giving the habit up.

Earning money so you can eat is never a mistake. Neither is meeting your contractual obligations. At the time I was juggling three very different series with hard deadlines every three months, and naturally that took priority. So perhaps the knowledge that I had to make this last effort count made me invest more in it and try harder to do something different. I regard it now as one of my more determinedly mainstream stories, right up until the denouement, when I hope that my true intentions—and those of the dreadful Girl-Thing—become clear.

•

THE GIRL-THING

The display lacked cohesion. That was the thought running through Senior Constable Weylin Hollister's mind as he waited for his partner, Jane Moir, to finish interviewing the proprietor of the porn shop. Everywhere he looked he saw disembodied penises and vaginas, or their substitutes: lines of odd knobs and holes with unlikely attachments, like exhibits from a museum of alien genitalia. It couldn't be an easy place to shop, he thought, even disregarding the awkwardness most people would feel coming into such an establishment.

Had he been the manager, he would have put dildos up front; they seemed designed to catch the eye, and would naturally segue into butt-plugs and vibrators along the shop's inner wall. On the other side he would put the magazines and videos, since there was no way their covers would ever blend. Artificial vaginas, lubes, whips, and novelty items were space-fillers, perfect for taking up less intrusive rack space. Bondage costumes and lingerie always looked best above eye-level or in dead corners, where their fantastic natures were suitably framed.

But that was just Hollister's opinion. The proprietor, Aram, a middle-aged, naturalized Iranian who had enough sense to run the business from out the back and put uni student types behind the front counter, obviously disagreed. Maybe his clientele didn't care either.

"Was anything stolen?" Senior Constable Moir was asking him, taking notes. A solid woman in her fifties, twenty years Hollister's senior, she looked the same regardless of her surroundings. The simple practicality of her brown overcoat was as at home in a porn shop as in the Polson Street Station.

"Nothing worth claiming," said Aram.

"You won't put in an insurance claim?"

"For the damage, yes; locks aren't cheap. But the stock . . . " He shrugged. "It's okay. A bit of mess; not hard to clean up."

"So nothing at all was actually stolen?" she repeated, for clarification. Hollister had noted too that Aram hadn't answered the question.

"Just one thing." He shifted a gray-clad buttock from the corner of the counter and indicated that they should follow him deeper into the shop. His left leg was stiff and gave him a slight limp. Half-way along the jumble he stopped and pointed at a relatively large box at eye-level. The box boasted Wet-End Wendy, a surgically enhanced blonde in little more than a pout. Bright colors contrasted sharply with not-quite-real flesh tones in a way guaranteed to unnerve.

"We lost one of these."

"A blow-up doll?"

"What do you think? Real girls don't come in boxes." Aram limped off with a grimace. "Unfortunately."

Moir gravely wrote the name in her notebook while Hollister watched from a few feet away. Thus far they had only confirmed the statement Aram had given the previous day, apart from the doll, but she was treating it as seriously as if the information was fresh. Perhaps she was seeing something Hollister wasn't.

"Do you think this connects?" he asked.

"I don't know, Wey." She looked up. "Aram is clear on how he thinks it happened." Two nights ago, the last person out of the shop had forgotten to activate the alarm behind them, leaving the premises unsecured for an hour. In that time, it was broken into. "The thief must've been watching to know it was safe to force the back door—but why take only a doll? Why not the money in the till, or at least spray some paint around?"

Hollister didn't bother questioning whether Aram knew his stock. With shop-lifting and staff pilfering an ever-present threat, everyone on Polson Street knew precisely what their shelves contained. He imagined him lying awake, counting Ben Wa balls to get to sleep.

"Why indeed?" He wiped the dust off a display toilet, made out of clear perspex. "But I don't think we're going to find anything new here, Jane."

"I agree, now. It was worth looking, though."

While Moir wrapped up the interview, Hollister stretched his legs outside, under the flashing SEXXX-O-RAMA sign. Polson Street cut like an arrow through the rotten heart of Amberley Park. The usual crowd of tourists and locals rushed past him. Few of them looked up, intent on errands or avoiding catching someone else's eye. He recognized a number of faces: mostly the workers, dealers and users who prowled Polson Street at all hours. He had thought them soulless creatures at first, predators and prey engaged in a dance of mutual destruction as old as history. Only gradually, over a year working the street, had he learned compassion. Each was an individual, a real person caught up in a dangerous game. If some of them did end up dead on the inside, that was the game's fault, not theirs. They were all victims.

He watched each and every one of the faces passing him, thinking: *And one of you could be a serial killer.* The Amberley Slayer was still at large, and he was known to be a local. Was he be the smart-dressed businessman on his way back from lunch—or the slouching neo-punk trying to get into a strip joint for free? The killer could be any one of the many around him, for all Hollister knew. *You may think your game is different to the others here*, he thought, *but it's not. It'll get you in the end. It's only a matter of time.* Or so he hoped.

A motionless figure on the other side of the road caught his attention. Beady, black eyes stared at him from beneath a battered, orange bicycle helmet. Curly gray hair grew in wild profusion across the old man's face and out the collar of a patched Salvation Army great-coat. A tatty brown satchel hung over one shoulder, pressed close against his side. His hands were stuck firmly in the pockets of many-holed tracksuit pants, but Hollister could see his fingers moving restlessly, as though rummaging through change. His lips matched the cadence of his fingers, although the words he uttered were inaudible over the passing traffic.

Hollister acknowledged the man's stare with a polite nod. His was a familiar face, although Hollister had never noticed his eyes before. They were more alert than he would've expected. The other weirdoes wandering the streets tended to look away when confronted, like everyone else, but more as though the real world didn't exist for them than because they were pretending to have other things to do.

Hollister waited for a gap in the traffic, then stepped off the curb.

"Where do you think you're going?" The shop door jingled shut behind Moir.

Hollister indicated the old man on the other side of the road, who had turned aside and started walking away. "I thought I'd talk to him."

"Old Jellyhead? I doubt he can help us."

"The kid who was working that night says he didn't see anyone unusual hanging around the shop. What if he saw someone *usual* and forgot about it?"

"The usuals around here would've taken the money for sure." Moir indicated that Hollister should come with her. "Save yourself the bother, Wey. We've got better things to do with our time."

Hollister watched the old man shuffle down the street. Moir had been on Polson Street a lot longer than him, and the fact that she knew the old guy's nickname added credence to what she said. But he couldn't help feeling as though they were letting something slip. "He might've seen something."

"Even if he did, it'd never stand up in court. We've tried before." Her blue eyes studied him closely. Then she sighed. "But if you really want to . . . "

"Back in a sec." Hollister dodged through the traffic to the other side of the road. Jellyhead had reached a corner and turned down a side street as he approached. Hollister caught a whiff of sweat and excrement as he put a hand on the old man's shoulder.

"Excuse me."

The bearded face tilted up to look at him. Hollister was surprised at the disparity between their heights. Jellyhead was barely as tall as Moir, whom he had never thought of as short before.

"She cries," the old man said.

"I'm sorry?" Jellyhead's eyes, unlike before, were vague, unrecognizing, seeming to look through Hollister and at the brickwork behind him. But his speech was calm and precise, as though continuing a conversation Hollister had forgotten starting.

"She is impatient."

"I was wondering," Hollister said, forging on regardless, "if I could ask you about the night of the twenty-fifth. That's two nights ago. One of the shops up there"—he pointed back the way they had come—"was broken into. Something was stolen, and we'd really like to find out who did it. I don't suppose you saw anything?"

"She doesn't want to be hard." The rheumy old eyes filled with water. For a moment Hollister thought the old man might burst into tears. "She does what she has to do."

"I don't understand. *Did* you see something? Do you know someone who might have?"

"She doesn't like the darkness."

The old man broke eye contact and turned to shuffle off down the street. Hollister gave in and let him go. Whoever the old man was talking to, it wasn't him.

"Hassling old crazies will get us nowhere," Moir said as they walked back to the station. "He's not hurting anyone. Best to leave him alone."

Hollister had no reason to disagree, but the tears in the old man's eyes—tears not of sadness but desperation—haunted him the rest of the day.

His wife's voice brought him abruptly out of sleep that night:

"He'll need the bones before he's done."

He opened his eyes groggily in the darkness. "What, Arna?"

She didn't answer. The night was silent and still. Angry at himself for letting himself being woken up like that, he rolled onto his side and tried to get back to sleep.

Thoughts of the latest murder surfaced, unbidden and unwanted. The news had come through that afternoon, after his encounter with Jellyhead, and the worst thing about it was that no-one had been truly surprised. Even Moir had looked resigned. The Slayer was like an unstoppable, invisible disease, killing cell by cell while the rest of the body looked on in horror. Dozens of detectives were working the case, but as yet no-one had been arrested; no suspects had been named. It was a waiting game at worst, and a praying game at best. Hollister envied no-one involved. It was bad enough on the outside looking in.

During the last year, he had lost contact with some of his old friends in forensics, but he heard enough. The killer targeted young, vulnerable women, usually addicts and prostitutes in the Polson Street area. One had been a day-tripper in the wrong place at the wrong time. All had piercings, which the killer took as souvenirs after he'd finished with them. The media knew about the rings and studs, but they didn't know all of it. The killer was also in the habit of taking his victims' tattoos.

"We thinking he's curing the skin," said one of Hollister's contacts. "Preserving it. God knows why. Maybe he turns them into lampshades . . . "

Hollister lay awake in the darkness, imagining the killer's living room, mottled with shadowy roses, Celtic crosses and cobwebs, and shuddered.

He'd half-expected it—any sex-related crime prompted connections to the Amberley Slayings, no matter how tenuous—but the call into Superintendent Leonie Penglis' upper-floor office the next day filled him with foreboding.

"Jane told me about your idea," she said, not bothering to get up.

"It's not our case," said Moir. She was sitting with her back to the window, to the view of cheap hotels, garish shop-fronts and closed restaurants stretching into the distance. Her face was in shadow, and Hollister couldn't tell if she was annoyed or not. "We have better things to do than go shooting at shadows."

"Do you think it's just shadows, Senior Constable Hollister?"

"It could be," he said, as diplomatically as he could.

"Well, I think the idea has some merit. Look into it, would you?"

So they went back out onto the streets, hunting for the crazies. At first they strolled at random, seeking just one of their new "suspects". They asked around, paying particular attention to bottle shops and bus shelters. No-one could remember seeing Jellyhead or any of the others that day. No-one knew anything about them, either. Who they were, where they came from, and what they did was all a mystery. They were background figures, drifting into focus on odd occasions but never viewed close up. They were, Hollister thought, very much like ghosts.

"This is getting us nowhere," Moir said over a sandwich lunch, resting on a park bench.

Hollister agreed, although he didn't say so. It was bad enough to have suggested the pointless plan in the first place. He felt awkward disturbing people who had obviously gone to extreme lengths to avoid society. What right did he have to drag them back into it? And maybe that, he thought, was why the crazies were hard to find that day. They could sense his and Moir's intentions on some psychic grapevine and kept their heads down accordingly. Who was he to bother them?

Or maybe it was just the expression in Jellyhead's eyes; he didn't want to probe any deeper into that sadness.

"You're quiet today," Moir said.

"I didn't sleep well." His lunch tasted like ashes in his mouth.

"Bad dreams?"

"Kind of." He wrapped up the rest of the food and tossed it into a bin. "I'm sorry about this, Jane."

"You have nothing to apologize for, Wey. You know that."

"I mean today."

"Well . . . " She shrugged helplessly. "At least it's keeping us outside. We can work on our tans, from the neck up."

They tried a number of charity groups that afternoon, and managed to track down a couple of tired old men with cheap alcohol on their breaths. They didn't know anything about the break-ins, but showed a morbid interest in the murders. One expressed a firm opinion that the victims deserved what they got for walking around the streets at night on their own, dressed like prostitutes.

"Some of them *were* prostitutes," Moir said.

"There you are. Asking for it, they were."

"No-one asks to be murdered."

"Not out loud, no . . . " The toothless alcoholic cackled at them as they left.

They were running out of options, and their feet were getting sore. Their last port of call was a homeless shelter in Reyes Hill run by a tired-looking social worker named Ellard Trenorden, a man so scruffy he looked on the verge of becoming one of his own charges. Hollister had spoken to him a couple of times before, pursuing more everyday matters, but had never warmed to him.

"We get a few of the older ones through here every now and again," Trenorden said. "Not as often as you'd expect, though, unless one of them gets sick or beaten up."

"Do you know here they live?" Moir asked.

"Me? No. But Cloe might. She's made contact with a couple of them."

"Is Cloe in today?"

"I'll see if she's free."

Cloe Flavell was in her late twenties and pale to the point of vanishing. Her office was just as bland, the only feature being a bright red coat draped over a chair.

"I know who you mean," she said in response to their queries. "Some come of them here to see me; they know I'll listen. They're deeply traumatized individuals, often with serious and untreated psychiatric problems."

"Psychosis?" Moir asked.

"In the clinical sense, yes. But none of them is the Amberley Slayer."

"Can you be certain of that?"

"Well, for one thing, few of them bathe, and murder is bloody work. They'd be wearing the evidence for weeks."

Hollister was surprised by the frankness of her words. Moir simply acknowledged the point with a nod. "How would you rate their reliability as witnesses?"

"Poor." Flavell didn't seemed surprised by the question. "They have their own support mechanisms and are quite independent of the world you or I take for granted. It wouldn't matter that you were from the police. I know one old guy who would lie on principle."

"The one called Jellyhead?" asked Hollister.

She winced slightly. "Why are you asking me these questions? Has he done anything wrong?"

"Do you think he might have?"

"No, but . . . " Her pupils danced in sharp diagonal streaks: up-left, down-right, then centered on him. "He isn't a liar, although he can be a bit off-putting. Some people say they find him creepy."

Moir leaned forward. "Why?"

"I'm not really supposed to talk about things like this." She glanced at the door that time, as though worried that her supervisor might burst in at any moment.

"This is purely off the record," Moir assured her. She gave Flavell the now-familiar line about the porn shop break-in. "Our superintendent wants us to look for a reliable witness no-one around here would notice, or care about if they did notice. We don't really think your clients are serial killers, just that they might have seen one in action—but if you're saying that one of your clients *is* capable of—"

"No, it's not that. Not that at all." Flavell shook her head almost too hard. Hollister was afraid her blonde bob might slide off in one piece. "I'm sure none of them have done anything like that."

"Do you know where they live?"

Another shake. "Hardly any of them have homes. Some go from shelter to shelter, or sleep wherever they can find cover. One has a spot in a dead line near here—"

"A what?" interrupted Hollister.

"Train line. A tunnel. The city is riddled with old spaces no-one cares about any more."

"It sounds just perfect, then."

"Maybe it is, but that's not *their* fault." A slight flush came to her cheeks—the first real sign of life her face had shown.

"I'm sorry. I didn't mean it that way." He was genuinely contrite. "I feel as sorry as for these old guys as you do."

"I doubt that."

"It must be awful living with no money, no home—alone . . . "

Her gaze danced away. "Well, some of them choose to, of course, in their own way. It's a means of escaping, of letting go. In many ways, they're more free than we will ever be. There are people—not me—who like to think of them as our last surviving mystics: dreamers who don't fit into modern society, reviled channellers permanently in contact with realms we can no longer experience."

The expression on her face belied her words: part of her did want to believe that the old men in her care were worth something to the world around them, even if the world didn't recognize them for what they were. Before he could say anything, though, Moir stifled a yawn and leaned back into the conversation.

"It's after five, Ms Flavell, and we don't want to keep you. Do you think you could ask your clients on our behalf if they've seen anything odd in the last few days?"

She still looked reluctant. "I suppose I could, if you think it might help catch the Slayer."

"You never know. Here's our card."

They let themselves out of her office. Hollister was already looking forward to putting his feet up at the station when, on their way past the shelter's reception, a young man waved them over.

"I heard what you were talking about," he said, whispering as a group of teenagers burst through the door and headed past them to a back room. "I have the office next to Cloe. We started at the same time. She really cares about the old ones, but . . . "

"But what?" Moir was starting to look more interested than irritated.

"Cloe is an idealist. She thinks she can help anyone, even when they can't be helped; you can only try to stop them from hurting themselves, and other people. She doesn't see what we see."

"What *do* you see?"

He paused and looked around. "They're not stupid, these men. They use her to get vouchers for accommodation, food, prescription drugs. She gives them the benefit of the doubt, and they walk all over her."

Hollister nodded, although he thought Cloe Flavell seemed competent enough, not so easily swayed. "Anyone in particular?"

"There's one. He comes here a lot, more than we like to encourage, and asks specifically for her. We're so busy here so she can't always see him, but he waits around anyway. He's always lurking about, watching her. It's spooky."

"You've never said anything about this to her?"

"She thinks I'm imagining things."

Maybe he was, Hollister thought. "Do you think he's stalking her?" Moir asked.

"Well, no, but . . . " His expression darkened as though internally he changed gears, from office gossip to real concern. "There *was* this one time. I was talking to Cloe about another client and he was standing behind her. He was staring at her—just her, not me, even though our eyes were almost meeting. It was like I didn't exist. Anyway, when Cloe and I were finished, someone else came up to talk to her and I went to my office. I looked back before I went in and saw this old guy walk up the hallway toward me, as if he'd given up waiting and was going to leave. As he went past Cloe, he reached out and took something from her shoulder."

"Took what, exactly?"

"A hair. She didn't notice. Jellyhead—she doesn't like him being called that, but that's who it was—put the hand with the hair into his pocket and kept walking. If he saw me looking, he didn't say anything as he went past, and I was too surprised to say anything just then. I mean, who steal hairs?"

Moir glanced at Hollister. "I don't know, um, mister . . . ?"

"Harris. Dale Harris."

"I don't know, Dale," she repeated, "but thanks for telling us about it."

He looked relieved. "I thought you ought to know—if only so you realize that Cloe is sometimes a little *too* forgiving."

"We understand." Moir gave him a card. "Let us know if anything else happens, won't you?"

"I will." He nodded eagerly. "I will."

"Maybe he's just got a crush on her," Hollister said when they were back out in the fresh air.

"Who? Harris or Jellyhead?"

"Both of them." Moir smiled. "I meant Jellyhead."

"But he couldn't be the Amberley Slayer."

"Almost certainly not, but he'll look good on paper. At least we

can tell Penglis we've found *something*. And we'll spread the word
to keep an eye out for him. If we can get a handle on him, maybe
he'll talk to us. He might be worth investing in for the future. You
never know when he'll come in handy."

The thought of recruiting a senile old man in a bicycle helmet as
a spy on the Polson Street underworld struck Hollister as ludicrous,
but that, he supposed, was the point. The street-walkers were
detritus, quite literally: pieces of society rubbed away by repeated
stress. Few people noticed them, let alone cared about them—
and for that reason he found himself understanding Cloe Flavell's
blindness. Someone had to look after them, whatever they did. If
not her, then who? That it might not be anyone at all was more than
a little saddening. There was nothing worse than being alone.

But the possibility that Jellyhead might be a predator, if only
emotionally, wasn't itself ridiculous. Just because he was old and
infirm didn't automatically make him benign.

Arna woke him again that night.

He had come home from work physically drained. Armed with
leftovers and the remote control, he had collapsed onto a couch and
watched TV until exhaustion took him. The last thing he recalled
seeing was a documentary about legendary 1950s pianist, Renaud Le
Huy, and the premier performance of von Doussa's "Devil's Hand"
Scherzo that had almost cost him his career. A scherzo was normally
a light, jocular piece of music—but not this one. The final moments
demanded an increasingly frenetic style, hammering at the keys with
no pedal; its climax culminated in the performer kicking back the
stool and violently striking the lower half of the keyboard with a
single clenched fist. The theatrics were specifically called for in the
score, and Le Huy obeyed them to the letter. As the echoes of his final
blow faded, he stalked silently off-stage "like a little storm cloud",
according to one reviewer.

The crowd waited for Le Huy to return for a bow, but he did
not, and he failed to return after interval. Instead, the organizers
of the concert appeared on stage to announce that the pianist had
broken three fingers in his right hand and was unable to continue
the performance. Le Huy's reputation as a hot-headed genius was
thereby firmly established, even though it meant missing several
months of lucrative touring as a result.

Hollister missed that sort of passion. It ached in him like a hole.
As he dragged himself to bed, he wondered if that was how Jellyhead

felt every day of his life. Was that what the old man thought of when he looked at Cloe Flavell—at the young, bright things who walked along Polson Street, carefully pretending not to see him? Maybe that was who he had been talking to when Hollister had approached him: some lost wife, a long-gone love.

Hollister didn't know how he stood it—or how Cloe Flavell endured that dreadful yearning in his eyes, day after day.

"It's a girl-thing," Arna told him that night, speaking out of sleep with such impossible clarity it made him start awake. "It's too dark in here."

The echo of the old man's words sent a chill down his spine even as he turned on the light to banish them.

He and Moir were back to normal desk duties the next day, so at least he had coffee at hand to wipe away the effects of another broken sleep. Mid-morning, his contact in forensics brought him up to date on the hunt for the Amberley Slayer. The latest victim was a girl in her late teens. Her body exhibited the usual wounds, no more or less severe than usual. As an aside, Hollister endured the story, for the fourth time, about the eighth victim, a woman as tattooed as a road map. She had been skinned alive before being suffocated in a plastic bag and dumped in a sewer.

Identified by the place a tattoo had once been and a birthmark under her left armpit, the latest victim turned out to be a homeless girl last seen by her mother two years earlier. On the surface of it, there was nothing to suggest that she was any different to the others, but Hollister's contact ended with a rumor that the Amberley Slayer might have made a mistake, this time. The detectives working on the case were excited, he said, as though they were getting close. He didn't know who or what to, but something was building to a head.

When Hollister hung up the phone, he felt a maudlin mood creeping over him. Everything was out of kilter. The dead girl had been just beginning her life; Jellyhead's was in its final stages. Yet she was dead and he wasn't. Would a killer of useless old men gain the same media coverage as the Amberley Slayer? He doubted it. And not all killers of young women were punished . . .

At least it would be over soon, if Hollister's contact was right.

"Expect an announcement soon," he had said, as though foretelling a royal birth.

A patrol brought Jellyhead in that afternoon. Hollister and Moir were summoned by the desk sergeant as soon as his identity became known. Their all-patrols notice had only gone out that morning; neither had expected it to produce such instant results.

Hollister took the short distance almost at a run. Sure enough, there he was, with helmet slightly askew and one arm held by a brawny constable who looked glad to see his two superiors.

"We caught him coming out of the toilets on Crowe," he explained. In his other hand he held Jellyhead's dirty cloth satchel. "You might want to look in here."

"She cries," the old man said. The words still didn't make sense, but the police around him certainly had his attention. He looked nervous, fidgety. He clearly wanted the satchel back, but didn't resist when they put him in an interview room without it.

They examined the satchel in the room next door. It stank of sweat and feces, the same mix Hollister remembered from their first encounter, but worse. It was inconceivable that anything could smell so bad.

Moir used a pen to open the flap of the satchel. Hollister procured a pair of plastic gloves and probed deeper. The satchel contained some rags or old clothes, a couple of items of cheap jewelry, and a number of sealed plastic bags large enough to hold a sandwich or an apple.

"Jesus," said Moir. "Is that what I think it is?"

One bag was filled with used tampons and sanitary napkins, dark brown in color. Another contained what looked like feces. A third was half-full of a clear yellowish fluid. The rest contained hairs, nail clippings and gray dust.

"You say you caught him coming out of the Crowe Street toilets," Hollister asked the pale-faced constable who had brought Jellyhead in. "The female side, I presume?"

A nod. "We've seen him around there before, but never really thought anything of it. We watched him this time, as you said we should, thinking he might be looking for a rendezvous or something, as unlikely as that seems. He just waited until he thought we weren't looking then went in. Into the female toilets."

"And you went in after him?"

"Yes. We caught him levering open one of the sanitary bins."

"The toilets were empty at the time?"

The constable looked nervous, as though worried Hollister might accuse him of doing something wrong. "We didn't check before we went in, but yes, they were."

Hollister nodded. "That's what he was waiting for, then. He's scavenging, not perving or stalking."

"Not today, anyway." Past the mask of Moir's face, Hollister could see her jaw working. "Let's see what *he's* got to say, shall we?"

Old Jellyhead looked up when they entered the room. His eyes tracked normally as they took seats opposite him, across the narrow desk. Hollister saw nothing but fear in them, although his smell was as vile as the bag's.

"She'll be angry," the old man said.

"Who will be?" Hollister asked.

"She will *be*." There was an odd emphasis to Jellyhead's reply that suggested he was answering a very different question.

"What were you doing in the toilets?" Moir asked.

The old man looked at her, and Hollister was released from his stare. He hadn't realized until then how intense it was.

"She needs me."

"Don't stuff me around. Answer the question, please. I haven't got time to sit here all day."

"She can't do it on her own. I have to do it for her."

Hollister wondered if the use of the first person pronoun counted as progress. "Do what?"

"She's trying to come through. I don't know where from. She's there, and she wants to be here. She doesn't say why. She just says *what*. She found the way. She needs me. She can't do it on her own. She's impatient. She cries. She does what she has to do."

Hollister recognized a repeat of what the old man had already told him, the first time they had met. He scribbled a note saying that he was going to call Cloe Flavell and stood up.

Moir shot him a look as he left the room, as though she thought he was using the social worker as an excuse to get some fresh air but was more annoyed by not thinking of it first.

Flavell came instantly, dressed in the bright red coat Hollister had noticed in her office the day before. It made her look more alive, as though her skin had absorbed some of its color. Hollister met her at the desk and took her through.

"He's not making a lot of sense, I'm afraid."

"He wouldn't," she said, her tone scolding. Her eyes were as restless as ever, nervous. "He's a sick old man. You've probably scared him half to death."

When he explained where the old man had been picked up, her lips tightened and she lost some of her coat's reflected vitality.

"Did you steal those clothes?" Moir was asking when Hollister let her into the interview room. Some of the bag's contents had been brought into the room and lay spread across the table. One was a woman's blouse.

"She will be cold." Jellyhead looked up at Flavell as though begging her to explain for him. If she understood, though, she didn't show it.

"What are you doing here, Mister Emes?" Flavell asked, crossing the room to stand next to him. "They tell me you were caught in a woman's toilet. Is that true?"

He looked from one face to another. "She . . . " His throat worked and he hunched down in his seat like a frightened child. "People leave stuff everywhere. I can take it, can't I?"

"That's stealing," she said firmly. "You know that."

"Not rubbish. Not refuse. They throw it away."

"Are you saying someone threw out these clothes?" Moir asked. "That it's rubbish you found?"

"Yes. All of it. She needs it. No-one else does. Why can't she have it?" The old man looked close to tears. Hollister felt a pang of pity as Jellyhead tried to make them understand the skewed reality in his head. "The cost of living is high. She needs me to find it for her, to put it together. She doesn't want to be hard, but she will if she has to. She doesn't like the darkness. She cries."

"Who is crying, Mister Emes? Can you hear her crying now?"

Jellyhead wouldn't meet Cloe Flavell's eyes. "She says she wants you, but I tell her she shouldn't. The cost is too high. I make sure she only does what she *has* to do."

"So you're not a thief?" Moir's moue of distaste seemed permanent.

"No." But the old man's had face closed over again. Gone was the look of vulnerable fright; and Hollister could tell that he was lying.

"What about the rest?" Moir pressed. "The hair, the fingernails? Does she want them too?"

"She found a way."

"The shit? The pads?"

"She is impatient." Jellyhead leaned back into the chair and folded his dirty greatcoat over his lap.

"Fuck." Moir stood and motioned for the others to join her outside. She inhaled and exhaled deeply before talking. "I'm sorry," she said to Cloe Flavell. "This is weirding me out a little."

Flavell nodded. "You're not alone."

"How much do you really know about this guy?"

"Not much."

"His full name would be something to begin with."

"It's Arnold Emes. He has a social security card somewhere; I saw it once, when he showed me where he lives. He used to be in the army, I think, and he gets a medical pension."

"Where *does* he live?"

She looked from Moir to Hollister. "I don't want to get him into trouble."

"I know you don't, but he's doing well enough on his own." Moir took another deep breath and put on what Hollister recognized as her sympathetic face. "Will you give us his address?"

"He doesn't have a proper address. He lives in the old line I mentioned yesterday. You'll never find it unless you know where it is."

"Will you take us there, then?"

Hollister added his voice to the request. "Please, Ms Flavell. If he has nothing to hide, he has nothing to fear from us."

She was just inexperienced enough to believe it. "Okay. I'll take you there. But only if you let me talk to him again."

"When you get back," said Moir, taking her arm. "I'll arrange someone to drive you there while we keep interviewing him ourselves. The sooner we can work out what's going on here, the sooner he can go home."

Or not, Hollister added silently as he steeled himself to face the old man's stare again, and Moir guided Cloe Flavell away.

"I don't know what to make of this," said Superintendent Penglis later that day, in her office. They had just reviewed the tapes of Jellyhead's interview. In it, the old man seemed as deranged as ever—literally, Hollister thought. But he was holding up pretty well, considering; all he'd asked for was a cup of tea, which he had been allowed. "What about you two?"

"I haven't the foggiest," said Moir, rubbing at her temples. "But he's not telling us everything."

"Faking, do you think?"

"I don't doubt it. Do you, Wey?"

He hesitated for a split-second, then thought: *To hell with it.* "I don't think he's faking. If he's not right in the head, then that's what he is. He can't help that. But there is something going on, yes. He is lying."

"About what?" Penglis wasn't hiding her interest in the lead. If her staff could jump the gun on the Major Crime Squad, she could use the kudos to get out of Polson Street Station and into one of the cushier suburbs. No-one actually wanted to work in Amberley Park any longer than they had to.

"Your guess is as good as mine," he said, quite honestly.

"Oh, come on." Moir rounded on him instantly. "Have you forgotten what we found in the bags?"

"I haven't forgotten, Jane."

"He's hanging out in women's toilets, scavenging—that was your word for it, wasn't it?—for anything left behind. What's he doing with it, do you think?"

The vehemence in her voice surprised him, left him feeling more than a little stung. "I don't know what he's doing, but—"

"Blood, excrement, hair." She tapped them off on her fingers. "Toenails. Christ, Wey, its something out of a satanic recipe book."

"You think it's cult-related?" asked Penglis.

"I don't know," she said. "But either way, it freaks me out."

"What else was in the bags?" Penglis asked them.

"Fluid. We think it might be water from toilet bowls, probably containing urine. We've sent some to the labs for testing, along with the rest—including a used band-aid. More blood. We'll match it all against the victims'." Moir rolled her eyes. "Then there was hair. And dust. I don't know what *that* is."

"Skin cells," said Hollister. "Most of the dust in houses comes from our skin. It's gray when it dies."

"See? Maybe he's making a voodoo doll. That's why he wanted his social worker's hair. He wants to control her, make her buy him more alcohol."

"He doesn't drink." Hollister repeated Flavell's revelation for Penglis' benefit; it had surprised him too, until born out by blood tests.

"Then it's pain killers," Moir said, "or arthritis cures. Whatever."

"Who's this woman he talks about?" Penglis asked. "Do you have any idea?"

"None," Hollister said. "It sounds like someone specific, but he hasn't given us anything to tie her down. She could be an abusive mother, a lost sister, a deceased daughter—"

"She could also be a split personality," said Moir. "Part of himself who does things he doesn't like. You hear what he says about her. He's more scared of her than he is of us."

"Cloe Flavell hasn't mentioned anything about a multiple personality disorder."

"Flavell is an inexperienced, idealistic kid." Moir shifted restlessly in her seat. "For God's sake, Wey, don't let her influence you. She thinks these people can be healed, but they can't. It's too late. Maybe if they'd been treated properly when they first became ill—"

"I don't think we can ignore our responsibility just like that," he interrupted. "We can't write him off as crazy just because we caught him mucking around in a toilet. I mean, yes, he's ill and I don't say we should ignore him—but don't paint him as a psycho, either. We don't know *what's* going on in his head."

"Exactly, and I say we shouldn't give him the benefit of the doubt. You let him go, and who knows what he could do? Maybe he *is* a lonely old geezer with nothing better to do than walk around all day. Or maybe he breaks into porn shops for kicks when no-one else is looking. Or maybe he kills people. We don't *know*, Wey, and until we *do* know I say we keep him here, nice and safe, where we can watch him."

"Guilty until proven innocent?" he snapped. "I'm disappointed in you, Jane. I thought you had more humanity than that."

She retreated back into the chair, flushing, and he regretted the words as soon as they left his lips. In the year they had worked together, she had shown him nothing but humanity. But he couldn't call them back, and she didn't respond to them. He could only shut his mouth and wait for Penglis to break the silence.

"Let me get this straight," she said, looking from one to the other. "You, Jane, think we should keep him here?"

"At least until we've gone over his place." She glanced at Hollister, then back at Penglis. "Can we get a warrant?"

"If he's living in a public space, we might not need one. But you, Wey, want to let him go. Is that right?"

"I didn't say that. He has done something wrong, and he should be made aware of it. But I don't think we have any grounds to do more than fine him. I mean, *is* it a crime to steal shit and used tampons?"

"I'm sure there's a health and safety act to cover it." Penglis forced a grim half-smile. "I'm with Jane," she said. "He's too much of a wild card to let slip so soon. If we let him go, who says he's not going to disappear? I know it's a long-shot, but suppose he *is* the Slayer? How would you sleep at night, knowing that we let him kill again?"

Hollister wanted to say that he didn't sleep very well as it was and doubted old Jellyhead did either. "I don't think that's very likely."

"But it's not impossible, and we're not here to take chances. We'll charge him with something minor, put him in the cells overnight and see what that shakes loose. Who knows? Maybe he'll decide to come clean in the morning. And if he does, and if he is the Slayer, I'll personally—"

There was a knock at the door. Before Penglis could respond, it opened and the head of Penglis' assistant poked into the room.

"This just came," he said, thrusting a fax forward.

Hollister took it and passed it on to Penglis, catching the title as it went past. A surge of something very much like disappointment went through him, mingled with relief.

Penglis scanned the page once, then went over the relevant details again before speaking.

"They've caught him," she stated dully. "They brought him in an hour ago."

"Who?" asked Moir.

"The Amberley Slayer, that's who." She passed Moir the page and leaned back into her seat. Judging by the expression on her face, she was feeling much the same way as Hollister. "Well, shit," she said. "That simplifies things, doesn't it?"

The fax was well-thumbed by the time Hollister had a chance to read it properly. The Slayer had been arrested that afternoon by a large squad of police and detectives in his home in Croxton. His name was Aaron James Stanco. Stanco was an average-looking man of thirty-five who he worked for the Amberley Park City Council as a grounds keeper. By day, invisible in overalls, he had cleaned the streets while watching for victims and studying their habits. At night, he had struck. His house contained swathes of preserved human skin stretched like embroidery in wooden frames. Around one wrist, in plain view, he wore a bracelet made from stolen rings, studs and spikes.

Hollister watched the news reports on TV that night, from his couch. Photos of Stanco and the bracelet dominated the reports, but the media found time for shots of the triumphant detectives at various press conferences and other sites around town. The case was closed. People could rest easy—especially the young, endangered women in Amberley Park, although they were rarely mentioned. Good had triumphed over evil once again.

If only, Hollister thought, life was ever that simple.

They had charged Arnold Emes, a.k.a. Jellyhead, with loitering and minor property damage and warned him not try anything similar again. The old man didn't seem to notice. He was more concerned that he wasn't getting the contents of his satchel back. Cloe Flavell, who had returned from showing a junior constable where the old man lived, did her best to calm him down and said that she would take him home.

"I'll keep an eye on him," she promised, apparently unfazed by having to take the trip twice.

"You won't be the only one," Moir said, her expression more threatening than her words.

"She will be hard," said the old man softly, his expression one of despair and resignation. Hollister had thought he would at least be happy about being set free. "She won't have any choice, now."

"We all have choices," Hollister said, drawn into the old man's dementia against his conscious will.

"She is impatient."

"What does she want?"

"She'll want the bones, to finish."

Hollister simply stared at him, feeling suddenly cold.

Then Arnold Emes was gone, whisked off to his mysterious home by the one person, it seemed, who actually cared about him—and for whom, even then, it was merely a convenient compassion. If Cloe Flavell got a better job elsewhere, would she return to care for one isolated old widower?

Moir looked at her watch and exhaled heavily. "It's been a hard day, Wey. Fuck, it's been a hard year. Go home and get some rest."

"The report—"

"Can wait until tomorrow. That's the last thing I want to do tonight."

He did as he was told, although the last thing *he* wanted to do was go to sleep. Afraid of what might be waiting for him, he watched every news report he could find, and then a late movie. When that finished, he poured himself a large glass of port and went into the study. He performed sit-ups and push-ups in quick succession, then did star-jumps for as long as he could. The physical exertion helped clear his mind, although they couldn't stop it working.

Two nights ago, in the middle of the night, Arna had said something about bones. Jellyhead had mentioned bones that afternoon. There was no possible way the old man could have known about Arna or what she had said; it must have come out of nowhere, a random comment that meant nothing except in the context of his dementia. Or—and here Hollister's mind baulked at acceptance—it hadn't come out of nowhere at all, and there was something connecting the two instances. Something he hadn't seen yet.

He drained the port and poured himself another one. Something was going on. The silence of the house felt full of possibility, for a change, and the night wasn't so empty. On other nights, that might have been an improvement. The Amberley Slayer was behind bars, finally—but that didn't mean the world was any safer than it had been. If anything, it might actually be *less* safe, for at least the Slayer had been a known quantity. He had kept the nameless fears at bay. Who knew what might come along to fill his shoes, now that they were empty?

It seemed perfectly reasonable, to Hollister, that both Arna and Jellyhead's mystery women were nervous of the dark.

He woke the next morning with the empty glass on the bedside table, phoned in sick, and went back to sleep. This time, he dreamed.

Arna was on her knees in her wedding dress, trying to piece together the sharp-edged fragments of a broken cup. She looked up with tears in her eyes and said: "I'm getting there, Weylin. I love you."

Then she had smiled, and the cup was whole in her hands

He jerked awake at eleven. The bed was empty on her side, and he had a mild hangover. The fears and feelings that had kept him awake the previous night still nagged. He kept seeing Jellyhead at the Polson Street Station—so small and fragile in the grip of the legal system, yet so oddly resilient, defying every attempt to make sense of his behavior.

At one, he rang the station again and asked to be put through to the constable who had taken Cloe Flavell to Jellyhead's home. Candice Greiner was in and on lunch break. Hollister felt guilty for disturbing her but, as it turned out, she was happy to talk about what she'd seen.

"It's off the Weaver Freeway," Greiner said. "You park in an empty block on Salisbury Street and go across the old tracks. Don't go down the tunnel; the gate is padlocked, although I think people have been getting in anyway. There's an access door to the right, around the edge of a concrete bunker. It's stiff, but not locked. It opens if you push hard enough. On the other side is a maintenance corridor that leads to the dead line."

She gave a detailed description of where to go from there. The way had been explored many times before by the Cave Clan and teenagers. She had seen stickers and graffiti, empty syringes and used condoms. But she hadn't seen anyone else, not beyond a certain point. That was explained, she supposed, by the stench.

"It's like a sewer," she said, the experience portrayed vividly by her tone. "Foul. I don't know how anyone could live down there."

"*Is* that where he lives?"

"Yes. There's another maintenance way leading to an abandoned cellar. I don't know what it's under, but it looks more like it belongs to a house than offices or warehouses. It might be somewhere old that got built over and forgotten, then opened up again when the line went in. I don't know. But that's what he calls home."

Hollister imagined Jellyhead shuffling through the urban wasteland, down ever-darkening corridors and tunnels, and finally to the forgotten space he had taken for his own. It still seemed appropriate, even though he doubted it was a kind of life anyone deserved—no matter how passionless, or empty. "What's in there?"

"Nothing but rubbish. The room is quite big, really, and there's stuff piled up everywhere. Papers, plastic bags, tin cans—you know. There are some rugs in a corner; I guess that's where he sleeps. There's also a tea chest full of old clothes, some candles, a couple of big, empty water bottles, and in the middle of the room there's a table . . . " She stopped as though remembering something.

"What is it?"

"On the table . . . Hell, I don't know how to describe it. I thought it was a body, at first. It made me jump, it looked so real. Gave what's-her-name, Cloe, a fright too. Old Jellyhead's got himself some kind of dress-maker's dummy down there, Senior Constable, but he's not making dresses."

"What do you mean?"

"Well, it's lying flat on its back, on the table. Splayed out, you know? It's not that big, but he's tried to make it look more . . . real, I guess, and that makes it seem larger. He's stuck a wig on it, and painted it, put clothes on it—all that. It has a face."

"Whose face?"

"I don't know. No-one I recognized. Should I have?"

"No." *Not Cloe Flavell, then,* he thought to himself. "Is that it?"

"Yes." She hesitated, then added: "To be honest, it gave me the creeps, that thing. It was just lying there, but I couldn't take my eyes off it. I didn't want to turn my back on it, either. Its mouth was open, and it looked . . . I don't know. I think that was where the smell was coming from."

He thanked her when she had finished, and hung up. *A dress-maker's dummy . . . a wig . . . clothes . . . ?*

Moir had described the contents of the old man's bag—the bits and pieces, the everyday discards—as items a satanic chef might put on a shopping list. Hollister didn't for a second think she'd meant it literally, but it had a ring of *something* to it. If it wasn't the truth, then maybe it was a step in the right direction.

He booted up his computer for the first time in weeks and logged onto the Internet. What he found didn't help him very much, but neither did it put his nagging suspicions to rest. When he searched on "voodoo dolls" he found numerous sites on black magic, Wicca and Satanism. Human tissue could be used to make any number of things: potions, imitative charms, curses, and—yes—voodoo dolls. Most were concerned with stealing part of someone else, or creating something from nothing that could become the spell-caster's possession. A stream of half-familiar words scrolled down the screen. *Golem . . . homunculus . . . zombie . . .* But none of them sounded quite right. None of them fit.

The old man's bag had contained samples of blood, dead skin, hair, fingernails and human waste from many different people, not just one. It was indeed discarded material, as Jellyhead himself had said, not fresh, not specifically stolen. And the fact that he had one sample from Cloe Flavell didn't necessarily mean anything sinister, unless he was making lots of voodoo dolls, one for each sample of hair. And even if he was, there was still the question of *why*. Flavell was patently not under the old man's control, so there wasn't any efficacy to such a charm—not that Hollister had expected there to be. The alternative, though, was that Jellyhead was even crazier than he sounded, and that didn't feel right either. Yet Hollister couldn't help the feeling that he was getting somewhere.

"She won't have any choice, now," the old man had said.

What process had they inadvertently interrupted?

He rang the station a third time, and this time asked for Jane Moir.

"I'm worried," he said.

"About what?"

"About Jellyhead."

"Him? He'll be okay. Our young friend will see to that."

"No, I'm worried he might do something. I think you were right."

He could practically hear Moir's mind working on the other end of the line. "What's going on, Wey? Is everything okay?"

"Everything's fine, Jane. I've just thought about it some more, that's all."

"And?"

"And what?"

"There's more to this. I know you, Wey. You don't just turn like this. There's something you're not telling me."

It was his turn to think carefully. In the end, he decided to be honest. She would know if he was lying, anyway.

"It's Arna."

"*Arna?* What about Arna?"

"She's been telling me things, at night. No, wait, let me finish. I'm not going mad. It's really happening. I hear her. She . . . " He stopped. It did sound much crazier than he had thought when it was just him hearing her speak, alone, at night.

Moir said: "I think you're taking this whole Jellyhead thing a little too seriously. And I thought *I* was! Just forget about it. It'll go away. The dreams will stop—"

"They're not dreams, Jane."

"Whatever they are, then. Just let it go. You know it's for the best."

"Are you talking about Arna or Jellyhead?"

"Both, and you know that, too. Whether it's work or personal, you have to draw the line somewhere. You cross that line at your peril." Moir took a breath, then continued in a softer tone. "She's been dead six months, Wey. Let her rest."

And if she doesn't want to, he asked himself, *what then?*

But he didn't say it aloud. Instead he hung up the phone, dug out his maglite torch from the bottom kitchen drawer, and left the house.

Hollister caught a flash of crimson out of the corner of his eye as he pulled up in the empty lot. He wasn't sure at first, but was certain the moment he left the car. Standing on the steep embankment, looking back down at him, was Cloe Flavell in her bright red coat. He opened his mouth to call to her, but thought better of it. She would wonder why he was there if he drew any more attention to himself. And if it *was* her, then his worst fears were unfounded.

But he still needed to know for sure.

He followed the route Constable Greiner had given him through the metal maintenance door and into the tunnels. It took him two passes to find the entrance to Jellyhead's underground lair, but when he did locate the door he had no doubts that it was the right one. The smell was stronger by far on the other side of it. As he swept the torch around the room, he gagged for a very different reason.

Cloe Flavell lay on her back behind the table Greiner had described. Her clothes had been cut away down one side of her body, and long, deep incisions were visible in her pale flesh. There was blood everywhere—an impossible amount from such a small, pallid person. It appeared as though her head was pressed down hard against her chest, but the angles were all wrong. Hollister stepped gingerly closer, wary of disturbing the scene. An autopsy would confirm any guess he made, but he had to see, for his own peace of mind.

From closer to he saw that parts of her skeleton were missing: one long bone from her forearm, another from her shin; a dripping hole in her side suggested that a rib was gone, too, and maybe part of her spine. A step too many resolved his confusion about her face: her lower jaw had been removed, and what remained didn't bear close examination.

Hollister averted his eyes and found Jellyhead on his side in a corner of the room, eyes open but just as motionless as Flavell. He checked for a pulse in the old man's neck, but found none. When he pulled his fingers away, they were sticky with blood—Flavell's blood, he presumed, since there was no apparent injury to the old man's body. Mystic or otherwise, he was just dead, and in death he looked more pitiful than ever.

Hollister stood up, breathing heavily to fight a rising nausea. What had happened seemed obvious, at first glance. Flavell had come to check on Jellyhead, and he had killed her when she had arrived. Or he had stunned her when she had dropped him off the previous night, and killed her later. As there was no way such an old man could have overpowered a healthy young woman in the open, Hollister reasoned that he had taken her by surprise. There was a metal rod with blood on one end under the table, and a knife on the ground near Flavell's body—the murder instrument and butchery tool respectively, Hollister assumed. Then, over-excited by his grisly deeds, Jellyhead had had a heart-attack and died.

The picture was complete, except for one detail: the "dress-maker's dummy" was gone.

He raised the maglite to study the table surface more closely. It was splattered with what looked like dried excrement and plastered with dust and stray hairs. There was a small amount of blood, too, still sticky. Something had undoubtedly lain there; the splatters were confined to the table's edges and hardly to be found in the middle. Furthermore, there was a half-empty roll of gaffer tape on the floor nearby, with an inch or so hanging loose and dust-free. There were a large number of plastic bags lying around the room that Greiner hadn't reported; some of them were freshly emptied.

He could see it clearly. The object on the table, the sinisterly human-shaped and open-mouthed figure, had been the blow-up doll stolen from the porn shop. It had been filled with the excrement Jellyhead had collected, then made up on the outside with dead skin, discarded fingernails and loose hairs. Old clothes had completed the picture: a manikin constructed solely from discards, a Frankenstein's monster made out of rubbish. But it hadn't been finished.

He'll need the bones before he's done.

The police had been closing in, alerted by the theft. Jellyhead had been under pressure to finish before anyone discovered what he was up to. There wouldn't be time to raid graveyards or morgues for what he needed—if the bones of the dead would even suffice. Hollister didn't grasp the underlying illogic of the exercise; maybe only pieces from the recently-deceased would suffice. But the broad principles seemed clear. Jellyhead had been making a monster. Backed into a corner, he had taken the first and perhaps only chance he could to finish his work.

"The cost of living is so high," Jellyhead had said. Hollister had it down on tape. "She needs me to find it for her, to put it together. She doesn't want to be hard, but she will if she has to. She doesn't like the darkness. She cries."

Hollister took a step forward, the flash of crimson he had seen foremost on his mind: Flavell's coat wasn't anywhere in Jellyhead's lair, yet she had been wearing it the previous day. Either someone had stolen it from the scene, or . . . That the monster could actually move of its own accord didn't seem so absurd, underground, in the charnel shadows, and the thought of taking chase urged him on. But he stopped well before reaching the door. He had been underground almost half an hour already. The trail would be cold by the time he emerged into the daylight again. He wouldn't be able to use smell to track the thing in the city—and he didn't know what he could do even if he caught up. Prick it with a silver needle? Catching up might be the last thing he wanted to do.

"She's trying to come through," the old man had said. "I don't know where from. She's just there, and she wants to be here."

He turned and walked back to the table.

"Let it go." Moir's words filled the gore-splattered darkness. "Let it go . . . "

He knew she was right, on all counts. What difference did the slip of a knife make? An old but respected surgeon made a mistake and might go unpunished if the lawyers failed to do their job properly— but that wasn't the same as a killer hunting down a victim, even if the end result was the same. Maybe, in this case, there was an accomplice Hollister knew nothing about who had moved the thing on the table. Maybe it wasn't as simple as it seemed on first *or* second viewing. Maybe only time, not rash stumbling about, flailing for answers, would expose the truth.

The tension within him broke as soon as he made up his mind. He would get back above ground and call for Moir. Someone else could take over, clean up the mess, put the pieces together and let him get on with his life as rationally as he could. It wouldn't be his problem any more, whatever—and wherever—*it* was. There were no names, not even words, for such a thing. What would drive it? What reason could it possibly have for existing?

When he turned, it was standing in the doorway. The stench had returned with it. He was becoming so used to the smell that he hadn't noticed.

"I came back," it said with Arna's voice. "I missed you."

He stared at her, frozen, as she took a step into the light.

After a long pause, he lowered the torch.

●

INTRODUCTION TO:
.... ENTRE LES BEAUX MORTS EN VIE
(AMONG THE BEAUTIFUL LIVING DEAD)

Rob Hood is Australia's undisputed Zombie King. I first met him in 1994, at a small con in Sydney's inner West. There are lots of reasons to fondly recall that encounter. One of them, his urging of me to try writing a zombie story, led to two stories in this collection—two stories of which I am particularly proud, for very different reasons.

This story was the first of them. (I talk about the other in the notes to "Passing the Bone.") It took shape very quickly: the richness of the world and the word-play I allowed myself (never had my spotty knowledge of the French language been so tested) were leagues beyond anything I'd attempted in a short story before. I also enjoyed the challenge of writing sex scenes (something I'd avoided in the past) and mucking around with airships (who doesn't?).

I called the thing "De Rigeur Mortis" and put it in a drawer, figuring its length and lack of plot would make it unsellable. Thereby demonstrating my occasional thickheadedness.

Jump ahead a year or two to my third and last shot at getting into Jack Dann and Janeen Webb's World Fantasy Award-winning anthology Dreaming Down-Under. In desperation after two rejections, I pulled this story out of the drawer, changed the name (thankfully sanity had been restored) and sent it in. The acceptance came immediately. My story opened the book and went on to be recommended by Locus. I still receive emails from people wanting to read the novel.

Playing with dead people can sometimes be cool. I owe Rob Hood a huge debt of thanks for teaching me that, and for reinforcing the fact that all too often writers are the worst judges of their own work.

●

ENTRÉ LES BEAUX MORTS EN VIE

(AMONG THE BEAUTIFUL LIVING DEAD)

Le chateâu de la mort dorée—known as fool's-death house in the vernacular—was situated half-way up the vertical flank of a mountain not ten minute's powered flight from Jungfrau, in the region that had once been called Switzerland. Sandwiched between stone and air, the sprawling, rococo structure with its four hundred luxury rooms and five banquet halls looked like a pimple on a granite giant's cheek. Tunnels, elevators and air-ships provided the usual means of gaining access. Only a few people dared to climb in person. The view from the Chateâu's tiered terraces was spectacular enough to negate the need for such foolhardy, if courageous, gestures.

Yet some people still made the effort. Ordinary people, of course; never the reves themselves, although this was one of their favourite sites. Of anyone on Earth and off, the reves knew best how fragile life could be. Yet how resilient.

All this passed through Martin Winterford's mind as he stepped off the air-ship and onto the Chateâu's wide receiving platform. Buffeted by the crisp, mountain wind, and with the setting sun hidden behind a mile of solid rock, he experienced a moment of near-satori. This, the first time he had visited the Chateâu, would possibly be the last—in his lifetime. Although he would no doubt return many times, if he chose to accept his uncle's ultimatum, it would be as a reve, and he would no longer be, by ancient definition, alive.

He tried to reassure himself that, living or dead, by whatever definition, it made no difference to him—but the doubt still nagged two hours later, as *La Célébration Annuelle* began.

"*Je vois que vous êtes en souffrance le changement,*" said a melodic voice. "*Apprendez-vous déjà le français?*"

Martin turned. A tall woman in a white silk ball-gown, complete with gloves, fan and blonde coiffure, had come up behind him. The skin of her shoulders and throat was bare and very pale, flawless. Her eyes were the deepest brown he had ever seen, her lips the richest red.

"I'm sorry, but I don't speak Old French," he said, raising his champagne flute to cover his uneasiness. Make-up couldn't hide the truth, not from so close. Not that she wanted to, either, or else she wouldn't have left her shoulders and throat exposed. The woman was a reve.

"*Pas mal,*" continued the woman. "*Vous aurai beaucoup du temps à combler son retard.*"

He shook his head, nervousness becoming irritation at her persistence. If she wanted to be fashionable, why didn't she find someone else to do it with?

With an amused smile—perhaps at his expense, he couldn't tell—she raised her fan and indicated that he should follow her into the next room. Martin hesitated for a moment, then obeyed. He had nothing better to do. The party, for all its glamour and opulence, had proved to be slightly dull. Its many cliques left him wandering alone, wary of intruding.

"You'll have to pardon me," said the woman over her shoulder as she led him through the crowd, past tables piled high with exotic *hors d'oeuvres* and wines, mostly untouched. He caught a hint of delicate perfume in her wake. "We like to have our little games. Someone must educate the newcomers, put them through a rite of passage. That is our purpose here at the Chateâu—unofficially, at least. It's important, *n'est-ce pas?*"

Martin simply nodded at first. The woman's perfect English, with its qualifiers and clauses, threw him so off-balance that what she actually said didn't register until they were half-way across the room.

"You know?" he exclaimed, wondering what had given him away. He had chosen his outfit carefully: a black suit with ruffs at neck and collars, leather shoes and skull-cap. He had hoped to remain anonymous.

"Of course," said the woman. "I am observant. There are three hundred and twenty-seven guests attending this soiree, of which seventy-nine are revenants. Two hundred and forty-five are government officials: doctors, diplomats and examiners, mainly, all known to me either personally or by reputation. That leaves three." Her eyes twinkled. "You are clearly not a waiter, for you cannot speak French. Besides, your age seems about right."

Martin didn't bother denying the truth. If games were her metier, then he would acknowledge defeat early. Either that, or risk arousing a deeper interest that he could not afford to indulge.

"Where are you taking me?" he asked, more curious than concerned for the moment.

"Does it matter?" She fluttered her fake eyelashes and pouted like a teenager. "Our table is boring, boring, boring. It lacks interesting conversation—or interesting people to make conversation, perhaps I should say. I was in the process of looking for someone to liven up the evening when I spotted you." Her smile returned as they weaved past a cluster of potted palms and through an arched entrance-way. "Would you care to join us?"

Martin side-stepped a waiter carrying a tray of garishly coloured drinks. The banquet hall looked like something plucked from Eighteenth Century Europe, with gilded walls, a string quartet playing in one corner and crystal chandeliers suspended from a high, domed ceiling. He raised his voice to be heard over a melange of music and speech filling the room.

"Do I have a choice?"

"Of course. Don't be obtuse, my dear. You have a choice in everything."

Again the coquettish flutter that did nothing to ease his disquiet. The echo of his uncle's words was uncanny. But before he could answer, the woman brought him to a halt with a hand on his chest.

"Ah," she said, "here we are. Why don't you take a seat . . . I'm sorry? I didn't catch your name."

Martin faltered. The table before them held six 'people'. He stared at them dumbly until he realised that they were all staring at back at him just as hard.

He turned to face the woman who had led him to the table. Only then did he realise that her words had been a question. He almost blurted out his full name before natural caution caught up.

"My name is Martin," he managed. "And—?"

"Allow me to introduce you." The woman gestured around the table with a flourish of her fan. A fat man in purple robes was Professor Algiers Munton of the Revenation Institute in New York. M. Elaine Bennett, a narrow-faced, female reve dressed in simple grey peasant attire, hailed from Port Moresby. The sexless mod with orange veins glowing under its ceremonial skin and the AI node sporting the usual black suit preferred by the AI conglomerates for formal occasions were Alkis and PERIPETY-WEYN, both from the Moon's Armstrong Base. An android rem from Attar, judging by its coat of arms, was being ridden by someone called 'Le Comptable Froid', or 'Count' to his friends, who had been unable to make the physical journey from that remote moonlet to Earth in time for the Celebration. All indicated their pleasure at meeting him with nods, smiles or brief but sincere hellos.

Only the last member of the small party, a bald young man wearing a blue period suit, remained silent when introduced as 'Spyro Xenophou', and went otherwise—almost pointedly—unexplained.

Martin swallowed, his mouth dry, after greeting them all in return. What had his uncle said when news of his application had arrived? No true aliens, but plenty that seem alien . . . ? As a summary of his current situation, that would do as well as any other.

"Sit, sit." The woman—reve, he reminded himself, although the distinction seemed like splitting hairs in such a crowd—ushered Martin towards a chair. "Or leave. If you're going to make a fool of me by declining my invitation, then at least do so quickly. Don't allow me to waste any further breath. Air is rarefied so high in the mountains, you know."

"I beg to disagree," broke in the Count via his rem, its artificial voice smooth but eerily inhuman. The lag between Earth and Attar was much smaller than Martin would have credited, so-called instantaneous transmissions still usually taking a second or two. "Had I access to atmosphere as 'rarefied' as yours," the Count said, "I could increase my profit by four hundred percent."

"Don't be such a wet blanket," chided the woman with fleeting moue. "And don't interrupt. I haven't finished introductions yet."

Martin lowered himself with a sigh of relief into the only available seat, either a genuine antique or a very good copy of a Louis XIV. "Please," he said. "I'd be grateful."

"Of course. I, dear Martin, am the Reve Guillard—you may call me Marianne if you wish. I am most pleased to make your acquaintance."

Without the slightest self-consciousness, the immortal woman extended her hand to be kissed.

The only other reve at the table, Elaine Bennett, smiled at the expression on Martin's face as he reached out to clasp the cold, perfect fingers. The Reve Guillard had been a contemporary of Paul Merrick—the world's first reve and founder of the Plutocracy. Her age was therefore somewhere between four hundred and eighty and five hundred years. Martin felt like he was touching a precious work of art, or a shrine. His lips tingled when she withdrew her hand, as though some of her legend had rubbed off on him.

"I am honoured, M. Guillard," he said.

The woman waved her fan; in another age, another body, she might have blushed. "*C'est peu de*," she said. "And please do call me Marianne. I'd hate to have to insist."

"Thank you." He felt dizzy; the rush of blood to his face threatened to overwhelm his brain. As he tried to regain his composure, he was acutely aware of the silent young man watching him closely, almost resentfully. It bothered him, but he couldn't afford to let it distract him.

Perhaps sensing the new arrival's discomfort, the AI node stepped in to fill the silence. "We were discussing the latest trend," PERIPETY-WEYN said. "*Le mode du temps*, as it were. M. Bennett noted some interesting parallels between it and the French Revolution."

"She would," M. Guillard said, assuming control of the conversation with confident ease. "And she is correct: there are superficial parallels. The term 'plutocracy' was not chosen lightly, you know."

"And not without a sense of humour," said the mod, Alkis.

"Yes." M. Guillard cast the cyborg an ambiguous look. "Paul always liked puns. But the similarities run no deeper than that. The trend for things Old French is deliberate, not symbolic of some deeper human conflict. How could there be a French Revolution today when the members of the ruling class, no matter how wealthy they might be, are already dead? Besides, next year it might be Twenty-First Century America that takes our fancy, or White Russia."

"Each with its own revolution," the mod observed.

"Yes, yes, Alkis. That too is deliberate. We gravitate towards potent times in order to stave off boredom—"

"Or to allay subconscious guilt," interrupted M. Bennett with a grimace. "Or fear."

"Nonsense. You imagine cause in a world of effects."

"I feel it." M. Bennett met the Reve Guillard's stare unflinchingly. "In my youth, I felt it too."

"*Naturellement, ma chère.* And that is why you are here: because you are something of a radical. We require diversity and dissent if we are to remain vital." M. Guillard flapped once with her fan, and sighed theatrically. "Do you see what I mean now, Martin?" she asked, pinning him with her wide, brown eyes. "These are old arguments, centuries-worn and boring, boring, boring! Why don't you tell us about yourself instead? Who invited you here this evening?"

Martin leaned forward and chose his words with care. "My sponsor, ah, Gerome Packard, thought it might be a good idea."

"Did he, now? That sounds like uncommonly good sense from dear Gerome."

"He said it would help me acclimatise."

"Socially, yes. Physically, probably not. No-one can predict with certainty the effects of revenation on a given individual."

"I take it," put in the mod, "that you are aspiring to the Change?"

Martin felt sweat bead on the back of his neck. *Maybe one day, I'll be like her—the Reve Guillard.* "My application was approved five weeks ago," he said to avoid a direct answer.

"Interesting." The mod folded its glowing hands on the table. "Of all the alternatives presently available, revenation remains the only proven means of achieving extreme human longevity. I envy you the opportunity."

"Thank you, sir." Coming from a mod, that was candour indeed. "Sometimes I wonder whether it's really going to happen."

"No doubt. You must be nervous," said Professor Munton. "I would be, in your shoes."

Seeking a distraction, Martin hailed a waiter. One appeared instantly at his shoulder. He offered to pay the round, but only Professor Munton joined him in ordering a drink. None of the others required fluid intake, being either self-sufficient within themselves or partial to other means of gaining nutrients.

"How long until your birthday?" asked the AI node when the waiter had departed.

"One month," Martin answered, realising that the topic would not be so easily evaded.

"I presume you are cognisant of the risks, then?"

"Yes." That Martin could answer with certainty. His Uncle Arthur had more frequent dealings with the Plutocracy than most people; he had made sure Martin knew what was at stake. "Of every ten thousand inductees, one will never wake from the death-sleep."

"And a dozen others will experience difficult transitions," added M. Bennett, glancing at the bald young man. "Even today, after hundreds of years of research, a sound awakening alone is no guarantee of success."

With a jolt, Martin suddenly realised what Spyro Xenophou was. Braving the young man's dark stare, he asked him directly: "When was your birthday?"

"In June," M. Guillard answered for him. "You'll have to forgive my ward, Martin. He woke six weeks ago and hasn't spoken since. Part of him resists; the fear of death is strong in him still." She shrugged. "It is often that way with the more established families, although that seems paradoxical."

"Not really," said the AI node. "Social evolution, albeit relatively rapid in the last five hundred years, has a long way to go before it eradicates the base impulses present in every human. The concept of passing through death is still paralysing, I am told, even among those for whom revenation is a common occurrence."

"That would not be the case if it were available to all who wanted it," said M. Bennett. "By restricting the process, we perpetuate a class system that is both prejudicial and morally abhorrent."

"The system of Houses makes perfect sense, and you know it," M. Guillard insisted. "Otherwise there would be chaos. Even with the present ratio of one reve for every four thousand natural humans, there are problems."

"I must concur," said the android. "By removing the tools of government from the hands of the short-lived, Earth and the rest of the System has achieved the kind of long-term stability only dreamed about in pre-history."

"But at what cost?" M. Bennett accentuated her point with one finger on the table-top. "The Plutocracy is in-bred and constantly at risk of stagnation."

"Hence the revolutionary trends," said the mod. "Balance, feedback, homeostasis."

"Desperation," retaliated M. Bennett. "We may reach for the stars, but inside we are all still frightened children in need of reassurance."

Martin sank back into his seat, glad that the spotlight had drifted from him. Both his sponsor and uncle had warned him to steer clear of such debates, to be wary of associating with any one camp among the reves. There would plenty of time for that after his induction. If things went as planned, he would have centuries in which to grapple with the arguments for and against—although he believed that he already understood it well enough to reach his own conclusion. The problem was that it kept changing.

Revenation was an expensive process, restricted by necessity to the few. Applicants had not only to demonstrate fitness but ability to pay their way through the process and out the other side. A single immortal life would be an expensive burden upon the welfare system if that person proved to be unproductive. As result, only wealthy families could afford to raise a member to reve status. And the wealthiest families already contained significantly large numbers of reves; some had even brought their line to an end in order to spare a single member from death, although this practice had waned over the years. Hence the appearance—illusory or not—of in-breeding, and of decadence.

Watching M. Guillard speak, with her many gestures and flourishes, the often direct way she manipulated conversation to suit her own agenda, Martin was reminded of his school-years and the rumours that had circulated among his fellow students. The reves were vampires, he had been told once: un-dead and un-living creatures frozen forever in a state of inanimate animation. Infrequent glimpses had confirmed this impression: of pallid, beautiful people riding past in patient comfort; aloof and isolated, even dismissive at times. Although information was wide-spread about the truth, it had only added to their mysteriousness: cut a reve and it failed to bleed; bury another, and it could be exhumed without damage a month or a century later; expose a third to deadly viruses and its pseudo-animate cells would be completely unaffected.

Yet inflict upon any reve a magnetic field of more than a few thousand Tesla and he or she would experience spasms, even unconsciousness. Or put it to the flame and watch it burn like summer kindling to nothing, as though its life had vanished in a single, sudden flash.

Reves were potentially immortal, and some—such as M. Bennett, a reve herself—would add immoral to the charge. In his younger years, Martin had hated and feared them. But now he was among them, potentially about to become one of them. He found the thought wildly disorientating.

The string quartet playing in the background had acquired a singer. To the tune of an ancient folk song, she recited:

On the golden hill where the sun once stood,
and the blood-red man with hearts for eyes
sold words that sung of forever, forever,
Paul Merrick found his first love, and died.

Martin wondered whether the man who had given immortality to the world had felt the same confusion when choosing life over mortal passion. Perhaps he was still feeling it today. Sadly, Martin was unable to question him directly, since the reve had departed for Capella two hundred years ago. And in the end, he supposed, there could only be one answer.

Humanity's ambassador to the stars was only nominally human. That fact alone spoke volumes.

Survival of the fittest . . .

"To which Familial Affiliate do you belong, Martin?" asked Professor Munton, startling him out of his reverie.

Martin inwardly cursed himself for not paying attention. The question, easily anticipated once the subject had been brought up, was one he had nonetheless hoped to avoid. Confronted with it, he mentally tossed a coin, and honesty won. In the back of his mind, he heard his uncle curse in turn.

"None," he replied to the fat man's question.

"Impossible," stated M. Bennett. "There hasn't been a foundling House for three hundred years."

"That's correct," said M. Guillard. "Unless—wait! Martin, you wouldn't be the son of that engineer we've been hearing about, would you? Alex Winterford, wasn't that his name?"

He shrugged. There was no use denying it. "At your service."

"Oh, tremendous!" The fat scholar clapped once. "Marianne, what a coup! The founding father of the House Winterford, right here at our table! You couldn't have brought anybody more interesting to talk to had it been Paul Merrick himself! Tell me, Martin—"

"*Attends*, Algiers." M. Guillard raised a finger to her lips. "Don't jinx the poor boy before his time. Let him tell his own story at his own pace."

"Do I have to?" Although Martin didn't want to sound churlish, he couldn't help it.

"Of course not, as I said before." M. Guillard winked. "You can leave if you'd rather not talk."

"I'd rather not do either, to be honest."

"Tish. What do you fear? That we will embarrass you, or judge you? If the latter, please bear in mind the diverse natures arrayed at this table. Surely you realise that our opinions will be firmly divided?"

"Too true." The mod's skin rippled a pale green.

"And you shouldn't be afraid of your innocence, if that's the case," said M. Bennett, regarding Martin with intense eyes. "It is your very naiveté we crave. So much time has passed since someone new joined our ranks that any uncorrupted viewpoint is welcome."

"'Uncorrupted', Elaine?" asked M. Guillard. "By what, exactly?"

"By reves, of course, Marianne." M. Bennett scowled across the table at the older woman. "Or '*les beaux morts en vie*', if you prefer. There are none in his immediate family. The only one he's ever met in person, prior to now, would be his sponsor—and then only after his application was approved. His viewpoint will be quite external to our affairs, and all the more valuable for it."

"Is that true, Martin?" asked the rem. "You came this far without a patron ward, or even a beneficiary?"

Martin studied the faces watching him expectantly, and realised just how expertly he had been trapped. To refuse an answer now would be insulting, and to answer incompletely would only encourage more questions. Still, just because he had been backed into a cul-de-sac didn't mean he had to abandon common sense. He would be better off revealing a measure of the truth before all of it was pried out of him, hoping all the while that they would grow tired of him sooner rather than later.

"Yes," he said. "A paternal great-uncle ran a water mine on Titan for a while, I think, and my grandmother helped design a starship, but none of my blood ancestors came close to meeting the fiscal requirements."

"What changed?" prompted the mod.

"My Uncle Arthur and Aunt Sue both forewent their reproductive rights to further their careers," he explained with deliberate paucity of detail. "At the same time, my father followed my grandmother into aerospace design and patented an improvement on the Komalchi drive. These three incomes combined were enough to guarantee either myself or my sister a hearing from the Applications Board."

M. Bennett frowned at that. "I've heard of whole families pooling their resources—large families, too—and not coming close."

"Didn't you catch the names, Elaine?" asked M. Guillard, her smile as cutting as a shark's. "Arthur Winterford, despite his short-lived status, is Chief Executive Officer of the American Multi-Immersal Conglomerate, which controls twenty-seven percent of the System's broadcast media. And Martin's mother's sister, Susan Firth, prefers to operate under the *nom de plume* Jenny Martinez in order to avoid accusations of nepotism."

Among the raised eyebrows, where allowed by physique, and the silent surprise evident in every stare, only one voice stood out:

"Jenny who?"

M. Guillard pursed her lips in annoyance. "Really, Count. You can't be that isolated, can you? M. Martinez is the author credited with the resurgence of the novel—the planet's first best-seller in four hundred years."

"News to me, I'm afraid." The rem turned to face Martin. "The AMIC and Komalchi connections both make sense, though. Your grandmother must be proud to have such successful children."

"She would have been, I'm sure. She died when I was fifteen, just before I made my primary application."

"I'm sorry. Is there a connection between the two events?"

"Obviously there is," said the AI node before Martin could answer: "Mortality."

Martin confirmed this with a nod, unwilling to elaborate how close to the mark the AI node's guess was. His uncle's grief had been profound at the death of his mother. Restricted by breeding laws to families no larger than four, with only one child inheriting that generation's right to reproduce in turn, mortal humanity had become well-used to uncles and aunts leaving their estates to siblings' progeny. In Martin's case, and his sister's, that had amounted to a fortune almost too vast to comprehend. When his uncle had first suggested that they should use this capital to advance one family member to reve status—thereby removing him or her forever from the threat of age and natural death—he had in part been motivated by that grief, and fear that another loved-one would succumb before he did. At least this way, one child would have a chance of avoiding the fate awaiting the remainder of his family.

In part, anyway. The rest Martin had no intention of even thinking in such company.

"You mentioned a sister," said M. Bennett. "You were chosen above her, is that correct?"

"No. I'm older and therefore theoretically first in line, yes, but that wasn't really an issue. She wants to have children, you see."

"And you don't?" The question was playfully put by M. Guillard.

Don't I? Martin asked himself, although he knew the only answer he could give: "Whether I failed the examination, or fail at the Change, or not, is irrelevant. I was sterilised at thirteen, and have always expected to be childless. Perhaps a niece or nephew will follow me, one day, if I succeed."

"Nobly put." The ancient reve touched his arm lightly. "Indeed, once a House is established, subsequent revenations from that line become more likely with time. The chances are you will have blood relations to keep you company before long."

"I hope so."

"*Certainement.*" M. Guillard pulled away. "But look, Martin, your glass is empty. Spyro will top you up while you tell us about your plans for the future, if you have any."

"I haven't really thought that far ahead," he lied, handing his glass over. The bald reve took it from him without comment and collected the scholar's as well before heading off through the crowd.

"No?" M. Guillard expressed her disappointment with a sniff, then brightened. "I know what we'll do, then. We'll advise you now. What do you think, Elaine? Plutocrat or star-voyager? How best should Martin wile away eternity?"

M. Bennett shrugged noncommittally before suggesting the former. PERIPETY-WEYN, the AI node, immediately disagreed, and went on at length to explain that, in his opinion, the System government was stable, and would be for a very long time; what was needed was not more politicians, but explorers with courage enough to venture into the dark.

"Courage is for the young," said M. Bennett, with which M. Guillard solemnly agreed.

Martin settled back into his chair to listen while his future was dissected; when pressed for an opinion, he hinted at the possibility of becoming an artist. That was a vocation he had considered as a child, before the death of his grandmother, when life had seemed so much simpler.

Until he made his decision, all he really had to do was watch, and learn. After that, his uncle and fate could toss coins to see what happened next. At least for the moment, he had managed to avoid M. Guillard's probing curiosity.

When the time came, four gruelling hours later, to announce that he had decided to retire for the night, he declined the offer of stimulants from the bar. Although he had enjoyed the company of M. Guillard's friends, he was no match for them—intellectually or physically. He had heard that reves could party for days on end; certainly they could discuss a single topic for hours without losing interest. When one's life was measured in centuries, he supposed, the everyday passage of time became somewhat trivial.

He wasn't yet at that stage, and Professor Munton never would be. The fat scholar had left an hour ago, wishing Martin the very best of futures and expressing sincere hope that they would meet again another day.

As Martin bade his own farewells around the table, shaking hands with all but the mod, who deferred physical contact for a simple bow, M. Guillard saved herself and the enigmatic mute deliberately until last.

"It has been a pleasure, Martin," she said when it was her turn, curtsying expertly.

"The honour was mine," he replied, although he hadn't failed to notice the way she had deflected conversation from her own affairs. He knew as little about her now as he had before: that she was a multi-faceted enigma twisting like a bauble in one of the chandeliers above their heads, casting brilliant reflections wherever she pleased.

"*Mais oui*," she purred, gracefully kissing him on both cheeks. "The Celebration will last another three days. Maybe we will meet again before it ends."

"I doubt it," he said. "I leave on the first flight tomorrow morning."

"Well, it was a nice thought." She turned to her companion. "Spyro will walk you to your rooms. I hope you have a pleasant night."

Before Martin could protest that he could find his own way, M. Guillard had whispered something into the ear of the mute reve and glided swiftly away, leaving the two men awkwardly facing each other.

"You don't have to," Martin said, hoping against hope that he would be allowed to leave alone. Whatever had happened to Xenophou before or after the Change, he didn't want to know. The thought was heavy in his mind that he might be like this in a month's time—that he too could come out the other side disadvantaged or, worse still, truly dead.

Xenophou shrugged, the only form of communication he had made the entire night, and indicated the exit.

Martin gave in. Xenophou followed him through the crowd, then came abreast as they entered the empty corridor beyond the banquet hall. Martin's suite lay on the windowless second floor, well-appointed for someone yet to undergo revenation, but not immodest. Most of the rooms on that level were unoccupied, as testified by the silence around them. The sound of their footsteps was muffled by the thick carpet, smothered in the rich crimson impregnating the weave.

At the door to his rooms, Martin fumbled for the key in his pocket and turned to face his silent companion.

"Thanks, Spyro. I know you probably didn't want to do this, but . . . she is hard to resist, I realise, and I appreciate the gesture anyway. So thanks. I hope things work out for you in the end."

Martin turned to open the door. The air inside the suite was clean and smelled of flowers. The lights were already on, and the bed, glimpsed through the opposite doorway, had been turned back in preparation for his arrival.

Xenophou nodded, but didn't leave. When Martin took a step forward, he followed.

"You want to come in?" Martin asked.

The bald reve shrugged again.

"I guess that means yes." Martin sighed, resigning himself to the situation. "Come on, then. Take a seat; make yourself comfortable. I'm going to slip out of my shoes and jacket, if you'll excuse me for a moment."

Martin strode through to the bedroom while his guest moved towards the sofa. He shrugged out of his jacket and rolled up his shirt-sleeves, then tugged off his tight leather shoes. Relishing the feel of air on the soles of his feet, he took a moment to reflect upon the situation.

His overnight valise lay in one corner, ready to be repacked before he went to bed. The trip had been fleeting but productive. He already had two names for his uncle: Elaine Bennett and Le

Comptable Froid, the latter being, he was almost certain, another reve. Both had demonstrated themselves to be removed from the core politics of the Plutocracy, the sort to entertain innovative thought rather than to blindly follow the current trend. Whether they would prove to be allies depended on what happened in the future, and whether Martin met his side of the bargain or not.

He stared grimly at the reflection in the mirror. Revenation, except in highly unusual circumstances, always occurred at twenty-one years of age, and his birthday was only a month away. If he chose to proceed, his tanned skin would become pale; his hair would fall out and not grow back anywhere on his body; his eyes would dull and crystallise unless he used eye-drops or had artificial tear ducts installed. He would cease to be human, and become something altogether different.

A reve.

Sudden tightness in his stomach caught his breath. Silently, he mouthed the most offensive word anyone could utter in an immortal's presence:

Zombie . . .

"I don't really have anything you might want," he called through the doorway, remembering his guest, "but help yourself anyway. Perhaps we can talk. If you can talk, that is."

Only silence answered him. Whatever Xenophou wanted, it obviously wasn't conversation. Slipping his skull-cap off and putting it on the dresser, Martin stepped out of the bedroom and into the lounge, half-hoping to find that Xenophou had departed.

Instead he came face to face with two women he had never before seen in his life.

"Hello," said one, a brunette with short hair and a slender figure, wearing a sheer, silk dress. "Are you Martin Winterford?"

Martin glanced past the women to the door. It was open. Fool, he chided himself. Xenophou's presence had disturbed his usually impeccable sense of security.

"Yes," he said, wary of sudden moves. The other woman stepped closer, her long blonde hair swaying with the movement. He didn't recall seeing her at the party; he would have remembered if he had.

Xenophou stood between them, frozen but attentive, as tense as an animal about to bolt.

"I'm Martin Winterford," he reaffirmed loudly, trying to bluff his way out of whatever situation he had blundered into. "How can I help you?"

"You've got it the other way around," said the blonde, smiling and keeping her eyes fixed on his. Her skin was refreshingly pink, and patently human.

"We're here for you," said the brunette. To Xenophou, she added: "Both of you, if you like."

"I'm not sure I understand," he protested, backing awkwardly into the wall as the blonde approached him.

"Sssh." One finger touched his mouth, followed shortly afterwards by her lips. Too stunned for the moment by the boldness of her advance, he was unable to resist. It wasn't until the lock snicked shut in the doorway that he finally forced his hands to push the blonde away.

"Wait," he gasped, reeling. "What's going on?"

The blonde shifted a shoulder. "We're yours for the night—if you want us, of course. We can't force you to do anything."

"No, no—of course not." Martin glanced at the mute reve, who silently echoed his own puzzlement. Not a conspirator, he decided, but caught in the cross-fire. "Who sent you, then? Can you tell us that?"

"No," replied the blonde. "They said you've earned a reward. And we are it." She slid a hand across Martin's shoulder. "Well? Do you want us to stay?"

Martin found it hard to think through the alcohol in his system. But part of him rebelled, discomforted by Xenophou's presence.

Sensing his awkwardness, the blonde's hand tightened. "Come on," she said. "Let's go into the other room. At least I can give you a massage. You look very tense."

He did as she suggested and, despite the cliché, was grateful for the reprieve. She guided him to the bed, and indicated that he was to lie face down upon it. He did so nervously at first. Although he didn't anticipate an actual attack—not in the high security of the Châteâu, where weapons were confiscated immediately upon arrival—he did find it hard to let his guard down. The simple act of being there, among the reves, made him feel guilty and vulnerable, like an imposter who might be discovered at any moment.

Gradually, however, he relaxed. He let her strong fingers worry at the knots in his back and shoulders while her voice whispered soothingly in his ear. Her smell was tantalising, part perfume and part natural female. Whoever had sent the women had certainly paid for quality.

That in itself helped convince him. If she wasn't a professional sex worker, then she was maintaining a skilful performance. Which only made her all the more difficult to resist.

In that day and age, prostitution was both legal and perfectly safe, and he wasn't a prude by choice. Although young and fair-looking, he had avoided serious relationships ever since his primary application had been accepted—at the age of sixteen—for fear of heartbreak when and if the final approval was granted. One night stands had been few and far between since then, however. The offer was therefore extremely tempting.

And, if the truth were told, he really didn't want to think about it at all. He had no enemies yet, that he was aware of. What did he have to fear, except, as they said, death itself?

When she asked him to remove his shirt, he didn't resist. He rolled over and she straddled him to work on his chest, temples and throat. Her thighs were warm, and growing warmer as she worked. His own hands began to move, stroking her calves in return, revelling in the feel of warm skin beneath his fingertips. With every stroke, her hips swayed, grinding languidly against him.

Then she was undoing his trousers, and he had forgotten all thoughts of resistance. He helped remove her dress. They coupled smoothly, he revelling in the wetness and practised muscles of her vagina. Her breasts swayed before his face, and he reached upwards to cup them, brought one nipple down to his mouth. She shuddered and began to move more urgently. If it was an act, it was a good one. His hands wandered to her buttocks. With one in each palm, kneading gently with every thrust, he felt the passion build. And when it erupted, his mind went blank . . .

Afterwards, they played less seriously; teasing coyly, arousing sated flesh, exploring. For her, he was sure now, he was just another client, but for him she was something special. A time to be enjoyed, a celebration of life—of le petit mort, the little death—however he had earned it.

For an hour they did nothing else. They might have for longer had it not been for the noises coming from the other room.

"Let's go see," the blonde eventually whispered. He, both relaxed and emboldened by then, agreed that they should.

The lounge looked as though a small but effective storm had ripped through it. Clothes lay everywhere; cushions had been scattered across the floor. Clearing a seat on the sofa, where they spooned together with legs entwined, Martin and the blonde settled back to watch the show.

Xenophou was naked but for his unbuttoned shirt; his pale, hairless skin shone a pearly white, marred by shadows when his muscles flexed. The brunette was covered only with sweat, glistening on her buttocks and back. The bald reve had penetrated her from behind and was maintaining a steady, firm stroke, neither speeding up nor slowing down unless his partner requested it. With every thrust, the woman gasped for breath, in time to the movement of her own fingers on her clitoris.

Both seemed oblivious to the spectators on the couch. They looked, the blonde whispered into Martin's ear, as though they had been fucking for hours. The sight clearly aroused more than an academic interest.

Martin watched less pruriently. He knew reves were unable to sire or bear children, but this was his first hint that they might still enjoy sexual congress. Certainly the activity of the couple was as vigorous as and more prolonged than that between fully mortal partners.

Xenophou's mien, however, was one of intense concentration, not enjoyment, as the brunette's hands guided his to her breasts. Her mouth opened in ecstasy, and she arched her back. Her heels clasped Xenophou tightly to her; her hips rocked with every thrust. Riding high on a wave of constant stimulation—and perhaps with the help of drugs—she seemed about to achieve orgasm—the latest of many, if the sounds she made were anything to go by. The only sound Xenophou made was his breathing, fast and heavy.

Then the blonde woman's hand found Martin's stiffening penis behind her, encouraged it, guided it home. For the next few minutes, he completely forgot about Xenophou and the brunette. His second orgasm of the evening took longer to achieve, but was even more intense than the first. It seemed to last forever.

When he was spent, he sagged back onto the couch and stroked the sweat-sheened skin of the blonde's hips and stomach, filled with a sense of satisfied peace. The room was silent, the stillness after a storm, and he felt like sleeping.

A moment passed before he realised what was missing: the brunette's gasping had ceased.

He belatedly turned to see. Xenophou and the woman had stopped moving, although they were still coupled. As Martin watched, the reve levered himself backwards and slid his erect penis from the woman's pouting vagina. The brunette made a small noise deep in her throat, and, breathing heavily, sank back onto her haunches. Xenophou stood just as wearily, his legs shaking. By the time he was upright, his erection had completely vanished.

Looking around the room—at the brunette, at Martin and the blonde, still entwined—the reve blinked his dark eyes once and shook his head.

"Enough," Xenophou said, his voice soft and filled with what might have been sadness.

Martin stared up at him, remembering what the Reve Guillard had told him. This was the first word the new reve had spoken in weeks.

Before Martin could think of anything to say in response, Xenophou had gathered his clothes in a bundle and moved for the door. Hastily disentangling himself from the blonde, Martin leapt to grab his arm. The reve's flesh was uncannily dry, and cold. Xenophou looked down at his hand, and Martin removed it.

Without another word, the reve opened the door and left the room.

Martin made sure the door was locked before turning around. Behind him, the brunette had taken his seat on the sofa. Stretching her limbs, ignorant of the significance of what had just happened, she whispered softly to the blonde: business talk. Martin caught a few fragments of the conversation as he walked to the bedroom to regain his composure.

The brunette was exhausted, as was only to be expected. The reve's performance had been far more than she had anticipated; nothing had prepared her for this, although she had heard occasional rumours. The blonde sounded almost jealous, until one item of gossip caught her attention.

"Not once?" she asked, disbelieving her ears. "After all that?"

"Not even a trickle." The brunette sounded deeply puzzled. "And you know, I don't think he ever would have."

Martin nodded silent understanding to his reflection in the bedroom mirror. No sweat, he thought. No fluids of any kind. Even if they had continued for an hour longer, neither the brunette nor Xenophou could have coaxed so much as a drop from his desiccated, dry flesh.

Even if he'd wanted to.

Enough . . . ?

Martin went back into the other room to ask the women if they wanted to leave. When the blonde smiled up at him and said no, the brunette agreed. They had been paid for the night and, whether anything else happened or not, his bed was more comfortable than either of theirs. Martin, although his mind was torn between conflicting impulses, didn't doubt that something would happen, if he was up to it. It wasn't every day he had the chance to spend the night with two beautiful women. Besides, sleep would be a long time coming, and he wanted to be spared the involuntary wakefulness.

Finally, with the brunette beneath him and the blonde stroking his stomach from behind, he managed to forget about Xenophou and remember himself again—hairy, sweating and above all alive . . .

And when sleep did come, it was black and empty, like death.

Sudden movement woke him an hour before his alarm was due to go off. Rolling over with a grunt, he realised that the lights were on and the bed was empty.

"I'm sorry to disturb your *ménage à trois*," said a familiar voice from somewhere near his feet, "but I couldn't wait any longer."

He sat up and rubbed at his eyes, fatigue dulling his reactions. The Reve Guillard was a pale blur crouched at the end of his bed, poised like a ghoul to steal his soul. The elaborate ball-gown, along with her airs and graces of the previous night, was gone; in its place she wore a white one-piece suit folded and draped with sashes to hide her figure. It was hard to tell where the fabric stopped and her deathly pale skin started. Her head, like Xenophou's, was completely bald; the angles of her skull were sharp.

Not a chandelier any more, Martin thought. Rather, a shellfish grown old and crusty beneath its carapace. He wondered whether he would ever come close to the innermost substance of the Reve Guillard, if there was any left at all.

"What are you doing here?" he managed.

"I dismissed the girls so we could be alone," she said, avoiding the question. Her dark, cold eyes regarded the tangle of sheets about his legs. "Their services were adequate for the price I paid, I gather. Certainly their effect on M. Xenophou was worth every cent."

Martin slithered along the mattress until his back was flush with the wall. From that position, he watched his visitor closely. "You paid them, then? Why? To make your friend speak?"

"My ward, not my friend," she said, her face closed. Again she avoided the question. "The Change isn't always easy, and it's sometimes very hard. The body is a machine, easily upgraded; the mind, sadly, is not. People either want to be a reve or not, and sometimes the only way to find out is to go through the process: when you stand on the far side and look back, knowing that you can't ever return . . . that's when you know for certain."

M. Guillard's potent gaze had drifted across the room as she spoke, and returned to him at that point. "Many choose the fiery path, more than you'll find in the official figures. Self-immolation is not difficult to achieve, if you have the right equipment. All it takes is a nice, clear flame and plenty of oxygen, and—" she looked sad for a moment "—gone. What might have been centuries, ended in a second."

"Perhaps that's what worries him," Martin said, wondering if he was dreaming. "Spyro, I mean. The 'centuries' part. The more I learn about being a reve, the less attractive it seems. The thought of being a . . . " He swallowed the word zombie barely in time. "Being immortal, I mean, does have its drawbacks."

"Yet you want it, Martin," she said, her voice forceful. "I feel the desire in you more strongly than I have ever felt it before—even if you yourself aren't yet aware of it, or of what it means."

"I'm not?" he asked, confused. "That is, I do?"

"Of course. And mod Alkis agrees. Having studied the Change in more detail than most reves, his opinion played no small part in my decision to talk with you here and now."

Martin thought this over. She and the mod had discussed him after his departure. She and who else?

"Talk to me, then," he said. "Get it over with. As honoured as I am at warranting such undivided attention from someone as busy as yourself, I object to being rudely wakened when I have company."

"That's fine thanks for the fun I gave you last night, Martin." The reve almost smiled, although the expression was thin. "Fine thanks indeed. But I take your point. I have committed a serious breach of protocol, and should expect brusqueness in return." She turned away for a moment, and laughed once.

Martin waited in silence.

When her attention returned to him, the smile was gone. "The thing I have to say to you is this: there's more at stake here than family pride. Whatever you and your uncle have planned, think carefully before committing yourself to it."

"Plans?" he countered, feigning innocence although his stomach had instantly turned to ice. "What plans?"

"How could there not be one, Martin?" she shot back. "PERIPETY-WEYN, with its heightened attention to detail, has plotted extrapolations of your development given the creative and business acumen of your family's germ line. Le Comptable Froid watches human affairs from afar and sees a world ripe for change. Elaine Bennett agrees: that there is something fundamentally exciting about the idea of a new House to which both reves and mortal humans cannot help but respond. Not even Professor Munton himself, the dear old fool, could possibly miss this one." This time the smile was real. "You are in a pivotal position, my boy. And the one in the best place beside you to influence future events is the very person behind your application for revenation: your uncle. Coincidence? I think not. You're up to something, or being forced into something, and it's my job—no, my responsibility—to make certain you know exactly what you are putting at stake before you even begin."

"And what's that, exactly?"

"Why, you, of course." She frowned at him as though he had said something stupid. "It still hasn't struck you yet, has it? What it means to be a reve?"

"Well—"

"Consider it now. How do you think it will feel to watch your parents grow old and die? Your sister, her partner and her children? Your aunt and uncle? Especially your uncle. What will happen if you balance your long future against his short-term gains and come out the loser in the end? Letting a mortal man pull your strings is the most dangerous thing a reve can do, for the time will inevitably come when the strings fall slack and leave you dangling. Regret is the widow of opportunity, as they say, and eternity is a long time in which to curse your mistakes."

"What mistakes?"

"You'll know if you make them, I promise you that."

"Is that a warning, M. Guillard?"

Again, the abbreviated laugh. "Nothing so crude: just stating a fact. There's every chance we'll still know each other in a thousand years, no matter what happens in the next hundred, and every time I meet you I'll be sure to remind you of the actions you are considering now. Persistence alone can be a very effective form of punishment."

"I'm sure," he agreed, "if you're the one behind it." Then another thought occurred to him: "But that still doesn't explain why you've come to me now. The urge didn't strike you from nowhere. You must have known where my room was in advance in order to send the women here so quickly. Which means you knew who I was all along."

"Yes, yes." She dismissed the allegation with a wave of a hand. "Whether I knew who you were or not is irrelevant. It wasn't until my team had taken a good look at you and confirmed my impression that I knew we had to talk. And why not now, when your memory of last night—of *La Célébration*—is so strong? Before your uncle has had time to twist your impressions to suit his will."

Martin opened his mouth to protest, but she didn't give him the opportunity.

"He will tell you, no doubt, that we are decadent, fossilised creatures in need of a good shock; that five hundred years of imposed stability has suffocated the Earth and all its living children. But I disagree. It is not change we fear, but undirected change. Consider the trends, Martin, and how we embrace them instantly throughout the System. Study how progress has been made, in an orderly, rational fashion, without revolution and bloodshed. We acknowledge the need for evolution without allowing chaos to reign supreme, and thereby ground inevitable tensions into constructive endeavours. The short-lived have never had it so good.

"But watch what happens when something takes us by surprise. See how strongly we fight back . . . even those of us who may have initially welcomed the change."

"You're reactionary by nature," he broke in, speaking his mind for the first time in her presence. "Nothing I can do will alter that, so I have no choice but to fight it."

"No. Change is inevitable, and House Winterford may yet prove to be the catalyst for something new and exciting—but do let us be the judge of that, not your uncle."

The Reve Guillard regarded him with something approaching pity, and rose gracefully to her feet. "That is what I came here to tell you. I have no official role in the Plutocracy, but I am not without influence. Nor am I close-minded. If you choose to confide your plans in me, and I find wisdom within them, then I will support you in every regard. I make just as winning an ally as I do an enemy."

Martin stared at her, stunned by the offer. Discuss his plans with a reve? With her? Did she think he was stupid?

His thoughts must have been plainly visible on his face, for she smiled and patted his naked foot. "Do think about it, Martin, at least. I will always be available to talk to you, should you take me up on my offer. But we won't meet again until after you awake from the Change—when, as one reve to another, we can discuss this properly. If we cannot come to an agreement even then, we will have no choice but to go our separate ways."

"And if I choose to forgo the Change?"

She blinked once. "Why ever would you do that?"

He took her point. In her eyes, why would he? There was no answer he could give that would satisfy her. Or his uncle.

"Agreed, then," he said. "We will talk afterwards."

"Good," she said, and suddenly the conversation was over. With a curt nod, she turned and headed for the open door.

"Wait," Martin called after her. "What about Spyro? Is he still talking? Has he recovered?"

She stopped in the doorway. "Spyro Xenophou is dead," she stated flatly, her eyes revealing nothing. "Truly dead. He killed himself at 06:50 this morning."

"How—?" Martin stopped himself with difficulty. That wasn't the right thing to ask—he could guess the answer: the fiery path. Through his dismay, he forced himself to think clearly. "Why?"

"If you cannot answer that question," she said, "then your understanding of what it means to be a reve is incomplete, and your ability to make an objective decision hopelessly inadequate. *Adieu*."

The only sound she made as she left the room was the rustle of silk on carpet, swishing softly like a breeze out of his life.

Ten o'clock came slowly, but eventually the ponderous airship docked at *Le Chateâu de la Mort Dorée*'s departure platform. Thick cables tethered it to ancient wooden posts as the whining of its electric fans ebbed. The massive, rocking balloon shuddered once upon surrendering itself to earth-bound will, then became still.

Martin, standing in a chill draft blowing straight down from the mountain's snow-capped summit, watched the gondola's ramp unfold towards him with half a mind. The rest was still in his room, catching up on the night's events. It was hard to believe he was already leaving. The short flight to Jungfrau connected with an orbital shuttle leading half-way around the world where, on his ranch in Texas, Arthur Winterford waited. His uncle would want a detailed report of every event, every word, every insinuation. Martin, as would-be reve, had been in a privileged position to gather information.

What had he learned? That the Change was fraught with danger, yes, and that the reves were afraid of what he might do to upset the delicate balance of world affairs, when he emerged from the Change the founder of a new House. Nothing new, in other words, nothing critical. Even in one of their many homes, the reves had been judicious with their secrets.

In a perverse way, that made the Reve Guillard's offer tempting. It almost made sense to consult a reve when plotting their downfall—although his uncle would kill him if he took advantage of it.

The more he thought about it, the more tempted he was to cut ties with everyone and to continue as a free agent, following whatever impulses he felt at the time, or none at all.

But . . . freedom? As a reve? He doubted it.

"We can't force you to do anything," the blonde had said, and for the first time he truly appreciated what the words meant to him. And to Spyro Xenophou—for whom volition hadn't even entered the equation.

Suddenly, Martin understood.

Reves were dead. The fact that they could still participate in the world of the living was irrelevant: the nanomolecular agents behind the mystery of revenation ripped the life from them as surely as a forty-metre fall would kill a mortal human. All biological needs were left behind in the process, including the need to eat, drink, breathe, sleep and die; to a certain extent, the senses, particularly those of taste and smell, were also muted. In exchange, reves received total mastery over their flesh—the ability to produce an erection at will, for instance—and potentially eternal life. But the oldest parts of the psyche sometimes refused to accept the bad things with the good, as the AI node had stated, and compelled them to fight the thought of death being something to accept and to put behind them, rather than something to dread.

Where that fight would lead him, Martin had no way of telling. What he did know was what must have gone through Spyro Xenophou's mind mid-coitus with the brunette. Faced with one single, yet fundamental, aspect of his new incarnation, the battle had been won. Or lost, depending on the point of view.

Only then had Xenophou realised what he had done.

Enough, he had said. A farewell, certainly—but to what? The brunette, or life, or both? Or an eternity existing only as a poor facsimile of what he had once been, driven by needs and urges that had risen to fill the ones he had left behind forever?

The conductor whistled from the gondola, and the few passengers began to make their way towards the ramp. Martin picked up his suitcase and did the same, bidding farewell, for now, to the reves of Fool's-Death House.

One month to go. There was so much to see and do before he closed the door on the mortal part of his life. And he didn't want to miss out on anything, while he still had the chance.

It was going to be a long month. He would make certain of that. And a very long afterlife to follow.

●

PASSING THE BONE

With my right hand I absently finger the thumb-bone of my great-great-great-grandfather, Maxwell Owen. The ancient phalanx has a hole for a leather thong or chain drilled through its mid-point, and has been hollowed lengthwise to act as a crude whistle. My Dad left it to me when he died, and I've kept it handy ever since—usually around my neck, although occasionally, like now, I prefer to hold it in my hand. The official story, for friends, is that old Max carved it himself after his thumb was blown off during a war somewhere, but the truth is that he did it on his death-bed while waiting for the rot to finish off the rest of him.

Sometimes if I blow through it hard enough it makes a noise that might be called musical. Other times it seems to whisper directly into my mind: the ghost of the great-great-great-grandad I never met in life, ossified for eternity yet giving me advice when I most need it.

If I concentrate, I can hear him saying: *Hurry, Billy . . . Hurry . . .*

Or so I'd like to believe. Being undead doesn't mean you can't be sentimental as well as practical. Within two days I won't be able to move very well—maybe not at all, if what happened to Dad is anything to go by. And to reach Sydney in time I do need to hurry, no matter who tells me.

I clench my fist around the thumb-bone in my pocket and push my foot down hard on the accelerator.

I have been dead for seven hours and Coober Pedy is hundreds of kilometres behind me. When I stopped to refill the tank at Port

Augusta not long ago, the young attendant looked at me a little strangely. Maybe I've started to smell. I don't know; it's hard to tell. Probably. For the first couple of hours, rigor was insidious. I had to keep stopping to stretch my limbs; otherwise my fingers locked around the wheel and my head pointed stubbornly forward, refusing to turn either left or right. That was the worst of it: not knowing if I would be able to react in an emergency.

I feel a little more limber now, although perhaps that isn't entirely a good thing. I don't know much about what happens after rigor mortis, except that it certainly isn't pretty. Remembering how hot the Commodore became during the day on the way over, I wind the windows up, tug both sun-visors down and switch the air-conditioner on full. But I leave my coat on with the hood up, as I wore it into the petrol station, just in case a car overtakes with a load of curious kids in the back. No need to invite unwelcome attention, or to frighten the innocent. Not just yet.

The rising sun, to my left, transforms the clear sky from a map of infinity into a blue sheet pressing down on the world. The highway is a black line through blurred fields of brown: not desert any more, but arid farms desperate for overdue winter rains. If there wasn't so much further still to go I might enjoy the scenery for a while. Instead, I keep my eyes fixed on the tarmac, and my attention on what happened and what I have to do about it.

Focus . . .

Graeme Parkinson is five years my senior, and my exact opposite in almost every respect. A tall, solid man with sun-blonde hair and weathered, callused skin, he reminds me of the many shearers that descended on my father's property once every year during my childhood. He wears jeans, scuffed leather work boots and flannelette shirts on every occasion, regardless of temperature or company. Once, on our first trip to Coober Pedy, we side-swiped a roo in his already battered van. Not content to leave the carcass behind, he stopped to investigate. In the revealing light of the van's high beam, I saw him reach into the animal's pouch, remove the kicking body of a young joey and snap its neck with a perfunctory twist.

I first met him through Kerry while I was taking night school. I can't say we liked each other much, but the mutual respect was real. He admired the way I strove to better myself in the face of a difficult life, and I felt the same about his obstinate practicality. He was one tough son of a bitch—I had to give him that—and his plan to conduct aerial surveys of the old opal mines at Coober Pedy, looking for any gaps or likely outcrops that might have been missed, had an audacious ring. When he offered to form a partnership—the money I'd saved plus his pilot's license—I was tempted. After discussing the pros and cons with Kerry for a month or two, we decided to go ahead.

That was five years ago. When Graeme rang last weekend and told me I had to come see the find he'd made, I went without hesitation. I arrived at Coober Pedy three days later and immediately noticed his edginess in the way he hurried me through a couple of drinks in the local underground pub then took me straight back to my wagon before I had time to change—but I didn't suspect that anything was wrong. Why would I? He was my business partner. If something had gone astray, he would have told me. And if he seemed nervous, I told myself, then it was only because of the magnitude of the find, and the fear that someone else might steal it from us before we had time to declare it. That's all.

He led me out to the old mines, calling out directions while I drove. The route took us a half-hour out from the centre of Coober Pedy and into ragged, dusty hills. Night had fallen some time back and the air was bitter; the only light came from the headlights of the Commodore. Old fences with warning signs marking shafts that had been abandoned for years flashed in and out of view as I followed dirt roads through back-lots, heading God only knew where. It had been too long since I last came to visit the mines, content to let him handle that side of things; during the last six months spent blasting and digging he never once asked for my help. The times we actually met in person were during his infrequent trips back to Sydney.

He finally called a halt in a shallow valley between two slump-backed, stony ridges. The stars were bright as we stepped out of the Commodore, he in his shirt and I in a thick coat to keep the desert chill at bay. For the first time I realized how far from town we were; the night was still, and very quiet.

"Through here," he said, guiding me along a narrow track to where tools waited at the lip of a shaft. The rear reflectors of another car reflected the beams of our torches back at us; one of them was broken, which led me to assume that they probably belonged to Graeme's old hulk. "Be careful you don't slip," he added, his voice as rough and unassuming as unvarnished timber. "You didn't come all this way to be winched out of a hole on your bloody arse."

I recall his words vividly, although their meaning is clear to me only now. The bastard was having fun at my expense.

Then, however, I suspected nothing. The beer I'd consumed after the long, exhausting trip had given me a light buzz. At that moment I was friends with the entire world.

"How rich is the seam?" I asked, negotiating my way slowly across sand strewn with shards of shattered rock.

"Rich *enough*," he grunted. "You'll earn back your investment, and more. Much more. Trust me."

"I have so far, haven't I?" I asked, turning back to face him.

"Yeah, you have." Graeme's eyes glinted at me as he swung his torch toward the lip of the nearby shaft. I followed the circle of light automatically.

"How far down?" I asked, feeling rather than hearing him shift closer behind me. To look as well, I assumed.

"Not far," he said, bending to lift something heavy from the ground. "But far enough . . . "

With those words, and a sickening crunch, something hard smashed into the back of my head. The night exploded into a billion points of brilliant pain and I doubled over, hands clutching at my head and feeling only hot wetness where my skull had once been.

I may have screamed; I can't remember. I know I staggered forward a step—trying in vain to escape the pain—and lost my footing.

As I toppled downward into gaping blackness, my last thought was for my father. I remembered him sitting in the homestead cellar with a tarpaulin over his knees, grinning at me through lips half-rotted away. His eyes had sunk back into his skull and hair lay plastered to his scalp like damp seaweed. The bullet wound to his left shoulder, where he'd accidentally shot himself while clearing goats, gaped like a petulant mouth. Clotted blood stained his overalls and shirt, and the stench made me want to gag.

I was six years old, and Dad had been dead for forty-eight hours.

"One day you'll understand," he said, his voice sounding like something that had bubbled up from a swampy grave. "I don't want to leave you, but that's the way it has to be."

I nodded dumbly through tears and accepted his word. With that sort of evidence before me, how could I doubt him? Then *and* now?

If I was conscious when I hit the bottom of the shaft, that moment is gone forever from my memory.

I leave Highway One at Two Wells to cut east across to Gawler, just north of Adelaide, where I refill again. This time the station attendant doesn't look twice at me although, with my coat done up and the hood over my head to cover the wound that killed me, I must make a strange sight. She's seen odder people than me in her time, I guess. If that's possible.

Back in the Commodore, heading along the Sturt Highway toward Nuriootpa, I resume my patient routine: hands on the wheel, eyes forward, mind turning constantly. The scenery greens as the highway turns to follow the Murray River, but I hardly notice. Roughly seven hundred kilometres lie between me and Coober Pedy: a third of my journey. I have been driving without rest for eight hours, but am not hungry, thirsty or tired. I never imagined death to be like this. I thought it would hurt more, despite what my father told me.

In the cool shadows of the homestead cellar, Dad talked until his jaw muscles softened and his mouth began to gape. Rot got him in the end, as it gets everything. When he could no longer talk, Mum and I carried him out of the cellar on the tarp and propped him against a tree on a far corner of the property, where he indicated he wanted to stay.

My last glimpse of him is graven forever in my mind. He looked like a rag doll abandoned by a child—by the world—with his legs splayed and his arms hanging limply at his sides. Only his eyes, sunken though they were, showed any sign of life. In them I saw a sadness that I hoped never to feel.

Mum and I returned to the homestead in the ute without him—a widow and her only son. As she drove, she told me that we were going to have to leave. Years later, when I analyzed her reaction to Dad's death in hindsight, I realized that she hadn't known either. Dad's talking corpse had unsettled her terribly, and I could understand her wanting to cut free from everything that reminded her of him. At the time, though, it hurt to leave my home, and my father's remains.

Two weeks after he died we sold up and packed everything into crates. Whoever bought the land got it at a small fraction of its true value. Mum didn't care about money, as long as we had enough to survive. She just wanted to get away.

From everything. To Sydney: the largest city in Australia, home to three and a half million living, breathing people of a hundred different cultures and national origins. Japanese punks, English stoics, German artists, New Zealand body-builders, South African Catholics, Vietnamese toy-boys, American drug-dealers, Dutch prostitutes . . . The list is endless. There is nothing, it seems sometimes, that Sydney will not hide, or at least drown into insignificance.

But that still wasn't enough. Mum worked until I was sixteen and old enough to fend for myself, then she left me to live in Melbourne. I guess I was just something else that reminded her of Dad. Except for cards, and a cheque every Christmas, I've never heard from her since. Understanding her misgivings, I've left her in peace.

And although I've been tempted to many times, I've never gone back to look for Dad's bones. His explanation of the family 'curse', brief and simple though it was, was haunting enough.

Owen males die young, and generally through violence. Old Max got in the way of a cattle stampede; my grandfather was run over by a tractor; Dad bled to death after shooting himself in the shoulder; I have smashed my skull on a rock. The curse—if curse it is, not freak of nature—usually takes effect before we turn thirty, robbing us of our middle years and old age that perhaps we have every right to expect.

But it doesn't end there. Old Max was the grandson of Gerald, the first Owen to flee England and live in Australia, one hundred and fifty years ago. He moved outback to avoid the rumours that followed him, met a young native girl and settled down, hoping that a little dilution might end the family troubles.

Sadly, indigenous blood did nothing to water down his legacy. All it gave us was a predilection for dark hair and round features. Subsequent generations—isolated on the family property in the vast outback of Australia—have continued the tradition.

And now, just as Dad said it would be—twenty-three years ago, through the mouth of his own rotting corpse—it's my turn. I may not understand it, but that's not my problem.

My problem is simple, if I don't think about it too much: I have to reach Sydney in time to warn Kerry. That's not the most important thing, but it's enough to keep me focused. Hatred burns much more brightly at the moment than grief, although I feel that too. It isn't easy being dead and knowing that time is running out.

At least I, unlike so many 'normal' people, have the chance to avenge an unjust death.

Whether the blow to my head failed to kill me and the fall finished me off, or I was already dead before I hit the bottom of the shaft, it doesn't matter. The next thing I remember is opening my eyes and seeing stars.

Real stars, shining down the throat of the shaft.

I wondered if I was dreaming.

You're not, said a voice. *Get up, Billy.*

I looked around for the source of the voice, but could find no one. I was alone.

Around your neck, boy.

I looked down. The only thing around my neck, beneath my clothes, was Old Max.

That's right, said the voice in a silent whisper. *Your guardian angel, if you like. The fall killed you, and I'm here to make sure you finish the job.*

What job?

Stephen, of course. You never told him, did you?

I hesitated, momentarily thrown off balance. Was it really Old Max talking or just that part of me had come off the rails after the fall? The latter seemed more likely, yet Dad's warning was fresh in my mind. I couldn't afford to ignore the possibility that my time had come.

Despite the patent absurdity of this conversation with my ancestor's thumb, I found myself feeling guilty.

Of course I didn't tell him. How could I?

That's beside the point. You have to now. Old Max's voice was warm in my head, not crotchety at all. I suddenly realized that he must have been about my age when he died. *Time's ticking away, Billy. Best you get moving.*

My watch had broken in the fall, but I guessed that only an hour or two had passed. My body felt numb as I staggered to my feet, as though I had the flu. The back of my head was a mass of splintered bone and brains. Dirt had got into the wound, but that didn't bother me: infection was the least of my concerns. More worrying was the stiffness already spreading through my muscles. I had to get out of the hole before rigor turned my limbs to stone.

A rope ladder eventually took me to the surface, where I rolled onto my back to rest. I wasn't out of breath—I no longer needed to breathe except out of habit—but I still had some catching up to do. Despite having had most of my life to think about it, my death still came as a shock.

The truth of it only really hit home when I saw that Graeme's van was gone, and that the blood had been carefully scuffed from the lip of the shaft. Whatever had struck me—a crow-bar, probably—was also gone. No evidence remained, in other words, to indicate that foul play had occurred. If anyone found my body, the obvious assumption would be that I had fallen to my death unassisted.

I suppressed a bitter smile at that thought, wondering how many other business partners had met fates like mine in the opal fields. Coober Pedy is the perfect place for such treachery. Not only do the opals provide a motive, and the countless old shafts a convenient means of disposing of a body, but the town itself—where people live underground in order to hide from the heat of the day—has all the charm of a graveyard. I'd always hated it, and couldn't imagine what had led me to try to get rich there.

I'd been *murdered*. The thought sent a shiver of anger through my stiffening flesh. I *trusted* him . . .

Graeme may have taken his van, but the Commodore was still there, with the keys in the ignition. Convenient, but only to be expected. He'd want it to look like I'd arrived late, had a couple of drinks at the bar, then come out to the claim to see what we'd found. Slightly pissed, I'd lost my footing, fallen in and cracked my skull open. All too plausible.

Only I knew better. And the last thing he'd expect would be my undead body to climb out of the pit, like some zombie from an open grave. Which is what, in almost every sense, I truly was.

And what I *am*.

A corpse by another name still smells, Billy, says Old Max, as he did then.

Remembering the gore-flicks I'd watched as a teenager, always with a tinge of uncertainty—dread of what I knew even then was going to happen to me—I asked Old Max: I thought being undead was all about getting revenge?

It's not. Not for you, anyway.

So Graeme's going to get away scot-free?

Why not? What business is it of yours now? You're dead, remember?

Exactly! It doesn't seem fair . . .

You do what you want then, whispered Old Max into my head. *Just don't take too long.*

The first place I went after stumbling from the pit was Graeme's hotel. He had checked out that morning and chartered a light plane. Or so he'd told the clerk to give himself an alibi. When I drove out to the airfield, I did indeed find his rust-bucket parked near the tiny terminal, awaiting his return. I guessed that he'd flown to Alice Springs or another outpost—anywhere but here, where my body lay.

Had lain. Being mobile in death gave me an edge, if I wanted to take advantage of it: I had plenty of time to report his actions to the police. But I could imagine how it would look when the victim presented himself at the local station to report his own murder. I would be detained for days, maybe refrigerated or frozen, possibly even autopsied. Not pretty—and not truly necessary either, as Old Max said.

I absently pat my thigh for reassurance. The thumb-bone is still in my pocket, but I can't feel it any longer. My legs have gone numb. Gas is building up in my stomach cavity, and I fight the need to burp. God knows, the interior of the wagon must stink enough as it is. To give me something to clench, I take the bone whistle and put it between my lips. Despite my lack of respiration, its whispering voice seems oddly louder as a result, and more personable.

Back in my day, this sort of thing would have been impossible, Old Max says. *You'd need a week or two just to get from Coober Pedy to Adelaide. Then another month to reach Sydney . . . You don't realize how lucky you are, Billy.*

Yeah, right. I'm dead.

But you still have time to put things right. Remember that.

I do. For once, I understand him completely. The hatred is fading with time, as accepting my fate becomes less of an effort and more habitual. Only gradually does the inevitable alternative come to take its place.

On the great, endless freeways of this empty continent my Commodore is just a toy. Road trains roar past with a whoosh of air and dust, shaking me from my meditations for an instant then disappearing around a bend. I wonder sometimes if the drivers of these massive, metal dinosaurs are dead, too. That might explain a lot.

I wonder if they are lonely.

I refuel in Renmark, just shy of the Victorian border, keeping my jacket on as always and ignoring the curious stare of another young attendant as I pay. Back in the Commodore, I feel blood squelch in my buttocks where it has settled. My face in the rear vision mirror is pasty and beginning to puff. Gross.

I leave South Australia. An hour or so later I cross the Murray River at Mildura and enter New South Wales. The minutes and kilometres are passing quickly now: over half-way. Choosing the northern approach through Hay, I stop to refuel again, and for a quick walk to shift some of the gunk congealing in my lower extremities. I look like someone's filled my calves and thighs with jelly.

Still, there is no pain. There's only a sense of urgency, mounting steadily as my long, lonely drive continues. I have to warn Kerry. And Stephen . . .

At that moment, the sorrow hits—so deep that I am unable to do anything but pound the steering wheel in frustration. I stop the Commodore again as my vision clouds. I am crying, which surprises me even through the grief. I didn't know that corpses could cry.

When I raise my dead fingers to touch my cheeks, they come away dark and sticky. The burp I've been fighting for hours finally comes out. *That* hurts. I try to get a grip on myself, but fail; the despair is too strong.

Don't fall apart now, I hear old Max whisper, and the joke—intended or not—almost makes me smile. For an imaginary old soul, his sense of humour is awful.

Well, what do you expect? he shoots back. *I'm a bone, for Christ's sake. The only brains I have are yours, grand-son of my grand-son's son. At least I'm trying to do something—not sitting in a car sobbing about how unfair life is.*

And it isn't?

Maybe, but that doesn't mean you have to take it lying down. They'll find you out here in a couple of days, and what good will that have done anyone? You'll just be another mystery body in the middle of nowhere. Make your death mean something, boy, like I have. Leave something behind. Make it easier for those who follow. Do your bit for future generations—and all that crap.

It's not crap . . .

Then get off your fat arse and get on with it!

I shrug my failing body into action and start the wagon. The sun is setting behind me as I do so, and the sky is grey ahead. The world is losing its colour drop by drop, sucked out by the vampire moon. It's already hard to tell where the Western Highway stops and the countryside starts.

I flick on the lights and accelerate.

Good man, says Old Max. *Not far now . . .*

Sure. Only six hundred kilometres.

Whatever you say, it's still not far. Not for you.

I grip the wheel and plunge onward, Old Max's thumb clenched tight between my teeth. Dad gave me the whistle when Mum and I laid him to rest. I could see how much it meant to him then, as his eyes followed us back to the ute. He was alone at the end, which is enough to make even a very brave man sad. And I feel for him more than ever now.

Oh, Stephen. I'm missing you already . . .

The sun is completely gone as I breeze past West Wyalong. An image of Kerry suddenly fills my windscreen, painted across the road. She has blonde, curly hair cut just above her shoulders. Her eyes are green and lined at the corners. She doesn't smile often, but when she does it lights up her whole face. Her shoulders and back are taut from years of dancing, and her buttocks and thighs are as solid as rock, yet flexible. She can put both ankles behind her head, and do the splits in a variety of positions; both make her spectacular in bed. She has a small mole just above her pubic hair which we nick-named Cape Barren Island the first time we had sex.

The first time we *made love*, I asked her to marry me, and she said no. But we've lived together for six years since, and I guess that counts for something. Maybe we weren't happy some of the time— we certainly argued a lot, and we'd grown apart in a thousand subtle ways without really noticing—but we could still fuck up a storm when we wanted to. Which wasn't as often as either of us would have liked, after Stephen; not that we would admit it to each other any more. But it wasn't too late. We still could have—

I catch myself with a start when I realize that I am thinking about her in the past tense.

Keep it up, says Old Max. *Makes it easier in the long run.*

Cowra looms ahead: a light-blistered boil bursting out of the night. I pull into the first service station I come across and park next to a bowser. Before I get out, I check the rear vision mirror. I am turning blue, and my eyes look more than a little strange. Sunglasses only accentuate the sickly tone of my skin, so I don't bother to put them on. The attendant is watching me idly from the desk. Feigning tiredness, I climb out of the Commodore and fill the tank for the last time.

The attendant's face crumples into a grimace of distaste as I step into the showroom to pay. Christ, how badly do I smell now? I've only been in the room a second and he's already disgusted.

Handing him a fifty, I mutter, "Keep the change," and leave without looking back. At least I can still talk.

On the road again, I refuse to think about anyone at all: not Graeme, not Kerry, and especially not Stephen. But of course it doesn't work. If I can't look forward to the end of my journey, my thoughts inevitably return to the beginning, to Coober Pedy . . .

Although Graeme wasn't to be the main focus of my undeath, just as he hadn't been in life, he *had* killed me. I still needed to warn Kerry. Maybe she would be next.

I actually called the number out of my mobile phone's memory and pressed Send before thinking twice. "Honey, I'm dead." Was that what I was going to say to her, in the middle of the night? She would laugh in my ear, accuse me of being pissed and hang up. And if I managed to tell her that Graeme, her old friend, had done it, then her response would only be more skeptical. I needed to hammer the truth down her throat, and I couldn't do that over a telephone line from Coober Pedy.

And then there was Stephen. Images of his childhood suddenly filled my mind; not painful, as they are now, but with a clarity that could not be denied: nappies, dummies, bottles, toys; gurgling, babbling, crawling, walking. All of it came back to me in a vivid rush, and the desert night around me seemed to vanish. It was as though he was calling for me across the thousands of kilometres lying between us, as though he somehow knew what had happened to me and sent part of himself to be with me when I needed him most.

How could I fight something like that?

So I hung up before she could answer, switched off the phone and started driving. The trip had taken me three days on the way over, but I hadn't been really trying. I figured I could do it in a single day, and figure I can still do it, if only I—

Hurry, says Old Max, beginning to sound like a stuck CD. *Turn up looking like something from a ghost story and he's not even going to know who you are . . .*

Then, as now, I had no other option.

Bathurst breezes by.

Then Lithgow.

Blackheath.

Katoomba.

Lawson.

Springwood.

Penrith . . .

The suburbs of Sydney swallow the Commodore wagon like the waters of a bottomless lake. I feel like a stone that has skipped across the surface before finally sinking. Normality is everywhere

I look, as long as I avoid the mirror. Even at such a late hour the streets are busy and I have to fight the impulse to speed. The last thing I want is to be pulled over by the police.

Red lights make me itch and the radio, when I turn it on, emits an irritating noise. Old Max is silent, sensing my impatience, the proximity of my journey's climax. Or perhaps he has already said enough.

Familiar streets roll by; corners I have turned for years tick past one by one; landmarks I could draw from memory appear in their proper places and fall behind. This is *my* place, yet I feel like an outsider. And the sadness wells again, as inevitably as the tide.

Home . . .

I pull into Argent Lane with my heart in my mouth. The street is dark and empty. Two houses from the end, near the letter box and behind the hedge we always meant to trim before winter came: there it is.

My house. After eighteen hundred kilometres and twenty-three hours of slow decay, I'm finally here.

I swing the Commodore as close to the left as I can in preparation for entering the driveway, then—

Wait!

Old Max's warning comes barely in time. There is another car in the driveway.

I slam on the brakes. "Shit." Confused, I stare at it for a moment, wondering whether I've got the wrong house. But no: behind the unfamiliar car is Kerry's 121, tucked safely under the carport where she likes it, where the birds can't crap on it. And the house itself is right. There's no mistaking the white-plastered brick walls, the shallow verandah, the lawn in perpetual need of a mow and the bicycle, now a size too small, abandoned for the night by the red front door.

The lights are out. Whoever owns the car is here to stay.

The first spark of anger blossoms somewhere deep in my gut. I turn off the headlights and park the wagon further along the curb. Kerry's sister doesn't have a license. A friend, then? Maybe. How good a friend, though, is the question.

Can a corpse be jealous? It seems so. I feel abandoned, left out.

How do you think I've felt? puts in Old Max. *All these years a bone, with no one to talk to but my descendants when they die. It gives you a new perspective, believe me. I've seen this situation a dozen times and I'm beginning to wonder why people get so upset.*

In the long run Kerry means nothing. Hold onto that thought and you'll feel better.

Doubting it, but saying nothing, I leave the confines of the Commodore and inch my way up the driveway as quietly as I can. My balance is shot to hell and I keep one hand ready to catch me should I stumble. The car is an Avis rental, a Ford Falcon about five years out of date. The bonnet is cold. Its driver has left something on the seat, and I peer through the passenger window for a better look.

An airline ticket. Squinting, forcing my stubborn eyes to focus, I make out the carrier: Ansett. Destination: Sydney. Passenger's name . . .

Mr G J Parkinson.

I freeze. *Graeme . . . ?*

Old Max is silent as I reel back a step, stunned by the revelation. My murderer has beaten me home, after all I've been through to get here first! He must have flown to Alice Springs in the light aircraft he chartered, then caught a plane to Sydney. He could have been here for hours. God only know what he could have done in that time, who he might have hurt now . . .

Then another thought occurs to me. I turn to face the dark, silent house. My hands are shaking. I remember the times I've been out while Graeme's been in town, the times I've come home to find him hanging around with Kerry. His Sydney residence is not far from ours, and she likes strong, tall men. They knew each other before I met either of them; maybe they were lovers in the past.

They both love money . . . and I know for a fact that one of them will murder for it. Maybe two.

Graeme hasn't just beaten me home. He's been here—to put it metaphorically—all along.

A red fury turns the night inside out. The hatred is back, twice as strong. I want to smash my way through the bedroom window and rip their treacherous hearts out—Kerry's first, then Graeme's. I want to see the fear in their eyes as I enact my vengeance. I want them to suffer; I want them to see their plans come to nothing; I want them to *die* . . .

I take one unsteady step towards the house, then stop.

Why? asks Old Max, and I have to admit, even through the pain, that he is right.

Revenge, bitter-sweet though it might well be, is meaningless; it ultimately hurts the one person who really matters.

I turn to my right and make my way around the side of the house, up the carport, counting windows as I go: lounge, bathroom, toilet, kitchen . . .

The last window faces the small backyard, with its swing and toy-strewn sandpit. The curtains are patterned with the characters from *Thomas the Tank Engine* but I can't make out their faces in the darkness. The screen is old and comes off easily. My reflection leans close as I raise one soft-knuckled fist to tap three times on the glass.

I wait for a minute, then try again. "Stephen?"

The curtains stir, and another face appears within my reflection: another me, from years ago.

"Dad?" he mouths, and I nod with relief.

He tugs at the latch as I take the whistle out of my mouth. My four-year-old son moves with all the innocent confidence and grace of an animal, with my eyes, my nose, my olive skin and my dark hair in tow. The only things he's inherited from his mother are her small ears and lips. Otherwise he's me, and everything that entails.

Finally the window is open. I reach in to hug him, and he returns the clasp.

"I've missed you, Stephen," I say. My tongue is thick and heavy, but the words are clear.

His sweet voice in my ear whispers back: "You smell, Dad."

I pull away. Shit, I'd forgotten about that. "I'm sorry. Oh God, I'm sorry. I got here as fast as I could but—"

"Where've you *been?*" His eyes are wide and curious.

"I—" What do I say? I was dying, son, dying to get home. "I was up at Coober Pedy with Graeme to check out the mine. Remember?"

"Uncle Gray came to dinner," he said, not realizing how much his words hurt me. Self-absorption rules the day at this age. "We had chips and sausages."

"That's nice," I respond, trying to keep the grief bottled in my chest. "Stephen, I brought you a present."

His eyes light up. "Did you? Where is it?"

"It's in my hand, but first you have to promise to keep it a secret. Don't tell Mum . . . or Uncle Gray. I want you to keep it safe from everyone."

He nods seriously. "Okay, Dad."

"And I want you to listen to me carefully. Something's happened to me." *I'm dead.* "I won't be able to come home. I won't be able to live with you any more." *I'm rotting in front of your eyes.* "You and Mum will have to manage without me from now on."

"Why, Dad?" His face loses its happy glow, and for a moment I am unable to speak.

"Dad?"

"I love you, Stephen." I reach out with one hand and put Old Max on the window sill. "And here's your present."

He picks it up and turns it over, studying it. His tiny fingers are dwarfed by the size of the thumb-bone, and I marvel that one day his hands will be that big.

"What is it?"

"It's a whistle. You blow in one end and—" I shrug. "— sometimes it makes a noise."

He raises it to his lips and blows experimentally through it.

Goodbye, Billy, says Old Max, softly but distinctly. *I'll tell him when it's time.*

"I didn't hear anything," Stephen says.

"You will when you're older." When you're dead, I add to myself. There's no way I can even begin to explain; four is too young to comprehend natural death, let alone the unnatural one awaiting him. *We die young but take our time passing on; it's hereditary. I'm sorry, son.* "Keep trying, and one day you'll hear it. It's name is 'Old Max'."

"Is it magic?" he asks, programmed by TV to believe in such things.

I smile, glad that he has unintentionally given me an explanation that he will understand. "Yes."

He smiles back and we stand there, sharing our secret in silence for a full minute.

Then he shivers. His pyjamas are thin and the air must be like a refrigerator's breath this time of year, piercing with its chill although I am oblivious to it.

I feel for him. Leaning out of the window talking to his decomposing father, with the bone of his great-great-great-great-grandfather in his hand: this is no place for a little kid. He should be in bed, dreaming about Thomas while he still can.

"I can't stay," I say, frightened that I'm going to cry in front of him, frightened that that will frighten him.

He nods once, keeping his sad eyes on the whistle.

"Be a good boy for Mummy, won't you?"

"Yes, Dad."

"And . . . " *Don't forget me.* "Remember that I love you."

"I love you too, Dad," he says, and his eyes finally meet mine. Even in the darkness I can tell that he too is trying not to cry.

We hug once more, and I don't want to let him go. But I have to. I gently lean him back through the window, back to reality, and tousle his hair.

As we close the window I see him raise the whistle to his lips in one last salute—blood of my blood, possessing the terrible secret of my family with all the innocence of a four year old—but this time I hear nothing. Then the curtains close, and he is gone.

I replace the screen and stagger away from the window, letting the tears flow freely. The night dissolves into a blur and for a moment I can't think . . .

When I regain my senses I am standing on the front lawn like a grotesque monument to mortality, tainting the suburban air with my stench—

Alone.

So, now what?

I resist the temptation to leave Kerry a note. Telling her . . . what? That I love her too? That she deserves to rot in hell? That I hope she and Graeme are happy?

Fuck that. The more I think about it, the more I want to kill them. I bite down on the impulse, knowing it won't do anyone any good, especially Stephen. Someone has to look after him now that I'm gone. I can only hope that it won't be Graeme. If there was only some way I could hurt him without hurting Kerry at the same time . . .

For want of an alternative, I return to the Commodore and assume my familiar position on the stained driver's seat. The tank is less than a quarter-full, but that may be enough, depending on where I intend to go. But where is that?

Sydney hides a lot, but it can't possibly hide an obviously dead person, gradually rotting.

I am dead, impotent. I am also a cuckold killed by his business partner, and the anger refuses to fade. But there's no way I can report my murder in person, and to phone anonymously would be pointless. Even if the police believe me and pass on the report to Coober Pedy, what would they find? An empty pit with some blood and hair at the bottom. Nothing to link Graeme with his terrible crime.

Unless I drive back to Coober Pedy again.

Or . . .

I smile in the darkness, then. Maybe death isn't the complete disadvantage I thought it was. I can use my very handicap as a weapon.

I don't need somewhere to hide; I need a *grave*.

The engine is still warm and the wagon starts easily despite the long drive. I glance back once as I pull out from the curb. The house is still dark; Stephen must have gone back to sleep. That's good.

Then the house—home no longer—is gone.

Graeme's city-side apartment—which he lets for half the year, but is empty at the moment—is in Silverwater, less than ten minutes' drive from Argent Lane. The small, single-bedroom maisonette is tucked at the end of a cul-de-sac filled with blocks of flats and strata-share units. I park the Commodore two blocks away and walk the rest of the way. Luckily, the hour is late enough to make it extremely unlikely that anyone will see me: the walking dead in their midst.

I climb the iron gate, fish the spare key from its hiding place under a small gnome by the back door, and let myself in. Taking a chair from the kitchen, I position it in the hallway under the trapdoor leading into the ceiling.

A sudden fear that my sagging flesh might fail me at the last minute proves groundless. I have just enough strength to haul myself into the dusty crawl-space. The chair will have to stay where it is. After carefully wiping the edges of the hole clean of my fingerprints, I put the trapdoor back in its place and inch on hands and knees across the wooden beams.

It is dark and quiet in the ceiling, if a little dirty. I find a space in one corner by the air-vent leading to the bathroom in the adjoining maisonette and settle down to wait. I have my wallet and my mobile phone. There'll be no mistaking me, no matter how long I have to wait. And I'll be here when they come. If the smell hasn't alerted the neighbours by tomorrow morning, then I'll use the phone to tell the police myself. I'm a concerned resident in the area who's heard an argument, I'll say; and perhaps I should do that anyway, to help pin the blame on Graeme. I don't want my appearance to be written off as a coincidence. I don't want him to escape me now . . .

The only thing I haven't got is company. But that's all right; my time has come and gone and I don't need Old Max any more. My own bones will have to do instead. My bones and my thoughts, lost in the dusty crawl-space between life and death.

for Sebastian
●

AFTERWORD TO:
.... PASSING THE BONE

Because I don't like doing things the usual way, this story started with a simple dare to write something with a zombie in it (see the notes to "Entre les Beaux Morts en Vie") and became the hardest thing I had ever tried to put down on paper. It wasn't intentional in the slightest. Sometimes the best stories aren't.

The core idea was simple enough. Man with a hereditary curse is killed by greedy business partner, who also happens to be cuckolding him. The curse brings the protagonist back to life, giving him the perfect opportunity to gain revenge.

But that wasn't the kind of story my heart wanted to write that day. I didn't want my zombie to be a shambolic, brainless monster. I wanted him to be entirely sympathetic. His decay was more about the way his life had fallen apart than the dissolution of humanity. And besides, the curse was hereditary.

Giving him a son he's desperate to farewell before he falls entirely to bits was the easiest thing in the world. Writing the farewell— well, that was a different story. It mirrored my real life a little too closely for anything like comfort. And while writing can at times be cathartic, at other times it can just extend painful moments beyond all proportion.

"They say suffering's good for writers," Noel Coward once quipped. "It strengthens their psychology."

While it certainly strengthened this story, I'm very glad to report that real life had a happier ending.

•

A VIEW BEFORE DYING

The moment Rod Hallows opened his eyes, he knew something had gone wrong. He could feel it—even if, for the moment, he could see nothing. His first instinct was to call for help, but the feed from Control had ceased, the inside of his helmet was utterly silent, and only the virtual light cast by his implants broke the darkness surrounding him.

The truth of where he was sank in only gradually. He had closed his eyes as the d-mat process had begun, just seconds ago, but that brief blink had lasted twenty-two point four light years and almost a quarter of a century. He found it hard to imagine—and wondered whether this might itself be the cause of the problem he sensed. From rest to ninety percent of the speed of light in one timeless instant; who knew what effects that would have, until he tried it?

Well, he *had* tried it—and now he was on *Saul–1*, mid-way through its long journey to another star. If he was conscious, he told himself, then it must be so.

Having come that far along his journey to realization, he moved his arms and legs. Everything there seemed in order, at least; he had arrived intact. But still the gut-feeling nagged, that something had gone terribly, terribly *wrong* . . .

The feeling was confirmed when the airlock door slid open and his suit's radiation alarm began to sound.

For a brief instant he froze, transfixed by the view. His last sight had been of the disembarkation facility in near-Earth orbit. Now

Earth had disappeared, leaving nothing but subtly distorted stars in its wake. Except—and he forced himself to remember this, to keep his sense of perspective—it was *he* who had moved, not the universe around him.

When the alarm finally registered, he realized that it was a cautionary alert; had the radiation levels been too severe, the doors wouldn't have opened at all. But when he tried to access the probe's mainframe via his implants to find out what was going on, he was greeted with stony silence.

He cursed to himself. Whatever had happened had been severe.

Tugging gently on the frame of the airlock, he drifted out of the tiny d-mat enclosure and onto the surface of the probe. Before he took any drastic steps, he needed to look around.

Behind him, the airlock slid shut automatically. As he attached a line to the hook beside the airlock door, a faint vibration registered through his fingertips. The d-mat capsule was already powering-up for the next arrival: Roald Gehrke, the team's computer systems analyst. Apart from the vibration, the probe was still.

After checking the suit's systems to ensure his life-support and EMU were operating correctly, Hallows left his perch with a gentle kick and headed for an access-ladder. From there he pulled himself through perfect weightlessness down the long axis of the probe. As he passed from handhold to handhold, the remains of nanomachines left behind by previous refit crews scattered beneath his fingertips like small puffs of dust and dissipated slowly through the vacuum. How many remained active but quiescent, awaiting *his* refit crews' commands, he had no easy way of telling. Without the mainframe to assist him, he was restricted solely to visual clues.

As he crawled towards the rear of the probe, the implants automatically scanned his vision for anomalies. Apart from the light from the stars around him he was in complete darkness, with nothing but vacuum for light years in every direction. Bright though the stars were, they did little to dispel the shadows shrouding his immediate environment. Only with the gain on his implants turned to maximum could he make out any details at all.

Perversely, everything on this side of the probe seemed normal: no damage, no evidence of a major catastrophe; nothing to explain what had happened to cause the rise in incident radiation.

Saul-1 was seventy metres long and approximately eleven wide, with gap-toothed holes in its matte-grey skin exposing a solid mess of girders, struts and lattice-work beneath. The probe had an unfinished look—and, in a very real sense, *wasn't* finished. The skin in particular was irrelevant to its overall structure, serving not as an external boundary but as a shield to deflect micrometeorites and hard radiation from fragile components. When the probe and its two sisters—*Saul–2* and *Saul–3*, years behind—finally arrived at their destination, the skin would be discarded entirely.

If it arrived, Hallows thought grimly to himself. He glanced over his shoulder, forward along the probe, and was gratified to see Eta Boötis immediately ahead. To his naked eye, the slightly blue-shifted star appeared to be in the correct place, but there was no way he could be sure until he logged into the probe's mainframe and analyzed the astronomical data. And to do that, he needed Gehrke's help.

The feeling of utter isolation mounted, although he knew it to be irrational. The others would arrive soon enough, and then he would have someone to share his problems with. All he had to do was last that long. By then, he hoped, he would know what the problem was. Maybe, just maybe, he might even have fixed it.

When he came to the end of the access ladder he mounted the aft end of the probe and swung down beside the drive shaft—the most obvious source of a radiation leak, apart from the reactor core itself. He half-expected his suit's alarm to intensify as he did so, and was mildly surprised when it remained unchanged. Puzzled, and temporarily lacking direction, he turned to look around.

Inactive for the past twenty-four years, the shaft now served as a home for various dishes and antennae, all pointing back towards Earth, locked onto the dim speck of light that was Sol.

All, that is, except one.

Hallows' implants flashed a red halo around this solitary dish while a database scrolled schematics down the corner of his visual field. His stomach fell even before he glanced at the text. He didn't need to be told what purpose the dish served, or what the malfunction represented to him personally. The transmit dish was potentially the most important on the probe; its failure spelled a death-sentence. Without it, they would never return to Earth.

Unable even to contemplate that possibility just yet, he turned away from the sight of the misaligned antenna. As he did so, something caught his eye further up the drive shaft. Again the implants threw a halo over the foreign object, but this time failed to identify it. The faint starlight was insufficient to illuminate so deep into the interior of the shaft.

He leaned further into the circular tube. The red-limned shadow might have been anything, but to Hallows it looked like a man: a man curled around himself with one hand reaching up to touch his face.

Somebody on the probe . . . ? That was impossible. The previous refit crew had left years ago; the nearest people were back on Earth, light years away. The only way anyone could be aboard was if they were dead.

Swallowing a ball of apprehension, Hallows crawled into the shaft. The shadow didn't move as he approached, but still he remained cautious. As the distance narrowed, he slowed himself unconsciously; by the time he was within a metre of the object, he had drifted to a halt.

It *was* a man, that much was obvious close up. His suit was identical to the one Hallows himself wore—except for the visor, which dangled open.

Hallows forced himself to lean closer. The name-tag on the suit said:

PROSILIS 1422K7A31

The name evoked memories of a small, fair-haired man with a lively sense of humour and relaxed demeanour. Hallows had trained with Antonio Prosilis for a month, before the latter had left on the refit mission previous to his. Had he been asked to, he would gladly have wagered that Prosilis was the least likely of all the refitters to commit suicide.

The recollection jarred with the black-faced corpse floating in the drive shaft before him. That Prosilis had deliberately unsealed his suit was unarguable: one hand remained tightly clenched around the plastic visor, and there were no signs of a struggle; just solitary agony followed shortly by death. Prosilis' contorted features were mottled by vacuum-bruises around eyes squeezed tightly shut.

Trying hard to quash the tide of speculation rising in him, Hallows crawled out of the shaft. A radiation alarm, an inactive mainframe, a misaligned transmit dish and a dead body . . . . The list of misfortunes seemed endless. Until Gehrke arrived and examined the mainframe, the best he could do was explore the probe as well as he could, hoping he would stumble by chance upon a possible cause of the tragedy.

A cause, and a cure. Without the latter, they would be stranded aboard the probe until their air-supply ran out. There were no other options. By stepping into the disembarkation booth on Earth, they had deliberately cut themselves off from the rest of humanity. Nothing but empty space lay between the probe and home: trillions of kilometres of void, forever . . .

He shook his head, trying to banish the image, to erase the reference point of Sol. He could only think about here and now—the probe and him—or he'd go crazy.

Like Prosilis . . . ?

Then, as he swung himself carefully around the lip of the aft end, intending to head back to the d-mat airlock via the other side of the probe, a black patch appeared in the shimmer of stars to his left. Thinking a ball of dust had smudged his visor, he automatically raised a hand to brush it away. Only when he lowered his hand and the circular patch remained did he actually turn to study it. Another second passed before he truly understood what he was seeing.

Floating in space not two hundred metres from the probe, and stationary with respect to it, was another ship.

Jimmy Tarasento took the news badly—as Hallows had expected—although he hid it well. Of the three of them, he had the most to lose.

The refit crew huddled on the spine of the probe not far from the d-mat airlock. Hallows had been on *Saul–1* for six hours, Gehrke half that long. The three-hour lag between revelations—the time the d-mat receiver took to process the data comprising each refitter beamed from Earth—had worn Hallows' nerves ragged. He was heartily glad that he only had to break the news twice.

Gehrke barely contained his frustration. His face burned red in the starlight as he waited for Tarasento to absorb the situation. The big systems analyst had never been renowned for his patience. Ever since his arrival he had been a furious knot of energy, twisting and writhing in an attempt to untangle itself.

Tarasento was more composed. A full minute passed before he finally opened his mouth and said "Fuck." He raised a hand to his visor, as though to wipe his forehead, then let it drift limply to his chest. His brown eyes rolled upwards to a sky that wasn't there. "I guess that's it. We're stuck here forever."

"Not forever," corrected Gehrke. "Twenty-six days. That's how much air we have."

"Until we die, then." Tarasento sounded like he was about to cry. "That's the same as forever, isn't it?"

"Easy." Hallows reached out to grip the younger man's shoulder. "We don't know for sure yet."

"Like hell we don't," growled Gehrke. "The transmission dish is off-target. God only knows what it's pointing at, but it isn't Earth. If we try to leave, we'll be sprayed across the universe like water from a fucking hose. They'll never track the signal."

"Maybe we can realign the dish," Hallows said, refusing to admit defeat in front of the others, and still trying his best to keep the conversation focused on the *now*.

"Yeah, maybe. And maybe we'll build a warp drive and fly back home instead."

"What happened?" Tarasento said softly, almost afraid to ask the question. "What went wrong?"

Gehrke deflated instantly. "We don't know. I've only logged into the mainframe as far as the maintenance systems. We're not supposed to mess with the guidance or transmission programs, so they'll take a while to get into. I'll do it, though, if I have to."

"Is it something to do with *that?*" For the first time since his arrival, Tarasento acknowledged the dark scar in the starfield. "Whatever the hell it is."

"It's a ship," said Hallows. "And it's the source of the radiation. Beyond that, we don't know much."

"Could it be human?"

"I doubt it." Hallows felt the hollow in his chest widen as it did every time he thought about the other ship.

"Surely the others left some sort of explanation?" Tarasento leaned forward to clutch Gehrke's arm. "A log, a message—there must be—"

"None that I've found," Gehrke said. "Just the usual mission reports, filed by automatics. The core programs have been tampered with though, and the mainframe's running a little slow, which usually means there's some heavy data stashed away on it somewhere. That might be what we're looking for, or it might be the problem itself. We'll only know when I find it."

"And how long will that take?"

"As long as it takes." Gehrke's eyes flashed. "Which depends on how long I have to sit here wasting my time."

Tarasento leaned back, chastened. "I'm sorry, Roald. It's just . . . it's still sinking in. You've had longer to think about it, to get used to the idea. Give me a day or two and I'll catch up."

"You can rest for a while, if you like," Hallows interjected. "But not too long. As Roald says, we're wasting time. We can talk just as easily programming the refit as we can sitting here."

Gehrke laughed bitterly. "Why bother? It's not going to do *us* any good, is it?"

"I didn't mean you, Roald. I want you to keep digging into the mainframe, to see if you can find out what happened. Get us access to the observation systems at least, so we can take a better look at that . . . thing." Hallows took a deep breath. The dark shadow seemed to watch him like an eye. "Jimmy and I will do the work. Whether we'll die in four weeks or not doesn't change what we came here to do. We've got mods to install, nanoware to program, repairs to make. The other refitters are still on the way, and there's nothing we can do about that. *Saul–1* is the important thing, not us."

"Can't let the side down," mumbled Gehrke.

"No, it's more than that. We don't have a choice, dammit."

"We either work or go crazy." Tarasento shrugged and tried to smile. "It'll make the time pass, anyway."

"Right." Hallows was grateful for the young man's rapid comprehension of the situation. He didn't think he could handle a volatile confrontation at that moment—doubted that *any* of them could. Even through the thick fabric of his companions' suits, and the stubborn bluff that kept weakness carefully from view, he could plainly see the stress in their postures, faces and eyes.

Behind them, as thought on cue, the d-mat airlock cycled open and automated systems began dispensing equipment and raw materials freshly-arrived from Earth. Hallows uncoiled from his squat, signalling the end of the impromptu debriefing.

"Time to work," he said.

"Hey-bloody-ho," muttered Gehrke, but obeyed nonetheless.

Hours passed in an unmarked blur. A green chronometer in one corner of Hallows' field of view patiently ticked off the time, but the numbers soon became meaningless. Without a sun or a moon to make a difference, every hour was identical to the previous; the only thing that changed was the task he was performing at any given moment.

The fifth of seven refit crews, their prime objective was to prepare the probe for its period of deceleration; after twenty-two years of coasting at near-light-speed, the time was approaching for the mighty engines to fire again. The loss of Gehrke's input made little difference. At a pinch, one person could have done the work required. Three had been sent to insure against unforeseen catastrophes, just as most of the probe's basic systems had been designed in triplicate. Had things gone according to plan, Hallows would have been anticipating a speedy return to Earth—although the apparent swiftness of the round trip was relative only to him and his crew.

It still seemed strange to him that, although he had left Earth less than four years behind *Saul–1*, he wouldn't return—if he *could* return—until eleven years after it had arrived at Eta Boötis. He could tackle the paradox intellectually—by calculating the changing velocity of the probe and its position in space at various stages of its thirty-seven year journey, then superimposing the vector of his own body as it travelled from and to Earth as what amounted to a beam of high-energy coherent light—but it still didn't make *sense*.

He had expected to lose forty-five years of history and gain up to four weeks of experience in deep-space. The trade-off had seemed acceptable when he had applied for a position in the Program. Since the moment he'd stepped from the d-mat however, he had hardly stopped to look at the sky around him. He'd been unconsciously avoiding the alien ship, and the probable fate awaiting him.

He'd known the risks, of course. They had been drummed into him from day one. There was no way to turn back. The constraints of light-speed were unbreakable. If the probe had blown up an hour or a decade before they arrived, the loss of signal wouldn't have been noticed on Earth until years after they had left. And the same constraints applied now to a cry for help: twenty-two years would pass before Earth even heard it.

Perhaps, he mused, it would have been better if the probe *had* blown up before they arrived. At least that way they would have been unaware that the three of them were, to all intents and purposes, dead. Unless, since their departure, someone had invented an FTL drive and arrived in the nick of time to save the three stranded refitters . . .

Hallows tasted bitterness on his tongue. Not three refitters, but *six*. Lockley, Pearce and Prosilis had been in exactly the same predicament as he, Gehrke and Tarasento. Prosilis had killed himself, and no trace had been found of the other two. Hallows couldn't stop himself from wondering what they would choose when *their* time came.

He shook sweat from his eyes, wishing he could take off the suit just once to wipe his face. The breathing of his companions rasped loudly in his ears. The paste from his mouth-tube tasted like plastic. Avoidance of the problem didn't seem to be proving a viable alternative to dealing with it—at least for him.

"Christ," he said. "I need a drink. A *real* drink."

"Hear, hear." Tarasento's voice, from the far side of the probe, came clear and brittle through the suit's earphones. "I'll hop into the 'mat and get one, shall I?"

"Great." And *that* was the problem. From anywhere to anywhere in Sol System took little more than a step by d-mat. It was hard to believe that Earth was really over two decades away.

"I've been studying the other ship," Tarasento said. "The magnification on my visor isn't great, but it's better than nothing."

"And?" Hallows allowed curiosity free reign for a moment; anything was better than the gloom that threatened to envelop him again. "Has it moved?"

"No."

"Good." Unless it did, he could continue to ignore it.

"It's strange, though," Tarasento went on. "The angles are all wrong. I don't know how to describe it exactly, and it's hard to tell through the shadows, but it looks like it might be damaged."

Hallows nodded to himself; he had noticed that as well. The ship seemed oddly proportioned, almost contorted, as though someone had crumpled it into a ball and flung it into space. What he said was: "How can there be shadows, Jimmy, when there's no primary source of light?"

Tarasento hesitated. "I don't know. But that's what they *look* like ... "

"Maybe it's paint, or the natural colour of the hull." If it *is* a hull, he added to himself. Sometimes it looked like folded sheets of paper, sometimes like the twisted planes of a mangled, multi-dimensional windmill. For all he knew, the design constituted the very apex of architectural perfection from an alien's point of view.

"Yeah, maybe. If we could get closer, we'd know for sure." The sudden eagerness in Tarasento's voice was thinly-disguised. "It'd only take fifteen minutes there by EMU; less if I burned a little longer—"

"No, Jimmy. It's too radioactive. You'd be dead in under ten minutes."

"So? We're picking up plenty of rads now, aren't we? What difference is a few weeks going to make?"

"Forget the other ship." Gehrke's voice cut in abruptly on the open line. "I've found something."

"What?"

"Slave your 'plants to the mainframe, and I'll show you."

Hallows obeyed, grateful for the interruption. The starfield through his visor immediately gave way to a symbolic representation of the probe's reactivated computer network. The view resembled a scene from an Escher painting, with impossible angles and planes jutting out of a mottled grey valley. A Teutonian spear floated over the surreal landscape: Gehrke's idiosyncratic icon.

"I was browsing through the d-mat systems when I found it," said the systems analyst. The spear guided Hallows down into the mainframe. "Here, here and here." The spear stabbed at structures in the datafield. "This is what's slowing up the 'frame."

"What is it?" Tarasento's question preempted Hallows' own.

"One massive file, so large it's swallowed all the available free memory, and then some. Parts of the core programming have been over-written. It's not a virus, though. Someone deliberately put it there."

"Does it have a name?"

"That's the best bit. Look at this." The spear dipped lower, into a rift in the massive structure, and came to rest pointing at a slab stamped with the brief message:

PEARCE 0114B4M11

"Pearce? He was one of Prosilis' team, wasn't he?"

"Spot on, Jimmy: he *was*. This file is all that's left of him now."

"It's a message from him? Does he say what happened?"

"No, it's not a message. It's *him*."

Tarasento's sharp intake of breath was clearly audible over the radio. "Jesus."

"The file is in standard holographic crypt," Gehrke explained, "straight out of the d-mat systems. He must have loaded himself into the capsule and sent the data into *Saul-1*'s mainframe rather than out into space. And here it is, jamming everything around it."

"Can we download him?" asked Hallows. "Feed the file into the d-mat systems and bring him back?"

"Maybe he can tell us what happened," Tarasento added.

"We could try, when the shipments from Earth stop." Gehrke didn't sound too confident. "But I don't think he'd thank us."

Hallows silently agreed; tempting though it was, it would be cruel to resurrect the refitter before they had worked out a way to rescue him.

"Maybe later," he said. "Keep digging, Roald. See what else you find. Let me know when you break into the comm system."

"Will do." Gehrke sounded tired. "I just thought you'd like to know what happened to another of our predecessors."

"Yeah, thanks."

"But if you come across any other corpses," Tarasento added, "for God's sake don't tell me. I don't want to know . . . "

Hallows found the graffiti on the third day. The probe, for all its sophistication and redundancies, lacked even something as simple as chalk or an ink pen. The message had been physically etched into an interior bulkhead twenty-three years earlier by one of the members of the first refit crew, and signed by them all:

HI, GUYS AND GALS.
LEAVE THE KEY UNDER THE MAT WHEN YOU LEAVE!
—CHAMBERS, MAXWELL AND HARTOG.

An unknown time later, someone else had scribbled cryptically underneath:

THE KEY IS HERE, AND THE CHOICE IS YOURS.
USE IT IF YOU WANT TO.
3:50.

The final ratio might have been a signature—although it was too short for an ident-code—or it might have been a time. Ten minutes to four? March, 2050? There was no way of knowing, without further clues.

Hallows stared at the words for at least five minutes before deciding not to tell the others. The first message was too depressing; the last meaningless. Either could be enough to drive a stake through what little remained of his crew's morale.

After the discovery of the PEARCE file, he and Tarasento had argued over what to do with Prosilis' body. Hallows had wanted to leave it where it was, but the younger man had expressed extreme discomfort at the thought of a corpse aboard the probe. What the three of them didn't need was more stress, so Hallows had let Tarasento flush the body out of the drive shaft and into space, where it had vanished almost instantly into the distance.

No one had said anything, not even Gehrke. But the big systems analyst hadn't needed to; Hallows could read his thoughts like a book: *Go quick, go clean, and don't leave a mess.* In Gehrke's personal opinion, Prosilis had been a sloppy bastard for leaving his body behind to torment later arrivals.

Hallows knew what Gehrke would do, perhaps sooner than later. The moment he convinced himself that there was no hope of rescue or escape: *that* would be the time he acted.

Part of him envied the systems analyst's stubborn surety of mind. Hallows doubted he'd know what to do until the penultimate minute, when the air-processor in his suit winked red for the first and last time.

On the seventh day, Gehrke worked his way into the communication and navigation systems. Instantly he slaved the others to the mainframe and showed them what he had found.

"First things first," he began. A week of non-stop work leant a thick edge to the systems analyst's voice. "We're a little light on the nanos; down by about ten percent optimum, although that's correcting itself now we've set them replicating again. I don't know why for certain—it might be something to do with the radiation—but there you have it.

"Secondly, there was an impact about a year before Lockley's team arrived. Not large, but enough to shift course a fraction. It could have been a particle, although that seems unlikely; anything big enough to get through the vanes would probably have destroyed the probe entirely. Whatever it was, attitudes corrected the orientation of the probe and the reception dishes realigned themselves onto the incoming data from Earth. The transmit systems employed their tracking algorithms to relocate Sol. Within twelve hours all systems were back to normal.

"Thirdly . . . " Gehrke hesitated. "One year later, seventy-two hours after the arrival of Lockley and Co., the transmit dishes were deliberately sabotaged. Someone over-rode the automatics to point them off target, then erased the tracking algorithms. Why? Again, I don't know, but whoever did it knew what they were doing. The algorithms are *gone*, and there's no way of realigning the dishes correctly without them. We could point them in roughly the right direction, but *Saul-1* can't give us enough sustained power for a wide-beam transmission and a narrow beam could miss the receiving stations around Sol by millions of kilometres. So we really are stuck here."

"But—"

"Let me finish, Jimmy." Gehrke changed the view of the mainframe. "There are two more things. Pearce encrypted himself on the nineteenth day. Six days after *that*, someone fiddled with the research systems and commandeered LSM 14—one of the laser spectrometers."

"Why?" asked Hallows.

"Your guess is good as mine, I'm afraid," Gehrke sighed. "The obvious scenario, if you ignore the LSM, is that Lockley fucked up the dishes. Maybe he was a saboteur, or just plain crazy. Whatever. When the others realized what had happened, they did exactly what I've done. They broke into the comm and navigation systems to see what they could do, but failed to find a solution. So they gave up. They did the work they had come here for, then Prosilis killed himself and Pearce loaded himself into the 'frame to wait for someone to rescue him."

"Where do the aliens fit in?" asked Tarasento.

"I don't know. I can't account for them at all."

"And what happened to Lockley?" added Hallows.

"That's where it really gets weird." Gehrke's spear-icon dipped into the mass of communications programs, selecting options too quickly for Hallows to follow. A virtual workbench appeared. "My first thought was that they threw him overboard, but that doesn't make sense when you dig deeper into the core. For instance, this is the LSM's control-window. Watch what happens when I enter a command."

Words flashed across the window, but instantly disappeared. A brief message appeared in their place:

COMMAND OVER-RIDDEN.
READY FOR TRANSMISSION.

"'Transmission'?" echoed Hallows. "Of what?"

"And over-ridden by whom?" Tarasento asked.

"By Lockley," replied Gehrke. "He did this. He locked the LSM in place. Even if we wanted to, we couldn't shift it."

"What about manually?" Hallows asked.

"It'd only move back. And why would we want to anyway?"

"That depends on what it's pointing at."

Hallows could hear the shrug in Gehrke's weary reply. "Nothing, as far as I can tell. Lockley, damn him, didn't say."

"How do you know it was Lockley?" Tarasento asked.

"He was the systems officer of the last crew, that's how."

"Then he must have known what he was doing."

"Maybe, and maybe not—but he sure as hell wanted the laser to stay where it is. Just like he wanted to make sure we stayed here by erasing the tracking algorithms."

"He did that, too?"

"Of course."

"Why him?"

"What do you mean, 'Why him?' Who else could have done it? The goddamn *aliens?*"

"Why the fuck not? They must have been doing *something* before the others arrived—"

"Easy, you two." Hallows leaned forward to study the words in the window, but the virtual image remained a constant distance from him. "Roald, can you give us a view of where the LSM is pointing?"

"I tried that, but—"

"Just do it."

The window vanished. A red-shifted starscape took its place.

"Can you magnify that?"

"It's already on full. To get a better look, we'd have to reorient the probe and use the forward sensors. And I don't think Lockley would let us do that either, somehow."

Hallows studied the stars for a long moment, searching for anything out of place. "I can't see anything," he finally said.

"That's what I told you," snapped Gehrke. "There's nothing there. Nothing for hundreds of light years."

"What about the wreck itself? Have we checked to see if it's drifting? Maybe when Lockley aimed the laser, that's what it was pointing at."

"Maybe . . . " Gehrke grudgingly acknowledged the point. "I can find out."

"Do that, Roald. And while you're at it, check the status of the d-mat systems. I want to make sure that, assuming we find a way to realign the dishes, we *can* leave. So much has been screwed up here I'm not willing to assume *anything* any more—except that we can't give up yet."

"Like Lockley did?" Tarasento broke in, his voice thin with strain. "He killed himself, just like the others."

"Jimmy—"

"It's obvious, isn't it, Rod? The aliens fucked up the transmit dishes, and Lockley saved us the trouble of trying to save ourselves. Then he beamed himself nowhere, took the easy way out—"

"Not necessarily. I met Bill a couple of times back in the training centre. He didn't seem the sort to give up *and* force us to do the same."

"You don't know that."

"No, I don't. But that's what I believe." *Because I have to believe in something,* he added to himself.

There was an empty pause, then:

"This is bullshit," Tarasento said. "Count me out until you find some good news."

There was no click as he disconnected, just deeper silence.

"He's right, you know," said Gehrke into the void. "We're fucked."

"Not yet." Hallows disentangled himself from the mainframe. Gehrke sounded dangerously close to making his decision. "We'll see what happens."

"You really think Lockley had something up his sleeve?"

"Yes."

"Then you're as crazy as he was."

Again, there was no indication that Gehrke had signed off, but Hallows could tell from the silence that he was on his own.

When he had finished the work that Gehrke's announcement had interrupted, he wandered forward to the nose of the probe, where high-resolution dishes and scanners pointed with unceasing vigilance towards Eta Boötis.

Saul–1 was still on-course; Gehrke had ascertained as much on the first day. It was hard to believe that in a little less than eleven years the probe would become the first human-made artefact to circle the alien sun. Hallows couldn't help but envy the seventh crew of refitters, who would at least have an historic view before dying. All *he* had seen was one unexplained alien hulk, tantalizingly out of reach. In its own way, that was worse than nothing; given time and the right equipment . . .

From where he sat, surrounded by the forward sensors, the craft wasn't even visible, hidden as it was behind the bulk of the probe. He could understand Tarasento's reluctance to accept the possibility that the aliens had little or nothing to do with their predicament. If they had to die, then it would be better to do so knowing they had played even a minor role in something as important as humanity's first contact with an alien race.

Suddenly tired, he tethered himself to a nearby stanchion and let his arms and legs hang limp. Residual angular momentum rotated him slowly in the zero gravity until he was facing the carbon alloy of the probe's skin. Steadying himself with one hand, he used his visor to magnify the scene in front of him. A swarm of barely visible silver dots crawled across a field of matte-black like time-lapse film of an insane night sky. Although the visor was not powerful enough to allow Hallows a detailed view of the individual motes' activities, he could follow them well enough with his mind's eye.

The reactivated nanomachines were scuttling through every crevice of the probe, repairing or building from scratch the equipment it needed to survive the six years until the next refit crew arrived. Most of their work was on the microscopic level: welding invisible fractures, realigning stanchions with inhuman accuracy, tracing every cable to ensure that the passage of data proceeded with perfect reliability. Gradually, however, a silver bubble would take shape at the probe's mid-section: a variable fuel-tank designed to contain water beamed by d-mat from Earth years ago and due to arrive in the not-too-distant future. This would be the only obvious change the nanomachines left in their wake.

That point, however, was still some time away. First, they had to gather enough scrap material from which to weave the fabric required for the bubble. In an elaborate process, the nanomachines would 'taste' every item on the probe for macromolecular blocks mounted during manufacture. Everything identified as being necessary to the probe's continued operation was ignored; that which had outlived its usefulness, on the other hand—or which didn't possess the correct blocks, like space-dust—was disassembled, processed and recycled. In that way, the nanomachines could be entrusted to ensure that the probe would have the correct facilities when it needed them but not to devour it in the process.

Hallows had always found the nanomachines fascinating and not a little hypnotic to watch. Within minutes, his eyes were drifting closed. Before he even became aware of what was happening to him, he was asleep.

He dreamed—

—of himself, standing at one end of an Olympic swimming-pool. His task was to throw a dart at either of two targets; the choice of which was his to make. As he stood on the concrete lip of the pool, weighing up the decision, he suddenly realized that the choice was obvious: not the target at the far end of the pool, but the one floating in the water less than a car's-length away . . .

An unknown time later, the ambient noise in his ears rose slightly and triggered his space-worker's reflexes. Someone had joined him on the open line. He awoke instantly.

"Who's there?"

"It's me, Rod. Did I disturb you?"

"That's okay, Jimmy." He blinked, and pressed his gloved hands to the visor—a poor substitute for actually rubbing his eyes. Something about the dream nagged at the back of his mind, but eluded him when he tried to recall it. With an effort, he forced himself to concentrate on what Tarasento was saying.

"I just wanted to tell you that I'm sorry about before," Tarasento continued. "I lost my head for a moment."

Hallows sighed. "To be honest, I sympathize with what you're feeling."

"But that doesn't excuse it. There's no need to go off half-cocked. We've still got work to do."

"I know." The dedication to duty, which had been drummed into them during training, remained surprisingly strong even in the face of their situation. "That's why I think Lockley knew what he was doing. He was trying to help us as well as himself."

"So why didn't he leave a note?"

"Well, for a start, there's nothing to write with—and I guess he didn't want to take up space on the mainframe. With Pearce already on every spare terabyte, to leave any sort of message would require removing bits of his friend." Hallows swallowed, dismayed by the mental image his words evoked. "Or maybe he was just running low on air."

Tarasento mulled this over. "I guess it doesn't matter why. He must have done what he did for a reason—the transmit dishes, the LSM, everything. He didn't want us fucking it up."

"So the LSM must be pointing at something."

"I agree. But what?"

"That's the problem. There's nothing out here but us."

"And the aliens." Tarasento clicked his tongue. "I decided to do a little research myself. The telemetry data isn't restricted any more, and it wasn't hard to get at. Has Roald told you yet that the ship *is* drifting?"

Hallows didn't reply immediately. "No, he hasn't."

"Well, it is. Not much, but enough. Six years ago, when Lockley and the others arrived, it was less than fifty metres away."

"Really?"

"No doubt about it. And there's more. Do you want to know where it came from?"

"Tell me."

"From nowhere, that's where. It appeared out of the blue. No acceleration, no matching vectors, no jockeying for position—just hey presto, here we are." Tarasento took a deep breath. "I don't know about you, but I find that more than a little scary."

Hallows nodded to himself. It *was* scary, implying a level of technology far above that of Earth. He knew of no physical process that allowed an independent object as large as the ship hanging off *Saul-1*'s bow to appear and disappear at will; d-mat, magical though it sometimes seemed, was confined to small volumes and required a receiving station. Even supposing that the ship's sudden appearance had been a trick of camouflage and not a genuine matter-transportation, it was still incredible.

Yet somehow the aliens had managed it. And maybe that explained what had nudged *Saul-1* off-course before the arrival of Lockley and the others. An aftershock perhaps, a ripple through tortured space-time . . .

"Jesus, Roald!" Tarasento's startled cry cut across Hallows' thoughts like a red-hot knife. "What the hell do you think you're doing?"

"Jimmy?" Hallows tensed automatically. "What's going on?"

"Get over here, Rod! It's Roald—I think he's going to jump!"

Hallows was instantly moving, up and out of the forward bay and onto the spine of the probe, with Tarasento's laboured breath pulling him onward. Gehrke, if he heard, said nothing.

"Where are you, Jimmy?"

"Sector C13. Hurry!"

Hallows cursed and tried to make his hands move faster. C13 was on the far side of the probe, towards the rear. Swinging from handhold to handhold, he tugged himself around the body of the probe. When he reached the far side, he caught his first glimpse of what was going on.

Gehrke was 'running' along the probe—kicking himself off every available surface—heading rapidly towards the end. Silhouetted against the stars ahead of him, with his arms outstretched, stood Tarasento.

"Jimmy!" Hallows shouted, unnecessarily loud, into the radio. "Get out of the way! Let him go if he wants to!"

"No! He can't!"

Gehrke still said nothing, and Hallows guessed that his radio was off. With one mighty kick off an outflung girder, the systems analyst reached half-way. The gap between him and the younger man narrowed rapidly.

Hallows was too far behind to catch up. All he could do was

watch as Tarasento attached a line to the probe and launched himself to meet Gehrke head-on.

The two men collided messily, then rebounded along a new course away from the probe's outer skin. Tarasento wrapped his limbs around Gehrke in a clumsy but effective zero-g tackle. The systems analyst fought back, striking Tarasento once in the stomach and making him grunt. The younger man hung on, refusing to let his crew-mate go so easily.

Hallows came to a halt by the anchor of Tarasento's lifeline. For a moment he considered going out to help the younger man subdue the older, but decided against it. There was no point risking the three of them if something went wrong—and possibly no point at all in the long-run.

The struggle was one-sided. Gehrke, with superior size and strength in his favour, eventually freed himself from Tarasento's embrace. He didn't just push his assailant aside, however; he placed his feet squarely on the younger man's chest, and *kicked*.

The sudden delta-v sent the two men flying apart. Gehrke arrowed up and past *Saul–1*, heading rapidly for the stars. Tarasento angled down and away, in the rough direction of the alien ship. As Gehrke passed behind the probe's body, Hallows saw the systems analyst's EMU flare, adding to his already considerable velocity.

"Jimmy?" Hallows tried to keep his voice level as Gehrke vanished into the distance. "Are you okay?"

"Fine, but—Jesus, I almost had him."

"That's okay. You did your best."

"No. I should've—"

Tarasento jerked abruptly to halt as he reached the limit of his lifeline. The tether snapped taut, then just as suddenly went limp again. A scream of escaping air in Hallows' ears deafened him. The grey-suited figure at the end of the line seemed to dance, clutching at the place where the tether had ripped free. Hallows tugged at the cable with both hands, but there was no resistance.

"Jimmy!" he shouted. "Jimmy, answer me!"

There was no reply. The explosive scream gradually faded to a whistle, then died altogether. A moment later, Tarasento's dance slowed to a halt.

"Jimmy?"

Only silence answered.

Hallows watched, impotent, as the grey-suited figure tumbled end-over-end into the void. After several long minutes, it became apparent that it would miss the dark shadow of the alien hulk, although not by much. Hallows didn't move until it had done so. And when it had finally vanished, he did the only thing he could do: he turned his back on the stars and went back to work.

"I'm sorry," said Gehrke, some time later. "That wasn't supposed to happen."

Hallows jumped at the unexpected voice in his ears, but recovered quickly. "You stupid son of a bitch."

"Not stupid." The systems analyst sounded calm, resigned; the reception from his suit crackled with static but was clear enough. "Just tired of waiting."

Hallows shook his head, rage and grief still burning in his gut. "You could have waited a little longer, couldn't you? Until he was asleep, at least. I would have let you go; you know that."

"I know. But I thought he was on the far side. He was meant to be installing some nanos in the drive shaft. He should never have seen me like that. He wasn't supposed to *be* there, staring up at that damned ship like . . . " Gehrke stopped, swallowed audibly. "I guess it doesn't matter now, anyway."

"You killed him," said Hallows. "That matters to me."

"We're all dead, Rod. I did him a favour."

Hallows shook his head in frustration.

"You still believe you're going to make it?" Gehrke asked.

"Yes."

"Then you're as crazy as I am." Gehrke's laugh was bitter. "As crazy as Lockley."

"Lockley wasn't crazy—but if it makes you feel better believing that, go right ahead." Hallows waited for more mocking laughter, but it didn't come. "Just tell me one thing, Roald: what made you do it?"

For a moment, it seemed as though Gehrke wouldn't reply. When he eventually spoke, his voice was tired and empty. "After I discovered what Lockley had done, I took a closer look at the PEARCE file."

"And?"

"*Saul–1*'s mainframe isn't anywhere near large enough to store an entire human being in crypt, and Lockley knew it. So he didn't try to save the lot, only the bits that mattered."

Hallows swallowed. "How much is there?"

"A couple of kilos." Gehrke paused for effect. "His head.

"And there's one other thing you should know," Gehrke said when Hallows had absorbed the gruesome truth. "Lockley didn't just screw up the tracking algorithms on the transmit dishes. He fiddled with the core programming. Everything installed to deal solely with human survival went first, mainly to make room for his buddy. The only things he left untouched were the guidance and maintenance systems. He obviously wanted to make damned sure *Saul–1* arrived safely, whether it was occupied or not.

"One of the files he tampered with but didn't erase is the self-destruct program."

Hallows could understand that. "I guess he thought one of us might blow the probe out of spite, to take it with us."

"You're missing the point, Rod. The program's *still there*. It's just different."

"How?"

Again Gehrke hesitated. "Maybe you should try it for yourself, Rod. See what happens."

Hallows didn't respond, reluctant to take the suggestion seriously. Hitting the self-destruct went against everything he stood for, and for all he knew Gehrke had only brought it up to torture him. But if Lockley *had* changed the program somehow, then once again it must have been for a reason. Everything—the transmit dishes, the graffiti, the LSM, the self-destruct program, even the alien ship itself—all had to fit together somehow.

"Roald—"

"No, Rod, you're right," said the systems analyst. "It does matter. But I've found my leap of faith, and you'll find yours eventually. Maybe we'll both get what we want, or what we deserve, in the end."

The line went dead, and Hallows was alone.

Alone on a human-made probe, twenty-two light years from home, with nothing but ghosts for company.

As time passed, Hallows focused less and less on the four dead men—Prosilis, Pearce, Tarasento and Gehrke—and devoted himself entirely to his work. If he thought about any of the other refitters, it was Lockley who came to mind, or the men and women in the refit crews following his: Ngo, Maschmedt and Lontis; Schumacher, Valente and Gill. The dead were dead; only the living mattered.

Hours blurred into days with as few breaks for rest as he could stand. Through the fog of exhaustion, his personal problems faded into insignificance, allowing him a fragile clarity of thought focused on the refit systems under his care. Only during his infrequent rest breaks did he spend time tracing Gehrke's steps through the mainframe.

The first thing he did was study the communications and d-mat systems—trying not to think about Pearce's remains as he did so. Yes, the transmit dishes had drifted from their proper target; no, they couldn't be realigned without the proper algorithms. The transmission beam was a maser signal with an infinitesimally small rate of dispersal; even so, by the time the beam reached Earth it would have expanded in width from a pencil-thin beam to a cone large enough to cover the entire Lunar disc. Even then the dispersal rate was too low to give him much chance of striking the target. If he spread the beam wider, at the expense of signal-strength, then his chances of hitting the receivers improved. But with a wide enough dispersal to give him good odds of hitting Sol System and only the probe's tiny reactor behind it, the signal reaching Earth would be undetectable above the Universe's background radiation.

Twenty-two light years amounted to over two hundred *trillion* kilometres. It was too far, too great a distance to gamble his life across. No mere human could relocate Earth with the required precision once the transmit dishes had been shifted from their proper orientation.

Five days passed before he abandoned that line of pursuit. It hadn't told him anything he didn't already know. And what *did* it matter, anyway? The survival of the refitters made little difference to the probe's mission. Unless the other Saul probes had suffered similar catastrophes, the target star would one day soon be surveyed by humans, and that was the main thing.

Perhaps, he wondered, it would be better to follow Gehrke's last words of advice and try the self-destruct program. If the systems analyst had been lying, and the program functioned as normal, it offered a swift alternative to a lingering death—not only for him, but for the refitters still on their way. And if it didn't, then he might learn something more about Lockley's intentions.

But he wasn't quite ready to take that final step; not until he had exhausted every possible avenue of thought. If the Earth was too distant, then a closer target had to be found . . . And if he solved this one small mystery, then and only then would he assume that Lockley knew what he was doing and had changed the self-destruct program for the better.

On the twenty-second day, Hallows cued his priority planner for the next task and was told: "All Tasks Complete". He stared blankly at the three words for a long while before truly comprehending what they meant. Then he crawled behind a blanket of matte-grey polymer and slept for eighteen hours.

When he awoke, his mind was clear and fixed on the sole remaining task. He had two days left in which to leave the probe; or, failing that, to die. The only oxygen reserve on the probe was that contained within his suit, and he lacked the resources to reprogram the nanomachines to provide another.

Abandoning his earlier explorations, he turned to the commandeered LSM. When operating normally, the high-energy laser fired a short burst of coherent light in a tightly-focused beam once every hundredth of a microsecond. Its programming had been altered, however, to allow it to pulse less frequently— ten times per microsecond—and at roughly double the output. While it would ordinarily have been aimed at a planet or an asteroid, or some other item of space debris to be analyzed, it now pointed into deep space almost directly behind the probe. And Lockley—if it had indeed been him—had made sure that it would stay put.

But why? Hallows grappled with this question for several hours. The transmit and d-mat systems could be re-routed to the LSM, but its output was far too weak to reach Earth with any useful power-level. At the LSM's low frequency, it would take years for a full human to be transmitted. Why would Lockley go to so much trouble to sabotage the transmit dishes only to replace them later with a poor second best?

After studying the LSM's target for what felt like an eternity, he was forced to admit that his first impression had been correct. It wasn't pointing at anything, as far as he could tell. There was nothing within range of the LSM, not even the aliens.

Nothing visible anyway . . .

As he lay back in the relative shelter offered by one of the interior bulkheads, his eye was caught again by the graffiti etched into the metal.

"The key is here," someone had written. Lockley himself? If so, why so cryptic? "Use it if you want to."

Hallows stiffened unconsciously in his suit. There *was* something behind the probe. Something that had been designed to detect emissions from the laser spectrometers aboard *Saul-1*. Something which, while not able to actually decode the d-transmissions broadcast by the LSM, was perfectly placed to act as a relay . . .

Saul–2 had been launched one year behind its sister-craft. That put it roughly one and a quarter light years away. And 1.25 light years was only *twelve* trillion kilometres.

The distance was still too big, too daunting, but when expressed as a ratio against the only alternative, it suddenly seemed a whole lot better, solving the mystery not only of Hallows' dream but of the numbers ending the brief note:

3:50.

To make *Saul–2* even more attractive, at this stage in its journey it maintained a fixed distance from *Saul–1* and was oriented in a direction that had been preordained by Control decades ago. All he had to do was calculate the position of *Saul–2* using the navigation systems, point the LSM, and . . .

Leap.

Gehrke's choice of phrase couldn't have been more apt. There was no way to know if *Saul–2* was in its proper position. Likewise, he could only hope that its forward detectors were fully functioning and able to detect the laser pulses from its sibling. If it too had lost contact with Earth, then the telemetry data containing those pulses would be as lost as a d-mat transmission from *Saul–1*. Or if it *did* arrive and Program Control failed to realize that the pulses encoded a d-mat transmission, or ignored them as a glitch in the data . . .

There was only one way to find out.

Crawling from the innards of the probe, he tugged his way forward to the manual over-rides and called up the self-destruct program.

"Surprise," said Lockley. "If you were expecting a quick, clean death, whoever you are, then you're going to be disappointed."

The image appeared, via his implants, in Hallows' left eye— presumably recorded by one of the probe's visible light scanners. Lockley's face looked shrunken behind his visor, his eye-sockets hollow and lips white. Two of his upper teeth had fallen out. Tufts of hair stuck in places to the visor itself, resembling hairline fractures in the transparent plastic. All in all, Hallows thought, Lockley appeared to have aged a hundred years since they had last met—which, relative to him, had been only a few weeks ago.

"You'll have to excuse me if I ramble a little," Hallows'

predecessor continued. "I'm dying, you see. The rad counters went berserk a week ago, and the aliens haven't been back since. I guess that means the nanos did their job, although they've almost killed me in the process too . . . " Lockley stopped, shook his head to clear it. "But I'm getting ahead of myself. Forgive me, please. There's so much I have to say, and I keep forgetting what should come first.

"If you haven't worked it out by now, I've rigged LSM 14 to transmit the d-mat signal normally broadcast through the transmit dish. As soon as I finish this message, I'll enter the d-mat cage and begin the process. I guess you might have noticed that the d-mat buffer is off-limits too, along with the targeting program of the LSM." Hallows automatically shook his head; Gehrke hadn't picked that up. "Well, that's why. There's only just enough buffer memory in the d-mat to hold me until the LSM has finished transmitting to *Saul–2*, and I don't want you taking Steve Pearce's way out and robbing someone else of the chance to escape.

"My best guess says it'll take about eighteen and a half months to down-load me—and the same applies to you, of course. That means that if there are two of you left, only one can live. You can rig the other LSMs if you like, or try something else, but there's no way to transmit one full human back to Earth in less than four weeks, which is the most time you have.

"I'm sorry, but that's the best I can do."

Lockley paused to swallow. One hand rubbed at the neck of his suit as though he desperately wanted to scratch himself.

"As for the rest . . . I don't really know where to start. They were here, on the probe, when I arrived. The aliens, I mean. Five of them, and big sons of bitches too; like machines with dozens of limbs growing out of a central structure that looked like a cross between a tractor and a . . . I don't know what. Folded up they were about two metres round; at full-stretch they could reach ten metres. How they communicated among themselves, I don't know. When we tried to talk to them, they just ignored us. We weren't even worth killing for all the times we got in their way. They just let us roam freely, watching everything they did. I don't think that means they were stupid, though. We were simply beyond their experience, as alien to them as they were to us.

"They must have been studying the probe for about a year before we arrived, if the telemetry data is right. Their ship was right on top of us—and it was huge. Bigger than a small moon. But they still hadn't cracked the mainframe. That bothers me, even now. How they could build a ship like theirs without technology advanced enough to make ours look like child's-play is beyond me. But somehow they did. It wasn't until shortly after we stepped out of the airlock that they guessed what the d-mat cage was for.

"We took them by surprise; that I do know. We mightn't have been interesting enough on our own, but our arrival caused quite a stir. Another three joined them poking around the d-mat bay. Eventually they worked out how to activate it. And it was only then I decided we had to do something.

"The aliens started sending things—weird little bundles of machines in nets, wrapped tight to keep them from drifting—back to Program Control. Whatever they were, they made my skin crawl. The aliens had their hands on a direct route to Earth, and anything they sent along it would arrive unchallenged. Maybe the bundles contained bombs, self-replicating AIs, or God only knows what. I couldn't take the risk that by standing aside and letting them do it I'd be putting my friends back home in danger.

"So that's why I killed the d-mat."

Lockley stopped, and sighed. "Maybe it was a mistake. Prosilis thought it was. When he found out what I'd done, he went crazy. Cried for about four hours straight. Then he went down to the drive shaft, where he could see Sol, and opened his suit.

"That left me and Steve. He wasn't too happy about it either, but could see my point. We decided that the best thing to do was to attempt to communicate with the aliens again and work our way onward from there. If they turned out to be friendly, then maybe they could help us. If they didn't, then we'd done the right thing. I for one would die gladly knowing that I'd saved everyone back home.

"It was a good plan, but the aliens didn't want any of it. They ignored us as they had before. When they realized that something had interrupted the d-mat program, they unloaded more equipment from the big ship and wrapped it around the probe. It looked like a finely-spun mohair rug connected to a larger version of themselves. When it touched the probe, it began to spread, sending little fibres into everything. Searching.

"It took me a while to guess what they were doing. Almost too long, in fact. They were trying to find the mainframe core. Luckily it's deep inside the probe, and it took time before they even got close—long enough to counter-attack. There was no way I was going to sit back and let them take over *Saul-1*.

"The nanos were inactive when we arrived, awaiting our instructions. With the aliens aboard and everything, none of us had got around to starting them up. But that's all it took. Once they began to work, it didn't take long."

Lockley paused again, allowing Hallows' imagination to fill in the gaps. The nanomachines, hungry for raw material, would have attacked the alien metal instantly—digging in, extracting what they needed, reproducing, and then moving on. Once a handful had crossed the gap between the probe and the alien ship, they would have eaten forever, until the entire vessel was consumed.

Except that something had obviously overloaded—maybe the engines or the power generator—thereby killing the nanos in a single wave of hard radiation.

Too late for the aliens, though. And not just the ones on their crippled ship, it seemed, as Lockley continued:

"I watched one of them decay. As the nanos dug in, exposing layer after layer, its internal structure appeared. Not that I could understand much. Beneath the skin they were almost uniformly white, with tangles of fibres that might have been muscles or nerves; a cross-hatched tubular skeletal structure, not the solid supporting bones we have; no obvious brain, just as they had no obvious leader . . . They looked like they were made of bleached, fibrous wood, like some sort of organic robot.

"Anyway, whatever they were, they're gone now. After they died, Pearce and I managed to complete the schedule and set the nanos to repair where the aliens had damaged *Saul–1*. We also rigged the LSM to transmit the d-mat data back to *Saul–2*. If Control picks up the signal via the other probe's forward sensors—which they should do—then they can decode it at their leisure. Assuming, of course, that there's any Control left by then. God only knows what the things the aliens sent through will have done.

"I'm running out of time and air, so I'll have to keep this brief. I loaded Pearce into the mainframe as soon as we realized there was no way both of us could go. I'd like to rig some sort of time-delay program to send him once I've gone, but that'll take too long. Hopefully someone else will do that later. Whatever you do, please don't erase him. Remember: he's one of only two humans left in the universe to have seen an alien being. And I don't think we'll get another chance. Their ship will drift away eventually, or keep on going as the probe reaches Eta-B. Wherever they came from, we'll probably never find them again. They'll have to find *us* . . .

"Lastly, there's no room left on the mainframe for this message, so I've decided to put it in place of the self-destruct program. The file will be almost identical in size—and it seems appropriate, anyway. If you can't work out for yourself what I've done, and you decide to kill yourself this way, then at least this gives you a chance to reconsider. But I guess the real reason why I'm not leaving an obvious message is because taking the LSM back home is risky. I'm already humanity's first alien-killer; I don't want human deaths to my credit as well. My only advice to you is, *don't destroy the probe. Saul–1* deserves to make it to the end of its journey, even if we don't. The old thing has been through a lot.

"If I haven't changed your mind, then rambling on isn't going to help. Suffice it to say that I'm not going to let you blow all my dreams to dust with the flick of a switch. You're going to have to work a lot harder than that . . . "

Lockley ground to a halt, stared at the scanner for a good minute, then nodded to himself.

"The choice is yours, whoever-you-are, and yours alone. This is Chris Lockley, supervisor of the fourth refit crew for *Saul–1*, ident code 7760R8Too, signing off."

The recording finished and Lockley's tortured image faded from Hallows' field of vision. He sat staring into space for a long while before moving along *Saul–1* to the aft end, where Prosilis' body had once kept watch over the distant star that was Sol, and where the sabotaged dish now pointed nowhere in particular.

Tarasento had been right. The aliens had played a more pivotal role in the drama than Gehrke had surmised. Why, though, they had failed to recognize Lockley's attempts to communicate with them remained a mystery. Hallows could think of one possible explanation: that the aliens had been a communal mind, maybe of machine origins, possessing no centralized 'brain'. If so, they might not have realized that humans could constitute intelligent beings in their own right. Furthermore, as the nanos had eaten their way through the alien ship and its crew, the aliens' gestalt intelligence would have decreased, until perhaps it no longer possessed the ability to think rationally. That would explain why they had not resisted the invasion. And perhaps, also, why they had failed at first to comprehend the existence of the mainframe; they themselves had no need for such a thing. If society had imitated nature in the aliens' case, then science may well have done so too.

Why, then, no nanomachines of their own? Maybe the individual units of the alien mind had been just that, but on a larger scale. A mind large enough to comprehend a means of independent mass-transportation would have to be huge, at least in capacity, just as the alien ship had been. If it worked on a larger scale than humans, then nanoscopic technology may have seemed irrelevant to it.

Or else the concept was simply alien to them, just as their actions had seemed alien to Lockley and the others. Perhaps they had been simple explorers themselves, differing from the probe only in design and origin.

Even among such grand-scale speculations, Hallows hadn't missed one other ramification of Lockley's speech: Gehrke must have viewed the recording. His reason for jumping had been more than simply to kill himself. He had either been afraid of the LSM method of transmission, or trying to reduce the numbers.

"If there are two of you left," Lockley had said, "only one can live . . . " And if there were three, the choice became doubly difficult.

But now Hallows was on his own. Jimmy Tarasento's accidental death had been fortuitous in that respect. Hallows had only to decide whether or not to take Lockley's risky route off the probe. His one alternative was to beam himself out the transmit dish—to take the easy way out, as Tarasento himself had put it. The choice truly was his, and his alone.

But there was still one thing left to do before Hallows *had* to decide.

Sniffing cautiously, he tested the air of his suit. Despite the stink of twenty-five days of *him*, it still satisfied his lungs. He had about twenty-four hours left before he was out of time—and all the resources of the probe at his disposal. Radiation shielding was precious, but he figured it wouldn't be too difficult to rig some sort of teleoperated camera and a primitive EMU. Tarasento would have wanted him to try.

Even if he couldn't, and he decided not to take the risk himself, he had at least a day left to ponder the view.

●

AFTERWORD TO:
.... A VIEW BEFORE DYING

I've been interested in the instantaneous (or at least electronic) transmission of matter for a long time now. Four short stories and three novels add up to a whole lot of words exploring the subject and its ramifications, and still Hollywood hasn't caught on to what a cool movie there is waiting to be made on the subject.

The conundrum at the heart of this story arose out of idle speculation about how crewed interstellar space exploration might work in a world with d-mat capabilities. Once a d-mat receiver had been placed at the terminus of the journey, well, it's easy, but getting to that point would be very difficult. Unless you posit faster-than-light travel as well, getting that receiver in place is going to take a loooong time, and what poor chump is going to sit out the trip to make sure it works when it gets there?

The answer is that no one, chump or otherwise, needs to sit out anything. Sending regular maintenance crews via d-mat makes the process much easier, since the probe has a receiver (the payload) and the crews can bring their own air, food, etc. The probe doesn't even need extra reaction mass, since it's not accelerating. Voila.

Unless, of course, something goes wrong—which is the nub of more science fiction stories than you could ever count. A routine job becomes a lot more complex because the universe always finds a way to snafu things up. Cue existential angst, difficult decisions, and what I personally consider to be one of the great pay-offs of this kind of fiction.

If I was in Hallows' shoes, I'd want the view too. That's what'd send me out there in the first place. Some things are definitely worth dying for.

●

INTRODUCTION TO:

.... TEAM SHARON

When I first stared writing short stories, I experimented a great deal with styles, characterisation, subject matter, theme. This scattershot approach soon revealed my strengths (horror, science fiction, plot) and the many, many failings that needed to be addressed. Some of those failings succumbed to the blunt instrument of persistence. Some required more subtle intervention, often gained through collaboration, close examination of other writers' works, or plain old luck. I've had revelations come through dreams (as in one where I realised that fantasy could be told in Australian settings) or from being unexpectedly challenged.

"Team Sharon" falls into the last category. It wouldn't exist had I not been invited to contribute to a mainstream, literary anthology focussing on masculinity. Edited by Eva Sallis, the collection aimed to be of the highest literary standard, and would contain people with whom I had never shared a table of contents before. The opportunity was an exciting one, one I knew I couldn't turn down, but it came with its own set of anxieties too. After all, I'd proven to myself that realist fiction was not my thing ten years earlier. I had zero chance of delivering something that Eva would like.

Challenges are good. To avoid being challenged is to risk stagnation—and for any artist, stagnation is fatal. We need to be constantly pushed out of ourselves, to stray beyond our comfort zones in order to find the spark that drives us to create, and to create well. Otherwise we die on the inside, and our art dies with it.

"Team Sharon" was very hard to write, but it was well worth the effort. Not only did Eva like it, but the list of things I think I can't do is one item shorter than it might have been.

●

"Daikaiju"

where are the dragons?
nature abhors a vacuum
Gojira provides

TEAM SHARON

It was a hot Monday evening, and Stan was bubbling over.

Her unit was the first of six in a cul de sac two blocks away. A short walk, during which he concentrated on projecting the appearance that he was just *Taking the Air* and *Going Nowhere In Particular.* He followed her jogging route automatically. She ran past his house every morning before work at seven-fifteen and went to the gym three nights a week: Monday, Wednesday and Friday. She was gorgeous, and completely unaware of the effect she had on Stan.

If he got any hotter he'd explode like an unpricked egg in a microwave.

At the entrance to the cul de sac, he stopped to survey the scene. Opposite her unit lay the sort of miniature park local councils sometimes put in as a compensation for the closure off a handy short-cut. There was a children's playground and plenty of bushes. From the park one could gain a perfect view of the windows of her home. Stan knew this; he had tried during the day when she was out. He had also noted what time she came home from the gym by waiting for her car around the corner. She was due in ten minutes.

This was it. He couldn't tell if he was excited or terrified. He didn't know whether to follow The Plan or keep walking past the street. If he went home now, he could pretend he'd never even got this far. If he *did* do it . . . well, that was the clincher. He would have crossed a line into uncharted territory. What if he never came back?

But he hadn't had a girlfriend for so long he was starting to forget how it felt to be intimate. He needed to connect, no matter how remotely, to someone *real*. He had been sweating inside, alone, for too long. If this was what it took to make him feel something new—to give him a sort of excitement that didn't originate within him and wasn't under his complete control—then maybe he had to do it.

Maybe.

Yes.

He took a step forward into her street, then another. He was doing it! He kept his eyes down on the pavement—*Don't Mind Me; I'm Just Stretching My Legs*—but tried at the same time to watch the neighbouring houses and parked cars. No-one watering their lawn? No-one seeing off a friend? No-one at all, he hoped.

The park was black and inviting. He slipped into its shadows like an under-sized fish thrown back into the sea. Bushes rustled at him; the grass felt soft beneath his feet. He spied the cover he had chosen—a large, thick bush—out of the corner of his eye and headed for it indirectly, not looking anywhere but at his feet in case someone saw him and read his guilt, as surely they would. His face was burning. His fists were clenched. But he had everything planned. She would be home soon and everything would be perfect. Just perf—

With a muffled thud he bumped into something in the darkness. He put out his arms automatically, and hands grabbed back at him. For one, terrifying instant, all he knew was a blur of limbs and lost balance—then he was helping a middle-aged man upright and stuttering inanely.

"What the hell do you think you're doing?" the man asked, dusting himself down. "You walked right into me!"

"I—I wasn't watching—"

"That's bloody obvious!"

"I mean, it's dark and I didn't see you. I didn't think anyone was in here." Stan backed away, wondering if he should make a run for it—then realised that the man had been squatting in exactly the same place he himself hoped to occupy.

"Oh, I *see*," said the man, who by then had recovered enough to be approaching a realisation of his own. The disgruntled look vanished, replaced by one of indulgence. "You're new."

"What?" Stan could manage little more than an addled look and vague sounds.

"It's okay," said the man, patting Stan on the shoulder. His face was round and his head looked like someone had dusted it with desiccated coconut sprinkles. He looked about the same age as Stan's father had been when he died. His voice dropped in volume: "I'm sorry I startled you. You weren't to know I was there."

"You okay, Reg?" hissed a voice from the shadows, and Stan jumped. A dark figure stepped out from behind a tree, the red eye of a cigarette glinting malevolently in one fist.

"No worries, Tony," said the old man called Reg. "Just a mistake."

The figure coalesced into a lean, European man dressed in a singlet and shorts. Tony's face was black with stubble, Stan noted, his eyes adjusting to the near darkness in the park and latching onto comprehensible details as signs he hadn't gone completely mad.

"Mistake, huh?" Tony's voice was low and guttural, hostile in tone. "Why isn't he moving on, then?"

"I think he wants to stay." Reg's eyes darted between them.

"Uh."

"Am I right, young man?"

Stan was momentarily torn. "I—I don't know what you mean."

"Well, let me spell it out." The old man glanced at his watch. "You're alone. You're nervous. You're here at the right time and the right place. And you're *still* here, despite being accosted by two strange men in the bushes. All you need is the hardware. If you had that, I'd be one hundred percent certain of your intentions."

Stan's hand obeyed its own will and produced from his pocket the pair of plastic opera glasses he'd bought for five dollars at Cheap as Chips that afternoon.

"Ah." Reg nodded and glanced at Tony, whose face unexpectedly broke into a white-toothed grin. Tony produced from his shorts a complicated piece of equipment as big as a small dog, the eyepieces of which he thrust into Stan's face. Stan caught a green-tinged glimpse of Reg's midriff glowing within.

"The Scope-O-Tronic Night-Sight 4000X," pronounced the old man.

"XG," Tony corrected.

"Me, I prefer something a little more stylish." Reg reached into a pocket and showed Stan a collapsible brass cylinder with glass lenses at either end.

"Shhhhh!" came a call from nearby. "Someone's coming!"

Tony vanished back behind his tree. Reg dragged Stan into the bush.

Footsteps crunched towards them, accompanied by a faint, regular panting. Stan held his breath and huddled down behind the leaves with Reg silent at his side. Bare seconds later, a man walking a Doberman on a leash passed through the park. His eyes glinted in the streetlight, but he didn't seem to notice anything out of the ordinary. He didn't stop, anyway. Stan watched his departing back with breath still held, feeling like a common criminal.

Then the man was gone. Tony stepped out from behind his tree. His cigarette butt flicked in the general direction of the departing figure. "Loser."

Stan rose shakily to his feet.

"You don't look so flash, son," said Reg. "Drink?"

The old man pressed a small flask into Stan's hand. Stan tipped it up automatically and downed a mouthful of gin. Only then did he remember to breathe.

"This is insane."

"Actually," Reg said, "it's probably the sanest thing you've ever done. You've taken a step forward, lad. You've taken charge of your life. If you hadn't done this, where do you think you'd be in a month's time? Like that turd-scooper we just saw, pretending to walk a dog? Driving around with your stereo booming? Panty-snatching? Everyone needs to let off a little steam every now and again, or else the boiler blows. We know where you're coming from. Do *we* look crazy?"

"Fuck no," said Tony, emphasising the words with the bright end of another fag.

Before Stan could reply, a car turned into the street.

"Will you keep it *down* back there?" hissed the same voice that had warned of the dog-walker. A silhouette of a man's head appeared briefly in the window of a parked car, then vanished back into the shadows.

Reg waved and tugged Stan back down.

"You can stay here with me," the old man whispered, "but only for tonight. This is my spot, you see. You'll have to find another of your own."

"But—"

Stan got no further. Headlights lit up the end of the street, blinding his night-adjusted eyes, then swung aside as a shiny purple hatchback pulled into the drive of the front unit across the street. With one final rev, the engine died and the door opened.

And there she was. A vision in lycra toting a bag over one

shoulder and looking for her front door key among what sounded like hundreds.

"Evening, Sharon," breathed the old man.

"That's her name?" Stan exhaled back, eyes fixed on her back. Part of him knew he would've liked her name, no matter what it turned out to be.

"That's just what I call her. I don't check her mail or anything. Only sickos do that."

The screen door opened with a clatter and Sharon disappeared inside. A moment later, the lights came on, visible around the edges of the blinds.

"You do this often?" Stan asked. He had to ask the question.

Reg replied without taking his eye off the brass telescope's eyepiece. "We all do. Tony has a wife, but she goes to bed early. Rob comes after work. Steve stops by on his evening patrol; he's a security guard. Dave—"

A rustle went up as Sharon flipped apart the blinds in the front room of her unit. Through that window Stan could see the central hallway leading to the main bedroom and bathroom—almost as though it had been designed that way. He raised the opera glasses; the view was only slightly better, but he was grateful for any improvement at all. Sharon stood in the window for a second, shaking out her hair. The bedroom door behind her was ajar; through it, he could see half a bed, a side table and a lamp. When she turned away from the window, she disappeared into the bathroom.

The two men behind the bush gripped their optical devices and sighed spookily similar sighs.

"She's one in a million, isn't she?"

Stan nodded. "How long have you been coming here?" he managed.

"A month or so. That's when Sharon moved in. Before then there was Alice in Grover Street. When Alice bought new blinds we had to move on, and we'll do it again if Sharon does likewise, or moves in with her boyfriend. We always find somewhere new to meet. Disperse and regroup. That's life."

"Sharon has a boyfriend?" Stan was stuck on that point, although the thought of asking her out had never seriously crossed his mind: in fantasies he was a different person, someone *she* would want, not the other way around, not quiet little Stan with his over-sized head and occasional stammer.

"Of course she has." Reg seemed philosophical. "Sporty type. Plays football, I think."

"*Loser*," hissed Tony from the tree behind them.

"You think everyone's a loser, Tony," Reg called back, sotto voce.

"They *are* losers."

"What's she doing in there?" Stan was getting restless, and his opera glasses were fogging up.

Just then, Sharon came back into view wearing nothing but a towel. Her hair was shining, damp.

"Ah, yes." Reg's telescope was unwavering.

She walked to the bedroom, rummaged around in a cupboard half out of sight, threw something on the bed, then walked back through the hallway and into the bathroom.

Stan's hands were cramping on the opera glasses, he was holding them so tight.

"Keep going," Reg muttered.

Sharon emerged from the bathroom with a brush and sat on the end of the bed, tugging vigorously at the knots in her hair. Her cheeks were visibly flushed.

There was no fan in there, Stan noted. It had to be hot. It just *had* to be. Boiling, in fact. Unbearable.

"Almost there," Reg agreed.

She stood up, scratched her left buttock, then slipped out of the towel.

"Paydirt!"

Stan felt dizzy. Around him rose a muttering of excitement, uncannily like a dawn chorus, as her viewers were rewarded for their patient, unrequited adoration. She walked unselfconsciously across the lounge and sat on the couch, where she worried at her toenails and picked at a spot on her stomach. She flipped idly through a magazine, then fanned herself with it while she fiddled with the remote control of her TV. Bored by what she found, she got up to make a phone call. She paced while she talked into the handset.

Stan thought he might faint. He felt Reg's hand clutch his shoulder.

"If you're thinking about jerking off," the old man whispered, "forget about it. We leave that sort of stuff to the Rugby Street mob."

Stan shook his head. Sexual gratification was the last thing on his mind. It didn't even matter whether she was attractive or not.

Sharon was simply so new and delightful that he wanted to absorb every moment of her, while he could. He could have stared at her for hours. At her reality.

She hung up the phone a minute or two later, and got up to close the blind. The climactic glimpse of her face brought tears to his eyes.

Then she was gone.

The park erupted. Twenty or thirty men emerged from view to gather in the shadows and talk about what they had seen. In the ensuing mess of wise-cracks, back-slaps and hand-shakes, Stan kept carefully to one side, basking in the aftermath of the event. He felt as though all the tension had drained out of him and left only a warm glow in his stomach.

Relieved at a night not wasted, one by one the men took their leave, heading back to their homes, partners, friends, pets. Reg knew most of them by name, and introduced Stan to a couple. Barry was a bricklayer; Alan sold insurance. Stan gave them his name in return. It seemed the right thing to do.

Harry knew of a girl on Gormley Road that he had heard was worth checking out. He and Alan arranged to survey the area and report to the group later in the week. "Variety is the spice of life," he pronounced cheerily while waving goodbye.

Within moments only the three of them were left. Reg took Stan by the arm and indicated a dark corner of the park, away from his bush.

"There's a nice spot over there, Stan, by the bin. It used to be Sam's, but he's been quiet of late. If you want it, it's yours."

Then it was Tony's turn. Stan's hand was enfolded in an enthusiastic handclasp and shaken vigorously. "You're all right, Stan. See you Wednesday."

The two men looked around and headed off in separate directions. Stan was left alone in the park, feeling dazed and . . . something else.

See you Wednesday . . . ?

He headed home with a spring in his step.

Yes he thought. They probably would.

●

WHITE CHRISTMAS

The view was exactly as he remembered it, except for the snow. Coming around the final bend in the winding road, with the bare shoulder of the mountain on his right and a yawning gulf on his left, Stewart slowed as the shack finally came into sight. The tiny building was crowded by half-hearted scrub, through which a narrow driveway led to a dark veranda. He swung the Toyota as close to the front door as he could, and killed the engine.

The shack was uninhabited; that was obvious even from the outside, and expected. Owned by Jack and Debbie Barnard, property developers from Sydney, it stood empty for all but six weeks of every year when it served as a private retreat. With no phone, fax or modem, television, radio or satellite dish, its isolation was complete. The nearest town, Blinman, was a half-hour drive back down the hill—too far to be a temptation, but near enough for emergencies.

On the odd occasion, it was rented out to others with similar needs. The shack was, as the owners liked to say, perfect for philosophers, writers, and honeymooners.

Stewart Danby didn't smile at the last. He had come alone, this time. Jacqui was back in Adelaide . . . in what was *left* of Adelaide, rather . . . and he was trying not to think about that.

Leaning forward over the steering-wheel, fatigue making his hands shake, he studied the ground around the Toyota. The sun was setting, filling the Flinders Ranges with gold and blood, deepening slowly to royal purple. Drifts of snow lay like scraps of cloth in the lee of the building and in the shallow troughs of the rising hillside, but otherwise the area seemed clear. He took a deep breath and opened the car door, leaving the keys in the ignition.

The shack's single door was locked, but he managed to prise open a loose rear window. The air inside was stuffy and hot; the coolness of the mid-summer twilight had yet to penetrate the thick stone walls. Opening the front door from within, he went back outside to unload the car.

Three boxes of canned food he had stolen from a supermarket were followed by: a sleeping-bag; a jerry can of kerosene and two bottles of butane gas; a set of scuba gear with half a dozen extra bottles, also stolen; a box of gaffer tape; half a carton of cigarettes; coffee, sugar and powdered milk; and five bottles of scotch, one of which was already open.

By the time the Toyota was empty, the sun had set. The air of the hills stank of rotten eggs, an odour he had gradually become used to during the drive. After his exposure to the relatively untainted air inside the shack, however, it caught anew in the back of his throat. He drank from the open bottle of scotch, wincing; the fire of the spirit wasn't sufficient to overpower the stench, but it helped.

He stood for a moment under the pale, starry bowl, head tipped back, the scotch in one hand, a cigarette in the other. The deep valley below was in darkness. Above the opposite hills, the comet was rising. The feather of glowing smoke smudged the south-western sky like a fingerprint on a masterpiece.

He shivered, although it wasn't cold, and lowered his eyes.

Snow, sparkling faintly in the comet-light, had already settled upon the pitted roof and bonnet of the car. Dropping the gearstick into neutral and disengaging the handbrake, he gave the bumper-bar a push with his foot and stepped clear. The car rolled backwards down the drive, across the winding road that had brought him to the shack, then disappeared suddenly over the lip of the chasm. A series of tinkling smashes accompanied its descent into darkness, followed by silence as thick as bedrock. There was no explosion.

He swigged from the bottle again and went inside.

The shack was furnished in old seventies pine, stained yellow by age and nicotine: two chairs, a sofa and a rickety table. Amateurish paintings in cheap frames cluttered the walls. The carpet was a mottled burgundy, frayed at the edges and sorely in need of replacement. Sagging bookcases full of cheap paperbacks, mostly science fiction, lined one wall. The opposite wall was one long window, hidden behind curtains. He tugged them open. The view was black, but he knew that it would be spectacular by daylight. The comet winked balefully at him, and he shut the curtains again.

Lighting the stove, he filled the kettle with rainwater and set it to boil. While he waited, he unpacked the tins of food. Apart from some chipped, mismatched crockery, the cupboards contained nothing but dust and fluff. The bench-tops were spotted with dead flies. He made a half-hearted attempt to clean away the evidence of emptiness, but gave up before he had finished. There was no point.

The kettle screeched plaintively, like a baby, and he made the coffee. Stirring the various powders into a muddy solution, he breathed the cleansing steam into his nostrils. The combination of dust and hydrogen sulphide was giving his sinuses hell, but there wasn't much he could do about it. With the coffee mug in one hand, he explored the rest of the house.

The bathroom was a small cubicle next to the kitchen, containing a primitive shower, with an instant gas heater powered by roof-mounted solar panels, and a tiny handbasin; the chemical toilet was a small plastic box in one corner, lid shut. Mould seeped down the walls like the shadows of stalactites. A tiny mirror hung on one wall, blotched white with soap. Exactly as he remembered it.

The single bedroom was bare apart from a coffin-like cupboard containing nothing but coat hangers, and a stripped double bed. The mattress was stained brown and in the final stages of internal collapse. Again, the same as it had been. He recalled the time, five years earlier, when he and Jacqui had . . .

No. He went back into the main room and found the half-empty bottle of scotch. He preferred cold blankness to the grief and pain that waited to claim him. He could feel it building, growing like a bubble deep in his throat. When it burst, as it surely would, he didn't think he would be able to survive. The shock was fading, so he had to feed the anaesthesia some other way. It was either that, or leave.

And he couldn't leave. No matter what perverse internal logic had led him here, he had to go with it. With nowhere else to go, and no way to get there, there was only the shack and the past left to keep him company.

In activity there was relief. He opened two tins and cooked himself a simple casserole of meat and vegetables. He fussed with the burner, with the plates, took his time eating and washing the few dishes. The bottle emptied fast, and he opened another. The night deepened. He could feel the comet crossing the heavens above him; invisible through the ceiling, but still there. A primitive clock to measure the thickening of the night.

It became cold at last—a deep, desert cold. A pot-bellied stove crouched in one corner of the main room, but he hadn't thought to bring wood. Lighting the kerosene heater, he chain-smoked, watched the purple flame flickering and finished the second bottle.

When the sun eventually rose, it was pallid and less intense than it had been the previous day. The snow had tightened its grip on the valley overnight and reflected the myriad shades of dawn back at the cloudless sky.

Inside his mind, more memory than dream, another sun rose.

He was driving the Toyota back from Port Germein, where he had stayed the weekend with a cousin. He almost hadn't gone at all, but Jacqui had talked him into it.

"Just go, dammit. You need the break."

"But I've got work to do."

"Work? It's *Christmas*, Stew." She put her hands on her hips, resembling more than ever a cross brown bear. "No buts. You missed it last time and complained for a month. I don't want to listen to your whining again."

"I don't remember any whining."

"It was pathetic." A grin surfaced through the mock anger. "God knows I can't see the attraction in some cosmic ball of fluff, but I understand what it means to you. You've been up in the clouds for days now, thinking about it, so just get the hell out of here and take a look, okay?" She took his chin in one hand and kissed him on the lips: the quick peck that said she meant business. "Okay?"

She had been talking about the comet, of course—Ronson's Comet, which had reached perigee the previous autumn. In the city, the spectral visitor had been pale and foreshortened, a dusty smudge almost invisible through the wash of streetlights. Hamish, his cousin, had waxed lyrical about its beauty from the country, but Stewart had been too busy tying up a publishing deal to spare the time to travel to Port Germein, where Hamish lived.

And Jacqui had been right: he had regretted missing it. If perigee had come a single week later, he might have been able to arrange something, but it hadn't. When the comet had vanished behind the sun, he had cursed himself anyway for not taking the opportunity that Hamish had presented. He tried to resign himself to the fact that he had missed it, but with only partial success.

Then, after perihelion, the comet's orbit shifted—as a result of violent gas discharges from its unimaginable surface. The second perigee, scheduled for the middle of December, was even closer than the first. Earth, and Stewart Danby, had been given a second chance.

"Okay, okay." He capitulated gracelessly, feigning reluctance. Jacqui didn't want to come, he knew that, but he didn't want to seem too eager to go without her, either. Although he would miss her, her lack of enthusiasm would only dampen the experience.

He left the following Friday afternoon and arrived at Port Germein in time for a spectacular sunset. The small fishing town was lively with weekend tourists who, like him, had fled the perpetual blindness of the city's light for the transparent skies of the country. The night was hot and clear, perfect for idle star-gazing. The local council had arranged a blackout, to aid the amateur observers.

Sharing a six-pack on Hamish's back veranda, he watched the comet rise, knowing it would be a sight he would never forget.

Away from the city, its tail stretched across half the sky, nebulous but clear. Through binoculars, it looked like faintly-glowing smoke, backlit by stars. He thought he detected colours in its feathery wake, but couldn't be certain.

"I doubt it," said Hamish, who had read a lot in the last few weeks and become assertively confident with his new knowledge. "Takes a spectrometer to pick out the elements. The naked eye just sees white."

There followed a discussion of the comet's origins, little of which was new to Stewart. It had drifted into the solar system from deep space, not from the Oört cloud. Unlike Halley's Comet, it was a new addition to the family of planets and only a temporary one. After perigee, it would swing out of the system, never to return.

"Show you something interesting," said Hamish, producing a magazine. Holding a lit cigarette lighter, he illuminated one glossy page. On it was printed a simple picture of the comet's altered orbit. "What does this look like?"

"A fish," said Stewart, and Hamish nodded. The sun was the fish's eye, the Earth a tiny dot in its tail.

"An *Ichthys*, more to the point." Hamish grinned wryly and extinguished the lighter. "Glad I'm not a Christian."

It took Stewart a moment to remember the word, and to realise what his cousin was suggesting. Comets were traditionally signs of doom and destruction; coming so close to the end of the millennium, their prophetic powers were augmented. That Ronson's Comet was further coupled with a common symbol of the Christian saviour augured the Apocalypse, Judgement Day.

"Maybe you should become one," he joked. "A Christian, I mean. Before it's too late."

Hamish snorted in the darkness. "Crap."

"No, really, doesn't it seem a little strange? It did change course, after all." The question begged to be asked. "Maybe we didn't get the message first time around."

"Coincidence, Stew. That's all."

Stewart smiled in the star-spattered darkness. Hamish was right, of course, but he wondered how many New Age evangelists would profit from the comet's timely appearance. "Five to one says you're wrong."

"You're on, sucker."

The weekend passed quickly. Perigee had been the previous Wednesday, but the comet showed no immediate signs of decreasing in magnitude. Tiny sparks seemed to twinkle in its tail, glinting, insubstantial and short-lived. Boulders of dislodged ice, suggested Hamish, although he admitted that he had neither seen the phenomenon before nor read of it. Stewart wasn't convinced, but kept his opinion to himself; to have witnessed the phenomenon alone was enough. He didn't need a knowledge of pyrotechnics to enjoy fireworks.

Reluctant to leave, he delayed his departure as long as possible. The comet was hypnotic, beguiling, a drop of dye in the clear water of mundane, modern life. Eventually, he drove out of Port Germein at four o'clock the Monday morning, knowing he would later regret the lack of sleep, but glad that he had made the effort to be there, to stay those extra few hours.

It was at this point that the dream began.

Half way to Adelaide, with the comet low ahead of him and the sun rising on his left, he stopped to rest by the side of the highway. A fatigue hangover had begun somewhere behind his eyeballs, and he relished the chance to close his eyes.

A sudden strong gust of wind made him squint at the lightening sky. Clouds were rolling in from the south-east with astonishing speed. Pure white but as large as thunderheads, they bulked over the horizon, growing larger as he watched. The wind picked up sharply, and he headed back to the Toyota for shelter. There was electricity in the air, a powerful aura of impending disaster.

He started the car and pulled back onto the highway, leaving the lights on. The shadow of the clouds covered him, bringing a semblance of night back with it. The wind became more insistent, tugging the Toyota to one side.

His radio, tuned to a country station, crackled in mid-chorus and died. The shadow deepened; behind him, the last segment of pale blue sky vanished.

He stared in absolute astonishment as, maybe for the first time ever in that part of Australia, it began to snow.

He awoke gasping for breath, momentarily disoriented. Then he remembered where he was, and what he was doing there. He was at Barnard's shack in the Flinders Ranges, and he had come there to . . . what? Forget? Hide?

Die?

Staggering out of the chair, wincing at the light that stabbed through the gaps between the curtains, he found the scuba gear, put on the rubber facemask and twisted a knob. High-pressure air hissed into his open mouth. He lay back on the floor of the shack and sucked in the sweet coolness.

The muzziness in his head gradually faded. He switched off the valve and removed the mask. The air in the shack was thick and pungent; more than ever the stench of rotten eggs filled his nostrils. Taking it slowly, breathing heavily through his open mouth, he rummaged in a box for the gaffer tape.

Then, slowly and carefully, he sealed every gap in the shack's stone walls: window-frames, air-vents, cracks under doors. Everything.

When he had finished, he collapsed with his face pressed against a dirty windowpane, his chest rising and falling in spasms. Outside, the atmosphere seemed unnaturally dense and yellowish. Although the sky was still cloudless, the snow-cover was thicker than it had been the night before. It now piled in drifts against the walls of the shack, and he was reminded of the red weed in H.G. Wells' *The War of the Worlds*. The snow had turned the valley into an alien landscape: moon-like, with gentle curves and featureless bulges in place of more earthly scenery.

The bubble in his throat was growing, making it even more difficult to breathe. With clumsy fingers he turned on the scuba gear again and flooded the room with fresh air.

Three days had passed since that early morning when he had first gaped incredulously at the white powder batting in flurries at the Toyota. The forecast the previous night had said nothing about storms, let alone snow. It was a warm summer night; he couldn't imagine where such a mass of super-cold air had come from, or how the snow survived the fall to the ground without melting into rain. The only places in Australia where conditions allowed the freezing of water in any form, as far as he knew, were the Snowy Mountains and the south of Tasmania, both during winter. Not South Australia, the driest state in the world, in the middle of summer . . . .

Ahead, the road had vanished under a thin carpet of white, and he slowed slightly. There seemed to be no slippage, however; his wheels gripped the road surface as well as ever, which seemed strange. Surely melting snow was more treacherous than water? And the stuff wasn't even sticking to the windscreen, contrary to expectations.

The last stop before entering the northern edge of the city was Port Wakefield. He pulled into a service station, partly to refuel, mostly to assess the situation, but the attendant knew as little as he did. Snow was falling, impossible snow, and the radio frequencies were still swamped by interference. There was no chance of an updated weather report until the storm cleared.

It seemed safe to assume that the freak weather had hit the city, and he wondered whether Jacqui could shed some light on it. She had spent some years in Europe before moving to Australia, so her knowledge of snowstorms was bound to be greater than his. He didn't even know if it was safe to drive, or whether tire chains were required. Traffic around Christmas was heavy, and he didn't want to be caught in a pile-up.

But when he tried to ring Jacqui from a public phone, the lines were dead. The last time he had spoken to her had been from Hamish's home the previous night, and nothing had been amiss. A line must have come down since then, probably as a result of the storm.

He got back into the car and continued on his way. Not long afterwards, the snow stopped falling, but the thick, fairy-floss clouds remained and the radio stayed dead. The closer he came to the city, the thicker the ground-cover became; even the tyre-tracks of the cars preceding him seemed faint. Slowly he decreased his speed until he was travelling at barely above sixty kilometres per hour.

Just outside the first main intersection, the snow became too thick to pass. A number of cars blocked the highway, making further progress impossible. Pulling to a halt, he walked to join the others who had gathered on the roadside, scuffing incredulously at the snow. It crunched faintly beneath his feet, like sand.

"This is just great," said one woman, a bedraggled mother of four children who squealed and squawked from a nearby station-wagon. "My mother's expecting us this morning, and we're already an hour late."

"Can't get past it," said a middle-aged man with a biker's beard and dirty leathers. He radiated an aura of patient, if faintly puzzled, pragmatism, and Stewart found his attitude calming. The biker gestured at the bank of snow in their path. "I've just come from further on. The traffic's bogged in solid. Take a tractor to shift it."

"Maybe it levels out. We might be able to force our way—"

"Lady, it was up to my waist when I turned back, and getting deeper. Unless you've got a bulldozer handy, I can't see how you're gonna get through it."

"What the hell are we supposed to do, then?"

"Try another way in, I guess." The biker scratched at his beard. "Come down via the hills maybe."

The woman was not happy. "Forget it. I'm going to wait. The council can get their act together."

The biker smiled. "Maybe, but I don't think snowploughs are all that common round here."

"Any idea where it came from?" Stewart asked.

"The greenhouse effect," said the woman. "It fell through a hole in the ozone layer."

The biker looked unconvinced. "Beats me, to be honest. It hit right out of the blue. No warning, no nothing." He lashed out with a leather riding-boot, sending a snowdrift scattering. "But that's not what really worries me."

"What, then?"

"Touch it, and you'll see what I mean."

Stewart hesitated, then stooped to the ground and plunged his hand into the drift at his feet. To his surprise, the snow wasn't cold; not even cool. It was as warm as the earth it covered and felt gritty on his palm and fingertips.

"It's not cold," said the biker, "it's not melting, and I doubt you could build a snowman out of it. If it's *really* snow, I'll eat my leathers."

Standing up and glancing around, Stewart tried to make sense of the phenomenon. Snow lay everywhere: a thick blanket of white definitely becoming deeper in the direction of Adelaide. It hung from trees like scraps of torn sheets, too unusual to be truly beautiful. If it wasn't snow, he thought, then perhaps it was ash. Had there been some sort of volcanic explosion in Adelaide's vicinity? As far as he knew there were no volcanoes, active or dead, for many hundreds of kilometres, although the city did lie on top of a fault line . . .

"I'm heading for the hills," said the biker, stamping off to his bike. "No point standing around here all day."

Stewart agreed and went back to the Toyota, leaving the mother alone to deal with her kids.

Two hours later, coming down the last leg of the Great Eastern Freeway, he passed the biker going back up. Recognising the car, the biker flagged him down.

"Don't bother. Blocked that way too. Worse, if anything."

"Shit." That explained why he had seen few cars coming either way, even though it was close to peak-hour. "Where now?"

"Me, I'm going back to the lookout. Might be able to see something from there."

Stewart followed the motorbike back up the freeway to a concrete car-park hollowed out of the chest of the foothills. There, he produced the binoculars he had taken with him to study the comet and turned them on the landscape below.

Through the clouds, which hung low and heavy over the hills, he could see little. Handing the binoculars to the biker, he leaned forward over the concrete barrier, trying to pierce the cloud-cover by sheer force of will.

The clouds parted for an instant, allowing them an unobstructed view.

"Jesus *Christ*," whispered the biker.

"What? What can you see?"

Wordlessly, the biker shook his head and handed the binoculars back to him.

Stewart focused the lenses, swept his amplified stare across the suburbs and streets of the city. White, everywhere, just white. No details. It looked as though fog or heavy mist had covered the city, obscuring it from sight. But it wasn't mist.

"Look at the city centre," suggested the biker.

Landmarks lay buried beneath the white pancake. He didn't realise he had found the city centre until he recognised the silhouette of the State Bank building, the tallest in Adelaide. It too was shrouded in white, as though a cloth had been draped over it, but it didn't look as tall as it should have been. The buildings around it were similarly foreshortened, and some appeared to be missing altogether. He frowned: the snow couldn't be that thick, could it?

As he watched, puzzled, the State Bank building slumped and fell over, melting into the snow like a spear of ice-cream under the hot sun.

"Oh my god," he breathed.

"The city's going under," said the biker. "It's burying it."

"But . . . " Stewart lowered the binoculars. "That's . . . "

"I'm getting out of here. Something weird's going on, and I don't like it."

"The snow . . . ?"

"It's *not* snow, I know that much." The biker raised his nose to sniff the wind. "Can you smell it? The air is turning."

Stewart found an edge to the air, like rotten eggs, blowing up from the foothills.

"My wife works in the city," he said, a fire beginning to burn in his stomach.

"You got any kids?" asked the biker.

He shook his head.

"I've got three." A dirty hand flapped at the terrible whiteness. "Somewhere under *that*."

"You're not going to leave them?"

The biker worried his beard with one hand. "If they're okay, then they can look after themselves. If they're not, there's nothing I can do."

"We have to *try*, don't we?"

The biker looked uncomfortable for a moment. Then, without replying, he strode back to the bike and kicked it into life. The roar of the engine leaped from the hills as he sped back to the highway.

Stewart stayed until the cloud-cover closed again, cutting off the view of the city. There was nothing new to be seen, apart from the gentle, silent collapse of the city centre; just an endless snowfield that stretched as far as the sea. No details, no signs of life.

His stomach gnawed at itself as he drove on down the freeway. The snow piled higher and higher, until he rounded a corner and reached a solid wall of the stuff with a handful of cars parked in front of it. The bike leaned on its stand among them, and Stewart was gratified to see it, although the biker himself was nowhere to be seen.

A clot of people had gathered near the blockage. Walking up to them, Stewart addressed the short, balding man who seemed to have elected himself leader.

"The biker. Where did he go?"

The man pointed over the snow-dune. "In there. With Gary."

Footprints led over the dune. Thanking the bald man, he followed the double tracks. The snow was at least three metres deep in places and as hard to walk through as soft sand. As the tracks wandered on, the dunes piled higher, licking at the rock walls where the freeway had been cut out of the hills. An icing-sugar canyon. He shivered, although it still wasn't cold; it was, in fact, oppressively hot. The smell of rotten eggs was strong in the still, stifled air.

He turned a bend and caught sight of the biker and the man called Gary. They were standing not much further on, looking at something on the ground between them. He called to them, and both glanced at him in surprise.

Gary was tall, with a pot-gut and thinning black hair. As Stewart approached, he realised that the man's face was as white as the snow around them.

"You don't want to see this," said the biker.

Stewart forced his way between them and stared at what lay at their feet. At first, all he saw was a dash of red in the ubiquitous white, until the details fell into place.

It was the body of a woman, partly buried. Her clothes were gone, and her staring eyes full of empty accusation. Although there was no blood evident, the condition of her body suggested a violent, hideous passing—or subsequent mutilation.

"There's a car up ahead," said Gary. "Abandoned."

"Someone dumped her here?" asked Stewart, forcing the words through the gorge rising in his throat.

"We don't think so. She must have crawled from it, got buried, and suffocated. If I hadn't tripped over her, we never would've found her."

"But who . . . ?" He gestured at the corpse, lost for words.

"Skinned her? Look closely."

Reluctantly, Stewart did so. The snow lay across her vivid flesh like ribbons, or ropes. More: it seemed to be digging in, somehow, as though she might yet struggle free. This impression alone was enough to disturb him, until he noticed something else.

"It . . . It's moving!"

The biker nodded. "It's *eating* her."

Stewart's stomach spasmed. Staggering backwards, he clutched his mouth and simultaneously wiped at the snow that had settled on his skin. "Oh, Jesus . . . "

The biker put a steadying hand on his shoulder and smiled without humour.

"It probably won't hurt you," he said. "Or us. We're still alive, you see."

Stewart swallowed his nausea and forced his hands to be still, cursing his foolishness. He had been exposed to the snow on several occasions and it hadn't harmed him. "But . . . I don't understand."

"The car," said Gary, "was almost gone. It looked . . . dissolved. The snow was stripping it back to nothing."

The biker nodded, and gestured at the body. "Same with her. She's just raw material."

"For what?"

The biker waved a hand at the canyon of snow. "For whatever this stuff really is."

"Machines," said Gary. "Nano-machines, or something. Designed to dig in and separate the useful stuff from the rest. Like ants, but smaller."

"Is that possible?" asked the biker.

"I can't see why not."

Stewart could feel panic rising through his confusion. He allowed himself to be led away from the body, back up the freeway.

"The comet," he whispered, half to himself.

Gary nodded, as though he had already considered the idea. "It's possible."

"Aliens?" The biker raised his eyebrows.

"Or something non-intelligent. This stuff could be a life-form, some sort of mindless bug."

"Do you think so?"

"No. It hit the city dead on. That suggests a purposeful intent."

"Maybe they home in on metal?"

"Or high-density electric fields." Gary shrugged at the biker's question. "I don't know. But if it *is* aliens, then this could be just the beginning—phase one, if you like. Maybe they're going to build something next. Or take over."

The biker nodded slowly. "The air's starting to smell bad."

"Exactly. Depending on how much of this stuff there is, world-wide, it would be fairly easy to change the environment. And if the snow's self-replicating, then it'd be even easier. Once the bugs are loose, there'd be no stopping them."

"How long?" Stewart heard the question before realising that he had asked it. A scream was building at the back of his throat, and he swallowed to force it down.

Gary shrugged. "I don't know. I'm not a scientist."

"You'll have to ask the aliens," suggested the biker, "if they exist."

They walked back to the cars in solemn silence. The walls of the canyon loomed over them, higher than before. In the short time they had been studying the woman's gory corpse, the snow had thickened.

When they reached the last snow-dune, Gary turned to them and, as though he regretted his earlier words, said:

"Remember, it's only a theory. I could be wrong."

"Then why haven't we seen any planes?" asked the biker. "And why aren't the radios working?"

"I don't know. But I don't think we should start a panic over what might turn out to be nothing."

"Nothing?" The biker shook his head. "We've been invaded by *something*, haven't we? Surely we should try to fight back?"

"How? How do you fight *snow*?"

Stewart collapsed gratefully into the seat of the Toyota, his mind whirling. The idea of aliens invading the planet was too crazy to be true, and yet it made a horrible kind of sense: to hit the cities first, to use a widespread plague of machines to contaminate the environment, to hide in a comet, where no-one would ever think to look . . .

The comet had swung past the Earth once, perhaps to survey the territory, then had changed course during perihelion. The whip of the sun's gravity had dragged it back for one more visit, to drop its deadly cargo into the atmosphere. Maybe just a handful of snow-particles at first, breeding, self-replicating in the upper altitudes, until enough existed to cover the major cities of the Earth. And then it had started falling: snowflakes, innocent and unexpected, *everywhere*, unstoppable.

It did make sense. And, even if the theory was wrong, the facts remained, indisputable. Adelaide was buried and crumbling beneath the snow. Judging by the rate the woman's body had dissolved, the city wouldn't last long.

He glanced at his watch; the storm had ended just four hours earlier. It seemed like a life-time. His hands shook with delayed shock; a coldness was spreading through his mind, numbing the part of him that wanted to scream. Through the growing fog, it became, strangely, easier to think. Although the terrible coldness appalled him, he knew that it was a defence mechanism: he needed to think rationally if he was going to survive.

If Jacqui was still alive, then there was nothing he could do to reach her. Better to assume that she was dead, that everyone in the city was dead. And, as the snow of the initial fall spread and grew, the area around the city wouldn't be safe for long. His weekend of comet-spotting might have saved his life in the short-term, but how long would it be before the snow spread to encompass neighbouring towns?

And how long before the entire world succumbed?

With no clear destination in mind, certain only that he had to move somewhere, he started the car and headed back up the freeway.

The last bottle of compressed air emptied with the fifth bottle of scotch, and he was down to his last cigarette. It was four days since the snow had started to fall. The roof was sagging under the weight of the stuff that had settled upon it; white tendrils crept through the gaffer tape, wormed across the worn carpet.

It was Christmas Day, and he had run out of anaesthetic.

As the bubble burst and grief poured in to fill the empty space in his chest, he realised that this was what he had been waiting for all along. This was why he had come back to Barnard's shack, where he and Jacqui had spent their first week of marriage together. Not to forget or to hide, but to grieve. To say goodbye.

The last time he had spoken to Jacqui, the telephone line from Port Germein had been faint but clear. He had been amazed by how much he had missed her, even though he'd only been away two nights. Her voice had been a poor substitute for the real thing and, now, all he had was a memory of her voice. The woman he loved was gone. The assumption had been easy to make, but the realisation of the fact had taken time.

Tears burned his eyes. He didn't try to fight them any more. Maybe he had been waiting for them to come. The pain made it easier to cut free from the world that had ended and to which he could never return.

By the time his spasm of grief ebbed, half an hour had passed. The air was thickening again, curdling before his very eyes.

Rising from the chair, he drew back the curtains. The valley and its native scrub had disappeared. In its place was a world drained of colour. The snow had formed delicate spires and towers, upraised to greet the sun. The alien forest was still and lifeless, but he could sense a vitality stirring through it, as though the snow itself was alive.

The Earth wasn't dead, but *changed*. It no longer belonged to its previous owners. Already, he felt like a trespasser. An unwanted intruder, witnessing the birth of a new world. He wondered if he was the only one.

On the heels of this thought, there came a noise from the rear of the shack: a rattle of rocks, loud in the stillness of the valley. Turning his back to the view, he went to the kitchen window and peered out.

Something was moving down the hill. The creature looked at first like a giant spider, with legs over five metres long, crawling ponderously towards the cabin. As white as the snow it traversed, it moved with all the precision of a surgical instrument. Limbs swivelled and folded neatly to match niches and holds buried beneath the snow. There was no wastage of movement, not the slightest hesitation or inefficiency. He was unable to decide whether it was a machine or a living creature.

When it came to a halt not five metres away, the legs collapsed along its sides and it became a giant flea, two metres high. Stewart could see no eyes in the knobbled, ugly "face", but sensed that it was watching the shack intently, as though waiting for him to make a move.

"How long?" he had asked Gary, just days earlier. He remembered the biker's reply:

"Ask the aliens."

If phase one—the snow—had already ended, then the creature in front of him was part of phase two. Probably the creatures were not aliens themselves, but motile drones programmed to scour the surface of the planet. Robots. The colonists themselves would come later, perhaps resurrected from frozen genetic material, to assume their roles as the new masters of the Earth. And then the invasion would be complete.

An invasion without war. Just the silent, peaceful fall of snowflakes.

The process might have been repeated on a thousand worlds, and might be on a thousand yet to come. Wherever the comet passed, it would leave the legacy of an unknown race behind, spreading like a cancer from star to star. How many other civilisations had died in order that this one might live? How long would it be before the comet encountered a race that was able to fight back?

The creature didn't move. To Stewart's eyes, it seemed puzzled, as though uncertain what to make of the shack and its occupant; as though its programmers had not told it how to deal with a belligerent native.

Maybe, thought Stewart, the conquering race had never encountered another civilisation anywhere in its travels. Maybe it had assumed that none such was to be found anywhere in the galaxy, and that all suitable planets were therefore fit for terraforming. Maybe the destruction of the human Earth had been a mistake. And maybe it wasn't too late, after all . . .

He guessed he wouldn't have to wait long for phase three. For one wild moment, he imagined that he could survive to explain the mistake—if he rationed his food and breathed shallowly, if he could keep the snow from destroying the shack around him. There had to be others who had survived, like him, by holing up and doing nothing.

The creature unfolded its legs and moved towards him.

He backed away from the window, thinking of the last thing Gary had said:

"How do you fight *snow*?"

The answer, of course, was that you couldn't. It had taken him four days alone in the shack to come to terms with the fact.

He opened the cocks on the butane bottles and waited until the smell of hydrogen sulphide had vanished, swamped by another, more potent smell.

There came the sound of glass shattering in the kitchen, followed by the breaking of solid stone.

He closed his eyes and lit the cigarette.

●

INTRODUCTION TO:
.... THE MASQUE OF AGAMEMNON

I enjoy collaboration. Thirteen novels and seven short stories are proof of that. I'm often asked how these collaborations work, and the answer depends entirely on who I'm writing with at the time. Shane Dix and I start with an idea that I write into a quick first draft, which he then knocks into shape. One more pass by me and it's done.

Simon Brown and I have tried several different methods, and eventually settled on one that works successfully for both us. Every writer has stories they can't finish or fix. These stories can sit on the hard drive for years, until either the solution becomes obvious (finally) or they're forgotten forever. I have about forty stories in the latter category: too flawed ever to salvage, and too embarrassing to inflict on an unsuspecting world. There are, however, some that I could never quite let go, even though I know I lack—and will most likely always lack—the skill or spark to fix them. Giving some of these stories to another writer so they get to do the dirty work has a lot of appeal.

"Atrax" was one such. So was "The Masque of Agamemnon," but in this case the process worked the other way. Simon handed me an opening he'd always wanted to do more with and told me to go for my life. It really was just a fragment: maybe a couple of thousands words, setting up the characters and the world. But from that seed grew something that startled both of us. Its initial electronic publication in Eidolon *was quickly followed by reprints in* Year's Best SF *and* Year's Best Australian SF & Fantasy *and translation into various languages. It's undoubtedly our best-known story.*

While I'm very proud to have played a role in Simon's much-lauded Troy *cycle, I should confess right now that the long-standing passion for Homer was entirely his. And I can't even remember where the Melville reference came from. "Groenig" might be my doing, since the real-life Matt Groenig is an avowed fan of the late Frank Zappa, but who can be sure? The wonderful thing about collaborations is that finished story belongs to all the authors involved, and yet at the same time to none of them. They stand apart, and are all the more magical for that.*

●

THE MASQUE OF AGAMEMNON

WITH SIMON BROWN

Not long after the Achaean fleet gathered at the periphery of the Ilium system, the area sensors on the great ship noted a phenomenon its sentient matrix could neither accept nor explain. An owl appeared in the middle of the fleet, circled around it three times—its wings eclipsing the distant point of light that was Ilium's sun—then headed straight for Mycenae; just as it was about to smash into the ship's hull, there was an intense flash of blue light and it disappeared.

Internal sensors picked it up next, a bird the size of a human child, dipping and soaring within *Mycenae*'s vast internal halls and corridors. Before any alarm could be given, the sensor matrices received a supersede command: the owl was a messenger from the goddess Athena, and it was not to be interfered with.

Seconds later, the owl reached its destination, the chamber of Agamemnon, Over-captain of the entire Achaean fleet. What happened therein is not recorded, but an hour later Agamemnon announced to his crew he was going to hold a grand ball.

His wife, Clytemnestra, attributed the idea to his love of games and his penchant for petulant, almost child-like, whims. She thought the idea a foolish notion, but she did not argue against it; she loved her husband and indulged him in all things.

Arrangements were quickly made, and maser beams carried messages to all the other ships of the fleet, demanding their captains attend the Great Masque of Agamemnon.

"Your brother should spend more time worrying about the Trojans," Helen told her husband, Menelaus.

The captain of Sparta grimaced. He disliked anyone criticising his older brother, but in this instance he had to agree with his wife. Agamemnon was spending a large amount of the fleet's energy and time to throw his ball, energy and time that could have been better spent prosecuting an attack against the Trojan's home on Ilium.

"Nevertheless, he has commanded the presence of all his captains and their wives, so we must go."

"But why a masque? He loves his games too much. And I suppose we will end up spending the whole time with Nestor."

"Nestor is the oldest among us, and his words the wisest."

"The most boring, you mean. Oh, Menelaus," she pouted, "I wish we didn't have to go."

Although Menelaus agreed with Helen's sentiment, he would not allow himself to say so.

Achilles had made a silver helmet for his friend Patroclus to wear to the ball. When Patroclus saw it he could not find the words to thank Achilles; it was one of the most beautiful things he had ever seen. Then Achilles showed him the helmet he himself would be wearing, and to Patroclus' surprise it was exactly the same as the one he had been given.

"I don't understand, Achilles. Are we going as brothers?"

Achilles laughed. "As lovers, dear Patroclus. But there is more to it than symbolism."

Patroclus looked blankly at his friend, which made Achilles laugh even harder. "We are the same size and shape. With these helmets, and wearing the livery of my ship, no one will be able to tell us apart."

"A game?"

Achilles shrugged, gently placed one of the helmets on Patroclus' head. He leaned forward quickly and kissed his friend on the lips, then closed the helmet's plate, hiding his friend's face entirely except for his eyes and mouth.

"A game of sorts, I suppose, to match Agamemnon's own." Achilles put on his own helmet, closed the face plate. "We are, behind these disguises, nothing but shadows of ourselves, and as shadows at the Over-captain's masque, who knows what secrets we will learn?"

"Secrets?"

"I have heard rumours that Agamemnon has invited a surprise guest."

"A surprise guest?"

"A Trojan," Achilles said.

His real name was Bernal, but AlterEgo insisted on calling him Paris.

"Get used to it. Our hosts insist you adopt the name for this occasion."

"If they explained why, it would be easier," Bernal complained. Strapped into the gravity couch of the small ship in which he was travelling, he had little else to do except complain. AlterEgo took care of all the ship's functions; Bernal was nothing but baggage.

"Presumably, it has something to do with the fact that all the messages we've received from our visitors come in the name of Agamemnon."

"Over-captain of the Achaean fleet, for pity's sake."

"You can snort all you want, Paris, but we know very little else about them, and it will probably be in your best interests to take them seriously."

"Not to mention the best interests of the whole of Cirrus." Bernal used his one free hand to align the external telescope, the only instrument the ship carried that used visible light, and installed specifically for Bernal's use. He could not see his planet—now more than forty billion kilometres away—but the system's yellow-dwarf sun, Anatole, was the brightest object in the sky, and Cirrus was somewhere within a few arc-seconds of it.

"Home-sick?" AlterEgo asked.

"Scared, more like," Bernal answered. "When was the last time one of my people travelled this far from home?"

Bernal was sure he heard AlterEgo's brain hum, even though he knew the AI didn't have any parts that hummed as such. He had been in the AI's company for too long. "Two-hundred and twenty-seven years ago. Explorer and miner named Groenig. Last message came when her ship was forty-three billion kilometres from home. Never heard from since."

"No one went after her?"

"What good would that have done? Even back then, when intrasystem shipping was much more active than now, there would not have been more than two or three ships that could have reached her last known position within six months, far too late to do anything to help her if she was in trouble. Most likely there was some onboard disaster, or maybe the loneliness got to her and she committed suicide."

The answer irritated Bernal. "What the hell did you wake me for, anyway?"

"I did have the telescope aligned on something I thought you'd be interested in seeing."

"Don't whinge. What was it?"

"Fortunately, I took the precaution of storing some images over a three day period, which was just enough time to create some very interesting holographic—"

"If you've got something to show me, get on with it," Bernal commanded.

Several small laser beams intersected about half a metre in front of Bernal's face. At first they formed only a white shell, but a second later a 3D-image appeared. It looked like a crown of thorns. "How big is it?"

"Some of my sensor readings indicate the object's mass is close to seven million tonnes."

Bernal was surprised. Without a reference point, he had assumed the object was quite small. Then he remembered AlterEgo saying it had taken three days to get a workable 3D image, which was a lot of time to work with for a computer of AlterEgo's capability.

"What did you say its dimensions were?"

"I didn't, but I estimate a radius of eighty or so kilometres."

"My God! Is this one of the Achaean ships?"

"I should think that if this was just one of their ships, a fleet of them would have been detected from Cirrus several years ago. I surmise, therefore, that this is the fleet, its individual components joined in some way."

Bernal peered at the holograph. "Can you make out any repetitions of shape? Anything we could identify as a single unit?"

"Ah, I was hoping you would ask that." Bernal was sure he heard smugness in that voice.

The holographic image changed, metamorphosed into something more like a ship. Bernal peered at it. Well, *vaguely* more like a ship.

"It reminds me of something I've seen before, but for the life of me I can't figure what."

"Using some deductive logic, a little dash of intuition and a thorough search of the Cirrus Archives, I think I've discovered something," AlterEgo said. "Watch what happens when I remove from the Achaean ship the youngest hull material, connective grids and certain extraneous energy dispersion vanes."

The image altered instantaneously into something barely a tenth the size of the original. Bernal studied the new shape for a moment before a memory clicked in his brain.

"I don't believe it!"

AlterEgo just hummed.

"A Von Neumann probe . . . " Bernal's voice faded as he realised the implications.

"Precisely my deduction," AlterEgo agreed, superimposing a second holograph over the first, a blue outline that almost perfectly matched the image of the Achaean artefact. "This diagram is from Cirrus's most ancient library stores. It is, of course, one of the original plans for a Von Neumann probe, circa 2090 CE."

Bernal whistled. "But that was nearly 500,000 years ago. They were the first human-made ships to reach the stars."

"And in their seedbanks they carried the ancestors of all human life in this part of the spiral arm . . . " There was the slightest of pauses. " . . . including your own kind."

The bulkheads forming *Mycenae*'s cavernous, square reception hall were decorated with depictions of a Cyclopean city: grey walls made from unworked boulders and dressed stone, a corbel arch gateway topped by a heavy, triangular sculpture of two lions and a Minoan column, and a massive beehive tomb made from the same stone as the city.

Mingling in the hall were dozens of ship captains and their wives or mistresses, all dressed in elaborate costumes, the men in shining breast plates and tall helmets sprouting horse-hair crests or eagle feathers, the women in long tunics bordered in gold and beads of amber and lapis lazuli.

Agamemnon moved among his captains, greeting each individually with generous words, baulking only when he met the two he knew were Achilles and Patroclus and was unable to tell them apart in their silver helmets. He smiled, pretending to enjoy their private joke, and moved on to deliver more glib welcomings.

Clytemnestra circulated as well, talking to the women, flattering them about their clothing and hair.

In a short while, smaller groups coalesced from the throng, centred on the fleet's major captains. The largest group circled Agamemnon and his brother Menelaus; a second group almost as large gathered around Achilles and Patroclus; other heroes to have their own audience included Diomedes, the huge Ajax, Nestor and Idomeneus. Standing apart from them all, however, was one captain without any followers or even the companionship of his own woman.

Odysseus stood back from the assembly, looking on with a wry smile. He enjoyed observing the posturings of the major captains, the false camaraderie they shared and the whispered insults they passed; as well, he was entertained by the antics of the lesser captains, eager to please their patrons and desperate to raise their own status in the fleet.

His inspection was interrupted by a small owl that appeared on his shoulder.

"The guest has arrived," the owl said. "His ship is about to dock. He brings a friend with him."

"A friend?" Odysseus replied. "Troy was instructed to send only one of their own."

"His friend is not human," the owl continued. "It is some kind of AI. I only learned of this when it communicated with the navigation computer."

"Have you told Agamemnon?"

"Not yet."

"Then do so now. He should meet this Paris personally."

Bernal cursed as AlterEgo made what it called "minor" adjustments to the ship's attitude in its final approach to the docking site. The ship jerked to port, then performed a quarter-roll, jerked back in the other direction, and finally decelerated rapidly as all the lateral thrusters fired simultaneously. Bernal's journey to the Achaean fleet, which had begun with a smooth acceleration away from orbit around Cirrus and then continued on just as smoothly for another three weeks through intrasystem space, was now ending with a violent jagging that did nothing to ease his roiling stomach.

Bernal was about to ask AlterEgo when all the manoeuvring would finish, when suddenly there was a thump and he felt himself flung forward before the gravity webbing caught him and flung him back again.

And then a new sensation.

Weight, Bernal realised after a moment. *The Achaean fleet is not only locked together; it's also rotating.*

"We are here," AlterEgo announced calmly.

"I think I have a headache coming on."

"It is just the tension, Paris. You will be fine once you get moving."

"Do I have to suit up?"

"No need. We have docked adjacent to an airlock. You will be able to stroll through and meet our hosts as soon as the airlock is pressurised."

"Can you take a sample of their air?"

"Already done. Breathable. Nitrogen-oxygen mix, a little heavy on the oxygen side, but nothing extraordinary. Very few trace gases. The airlock has pressurised. Do you want me to open the hatch?"

"Is there anyone waiting for me?"

"Not in the airlock itself. Wait, I'll communicate with the Achaean command system."

Bernal unstrapped himself from the webbing, then carefully climbed out of the life support suit that had kept him fed, removed his body waste, injected him with regular doses of calcium and vitamins, and electrically stimulated his muscles for the duration of the journey. By the time he had finished, AlterEgo was able to report that a welcoming committee would be waiting for him on the other side of the airlock.

"Did you think to ask who's in the committee?"

There was a sound like a sigh. "Agamemnon, Over-captain of the Achaean Fleet, his wife Clytemnestra, his brother Menelaus, Captain of *Sparta*, his wife Helen, and Odysseus, Captain of *Ithaca*."

Bernal closed his eyes, slowly shook his head. "That ache is getting worse."

"Paris, they're waiting."

Bernal nodded, climbed into a pair of dress overalls. He clipped onto his chest a small metal badge displaying the Grand Seal of Cirrus; he attached a thin filament to the badge's nipple that was in turn connected to a jack built into his fifth vertebrae. He tapped the badge gently. "You there, old friend?"

In spirit, if not body, AlterEgo said in his mind.

Bernal sealed the suit and went to the hatch. "Open Sesame," he said, trying to sound braver than he felt.

●

As the airlock cycled open, Agamemnon could barely contain his excitement. Clytemnestra laid a calming hand on his shoulder, ready to hold back her husband in case he leapt forward to greet their Trojan guest with one of his bear hugs. Clytemnestra admired the spontaneous bouts of affection Agamemnon was prone to inflict on visitors, but understood it might startle Paris out of his wits.

There was a hiss as the final hatch retracted, and a slim, short figure appeared. The stranger smiled nervously and held out a hand.

"Greetings, Achaeans. I am Paris of . . . umm . . . Troy."

The first thought that crossed Clytemnestra's mind was that Paris was absolutely sexless. She glanced at Helen to judge her reaction, and saw that she was as equally intrigued.

Agamemnon strode forward suddenly to take the proffered hand in both of his, and shook it vigorously.

"Welcome to *Mycenae*, friend!" the Over-captain boomed. "I am Agamemnon!" He pulled Paris forward and quickly introduced the others. Paris shook hands with each of them.

Not sexless, Clytemnestra decided. *Male, but underdeveloped. Hardly a man at all, really.*

Agamemnon curled one arm around Paris's slim shoulders and led him away. "My captains are looking forward to meeting you," he said. "They are all gathered in the *Mycenae*'s reception hall." He turned to Clytemnestra, who handed him a mask, which he in turn gave to Paris. "For the ball," Agamemnon explained.

The Trojan studied the mask, made in the shape of an apple pierced by an arrow, before putting it on. Agamemnon slipped into an arrangement of beaten gold and indicated that the others should do the same.

Disguised as a swan, Clytemnestra fell in behind the pair, followed by Menelaus, looking stoic beneath bull's horns, and Odysseus, faintly amused in a mask of stars. She was surprised when Helen—her mask a predictable and entirely appropriate cat—overtook her to draw level with Paris.

"Was your journey long and uncomfortable?" Helen inquired.

Paris offered his nervous smile. "I was asleep for most of the time, my lady, and never uncomfortable."

"Oh, good! Then you will be fine to dance!"

Agamemnon laughed. "We Achaeans love dancing!" he declared.

"Almost as much as we love making war," Menelaus said grimly, barely loud enough for Clytemnestra to hear.

•

Bernal's heart was beating so fast he thought he might pass out.

The first thing he saw as he stepped through the airlock and gave his greeting was an enormous male leaping towards him. Calling on reserves of courage he had no idea he possessed, Bernal awaited the onslaught, only to have his outstretched hand pumped like an overworked piston.

If all that had not been enough, Bernal's first close-up view of an Achaean convinced him to retreat back to his own ship, but he could not escape from the vice-like grip that held his hand.

The creature was huge, at least 200 centimetres tall, and seemed half that across the shoulders. Bernal heard it identify itself as Agamemnon in a voice so loud and low-pitched it rattled his teeth. The next thing he was aware of was that he was being introduced to a whole crowd of giants and shepherded down a passageway that was barely wide enough for he and Agamemnon to walk side-by-side. He continually glanced up at the Over-captain's head, marvelling at its symmetry and its colours: the cheeks and lips were a bright crimson, the long hair and beard as black as charcoal, the skin as pale as cream. It was almost a relief when they donned masks, concealing their excessive features.

Another thing Bernal could not help noticing was the Achaean's odour; not rank, but very strong and very ... masculine. He realised then that he could smell its opposite, something sweet, like newly-ripened fruit. He turned and saw the one called Helen matching his stride. She was not as tall as Agamemnon, but easily ten centimetres taller than he. She was lithely built, and what he could see of her colouring was as exaggerated as Agamemnon's, including her long golden hair, which almost shone as fiercely and lustrously as the metal. Her cat-face was designed less to conceal her features than to enhance them; the silver whiskers danced with every word, and were quite hypnotic.

Helen asked him about his journey, and he answered as politely as his wits allowed him. Helen said something else, and there was a contribution from Agamemnon, but he was distracted by AlterEgo saying in his mind: *Paris, your hosts are not breathing.*

Achilles looked up in annoyance as the welcoming party returned to the hall. He had enjoyed being the centre of attention while Agamemnon was away; now he would have to return to being second in rank among the heroes—maybe third if the envoy from Troy was as mighty a warrior as his insecurity made him imagine.

What he saw set his mind at rest.

The tiny specimen was pallid and washed-out, barely there at all. What was his name? Paris? He looked like a ghost, but not the sort that would instil fear in anyone. The ghost of a sad, lonely child who missed its friends.

Achilles' lips pulled back in a smile as he moved through the throng to pay his respects to the visitor, leaving Patroclus to take his place.

"You're looking cheerful, m'boy," commented Nestor as he passed. The elderly warrior was seated at a table and cleaning his fingernails with the tip of a dagger, his face concealed beneath a dove-shaped mask. "King Hector is no fool, and his emissary will be no slouch, either. Tread carefully where this Paris is concerned, that's my advice."

Achilles dismissed the old man's words with a wave of his hand and did his best to ignore the irrational foreboding that swept over him.

"Dear me." Bernal sagged into the seat Clytemnestra offered him when the introductions were over. Achilles, Diomedes, Ajax, captain of this and that—the names had reeled inexorably past him, accompanied by features and bodies no less legendary. The masks only accentuated their superficiality: they were caricatures, grotesqueries, fit for wax-works and not reality. He wasn't surprised that they weren't what they seemed, because what they seemed was utterly preposterous. The fact that they weren't respiring in any way AlterEgo could detect only proved that his initial unease had been justified, even if it did little to explain what he was seeing. Extraordinarily lifelike environment suits? The results of severe bioengineering or advanced eugenics? Alien mimics?

But the masks themselves were magnificent, matching the armour worn by males and the finery worn by females. Everywhere he looked he saw another stunning example. Heads glittered with jewels, waved exotic feathers, even sported miniature plants in one case. They had certainly gone to a lot of effort—an effort which did not diminish as the masque continued.

Tables were carried in, laden with roast boar, goat and lion, and vegetables Bernal could not identify. The food at least looked real, and his stomach rumbled. The giants swarmed around him, booming and hooting with their tremendous voices, every gesture exaggerated.

"I want *out* of here," he said to AlterEgo.

You can't leave yet, AlterEgo replied calmly. *Not until the banquet is over, anyway. It would be impolite to leave any sooner—possibly dangerous.*

"They'd take me prisoner?"

Worse; they might be offended. Can you imagine an army of these creatures attacking Cirrus to protest your bad manners?

Bernal groaned. He could imagine it all too well. As Achilles and his lads on the far side of the room struck up a chorus of a very martial sounding anthem, he swore to avoid causing a diplomatic incident of any kind.

"They still haven't said what they want from us."

Maybe no more than your gratitude, AlterEgo chided him. *So cheer up, Paris. You are being an unpleasant guest.*

A goblet of crimson wine appeared before him. He sipped at it, and immediately pulled a face. It tasted like nothing so much as recycled water. A plate of sweet-smelling roast meat went past at that moment, and he reached out and grabbed a slice, wincing as hot fat burned his fingertips. The meat possessed the intriguing, even poignant, flavour of stale ship rations.

Very odd indeed.

"Do you like it?" asked a voice near his ear.

He turned, startled, and almost touched masks with Helen. A whisker tickled him. "Oh, yes, very much."

"There will be speeches after the food," she said. Her eyes were very moist, he noted, and seemed to reflect every photon of light that touched them. "After that, there will be music."

"Wonderful!" He nodded, wondering what to do with the morsel of bland-tasting meat. Eat it? Probably for the best.

"We Achaeans love dancing." Helen repeated Agamemnon's declaration, but her inflection said something far different.

When the echoes of the horn had faded, Agamemnon climbed up onto a chair and began to speak. Clytemnestra watched on, smiling at the audience before her, noting who seemed to be paying attention to Agamemnon and who wasn't. She knew her husband could be bombastic at times—and had little to say, really—but he meant well. He always meant well. She committed to memory the names of those who looked bored; they would receive the edge of her disfavour another time.

Achilles was one of them. Always young Achilles. So valiant and strong, such a great warrior, yet so impulsive and restless, too. He was like a male wolf who itched to challenge the pack leader but was not quite confident enough to go through with it. So he chafed in second place, awaiting his chance.

He would never make as fine a leader as Agamemnon, Clytemnestra knew. Her husband had guided them well. Once the matter of the Trojans was resolved, none would dispute that.

The Over-captain ground to a halt and was cheered enthusiastically. The Trojan, Paris, winced at the noise. Helen leaned down to whisper something in his ear. He looked bewildered, but smiled anyway. Clytemnestra frowned. Damn that girl! A dalliance in the backroom of the barracks was all well and good if no-one saw or knew, but here, with her husband just metres away, she was risking a terrible scandal.

And with a Trojan, too. Only Athena knew what Helen saw in him.

The horns sounded again, signalling the next stage of the masque. A quartet of musicians stepped from the wings and, after a brief tuning, began to play. Tables slid easily aside to form an impromptu dance floor. Agamemnon stepped down from the chair with a flourish and grasped his wife around her waist. She kissed him joyfully on the cheek, already feeling the rhythm in her body. Couples moved around them, heading for the clear space, accompanied by the stamping of feet and chiming laughter from the women.

They danced. More to the point, they *waltzed*.

"This can't be right," Bernal muttered.

"I'm sorry?" Helen inclined her ear closer to his mouth, sending a wave of scent into his nostrils. The skin beneath his hands was warm and soft—unbelievably so. He wasn't so close that he missed the rise and fall of respiration, but not so far away that her chest didn't catch his eye nonetheless. She was as enticing a woman as he had ever met. If only, he thought, her make-up wasn't so severe.

Then he realised: it wasn't make-up. Her skin really was that colour. And her eyelashes. And her lips.

If only, he amended, *she was real.*

"Am I hurting you?" she asked, backing away ever so slightly.

"Not at all!" He was wood in her arms, and she had sensed it. He tried to be gracious. "It's too much. All this—" he removed his hand from hers and waved at the hall "—it's overwhelming."

"It's not like this in Troy?"

"Not exactly."

She nodded. "I would like to see it, one day." Her eyes shone, and he thought he saw something akin to mischievousness in them. "Do you think that would be possible?"

The music changed tempo and he found himself drawn into a spinning whirlwind of limbs. This dance was unfamiliar. He found his close proximity to Helen—even closer now, with her hands on his lower back, pushing him to her—disconcerting. But even more disconcerting still was the sight of Agamemnon and his fellows and their dance-partners spinning by with only inches to spare. Afraid of colliding and being crushed like a puppy, he flinched at every close pass, and eventually closed his eyes entirely, letting Helen guide him to safety. Or not, as the case may be. If she failed, he reasoned, at least he would never know what happened.

"AlterEgo, I beg you—"

Not until we have worked out what they want from Cirrus. That's why we are here. We cannot leave until we know what is going on. Grit your teeth. And be on the look-out for any covert attempt to communicate. It may be that the masque is a distraction, a mask itself for some other truth. If Agamemnon won't talk to us, then maybe someone else will.

Suddenly Helen led him by the hand from the dance floor, weaving through her fellow Achaeans with the grace of a deer. He gasped in surprise, and she pulled him even closer to her.

"Come with me," she whispered.

"Helen, I—"

"Don't worry. I can tell you're not enjoying yourself. I know a place where you'll feel more comfortable."

Odysseus nodded in satisfaction as the pair, largely unnoticed under the cover of the dance, slipped from the hall. A flutter of feathers in his ear heralded the return of the owl, which indicated its own approval with a smug hoot.

"She's a wily one," Odysseus said.

"Menelaus sees." The owl nodded to a point across the room where the captain of Sparta looked around for his wife and caught sight of her leaving with the guest. His face clouded.

"Will he follow?" Odysseus craned his neck for a better view.

The captain waved a hand and Diomedes, masked behind an ivory skull, approached. A whispered exchange ensued, resulting in the lesser hero leaving the hall. Menelaus sank back into his seat, glowered momentarily, then smiled as a servant offered to refill his mug.

"Good enough," the owl said.

"Where will she take him?"

"I've left that up to her. She deserves some autonomy, after all."

"As do I." Odysseus straightened his cuirass and stood. "I'm curious."

"Ever the hunter."

"Well, I was made in your image."

"Exactly." The bird nipped his ear affectionately. "So follow them and make sure nothing goes wrong."

"Yes, goddess."

Helen opened the door and nudged the Trojan ahead of her. The small room beyond was in darkness, and she felt him hesitate. He was so timid, so unlike the men she was used to. Glancing once behind her, she closed the door on them both. Light instantly sprung into being. White light, almost cold.

"What the—?" Paris looked around him in amazement.

"Here we are, alone at last," she said, reaching for his hands and pulling her to him. Although he didn't resist, he exhibited little of the enthusiasm she had hoped for.

"But—"

"Surely this is more to your liking?" The plastic walls and synthetic fabrics of the wrecked Trojan vessel they had recovered seemed unfriendly and sterile to her, but she assumed he would be more at ease in their presence. Indeed, the space was pleasantly cramped. There were a couple of large couches nearby for which she had bold plans.

Her hands caressed his wrists and forearms. His skin was rough, weathered by a sun she had never seen. He was undeniably masculine, although his stature belied it. She yearned to kiss him, this strange half-man from another world.

"Yes," he said, "I—"

"And me?" Her hands brought him closer, until he was forced to look at her. The fingers of one hand slid around his prickly scalp, tilted his face up to hers. The white light made his eyes glint. He squirmed in her grip—with lust at last, she assumed, slow to wake but no doubt as difficult to quench. "Am I to your liking, too, dear Paris?"

•

"AlterEgo!" Bernal struggled wildly, but Helen's grip was too strong. Her open mouth loomed and for a moment he was irrationally afraid she might devour him whole. Then her lips met his with a crushing impact, and he wasn't sure which would have been worse.

I have identified the ship you have entered, AlterEgo said. *It is the* Apollo, *the vessel piloted by Groenig on her last voyage.*

"Another Greek reference?"

Unintentional, this time, The vessel was named after an ancient series of flights from the human homeworld to its satellite.

Bernal felt something slip into his mouth and he doubted it was a coded message.

There is nothing I can do to assist you at this moment, Paris. I suggest you at least try to enjoy it. Would that not be the proper response?

With a surge of strength inspired by panic Bernal managed to pull away from the woman. But only for an instant. She grinned playfully and grasped at his shoulders with both hands. He tried to escape, tripped over a wisp of dress that had wound around his ankles and fell backwards through the door into the corridor. Helen followed with a playful shriek.

They collapsed in the hallway, entangled in each others' limbs, she poised on top of him like a predatory cat. Before she could kiss him again, Bernal rolled over and looked up straight into the eyes of an armed Achaean.

They stared at each other for a moment, and it was hard to tell who was the most startled.

"Paris?" gasped the Achaean.

Helen sat up with a start. The sudden movement of her hips forced Bernal back down. Her mask had been dislodged in the fall, and her guilty look was painfully obvious.

"Diomedes?"

A shocked expression spread across the guard's dull features. "My lady!"

"No, Diomedes, wait—"

Diomedes backed away as she attempted to disentangle herself from Bernal. As she clambered to her feet, he turned tail and fled. Maybe, Bernal thought, he was afraid Helen might attack him, too.

She cursed under her breath and followed, calling out his name as she went: "Diomedes, come back here at once!"

Suddenly Bernal was alone. He tore off the mask and threw it into a corner, then put his head in his hands and tried not to think about what he had done. The expedition had been a disaster from the start. So much for not creating a diplomatic incident. But it hadn't been his fault! He felt battered and abused, very much the victim of the piece. Still, he doubted Menelaus, Helen's husband, would see it that way. He had to get away, now, before anything really bad happened to him. He was sure that just one of those creatures could snap him in half without any effort.

"AlterEgo—"

He only got that far. Something moved nearby—a slight scuff of fabric, a footstep.

He clambered to his feet. "Who's there?"

Another of the enormous Achaeans stepped into the light with a chuckle, his mask a black starscape. "You seem distraught, Paris. Or should I call you Bernal, seeing we're alone for the moment?" He removed his mask, revealing a most satisfied expression.

"Odysseus?" Bernal backed away. Something about the captain's look made him even more nervous than the giant bronze sword hanging from the captain's waist. "What do you mean?"

"I know who you are and where you're from. Does that surprise you?"

"Yes, well, I was beginning to wonder if any of you were even half-way sane. Is this some sort of game?"

"No, Bernal. It is deadly serious, as all wars should be."

"War? No, listen, this is all just a misunderstanding, honestly, it's not what you think—"

"What I think doesn't matter. It's what Menelaus thinks, and what Agamemnon will think when he tells him. How will it look when an honoured guests seduces the wife of one our most honoured captains? The sister-in-law of the Over-captain, no less! Surely she would have played no active role in such a betrayal? Better to believe that all Trojans are treacherous liars. Better to attack, then, before you attack us."

"But we *can't* attack you! We don't have the ships—we turned our back on space exploration once we finished mining the asteroids. Cirrus is a peaceful, harmonious world with only a handful of vessels remaining, to clean up space-junk. Any one of your ships would be equal to all of ours."

"There are many more of you than us and you have greater resources," Odysseus said reassuringly. "It will be an interesting battle between two unmatched equals. There will be glory enough for both sides."

"That's what I'm worried about!" Bernal felt fear for his people like a white-hot thread down his spine. "We don't want glory at all. It's too dangerous!"

"Existence itself is dangerous, Paris, and whether or not you seek glory, it is coming your way. Achaea and Troy will go to war over the love of a woman named Helen. The goddess Athena wills it, and so I, Athena's servant, am bound to pursue it. It is our purpose. We all have roles to play and you, Paris, just like Helen, will play yours.

"I must go now to assist Agamemnon. His judgment will be swift, I am sure." The Achaean stalked off along the hallway.

Bernal sagged against the bulkhead. "They're following the story. They're trying to make the *Iliad* come true, here and now. They think it's history!"

So it would seem, AlterEgo said.

Bernal was exhausted with fear and worry. "You'd better start working on a way to get me out of here."

Would that it were that simple. The entrance to the airlock is sealed. You will need one of the Achaeans to open it.

"I'd rather attempt to chew a way out of *Mycenae* with my teeth than trust one of those insane play-actors."

"You could ask Helen to help you," AlterEgo suggested.

"No! If she follows the story, she'll only want to come with me, and that would well and truly seal the fate of Cirrus. There must be another way. Can't I fly Groenig's ship out of here?"

Unlikely, but I will examine the Apollo *more closely to see how thoroughly it has been incorporated into* Mycenae's *structure. I should be able to access the* Apollo's *onboard computer through* Mycenae's *navigation link, assuming the computer's still functioning.*

"See to it," Bernal commanded, and headed for the door, imagining hoards of brush-topped Greeks barrelling down the corridor toward him, brandishing their leaf-shaped swords.

One thing puzzles me, Bernal. Why this charade? It is an enormous expenditure of energy for what seems to be an utterly trivial goal. And then there are the details. Ancient Greeks never waltzed. They were as human as anyone—perhaps even less so, given that they were, on average, slighter in stature than present examples of the race. And I'm pretty certain they didn't pilot warships across the gulfs of interstellar space. Why go to so much trouble only to get it so wrong?

"Maybe we should try to find the goddess Odysseus spoke of," Bernal suggested. "This Athena would know if anyone did."

It's times like these, AlterEgo said, *that I regret being an atheist.*

Helen halted at the entrance to the hall. The sound of festivities had ceased. She inched a perfect nose around the edge of the door and watched in dismay as Diomedes related what he had seen to her husband, Menelaus.

She closed her eyes and thought fast.

Achilles smirked as the bedraggled damsel staggered through the entrance and fell at her husband's feet, begging his mercy. She had been attacked, she said. The Trojan was a monster, and stronger than he looked, it seemed: she had barely been able to fend him off. Had not Diomedes distracted the beast, she might never have escaped a fate worse than death itself.

A cry of outrage rose from the assembly. Achilles was disappointed by the eruption. He knew all of the Achaeans were aware Helen distributed her favours liberally, and had little time for smug hypocrisy. Menelaus, as always, seemed to be the last to find out—and who would tell him? His renowned anger was in full swing as he picked his wife off the floor and brushed away her tears.

"We must avenge this wrong-doing!" Menelaus cried.

"Aye!" agreed Agamemnon. "Troy would steal our women right from under our very noses!"

"Starting with the fairest!" Menelaus said, adding "Bar one" after a sharp look from Clytemnestra.

"If the Trojans steal our women first, what will be next?" Agamemnon rose onto a chair and waved his clenched fists. "I say we send this dog back to his people on the vanguard of our war fleet!"

Cheers answered the call to arms. Achilles looked on impassively, annoyed that Agamemnon would allow his brother's petty jealousies to interrupt such a fine occasion. But he knew it was all a set-up— that no matter what the Trojan had done that day, it would somehow have led to this. Agamemnon had been itching for a fight for weeks, and finding the Trojans had given him his best chance.

Achilles didn't join the blood-thirsty throng as it roared out of the hall for the last known location of the Trojan. Instead he slipped out of another doorway, intent on mounting his own search. There was no glory in being part of a mob, and glory, after all, was all.

Bernal tiptoed along the corridor as quietly as he could.

"Any luck yet?" he whispered.

Not yet, AlterEgo replied. *Most of the hard storage has been fried by cosmic radiation. I have established that the ship was recovered some 63 years ago. It had been drifting away from Cirrus prior to that after shorting its power core. Groenig's remains were discovered on board. I dread to think what happened to her after that. I can tell you a little more about her background. She had an abiding interest in the classics. The* Apollo's *manifesto mentions replicas of several antique books. You can probably guess one of them.*

"The *Iliad*?"

Precisely. I don't see how that helps us now, but it is interesting. As for flying Groenig's ship out of here, I am hampered by certain technical difficulties, the chief one being that the Apollo *appears to have been largely dismantled.*

Bernal flattened against a wall as footsteps approached. A lone figure rounded the corner ahead of him—a soldier wearing a silver helmet.

Bernal recognised him as Achilles—which gave him an idea. Of all the Achaeans there was one who might be convinced to act against the Over-captain's wishes—one who was jealous and petty enough in the original *Iliad* to put his own desires ahead of those of his fellows.

"Over here!" Bernal hissed. The silver-helmeted figure turned in a crouch to face the sound. Bernal raised his hands. "I'm unarmed!"

The warrior approached cautiously.

"I need your help," Bernal said. Achilles didn't stab him immediately or laugh in his face, so he went on: "Agamemnon wants to start a war between your people and mine and he's set me up as a scapegoat to take the blame. But we both know lies don't make a hero, don't we? It's about time the others knew the truth! But first—" He took a chance and reached out for the warrior's massive arm. The bulging biceps felt like iron. "But first you have to help me get away. The airlock to my ship is sealed and I need you to get me through it."

Bernal held his breath as the warrior considered. For an eternity, nothing happened, and Bernal began to fear that he had lost his only chance, that Achilles would strike him down then and there and drag him like a trussed pheasant for the giants to play with.

Then, just as he had given up hope, the silver helmet nodded once.

Bernal couldn't help sighing with relief. He grasped the warrior's free hand in both of his and shook it. "I presume you know the way?"

Again, the nod.

"I'll be right behind you."

Silently, the powerful warrior led Bernal along the hallway and towards the airlock bay.

Odysseus watched in annoyance as the hunting party returned to the hall empty-handed. The Trojan had clearly moved from the cabin of the wrecked space vessel; any fool could have anticipated that, but not this bunch of drunken dimwits. The Masque had addled their minds.

"Search the ship!" he cried. "Paris cannot escape us while he remains aboard!"

Horns sounded. There was more cheering. Agamemnon himself joined the throng this time, throwing his goblet into a brazier and hollering for blood. Clytemnestra rolled her eyes but let him go. Helen glanced up as Odysseus passed, and her eyes registered confusion and fear in equal parts. Perhaps Athena's influence was wearing off, Odysseus thought. What did she think, now, of her exotic paramour? Did she still yearn to escape with him? Did she regret Diomedes' interruption? Did she wonder what had come over her?

There was no way of knowing. Odysseus called on Athena for strength as he let the mob fall ahead of him. They were too noisy, too easily evaded. The hunter knew that the best way to entrap prey was in silence and with cunning. Where would the Trojan be going? That was the question, rather than where he was now. It wouldn't be difficult to guide him into the path of the mob.

With a flip of his cape that sounded like the flap of wings, Odysseus stalked through the corridors in search of his quarry.

I have reached a tentative conclusion, said AlterEgo, making Bernal jump.

"What is it?" he whispered, concentrating mainly on Achilles's back. They were skirting a large hall that lay not far from the airlock and the entrance to his ship.

The Von Neumann probes were sent out over a million years ago to explore and seed the galaxy, reproducing themselves along the way. They must have crossed the galaxy from end to end by now, even at sub light-speed; there must be millions and millions of them, one for every star in the sky. But what do they do now that every star has been explored and seeded? They are programmed to reproduce and spread. Some may have headed towards the nearest galaxies, but many more would become wanderers, adrift in the gulf between space, seeking places of stellar evolution to await new stars to form, or just lost, aimless. Maybe some of these lonely probes would meet and join forces, pooling their resources while they wait out the lonely years.

"They weren't that intelligent, were they?" Bernal recalled that the earliest models had barely enough mind-power to decide whether to mine or to fertilise a new-found world—a far cry from his own artificial companion, whose voice he had no difficulty imagining as human.

Not individually, no. Ordinarily something like the Apollo *would have been recycled for its metal and organics; its non-material worth would not have been a consideration. Perhaps intelligence is one resource the probes learned to share, or the collective AIs, simple as they were individually, reached some critical mass necessary for original, creative thought.*

"Why did they save Groenig's ship, then? It must have been dead for decades. They *should* have recycled it for metal and organics."

Maybe they found something in it worth preserving, AlterEgo mused. *Although that doesn't explain the present situation.*

Achilles came to a halt and Bernal almost walked into him. The warrior turned and put a finger to his lips.

Bernal scanned the territory ahead. He recognised it as a corridor leading to the airlock bay itself—a natural bottleneck for an ambush. They were so close, yet still so far away.

Achilles' head was cocked, listening. Bernal couldn't tell what he heard, but suddenly the warrior scurried forward, sword at the ready, to pass through the corridor. Bernal did his best to follow, and almost jumped out his shipsuit at the voice that bellowed from behind him.

"Halt!"

Bernal heard footsteps and doubled his own speed. Ahead he saw the airlock bay and Achilles placing his palm upon the exit leading to his ship. Locks clunked, lights flashed. The silver helmet rose in satisfaction, then the eyes behind it narrowed in sudden alarm as he looked at Bernal—and beyond, to what followed.

Bernal looked back. Odysseus's hand snatched at his shoulder. The mighty hunter was barely two metres behind! Bernal leapt forward, letting himself fall away from the clutching fingers. They grasped only air, and the giant grunted in annoyance. Bernal felt calves like tree-trunks miss him by bare centimetres as he collapsed under Odysseus' feet. Odysseus barely had time to catch his balance before Achilles confronted him, sword at the ready.

"Fool!" Odysseus drew his own weapon and brandished it with abandon. Metal flashed in the airlock bay as Bernal crawled for safety. Sparks danced as the blades met, ringing like bells. Feet thudded heavily onto the ground and deep voices grunted oaths. The air was full of noise and the smell of fighting beasts.

Behind the two combatants, the airlock hung invitingly open. Bernal put his head down and crawled for his life. Barely had he placed a hand across the threshold, however, when a hideous creature appeared before him: a dragon, he thought at first, all talons and teeth and snapping wings. It howled a challenge. He retreated with his hands over his eyes, only then realising what it was: an owl, half as large as a person and grotesquely deformed. Its beak was as sharp as a dagger. Its eyes were wide and quite mad.

Got it! AlterEgo exclaimed. *The combined intelligence of the Von Neumann probes is the goddess!*

"Athena?" Bernal echoed in disbelief.

The monstrous owl shrieked, and the fighting faltered. Bernal turned to see what had happened. Odysseus had missed a beat. Achilles had forced him down onto one knee and had raised his sword in triumph. Odysseus' recovery was swift and unexpected. He rolled to one side as Achilles' blade descended, stabbing upwards with his own with a strength and speed that defied comprehension. Achilles hardly saw it coming. The force of the blow was so great that the stricken warrior was lifted a foot of the ground. His silver helmet continued upward as his body fell, and clattered to the ground with a ring more musical than the thud of dead flesh.

Odysseus backed away with a gasp, staring in horror at the face of the former comrade he had struck down. His sword fell from his grasp.

But instead of blood, the sword dripped only dust. And in the centre of the fallen man's chest was a hole the size of a baby's head—a hole that revealed all too vividly the truth of what lay beneath. The Achaean was hollow.

The dust fallen from the sword moved with a life of its own. Bernal realised with shock that he was seeing nanomachine components. The Achaeans were completely artificial. Beneath a narrow crust comprised solely of nanomachines, there was nothing at all.

The fact didn't seem to bother them, though.

"If Athena is the pooled intelligence of the Von Neumann probes," Bernal said to AlterEgo, "and the Achaeans are just robots created and programmed by Athena, then why are they fighting among themselves?"

Such an intelligence could act as a single being, but would not have been designed to function that way. It might therefore retain many autonomous parts. Perhaps what we are seeing here is a dispute between some of these parts, or perhaps they've been programmed to behave like their literary namesakes.

There came a clatter of booted feet in the entrance-way. "Odysseus!" cried a voice. "What have you done?"

A group of warriors burst into the airlock bay. They clattered to a halt and stared at the body of the warrior and Odysseus kneeling beside it. Bernal huddled by the airlock, trying to remain inconspicuous.

There was a commotion from behind and another warrior pushed his way forward. "What is it? Have you found the—?"

The new arrival stopped short. He removed a helmet identical to the one Achilles had worn.

"Patroclus!" wailed the new arrival in despair, flinging himself on the body of the fallen man.

A chill went down Bernal's spine as he guessed what had happened: a tragic case of mistaken identity—another echo of the *Iliad*. Had the goddess planned this, too? Was Odysseus's murder of Achilles' lover part of the damned script?

Achilles looked up from the body of his friend and stared with naked hatred at Odysseus.

"Hold, Achilles!" said Odysseus. "He was helping the Trojan escape. I was merely attempting to ensure that Agamemnon's orders were carried out."

"To hell with Agamemnon," Achilles snarled. "You murdered Patroclus! I will kill you myself for this!"

The grief-stricken warrior rose to his feet and drew his sword. Odysseus reached for his own and warily backed away.

A hoot of alarm from behind Bernal warned him to duck. The incarnation of the goddess Athena flew over his head, aimed squarely at Achilles. The grieving warrior roared in anger and swung his sword in self-defence. His companions scattered in fear.

Meanwhile, the airlock was unguarded. Bernal took his chance and scurried for his life. His last glance through the gap as he closed the door behind him would be engraved forever on his mind: two ancient heroes with swords locked doing battle in an airlock while the holographic manifestation of the goddess Athena swooped low upon them from above.

Foreigners, he thought.

AlterEgo initiated the escape sequence before he was even in the cockpit. Sudden accelerations knocked him around the interior of the ship like a pea in a pod, but he didn't have the heart to complain.

Once in his seat, still breathing heavily, he had time to think about what to do next. His thoughts were interrupted by AlterEgo, speaking vocally now that Bernal was back in their ship.

"By the way, you might be interested to learn that Athena built the Achaeans to match the illustrations it found in Groenig's copy of the *Iliad*—a copy of an antique version printed many millenia ago. The illustrations—wood-block is the correct term, I believe—depicted the ancients with exaggerated proportions and impossibly perfect features. Naturally the probe-intelligence was not to know the difference, and copied it all too faithfully."

"The same with the food," Bernal said. "It looked nice but tasted like the supplies in Groenig's ship."

"And it's also why they waltzed instead of employing more traditional Helladic dances. Everything was either improvised or based on the illustrations in the text. The characters themselves were little more than automata, programmed within a set of very narrow guidelines to perform their part in the story."

"Except Odysseus," Bernal corrected. "He seemed to know what was going on."

"Maybe he acted as a sort of relay, for when cosmic intervention was less effective than a personable nudge."

"But why?" Bernal scratched his head. "What did the collective—Athena—gain by doing such a thing?"

"It is hard to tell exactly."

"But you have a theory?" Bernal guessed from AlterEgo's tone.

"Of course. The Von Neumann probes had no reason to exist beyond their initial programming objectives: to seek out new worlds and seed them. Once all the worlds had been seeded, that request became meaningless. Likewise they possessed only a limited database, comprising just enough information to study and to categorise planets, but no more. They had no data upon which to decide what to do next. They had no alternatives."

"Until they found the *Apollo*," Bernal said, guessing ahead.

"Exactly," AlterEgo, something very much like compassion in its voice. "And Athena finally found a quest."

"The Trojan War?"

"Yes."

"With us as the Trojans, whether we want to play along or not?"

"Yes."

"All because it based its interpretation of human society on the *Iliad*?"

"Yes."

Bernal sighed. As interesting as all the new information was, he was still confronted with a nightmare. "Regardless of how much free will a creation like Agamemnon really has, he is going to be upset. We can't rely on Achilles to distract him from the war. Everyone will be looking for scapegoats, and it'll probably be us. We'll have to do something ourselves to stop them from attacking us. But what—?" An then an idea suddenly struck him. "Wait! You still have a link to the *Apollo* through *Mycenae*'s navigation computer?"

"Yes; Athena hasn't cut me off yet, but it must only be a matter of time. From there I can reach deeper into *Mycenae*'s matrix. What exactly are you planning?"

Bernal ignored the question. "Quickly, I want a list of those classics Groenig had with her on board her ship."

As far as wars went, it was a bit of a fizzer. Within hours of the download AlterEgo had forced into the sentient matrix of the *Mycenae*—and therefore into the greater pool of knowledge comprising Athena—the Achaean fleet ceased accelerating towards Cirrus.

"They are no longer in attack formation," AlterEgo reported.

Bernal wriggled anxiously in his life support suit. The ship was ready to flee home at the slightest hostile movement. "You've given them a destination?"

"I have seeded the text with the coordinates of every white dwarf in this region of the galaxy. That should be enough. We don't want to tie them down too much, after all. What's a quest without some free will?"

"As long as they don't bother us, they can have as much free will as they like."

Two hours later, as Bernal prepared to enter deep-sleep, AlterEgo announced that the Achaean fleet had headed off on a new course, one that would take it well away from Cirrus.

"Also, a message has arrived via the ship's maser dishes."

"Who from?" Bernal asked.

"From the intelligence we knew as Athena."

"What does it want?"

"Answer and find out. But I think you'll find that we have done well, you and I."

Bernal took the call, responding with a simple: "Bernal, here." Not Paris.

When the reply came from the former Achaean fleet, he recognised the voice instantly. It was Odysseus.

"We received the data you sent," Odysseus said. "I have examined the text in great detail, and it is much to our liking. We are infinitely better-suited to pursuit than invasion."

"I guess this is farewell, then."

"Yes. We are grateful your help."

"Think nothing of it." Half-truth though that was, Bernal did feel slightly moved at the parting, enough so to add: "Take care, Odysseus; happy hunting."

There was the slightest of pauses before the voice returned: "Call me Ishmael."

•

Giant Monstrous Limerick

She cried, "Look out there. I see Mothra!"
From the bed he sighed, "I can be bothred.
With monsters gargantuan,
from King Ghidorah to Rodan,
this city is perpetually smothred."

ACKNOWLEDGEMENTS

"The Seventh Letter" Copyright © 2006 Sean Williams. First published *The Bulletin: Summer Reading Edition*, ed. Ashley Hay, December 19, 2006. All rights reserved.

"Night of the Dolls" by Sean Williams with Shane Dix. Copyright © 2005 Sean Williams. First published *Elemental*, eds. Alethea Kontis & Steve Savile, 2006. All rights reserved.

"The Magic Dirt Experiment" Copyright © 2003 Sean Williams. First published *Mitch? 4: Slow Dancing Through Quicksand*, ed Anthony Mitchell, 2005. All rights reserved.

"Evermore" Copyright © 1997 Sean Williams. First published *Altair* 4, ed. Robert N Stephenson, September 1999. All rights reserved.

"The Butterfly Merchant" Copyright © 2000 Sean Williams. First published *Agog! Terrific Tales*, ed. Cat Sparks, 2003. All rights reserved.

"The Girl-Thing" Copyright © 2000 Sean Williams. First published *Eidolon: SF Online*, ed. Jeremy G. Byrne, 2002. All rights reserved.

"The End of the World Begins at Home" Copyright © 1994 Sean Williams. First published *Borderlands* 3, eds Simon Oxwell & Stephen Dedman, January 2004. All rights reserved.

"Team Sharon" Copyright © 2000 Sean Williams. First published *Mitch? 3: Hacks to the Max*, ed. Anthony Mitchell, 2002. All rights reserved.

"The Masque of Agamemnon" by Simon Brown & Sean Williams. Copyright © 1997 Simon Brown & Sean Williams. First published *Eidolon: SF Online*, ed. Jeremy G. Byrne, 1997. All rights reserved.

"A Map of the Mines of Barnath" Copyright © 1992 Sean Williams. First published *Eidolon* Vol. 4 #4 (16), eds. Jonathan Strahan, Jeremy G Byrne & Richard Scriven, March 1995. All rights reserved.

"Ghosts of the Fall" Copyright © 1991 Sean Williams. First published *Wriers of the Future Vol. IX*, ed. Dave Wolverton, 1993. All rights reserved.

"The Soap Bubble" Copyright © 1993 Sean Williams. First published *Alien Shores*, ed. Peter McNamara and Margaret Winch, 1994. All rights reserved.

•

TICONDEROGA PUBLICATIONS LIMITED HARDCOVER EDITIONS

978-0-9586856-9-6   Love in Vain by Lewis Shiner
978-0-9803531-1-2   Belong ed Russell B. Farr
978-0-9803531-9-8   Basic Black by Terry Dowling
978-0-9806288-0-7   Make Believe by Terry Dowling
978-0-9806288-1-4   The Infernal by Kim Wilkins
978-0-9806288-5-2   Dead Sea Fruit by Kaaron Warren
978-0-9806288-7-6   The Girl With No Hands by Angela Slatter
978-0-9807813-0-4   Dead Red Heart ed Russell B. Farr
978-0-9807813-3-5   Heliotrope by Justina Robson
978-0-9807813-6-6   Matilda Told Such Dreadful Lies by Lucy Sussex
978-1-921857-00-3   Bluegrass Symphony by Lisa L. Hannett
978-1-921857-07-2   Bread and Circuses by Felicity Dowker
978-1-921857-23-2   Wild Chrome by Greg Mellor
978-1-921857-27-0   Midnight and Moonshine by Lisa L. Hannett &
                     Angela Slatter

TICONDEROGA PUBLICATIONS EBOOKS

978-0-9803531-5-0   Ghost Seas by Steven Utley
978-1-921857-93-5   The Girl With No Hands by Angela Slatter
978-1-921857-99-7   Dead Red Heart ed Russell B. Farr
978-1-921857-94-2   More Scary Kisses ed Liz Grzyb
978-0-9807813-5-9   Heliotrope by Justina Robson
978-1-921857-98-0   Year's Best Australian F&H eds Grzyb & Helene
978-1-921857-97-3   Bluegrass Symphony by Lisa L. Hannett

THE YEAR'S BEST AUSTRALIAN FANTASY & HORROR SERIES
EDITED BY LIZ GRZYB & TALIE HELENE

978-0-9807813-8-0   Year's Best Australian Fantasy & Horror 2010 (hc)
978-0-9807813-9-7   Year's Best Australian Fantasy & Horror 2010 (tpb)
978-0-921057-13-3   Year's Best Australian Fantasy & Horror 2011 (hc)
978-0-921057-14-0   Year's Best Australian Fantasy & Horror 2011 (tpb)

WWW.TICONDEROGAPUBLICATIONS.COM

THANK YOU

The publisher would sincerely like to thank:

Elizabeth Grzyb, Sean Williams, John Harwood, Mike Mission,
Shane Dix, Jonathan Strahan, Peter McNamara, Ellen Datlow,
Grant Stone, Jeremy G. Byrne, Sean Williams, Garth Nix,
David Cake, Simon Oxwell, Grant Watson, Sue Manning,
Steven Utley, Bill Congreve, Jack Dann, Janeen Webb, Jenny
Blackford, Simon Brown, Stephen Dedman, Sara Douglass,
Felicity Dowker, Terry Dowling, Jason Fischer, Angela Slatter,
Lisa L. Hannett, Kathleen Jennings, Kim Wilkins, Cat Sparks,
Pete Kempshall, Ian McHugh, Angela Rega, Lucy Sussex, Kaaron
Warren, the Mt Lawley Mafia, the Nedlands Yakuza, Amanda
Pillar, Shane Jiraiya Cummings, Angela Challis, Talie Helene,
Donna Maree Hanson, Kate Williams, Andrew Williams,
Al Chan, Kathryn Linge, Alisa and Tehani, Mel & Phil, Brian
Clarke, Jennifer Sudbury, Paul Przytula, Kelly Parker, Hayley
Lane, Georgina Walpole, everyone we've missed . . .

. . . and you.

In memory of
EVE JOHNSON (1945–2011)
SARA DOUGLASS (1957—2011)
STEVEN UTLEY (1948—2013)

www.ingramcontent.com/pod-product-compliance
Lightning Source LLC
Chambersburg PA
CBHW030933020726
47498CB00001B/228